Maggie ☺   £1·69
                    81/WG

A Sort of
Homecoming

01394 383555   8

SCEPTRE

A Sort of Homecoming

ROBERT CREMINS

SCEPTRE

First published in 1998 by Hodder and Stoughton
A division of Hodder Headline PLC
A Sceptre Paperback

10 9 8 7 6 5 4 3 2 1

A CIP catalogue record for this book is
available from the British Library

ISBN 0 340 71723 8

Typeset by Palimpsest Book Production Limited,
Polmont, Stirlingshire
Printed and bound in Great Britain by
Clays Ltd, St Ives PLC, Bungay, Suffolk

Hodder and Stoughton
A division of Hodder Headline PLC
338 Euston Road
London NW1 3BH

In memory of my father
and for my mother
– and for Melanie and David too

And I have no compass
And I have no map
And I have no reasons
No reasons to get back

And I have no religion
And I don't know what's what
And I don't know the limit
The limit of what we got

U2, 'Zooropa'

Advent

I'm the last passenger to deplane.

'Happy Christmas, safe home,' says the ancient Aer Lingus hostess at the cabin door. I respond by repeating something she said over the PA as we were taxiing in, 'See you again soon.'

Bitch of a line at immigration control. The plastic jacket of my passport is torn from frequent flying. I open it (nothing better to do). Skipping over the thorny Irish text, I read the blurb in English on the inside cover,

> The Minister of Foreign Affairs requests
> all whom it may concern to allow the bearer, a
> citizen of Ireland, to pass freely and without
> hindrance and to afford the bearer all necessary
> assistance and protection.

Well, who'd mess with an Irishman after reading that? A lot of good the Minister of Foreign Affairs – search me who it is now: I think another coalition has collapsed in my absence, part of the fallout from that Fr Golden scandal –

a lot of good Mr Micky Minister did me back in September when I got detained under the Prevention of Terrorism Act at Heathrow.

Five fucking hours the British cops had me in that windowless cube. Not that I can blame them too much for taking their time (I may be a hater, but I'm nothing so obvious as a *Brit*-hater). My story sounded pretty implausible – a twenty-two-year-old Irish guy, carrying enough traveller's cheques to buy a sackful of Semtex (the drug or the explosive), claiming that he had no business in life other than flying. I would have stopped me. Maybe I should have obeyed my friend Roderick de Brun's First Law of London: wear a tie going through Heathrow. But I'm not much good with laws.

I turn to the laminated main page of the passport. It says my forenames are Tomás Michael. But it's more accurate to say that those are *his* names – the chubby-cheeked, round-shouldered, ugly duckling seventeen-year-old there in the photograph. The Heathrow heavies had a hard time believing that boy was me. I have a hard time believing it myself.

So who am I now? You can call me Tom – don't even *think* of calling me Tomás – but mostly the world calls me by my surname, my essential name, my true title: Iremonger. I love its snarl and swagger. That name is the best part of my inheritance, better even than my grandfather's money. And I'm more of an Iremonger he ever was; certainly more of an Iremonger than my father. The name has been waiting for me.

I flick through my visas. Okay, I've got stamps for Helsinki, St Petersburg, Belize, Tangier, Toronto, to name but a few; but they tell only half the story. Barcelona, Trieste, and Los Angeles have left no imprint on these harp-watermarked pages. There's no mention of the trip I took from Athens, Greece to Athens, Georgia. Copenhagen might as well not have happened. Arriving in an EC city these days, the immigration cop barely nods when you wave your Burgundy-red passport. You're cleared for the States before you leave Irish soil. What is the world coming to?

I relish that *chu-chink* of arrival. I need it. Right now, for example, I *think* I was in Florence this summer. I distinctly remember watching a fire-eater perform on a narrow street near the Uffizi. But maybe I'm getting mixed up with the time I went there years ago with my parents. Maybe this time I did no more than touch down and take off. I've done a lot of touching down and taking off again these last six months.

Maybe I'll buy myself a video camera for Christmas, among other treats. In the New Year I don't want any of this confusion. After all, I'm having the time of my life.

The line has moved quickly. I expect to get a stolid nod from the bald, plain-clothes cop standing beside the Tensa-barrier bollard when I hold up the harp – he must have seen a hundred thousand of these today – but to my surprise he takes it from my hand. He compares me with the boy. I guess he recognises me from the poster (coming up real soon). He must pass Iremonger going home every day.

'Where are you coming from?' he asks.

I shrug. 'Everywhere, I guess.'

'You sound like you're coming from New York, but you can't be that slow getting off a plane. So be more specific, sonny.'

He's got the dress-sense of a bachelor farmer; I guess they're not called plain clothes for nothing.

'Paris.'

'I'd believe it,' he grunts.

I take the escalator. All the way up are illuminated posters of folk singers and sentimental tenors dressed in knitwear. Imagine, this is the first taste of Ireland foreigners get when they deplane. If I were Taoiseach I'd ban this crap. Not that I'm ever going to be Taoiseach. I believe one of the requirements of the job is that you are prepared to live in Ireland. I am not. I know too much. I know, for example, that if these wispy-bearded old bastards, the Padraig Pearse Project, had any guts they wouldn't be calling their CD *An Emerald Welcome* but something like *IRA Forever!* Time to come out of the provo closet, lads. Must be quite a crush in there.

For a stretch at the top of the escalator all that divides Arrivals and Departures is a glass wall. I stop and watch this guy in stone-washed jeans walk onto a pathetic replica of the Ha'penny Bridge – gateway to the departure gates. Part of me, most of me, wants to smash the glass and follow him. See, I have my own project. The Tom Iremonger Project. That's what I've been up to for the last six months – an anti-odyssey acting out the Iremonger philosophy, which I've been honing for close on five years.

The philosophy runs something like this: make the present moment a work of art. Fuck sitting in dark recording studios or in a poky room writing a book (I have been, since graduating from Trinity, a post-literary individual, and even there I tried to stick to criticism as much as possible). Dive deeper into the present than you've dared to do before. Wake up and realise that the only thing worth investing in is *living*. And don't let the past and the future, the bully boys of existence, push you around. That means, for one thing, taking a pretty dim view of tradition. In my opinion, tradition gets away with murder. Tradition needs to be questioned in a windowless cube in the bowels of Heathrow airport on a regular basis. Take, for example, Christmas. Why do we all have to come back, like some refugee crisis in reverse, to see our folks during this miserable mid-winter week? I'd much rather breeze back into Dublin, unannounced, for a weekend in June or July, a time of year when I find the place approaching the condition of bearability. But no. Everybody has to have their Christmas in December. Even me. Charming.

But I do have the poster to look forward to, my poster. According to my friend Dylan Carraig-Dubh – yes, son of Carmel Carraig-Dubh, the *Ireland on Sunday* social columnist – it's at the end of the long corridor that leads to baggage reclaim. He saw it when he came home from Manhattan for a few days last October. At least eight strangers I've met on my travels – and not all of them Irish – have told me they've seen it too. Only last night a girl from Cork walked up to me in Godot's on rue Mouffetard and asked me if I was the guy in the IDA advertisement. I shyly confirmed that I was; it turned into a one-night stand. My father mentioned on the phone – I think it was the call I made to my parents in August – that several of his former colleagues at American Machines have noticed it also; he joked that he felt like taking a trip to London just to see his son.

I see myself, Iremonger illuminated, as soon as I turn the corner. A red paisley tie (Oscar's, £29) offsets the dark-blue tailored suit (Louis Copeland, £499). I carry a cell phone in one hand, a copy of *The Irish Times* in the other. The other me walks faster, weaving around other passengers. The day after the photoshoot in June I saw that image circled on a contact sheet, but I left Dublin too early – graduating *in absentia* – to see the polished product, embossed with copy. But I can see it all now. *Our Greatest Resource*, reads the slogan at my feet. The creatives from Ascendancy have done one hell of a job. I bet they'll get some kind of industry award for this.

I stop right in front of the poster (out of the corner of my eye watching other passengers do a double-take at its living reflection as they walk by). I take a close look at my face, at my flawless post-adolescent skin, sky-high cheekbones, young-god jaw, guilt-free eyes, pleasure-ready smile. It's odd to think that all this time I've been away, no matter what I've been doing – getting tied down in the Italian Alps, hallucinating in an isolation tank in Toronto, partying with the Red Hot Chili Peppers in Venice Beach, and flying, flying, flying – I've also been right here, not moving a two-dimensional muscle, staring confidently at every arrival, welcoming the world to Ireland.

Sure, I do wish I were the poster boy for a cooler product than the Industrial Development Authority – the Ray-Bans hanging around my neck, for example. But I can live with it. Ultimately I'm advertising myself. If *Cara*, the Aer Lingus in-flight magazine, is to be believed, a quarter of a million people will have seen me in the last few days alone. As Dylan said to me one night in New York, only half-joking, 'You're entering the collective unconscious, Iremonger.'

If that's true, it applies to Mainie too. Mainie Doyle, one of my oldest flames. She's the model in the female version of the advertisement, the other half of the campaign. Ascendancy placed her in *Cara*. This has been the first time I've flown Aer Lingus since leaving Dublin in June, so I checked her out as soon as I got seated on the ground at Charles de Gaulle (I haven't seen her since June either). There she was, in between an article on Romy Dorgan, the Wall Street arbitrageur from Mayo, and an advert for Kells (*Sacred for Centuries*), the new cream liqueur.

Mainie wears a sleek beeper and sparkly Celtic brooch. She looks great. True, they've elongated her a little; Mainie doesn't quite have the height for the big time, a fact that has never phased her since she's never been hungry for a career on the catwalk; it was just one of those sidelines in her ever-busier life that brought her, as usual, further success. Mainie has the Midas touch. No, Mainie has the Mainie touch. I had forgotten that. I had forgotten how evil she can look, especially with a tad of distortion. Ascendancy was right on the money with Mainie Doyle. One look at those big black tax-free eyes and executive vice-presidents will be lusting after Ireland as a location. CEOs will be lining up to invest in those bold, arching, mannish eyebrows. That ahead-of-schedule smile will be responsible for many a white elephant. Mainie's is a face that will launch a thousand joint projects. And she'll be proud, very proud. See, that's the difference between Mainie and me: she believes in what she's selling (besides herself), she believes in the Industrial Development Authority. Mainie Doyle could very well be Ireland's Greatest Resource. Hell, she even wants to come back and live here.

I checked her out several more times during the flight – nothing much else to do. *Your copy to take away*, it said on the cover of the magazine. I took it.

Baggage reclaim is insane, mental. You'd swear they'd discovered gold in the Dublin Mountains. The departure gate at Charles de Gaulle was nothing compared to this: I recognise somebody every thirty seconds, and sense I am recognised every three. Not a problem. What gets me is that, in a sense, I know everybody here, I recognise every face. Just the other night in the Chelsea Hotel I was giggling at an advert on cable TV. It was for a product called Galway Morning, a soap you will not find in any Irish bathroom. The camera crew had obviously gone back in time to shoot the commercial. But what really cracked me up were the actors with their in-your-face Irish faces: flaming red hair, freckles by Jackson Pollock, eyes so twinkly I swore they'd been smoking the same stuff I was. These airport faces are not clichés, but they are emphatically Irish. I can't say what the common denominator is. Perhaps it is their heart-sinking familiarity. I'm surrounded by the plain people of Ireland.

Despite the crowds, there is no shortage of baggage carts

(no expense has been spared to get everyone in and out of the country efficiently), but I don't need one. I'm travelling light – just this Coach carry-on and one suitcase – because I'm not staying long. The rest of my wardrobe is back in Paris, in my apartment on rue du Guignol (in the *troisième*, two blocks from the Pompidou). I share it with a rich kid from Orange County, Step Purchas, who claims to be writing a screenplay on Jim Morrison's last days, though *share* might not be the right word: I've spent no more than twenty nights there since June.

Christmas lights, pine sprigs and ribbons are festooned from the ceiling. In the middle of every baggage carousel stands a Styrofoam snowman. I find the carousel advertising the baggage from flight EI 407. It looks like luggage from a Milan flight is still circulating, so I hover at the edge of the crowd. Our snowman holds a sign saying *Hurry Up – I'm Melting!*

Somebody taps me on the shoulder. Don't tell me it's that engineer from Kildare I sat beside on the plane. Quite the charmer when I'm up in the clouds, in my element, I easily form these air-friendships; but they have no weight on the ground, for me at least. First Rule of Cool: don't end a journey with more baggage than you started with.

I turn around. It's Roderick de Brun. Coincidence? Not in my world, sweetheart. Things like this happen all the time, particularly at airports. Airports are my local pub.

'So it's true – Iremonger's home. Slaughter the fattened calf.'

'It's the very least you could do.' I smile.

Usually when Irish guys go away they lose weight – I know I'm leaner than ever before – but not Roderick. He looks exactly like he did six months ago: a combination of the well-fed barrister his father is and the rugger-bugger Roderick used to be. But Roderick, who is even taller than I am, carries it well. Girls find his girth a turn-on. I won't deny it, the guy's got presence. A few years back, Roderick came that close to being cast as the piano player in *The Uncommitted*, this (pretty crap) movie about a bunch of Southside guys who form a jazz band. They were crazy not to pick him. If it weren't for his congenital geniality, I think Roderick would be a kind of rival Iremonger. As it is, he is my long-time partner in crime, a founding member of the mad pinting gang, of which Dylan is the other essential element. God knows how long Roderick has been flying, but he's still looking pimp, wearing his signature oval Oliver Peoples glasses, and a new gilded toque.

'I like the hat,' I say.

'I like the jacket,' he replies.

He's talking about Nico. Nico is the name (the secret name) of my black leather jacket. You've got to give a name to something you love. And this was love at first sight. I saw Nico in the window of a vintage clothes store on Perry Street in Greenwich Village last August, and realised I'd been looking for her for years, probably ever since I heard that Leonard Cohen song 'Famous Blue Raincoat'. Well, Iremonger's defining item of clothing ain't torn at the shoulder: it's in mint condition. Nico is a 1950s Swedish motorbike cop's jacket with detachable lambswool lining. $850 I paid for her, and I would have paid double. She's been on my shoulders every day since. This jacket is my second skin. My one true love.

'So what the hell are you doing back?' Roderick asks me.

I shrug. It's an evil question. 'It's Christmas,' I say. And that's a bad answer. *I'm* not satisfied with that answer. Christmas means nothing to me, yet here I am – in Dublin. And that's not all, that's not the whole story . . . Spit it out, Iremonger: I have come back on the return portion of the ticket I flew out from Dublin on in June. I found it last week in a torn Diaspora

Travel disposable wallet I thought I had disposed of in Aix-en-Provence.

'I heard there was no way you would be back, Tom.'

'What exactly did you hear?'

'Well, a number of things. Someone said you were on location with Wim Wenders in Alice Springs; Vogue Fitzgerald told me that you were in a drug rehab facility in Santa Cruz, California; last week Dylan was adamant that you would be spending the holidays with Isabel Adjani's sister in Cannes; there was even briefly a rumour that you had died in Egypt.'

I can't help but smile. I love this stuff. I live for it. The more gossip, the more fictions, the more myths out there about Iremonger the better. If it could be bought, I'd gladly spend my whole inheritance on the power of bilocation. As it is, I have to settle for the odd morning when I half awake in two places – head in London, say, body in Los Angeles. But the sensation lasts no more than a few seconds. Before long all of me is falling out of somebody else's bed in Islington. But it's sweet while it lasts, that spatial *déjà vu*. Must be the drugs.

Roderick is still going on about how neat it is to have me back. So I change the subject,

'Enough about me.' Those words don't come easy. 'How was Argentina, for god's sake?'

'Excellent. I had this nightly gig at the Ulysses Bar in Buenos Aires. I learned how to ride a horse. I slept with one of Borges's granddaughters. I ate a lot of steak.'

'So no regrets about not doing King's Inns?'

Maybe you'll get the import of that comment if I tell you that Carmel Carraig-Dubh, in one of her more generous moments, called Roderick's old man 'one of the living legends of the Law Library, the tort king of Dublin'.

Roderick gives me a steely smile. 'No way.'

'How long are you back for?'

'Oh, a month at least. I got one of those McGowan visas in the lottery.'

'You did that?'

'Yeah, I sent 1,150 letters to the post office in Danforth, Maryland. It did the trick.'

'I should hope so. But why are you sticking around for a month?'

'You're not fit to be an American unless you've got clean blood and clean lungs. Got to get those tests done before the interview. That's on the 22nd of January. Then I'll be off to validate. What about yourself?'

'Well, let me see. I picked up two hundred Rolands in duty-free this morning. That might last me till New Year's Day.' (Right now I'm T - 192.)

Roderick smiles. 'Which conveniently means that you'll still be here for Mainie's party.'

I put on a sceptical expression. 'Yeah, but I'm not sure I want to go. Christmas in Dublin is going to be difficult enough without a Mainie Doyle affair.'

This is an excellent improvisation, if I say so myself, because I have *no idea* what Roderick is talking about. There's a chance he's just kidding – I usually know about parties on other continents, in alternative universes – but I can't take the risk of showing up my ignorance of what, axiomatically, would be a major social event. All of a sudden, I have something pretty close to a purpose in Dublin. If that party's on, I must be there.

'You know, it's a gas seeing the two of you in those adverts, the poster especially.'

'Isn't it just?'

'It's like you're watching over us or something, Iremonger.'

Adopting a heavy Polish accent, I respond, 'Young people of Ireland, I love you.'

Roderick chortles; sometimes I think he really is meant for the Law Library.

'Listen,' he says, 'it looks like fresh blood has come onto my carousel, I'd better go. I hope you're in the mood for some mad pinting later on.'

I smile. That's exactly the mood I'm in, now that logical old Roderick mentions it. For a moment it almost feels good to be back. 'I have no commitments.'

'Very funny, Iremonger. Anyhow, here's the deal: I'm going home to lick this jet lag, but I'll be meeting Dylan at six in Keogh's.'

'I'll be there.'

'Excellent.'

Roderick's gold-threaded toque bobs through the impatient crowds. I squeeze and BS my way to the edge of my carousel. I light up a Roland. This is a serious cigarette, sweetheart – unfiltered, densely flavoured, refreshingly addictive. You should try one. The brand has only been around about a year; I'd never heard of it till last June. The day I left Dublin I was riding the RER into Paris and saw an advert above the sliding doors. *Le Mort du Fumeur*, the copy read. I bought a packet in Relais H as soon as I got to Les Halles. After a couple of drags I was ready to convert.

A frizzy-haired woman caresses a navy-blue suitcase, but lets it move on. I don't want to see her fingering mine. I guess I'm a little touchy about my luggage. Blame it on Las Vegas. In Las Vegas my suitcase didn't show up. Not on the next flight, never. A caseful of Hugo Boss, Donna Karen, Ralph Lauren, Giorgio Armani – gone (thank god I was wearing Nico). As I speak some baggage handler from Iraq is probably changing into designer threads in the locker room at La Guardia. The cheque from Maverick Air didn't come close to covering the loss. Some items I will never replace. Now I know how Hemingway felt when that suitcase full of stories was stolen.

I light another Roland. Fewer and fewer items of luggage

are coming through the rubber curtain. Most of the Paris passengers, my air-brothers and -sisters, have deserted me and headed for customs. The latest Heathrow sortie is surrounding me. All that's left on the carousel is the sad baggage – cases held together with string and masking tape, bags that look like they landed on Lockerbie, coffin-ship trunks. Maybe their owners are in a state of denial. The same beat-up box marked FRAGILE has passed me by six times. It's times like this you notice all the faded ID tags smoothed into the rubber of the conveyor belt. This is not fair – in terms of airline logic, Iremonger logic, my case should have been the first one out since I was the last passenger to check in. But something tells me my suitcase is coming in on the next flight, or may be spending the night in Paris. If that's so, I'd gladly swap places.

Forget it – here it is. And I tell you, it's nothing to write home about, this suitcase. I really must go back to Galleries Lafayette and replace the leather-trimmed Louis Vuitton I lost en route to Vegas. In the last month I just haven't had the time. Instead I've been using this synthetic St Brendan I left Dublin with in June. As one edge nudges my shin, I reach down, grab hold of the case (feeling the tug and slide of the rubber current), flip over the tag – a finicky habit of mine – and see my father's symmetrical writing:

IREMONGER
29 CEDAR-OF-LEBANON RD
OWENSTOWN HILL
CO. DUBLIN
REP. OF IRELAND
PH: 353–1–2889434

The rubber current is beginning to win; hurriedly I haul the case off the belt.

My taste in EC customs is similar to my taste in cable TV – it's the blue channel for me.

I'm clean, I swear. There was a time in my late teens (ah, those early Iremonger days) when I got off on smuggling a little hash back from London or Amsterdam, but not any more; I've lost that innocence, I'm afraid.

I find myself eyeing one of the customs men – I'll flirt with anyone – daring him to stop me, delay me. Is it too late to get arrested under the Offences against the State Act? Some people would say that I *am* an Offence against the State (and I'd take it as a compliment). Maybe the authorities could hold me for the maximum seven days. Christmas in Dublin Castle might be more fun than Christmas in Owenstown Hill.

I get the dreaded nod – yes! I hope they look inside every one of my Paul Smith socks. For the first time in my life, I would welcome a strip search. Anal examination? Be my guest – it would be less painful that the interrogation I'm going to get from my mother. Maybe I should blurt out that I've just swallowed ten little bags of smack, then later tonight plead insanity and ask to be deported.

I put my carry-on down on the counter and start to unzip it. But my heart sinks when the man in blue waves a negating finger. Looking at me close-up he says with a leery smile, 'You're the fella in the IDA ad, aren't you?'

Too readily, I confess.

I walk around the flimsy wall that divides customs and the entrance to the waiting area. My heart – that uncool organ – is thumping as I reach the threshold. Its sliding doors are frozen open by the volume of arrivals.

I cross over, and feel like I've walked on stage. But this is not the feeling I got the last time I actually did so, strutting down the runway at the Smirnoff Young Designer of the Year Show back in May, one of the highlights of Trinity Week. This is more like the fear I felt walking on stage for the *first* time – doing my bit part in the fourth year production of *Julius Caesar* at Berchmans, St John Strongbow sneering in the wings. And I don't like that. I don't like it at all. I will not put up with any hassle from the past on this trip.

The waiting crowds are disturbingly well-ordered. No one, not even a small child, is out in front of the chrome barriers; nor is anybody stepping over the blue lines marking the passenger exits. For a moment I think I've landed in Switzerland, until I see a no-nonsense ban-garda (a cutie) to my right. Heads bob in anticipation. Countless eyes check me out. At first I think it's the poster. Then I realise it can't be. Most of these people, wrinklies and babies, won't have seen it, won't have walked the *via dolorosa* from air bridge to baggage hall – they are the ones left behind. So they must mistake me, momentarily, for their brother, son, lover, whatever. Though I'm not actively looking for them, I'm uneasily aware that I haven't made eye contact with my parents.

I exit the homecoming stage. After the sardine treatment behind the barriers, people don't hold back. They squeeze out of the audience and speed to their loved-ones. Reunions reel around me – I hear the inarticulate speech of recognition, see fingers splayed on backs, negotiate abandoned carts. But I still don't see my parents. How ironic if, in her excitement, my mother has taken the flight information down wrong. And how annoying. It's going to be murder getting a taxi today. And I'm not getting the bus. I don't *do* airport buses.

But here they are, of course – here come my mother and father; they must have been doing the sensible thing, as usual: sitting in the rows of cushioned seats to the side of the homecoming stage. My mother's wearing a pretty smartly cut carbon mélange tweed jacket, sort of third-generation Emanuel Ungaro. My father's wearing his Bavarian hat, a mottled-brown monstrosity with a fly-fishing feather in the band that even as a child I knew to be a crime against fashion. His famous grey raincoat is no more than a misdemeanour.

As I lower my case to the ground, I take in the tentative optimism of my father's smile, the wrinkled innocence of my mother's expression. I'm not prepared for this. A splash of soupy emotion in my chest unsettles me – these days my feelings are usually designed, procured, swallowed, snorted. So I go for the classic Iremonger smile, the one orchestrated by the ridge of tough muscle either side of my lips.

'Hi, people,' I say.

My parents don't say anything. My mother reaches me first. Or rather the violently nice smell of Aisling, her scent of choice, reaches me first. I kiss her daintily on the cheek. Flakes of her bisque foundation come off on my lips, which makes me want to recoil. I don't. Instead, my arms virtually encircle her. Meanwhile, one of her arms clambers around the carry-on, which I still have slung across my shoulder, and joins the other one across my spine. She holds me tight and pulls me towards her, as if she were trying to wrestle me to the ground.

My father is standing behind her, his own arms outstretched tentatively, like that way of saying the Our Father that was becoming trendy when I stopped going to mass. He's actually lost a little weight, but I can't say he looks healthy. There's this yellow tinge in his complexion, not a smiley-face yellow but undeniably amber. There's even a hint of it, behind his square bi-focals, in the white of his bulbous grey-blue eyes. Is this what they mean by a jaundiced look? Is this what nine months of retirement does to you?

My mother is still clasping me, silently.

'Say something, Mum!' I demand good-naturedly.

Immediately she releases me. Her eyes are dry, almost. She looks me up and down, smiling and shaking her head.

'Would you look at him, Risteárd,' she says, 'skin and bones.'

'It's the starving-artist look, isn't it, Tom?' my father replies as he finally moves in for his reunion hug.

'Exactly, Dad,' I say in the midst of a lot of back slapping.

But my mother goes on. 'Your cheekbones, Tom. I can't get over your cheekbones. Have you been feeding yourself at all?'

I don't want to know about it. I want to know about *his* cheekbones – why they are visible, for example. But I don't say anything.

'Sure, I have, Mum. Never skip an airline meal.'

'Well, you can forget about airlines and airports for the next few weeks.'

The next few *weeks*? Well, I guess I don't want to cause a scene straight away explaining that I'm out of here ASAP. So I don't interrupt as my mother continues, 'You know where you are now, I hope.'

My father speaks for me, 'Of course he does. It's Saturday, it must be Dublin, Ireland.'

I slap my forehead. 'This is *Dublin*?'

My father smiles, my mother doesn't. She says, 'A pity you couldn't have managed to get here yesterday.'

'Why yesterday?'

She looks perplexed, and a little scandalised.

'Why yesterday? Because of your uncle! Because of Columb!'

'Of course, of course. I just forgot he got in *yesterday*.'

My mother looks sceptical. Well she might. It had slipped my mind entirely. When I phoned a few nights ago to say that I would be coming back, she did tell me that there would be another guest staying at Cedar-of-Lebanon Road over Christmas. Uncle Columb, my father's younger brother and only sibling. He's a Jesuit, and that's one of the big reasons why I went to Berchmans, though I'm not going to hold that against him. Lives in this tiny, super-poor central African country called Remoko that still manages to produce very colourful postage stamps. I guess he's passed through my life four or five times. How do I remember him? Tall, thin, a little creepy, a kind of haggard Jeremy Irons. Last time he was home was just before my Leaving Cert, when the old man died. Time before that? Must have been the pope's visit. Funny – now that I think of it – this will be the first priest I've talked to in fucking *years*.

My mother is going on about what an exhausting flight Uncle Columb had, coming all the way from Remoko.

'He wanted to come out to the airport today, but I told him that he was mad, that he should go back to bed. And he listened, would you believe. But he's dying to see you, Tom. Everybody is – Triona and Finbar and the kids. Dying to see you.'

'And I'm dying to see them. So let's get out of this airport, shall we?'

This time both of my parents smile.

Leaving, I notice one final reunion scene. It's impossible not to. The grouping has this awful aura about it. Three people, probably a brother and two sisters, all in their thirties. The brother, who has his hands scrunched into the pockets of a shabby brown bomber jacket, looks away, as if ashamed, while the woman beside him clasps her sister's hands, delivering a dismal monologue. The arrival's eyes are slick, though no tear has yet taken the dive. If I went over and wheeled away her chaotically loaded cart, I don't think any of them would notice.

'Count your blessings,' I hear my mother say.

According to my Tzara (genuine, bought in Geneva), it's

only 1:55 – no, wait, I'm still on European Standard Time – it's only 12:55, but the daylight is already looking tired. When I left Paris this morning it was seriously cold, but a high, clear sky more than compensated for the chill. In Dublin I look up and see that constitutionally guaranteed grey sky. Cloud cover is absolute. For a strange second I wonder if I'll ever penetrate it again.

We cross the road to the car-park pay point. On the roof is this giant red-ribboned gold-lamé box balanced on one edge. It reminds me of the gift-wrapped presents I got for my family in Bloomingdale's last weekend. I really splashed out – must have clocked up something like $500 on my Wanderlust card (don't go into exile without it). On top of that, add another hundred bucks to CeltEx the crap to Dublin at this time of year. They'd better like what they get.

For my father it's a big deal that the computer that eats your ticket and tells you what the damage is was made by American Machines. Back in the terminal, he took my modest suitcase before I could stop him, but in the car park he wheels it along as if he were dragging a dead body. At last he stops and puts it down and takes a remote control out of his raincoat.

'I've got it,' I say, when he reaches down for the case again.

He doesn't argue. Instead he aims the remote in the direction of a shiny metallic-green Senator. He clicks and the locks stand to attention with a sharp chirp. That sound – music to my ears – is a reminder of how wise my father, his father's executor, was to wait five years, to wait until Dublin house prices sky-rocketed, before selling the old man's investment property on Raglan Road, a quarter of which had been promised to me in his will.

'So this is how you guys are spending *your* inheritance.'

'There are no more company cars, Tom.'

'Yeah, but still, this is a pretty nifty replacement for the Chieftan. I'm proud of you, Dad.'

'Well, I reckon this one will last me.'

'You sit up front, Tom,' my mother tells me, opening the back door on the driver's side.

'As soon as I've loaded the luggage,' I tell her.

I turn to my father and say, 'Great engine. But doesn't this model come equipped with at least a radio?'

'Stolen last week,' he replies. He lets the handbrake off and starts to back out, sucking air, fart-like, in through the side of his mouth, a side-effect he gets from grave concentration. For some reason, I find this as funny as when I was a kid. I fold my lips to stifle imminent giggles.

'It's the *second* time it's happened since we got the car,' adds my mother from the back. 'The insurance money for the first one hasn't even come through yet.'

'Twice in six months?'

'It's happening all over the Southside, Tom. They come around about four or five o'clock in the morning and smash the side window.'

'What about the alarm?'

'Alarms don't mean anything to them. When it went off the other night, Daddy got out of bed and started banging on the window. And the little pup just looked up and *waved* at him, didn't he, Risteárd?'

My father doesn't say anything, just makes the sucking sound. My mother is undeterred, 'The place has gone crazy. Joy riders wait for each other in the church car park and then go racing down the Ascent. A house on Belvedere Road was broken into while the family were out at a funeral. Old Mrs Neary down on Folly Lane had her handbag snatched on her way to Mass.'

'What about the cops? Have they caught anybody?'

My father sighs. 'You've been away a long time, Tom.'

The Senator speeds south along the motorway. I guess incoming tourists must think all the roads in the country are going to be like this, that there's going to be some Irish autobahn system. Well, they'll be much the wiser leaving. The Dublin Mountains – now there's a place to hide – smoulder in the distance ahead. To my left I can see Howth, rock-like from this point of view, with the Northside suburbs I might be able to name if you put a gun to my head in between. I'm used to looking at Howth from the back bedrooms of Cedar-of-Lebanon Road, whale-like across the water, the strong arm of the sheltering bay.

The interrogation has begun.

'So when you phoned two nights ago, you were still in New York?'

'No, Mum, I got a flight out of JFK last Monday night.'

'To Paris?'

'Yes.'

'But that's not where you phoned from.'

'No. I phoned from Brussels. I was staying with some friends.'

'Irish friends?'

I laugh. 'That's what you always want to know. Is there something morally superior about Irish friends?'

'No,' she replies with laboured patience, 'I was just curious to know if you met any Irish people in Brussels.'

'I meet Irish people everywhere. It's impossible not to meet Irish people. I don't even blink when it happens now.'

'Meabhdh Pembry's daughter is there.'

'That's nice.'

'Working for the EEC.'

'EC,' my father corrects her.

'Doing very well,' my mother adds.

As we run out of motorway I'm running out of time to make a crucial request. Soon my father will be turning for the toll bridge, gateway to the southern suburbs. I've got to keep him heading towards the city.

'Hey, Dad,' I say nonchalantly, 'would you mind dropping me off in town?'

For a long moment the only sound is the powerful thrum of the Senator's engine. Then my mother says, 'What do you mean *Would you mind dropping me off in town?* Columb's waiting to see you! Triona and Finbar and the kids are coming down to see you at three o'clock!'

'They are? Well, I've still got to buy a present for Uncle Columb.'

'I'll drive you to Stillorgan after lunch. You can do your shopping there.'

'Yeah, but lunch is the real problem,' I lie. 'I promised Mainie Doyle I'd meet her at Bewley's, Westmoreland Street at 1:30.'

'Mainie Doyle?'

'Yeah.'

'I was talking to her mother at the Lady Captain's dinner, and I got the impression from her that the two of you were finished.'

'Mainie and I will never be finished,' I say as calmly as I can, wondering what my mother knows that I don't. 'It's not in the nature of our relationship.'

'But I told the kids you'd decorate the Christmas tree with them.'

'You haven't decorated the tree yet?'

'No. Of course not. We were waiting for you.'

'Well, Mum, that's a touching display of faith, but I made arrangements to meet Mainie for lunch on Christmas Eve months ago. I never made arrangements with *anyone* to decorate a tree.'

'Months ago? So you knew you were coming home for Christmas the whole time you were away.'

For a moment I don't say anything, just stare at an ugly redbrick church that's coming up; we're on the Swords Road now. They've put up a lot of ugly churches here in my lifetime. The Renaissance, Dublin-style.

'Yes and no,' I shrug. 'Difficult question to answer.'

We're coming up to the junction with Collins Avenue, the *crucial* junction: if my father gets into the left lane, Owenstown Hill here we come.

'The kids will be very disappointed,' my mother adds. 'And besides, your father and I wanted to talk to you about something.'

Oh, that does it – I'm walking into town now if necessary. Luckily, my father comes to the rescue,

'Let it go, Sinéad,' my father says quietly. 'Let *him* go.'

'Oh, off with him,' she replies.

My father doesn't switch lanes, the lights stay on our side, the Senator cruises through the crossroads, but still I'm not satisfied. The way they're talking – it's like I'm not really here. And I get the feeling they've had this conversation before.

This is not the scenic route. The soggy litter in front of MISSISSIPPI FRIED CHICKEN on the Drumcondra Road makes me temporarily nauseous. The Royal Canal is cynically named. I'd forgotten what a toilet Dorset Street is, but it's Park Avenue compared to Upper Gardiner Street. The front garden of a boarded-up Victorian house is full of rubbish – furniture foam, rusted bedsprings, broken toys, smashed-up prams.

'Jesus,' I mutter.

'Indignant?' My father smiles.

I shrug. 'Who wouldn't be?'

'Do something about it.'

'What can I do!'

'Write a letter to *The Irish Times*.'

For a moment I think this is some weak reference to the IDA poster, but then I remember something else. Oh, that man has quite a memory. I wrote one letter one time when I was fifteen to the paper protesting the demolition of this abandoned Big House in Blackrock. (Strongbow gave me a hard, sarcastic time about it, of course.)

'Anywhere down by the river would be great,' I suggest.

Lower Gardiner Street is another story. Lower Gardiner Street reminds me of the Lower East Side – heavy gentrification is going on. They've got these new apartment buildings pretending to be the old Georgian houses that they pulled down to make way for redevelopment.

'Those apartments are meant to be gorgeous inside,' my mother says.

I know what she's getting at.

'Yeah, well, the facade lacks architectural integrity, if you ask me.'

Mainie said that one time about some building in Berlin.

'They're meant to be a bargain.'

'I should hope so.' How can I tell her that I'm not sure I have enough dough left to make a ten per cent downpayment? That I've spent maybe seventeen grand on my anti-odyssey out of the twenty-one I inherited?

Now my father gets in on the act. 'It's a Section 42 development. There was a similar scheme back in Daddy's day. That's how he got Raglan Road.' I am tired of them hinting at what I should do with *my* money. 'And, you know, without Raglan Road—'

'Please,' I say, 'I appreciate your interest, but I don't see myself living around here.'

'You're as safe here as you are in Owenstown Hill,' my father mutters.

'Maybe Triona and Finbar should invest their money here. It's just a few blocks from the Financial Services Centre.'

'They already have,' my mother informs me. 'They're renting it out to a very nice couple from England. Well, he's nicer than she is.'

My father stops the Senator down-river of the Custom House. I open the lock, and turn to my mother. 'I'm not sure I'll make it home for dinner. But don't worry, I'll get something in town.'

She's busy lighting up an Extra King-Sized Gossamer. 'Oh, I'm not worried at all.' She lowers the whiny power window a little, and blows a deft jet of smoke out through the opening. I've always liked the way my mother smokes, I have to admit.

'Okay, well, I'll see you guys when I see you.'

I hook my fingers around the door handle, but her voice stops me from pulling it. 'I suppose it wouldn't interest you to know that you uncle is concelebrating Midnight Mass at Berchmans tonight. I think he was hoping you'd do one of the Prayers of the Faithful.'

I turn to her and smile. 'I don't think I'm the right person to ask. But, hey, say a prayer *for* me, if you like.'

She nods thoughtfully. 'I will. To St Jude.'

I laugh. 'Why St Jude?'

'She's the patron saint of hopeless causes, Tomás. Here, take my house keys for now.'

I pluck them from her hand. 'It's Tom, Mother, Tom.'

I open the door. My father touches my arm. 'One *more* thing.'

I feign patience. 'Yes, Dad?'

'Bet you don't have any Irish money.'

'Bet I have my Puntpower card with me. I'm still a Tara Bank customer in good standing.'

'Well, then, you're set, aren't you.'

'Hope so. Say hi to everybody at home.'

As I watch the Senator drive down-river towards the toll bridge, I feel a twinge of regret I haven't gone with them. But it's better this way. Going straight back to Owenstown Hill would be too much, too soon. I would get the emotional bends. Town will be my compression chamber.

I walk up-river. On my left is the black Liffey, on my right the restored brillance of the trade temple (I've blanked on the name of the architect). If more of the city looked like that, maybe I could live here, from time to time.

Now that my father has mentioned it, I am anxious to get some Irish cash, get liquid again. Besides my Puntpower card, I have a small basket of foreign currencies in my Gucci wallet, but my favourite line of credit, my peerless Wanderlust, I left in the pocket of a corduroy J. Crew shirt, which I stuffed into my carry-on, which is in the boot of the Senator. So I divert to the nearest Tara Bank branch I can think of – Abbey Street, where the Christmas decorations look like they've been up since last year. Dodging a beggar, I swipe my card and gain entrance to the Puntpower lobby.

But as I queue up to use one of the machines – third person in line – I have a sickening epiphany: it has been six months since my last automatic teller withdrawal; I cannot remember my personal identification number. Second person in line – all I can remember is that I had some kind of mnemonic for it, but what? Some short word composed out of the first nine letters of the alphabet. HIGH? HEAD? DEAD? I translate them into numbers, but no combination sounds remotely right. The machine is free. I step up to it and fatalistically feed it my card. It asks me for the one thing I haven't got. Blankly I look down at the demanding screen until I can't ignore the rustle of impatience behind me. There's nothing else for it but to free associate: I punch in the first four numbers that come to my fingers.

The machine swallows my card.

Apply to your branch for retrieval, it tells me. On the way into the lobby I've seen a notice informing customers that Tara Bank will reopen on Wednesday.

'What? Not even a second chance?' I bark. 'You're meant to give me three goes, you bastard.'

'Not at Christmas,' says a deep Dublin voice behind me. 'Too many robbers.'

'Great.'

I turn around and stalk out of the lobby, finding myself back on the bustling, darkening, crummy streets of Dublin – without plastic, without a PIN, without a bloody punt.

2

No Room

What a profitable afternoon it's turned out to be. It's like
. . . Christmas. My location? The Shelbourne Hotel. Interior. Early evening. I'm sitting in a deep armchair in the
Lord Mayor's Lounge. A swanky location – not Manhattan
swanky, of course, but respectably plush – stucco, chand-
eliers, furry wallpaper, calm landscapes from the days when
the Brits were calling the shots. Chick radar picked up on
me as soon as I walked in the room, even old Protestant
lady chick radar. Afternoon tea is being served but I'm
drinking Furstenburg, Dublin's own on-tap German beer,
the basic fuel of the mad pinting gang. Snorting sneachta
(I do remember the Irish for snow) does two things to me:
leaves me with an evil thirst, and kills whatever appetite I
have. So even though those fat scones and prissy sandwiches
look good enough to be photographed, I'm not going to
touch a single one. But I'm sure my guest will, when she
finally arrives.

It didn't take me long to figure out what I had to do. So
my card had been kidnapped, big deal. There was no need

to panic (there's never a need to panic). I knew of a more dynamic institution than Tara Bank, one that was open on Saturdays. For six months I've been picking up mail, cashing traveller's cheques, and changing money at Wanderlust offices worldwide. Today would be no different.

I headed for Westmoreland Street. The Christmas tree on O'Connell Street was . . . well, let's just say it wasn't quite Rockefeller Plaza. It was slow going over O'Connell Bridge. Besides the flow of shoppers north and south you had all these kids – bedraggled Goths, non-designer grungy types, hyper-alert urchins in shiny track-suits – standing around display cases of cheap jewellery and the same old useless U2 bootlegs (not that I think there's such a thing as a use*ful* U2 bootleg). The first time I ever tried to buy ganj – we're talking pre-Iremonger days here, the days of wishful thinking – was from one of these hawkers. I had been informed by a guy the year below me at Berchmans that you could score a ten spot by asking the hippie with the Benny Hill hat for a packet of crisps. This proved not to be true. I chose not to replay the full incident on my memory-video. I was glad to hit the Southside. The tracksuits started to thin out.

Wanderlust was open but quiet. I got served straight away at the Bureau de Change. I didn't need my card. From my Gucci wallet I pulled out sixty francs, five hundred drachmas, three thousand lira, and two dollars. I came back out onto Westmoreland Street with a ten-punt note – the one with Joyce on the cover – and some loose change.

Now what would the average guy, the sensible guy have done? He would have walked straight over to the 46A terminus on Fleet Street and gone home. But being sensible has very little to do with being smart in the Iremonger bible. Okay, I could have taken that Bombardier back to Owenstown Hill and made a cameo appearance – putting a bauble or two on the tree then splitting again with my Wanderlust card and some borrowed cash. But I knew it wouldn't have turned out like that. I can get past my mother or my father, or even my mother and my father, but all those Iremongers together, including an uncle I haven't seen since I was seventeen – that would have been too much, even for me. No, I'm not being modest when I say I don't think I could have escaped the collective mass of my family. And besides, instinct, my infallible Iremonger instinct, told me that evil things would happen if I stayed in town. And, let's face it, what evil things were going to happen to me back in Owenstown Hill? All I had to look forward to there was the Big Conversation my mother had promised me in the car. I could guess what that was going to be all about – another lame attempt to trash the Iremonger Project, to inject me with self-doubt, to make me *stop and think*, to pay homage to that ultimate fiction, the Future.

I had only ten quid to improvise with, but wearing Nico I felt like a million dollars.

It was the right move.

I am doing something out of character. I am waiting. I cannot remember the last time I waited for someone. Not only that, but I was *on time* for this rendezvous. As a rule I like to be running late. Since graduation I have been running late all over the planet. Tardiness – except for certain crucial flights – is one of my few scruples. I remember something I once heard Simone de Beauvoir say in a television interview: if J-P Sartre said to you, I will meet you at the Acropolis this day ten years from now, he would be there. Well, so would Iremonger. With one difference: I would get there twenty minutes after the appointed hour.

So this is going totally against the Iremonger code, I admit it. But look at it this way: unexamined, a code can turn into a tradition. It's healthy to make an exception from time to time. Especially when the exception is Mainie Doyle.

Even more extraordinary, Ms Conscientiousness is late,

fifteen minutes late, but that doesn't bother me too much. It's busy in here but it's crazy out there – the last shopping hour before Christmas, need I say more? I can deal with Mainie Doyle being late. I'm not going to get stood up. You see, there are two types of people in this world: the stood-up and the stander-uppers. A long, long time ago I used to be one of the stood-up (though I barely remember what that was like). The important thing is that both Mainie and I are very definitely stander-uppers (that she chooses not to use this power is beside the point). And it is impossible for one true stander-upper to stand up another, if you get my drift. It's just not going to happen. Mainie just has a lot of shopping to do.

What's really irritating me is that old fart of a piano player a few tables away. Right now he's doing a muzak remake of 'O Come, O Come Emmanuel'. I can't stand Christmas carols, even when they're played right. They're worse than U2. (You really want to get to Iremonger? Play me a CD of U2 singing Christmas carols. That should destroy me right on the spot.)

Ah, Trinity – Iremonger's nurturing mother. They had that scaffolding back up in front of the old facade; I guess they're in a no-win situation with that acid rain crap. They should do what they do in Paris – put up a giant camouflage canvas depicting the building; it looks better than the real thing.

As usual there was a bunch of people hanging around the front gates trying not to look like they'd been stood up. I saw one or two of them glance up furtively at the blue clock. The only people who didn't look like they'd been stood up were Goldsmith and Burke, up there on their pedestals. I've always liked those guys, even though they were basically literary figures. They've got attitude. They aren't waiting for nobody. Who knows, maybe in a hundred years' time they'll have Iremonger up there. Isn't that how Ireland rewards its revolutionaries? I've got some poses that would look evil in bronze.

Front Arch was closed. I knocked confidently – a little experiment in reverse psychology. This was important because there were one or two porters who might not be so delighted to see me back at the old alma mater, who might have ideas about not letting me back on campus. But the experiment was unnecessary. Bosco answered.

'Jaysus, would yeh look who it is!'

A four-hand shake followed. I was very glad to see him. I owed Bosco a lot, and he owed me small amounts of money. I was not at all interested in reclaiming that cash because Bosco had done me many favours over the years, including personally raiding my rooms on the evening of the last Trinity Ball and failing to see half a dozen ticketless people with joyces up their noses. He's a good man. As a rule he doesn't approve of students, but he makes exceptions for the likes of me. Most of his working day consists of guarding the newspapers in the lounge of the Phil. I used to go there a lot to crash on the sagging couches in the afternoons.

'Bosco, how come you got stuck doing front arch?'

'Ah, skeleton staff, Tommy, because of the holidays. And I tell yeh, the last purson in the wurld I expected to be lettin' in was Tom Iremonger. Sure they told me all sorts of tings about yeh.'

'What did they say?'

'One gurl said she knew for a fact you were livin' in Cork. Someone else said you'd joined a cult in I-ran or one of dem places. You wouldn't know wha' to believe.'

'Believe it all, Bosco, believe it all. Anyway, I need to find out something. I'm here to see my friend Ardal McQuaid. Could you look up in the book where his rooms are this year?'

This simple request provoked a very rich smile. 'Oh, I don't need to look it up in the book. Try 18.3.1 over in

Rubrics, though you'll be lucky if his eminence is still there.'

We wished each other happy Christmas and I went through Front Arch into college proper. A year ago this place had been my little kingdom. Now it was a forgotten province of my hastily conquered empire, left to the strongest to rule in my absence. But the symmetry, silence, and cobblestones got to me all of a sudden. For a moment I found myself wondering if I wouldn't like to trade it all back – the money, the rumours, the frequent flyer miles – for something a little less . . . hectic. Then I told myself to stop being ridiculous, remember what Lloyd Cole said, Don't look back.

I saw those flames of red hair coming towards me along the Phil side of Library Square. The Bish's head is the spitting image, I swear, of the Versace trademark Medusa. Bish had his chin held high, staring at the world as if it were a bad waiter. But when he saw me his expression changed. Bish and I go back a long way – four years. We embraced by the Campanile.

'I knew it,' he said, 'I *knew* you'd be back.'

'You did?'

'Yeah, I read what Carmel Carraig-Dubh wrote about you and that princess, and I said to myself, Lichtensteinian royal family or no Lichtensteinian royal family, he'll be back.'

'What made you so sure?'

He shrugged. 'Birds fly south in winter.'

'Ever the philosopher, Bish.'

This was more than a joke. Go to the Department of Mental and Moral Science in Trinity and they will tell you all about Ardal McQuaid – he's the poster boy of the Anglo-American analytical tradition. By some minor miracle, having read nothing but criticism and biography for four years – and not very much of those either – I ended up with a 2.2 last summer in Pure English. I can proudly say that I am a college graduate, and proudly add that I have never read an entire book published before 1945. Bish got a first and some mother of a gold medallion. Having said that, consult Carmel Carraig-Dubh's column in *IoS* and you will find Ardal McQuaid being described as a mover and shaker in Dublin's alternative club scene. Consult the Bish himself and he will tell you that he is a 'post-modern impresario', whatever that means. (He might grudgingly acknowledge his status as a doctoral student at TCD.) But I will tell you what he essentially is: Bish is a pusher. That's right – he's one of those pioneers who's broken an old taboo by running both clubs and drugs, though not, he insists, at the same time. What can I say? I wasn't there to dance. The Bish was my greatest resource.

'So where are you off to?' I asked.

'There's an Almodovar retrospective on at the IFC. I'm going down to catch a matinee of *Matador*.'

'That's a pity because I really need some advice.'

'Some advice? Why didn't you say so? I've got a few minutes. I've always got time for Iremonger.'

So we went up to his rooms. And when I say rooms, I mean *rooms*. I had always thought the phrase 'living in rooms' to be a figure of speech. When I lived on campus last year – over on New Square, pretty close to where Beckett used to live – I had my own bedsit but had to share a kitchen and bog; those living in a suite of rooms shared everything but their bedroom. As a scholar of the college, Bish had been living on campus since our third undergrad year and had always had a big say in what rooms he wanted. Last year he'd shared a charming little apartment in Botany Bay with some other brains. But this year Bish was out on his own. He had managed to get a set of rooms all to himself on the top floor of Rubrics. For Christ's sake, the guy was living in a seventeenth-century penthouse in the centre of Dublin, rent free.

'Bish, how did you get this place?' I asked, trying to dampen down the awe in my voice.

'I threatened to leave the department and go to Stanford.'

I didn't know whether to believe him. There was more to it than just living space. In his living room Bish had a Mac, a laser printer, a television, a VCR, and a fax-telephone. Other old rooms on campus had barely left the age of candles. In the time I'd been away, it appeared that Bish McQuaid had become a big operation, a very big operation indeed.

'Take a seat, Tom.'

I sat down in a leather director's chair – not college furniture, to be sure; nothing here was college furniture.

'I've just got to check out Ardal's pharmacy.' He smiled.

He went into another room. I flicked through a glossy black copy of Adorno's *Minima Moralia* I found lying on the glass coffee table in front of me – not reading, I hasten to add, just *flicking*; I find it soothing sometimes. Bish came back a minute later carrying a silver tray. He put it down on the glass and sat down in a twin chair. On the tray were little transparent bags of powder and tiny porcelain bowls, each containing several tabs. I felt a little glow inside me. I knew this was good shit, almost as good as anything I could pick up in Paris or Berlin or LA. You see, Bish is strictly designer, strictly Class A. Go down to any pub on the docks if you want to get fuckers or rolling stones, sub-standard unicorns or apollos, lines of nirvana cut with baking powder. Bish, with his London contacts and his New York network, is interested in a more refined high. He knows that what passes for ecstasy in Tallaght feels like melancholia in Dublin 4.

I leaned over and took a closer look at the contents of the tray. I recognised the old reliables straight away: cranberries, green cards, altar boys, charliebirds.

'Feel the quality,' Bish said.

'I'm sure they're great. But my dancing days are over. I

think it's sneachta time. In fact, I think I might just let it snow, let it snow, let it snow right through Christmas.' I picked up a packet and wiggled it. 'What's this?'

'Your old favourite.'

'Semtex.' I smiled.

'Yes, but that's not what I would recommend.'

'Why not?'

'I have concerns about tolerance.'

'Based on what?'

'Well, your face for a start, Iremonger. Look at those cheekbones! You look comparatively plump in the infamous poster.'

'Who are you, Bish, my mother?' On the surface I was being very joky.

So was he. 'No, but I do want what's best for you. That's why I would suggest this product, just in from London, BNF, British Nuclear Fuel. Or even better, something that took a circuitous route to reach me – Bogota via Belfast – my taster's choice, my Christmas blend, the B-Special.'

He handed me the baggy. I stared at the powder. The white reminded me of the restored Customs House. The good shit detector in my gut was going off the chart.

'How much?' I asked.

'Eight jimmy joyces a bag. You'll get three lines out of that.'

So there had been a little inflation going on in the time I'd been away. But I knew better than to complain about prices to the Bish. He simply refused to do business with people who were looking for a cheap high, or even a reasonably priced high. And asking for credit would only earn his contempt, although I saw from the swipe hooked up to his computer that he now took credit cards. There was only one possible alternative to walking out of here empty handed.

I said very matter-of-factly, 'Okay, I'll sample it now, get back to you later about a transaction.' I held out the bag. This was an example of Iremonger *chutzpah* because although this had been our procedure in the past when Ardal was starting me out on a new product, the treat was always his suggestion. The Bish is a touchy kind of guy, and you can never be quite sure what he's going to get touchy about.

But he took the bag. 'Of course. Let me be mother once again.'

He unsealed the bag and shook out a fat line. While he was concentrating on that I slipped the joyce out of my thin wallet. And while I was shovelling up the sneachta, Bish went over to his desk and came back with a flyer. I stood up. I had to stand up.

'Well, what's this?'

'It's for the club I'm running between now and New Year's day – 1916, at the old Tivoli Hotel down on Fleet Street. Major investment. We did a big promotional thing yesterday in front of the GPO.'

'Very clever.' And it was – the flyer was a piss-take on the Proclamation. 'But why 1916?'

'It's only going to last a week.'

I exploded with laughter, but I think we both realised that it was mainly the B-Special kicking in.

'So you know where to find me, Tom.'

'Thanks, I appreciate it.' And I truly did, and do – when he really gets into running a club, drugs go on the backburner for the Bish.

'For you, Iremonger, anything.'

'I better get out of here, Bish. I feel like I've got half a dozen fucking Rottweilers chasing me.'

'I better tidy up.'

Letting me out he said, 'Oh, by the way, nice jacket.' Lightly, almost reverently, he touched Nico's shoulder. 'Where did you get it?'

I laughed again. 'That would be telling now, wouldn't it?'

*　　*　　*

The pianist is wearing a toupé. A pretty subtle one, but he's no less bald. This strange gift for sussing out rugs – I can spot them twenty rows away on a plane – is something I've inherited from my mother. It may be her greatest legacy. But it's small consolation now for the for emotional distress Rugman is causing me by playing this endless Richard Clayderman inspired version of 'Angels We Have Heard on High'.

I giddily recrossed the cobblestones, the Rottweilers in hot pursuit. Bosco let me out through Front Arch and I started to glide up Grafton Street. The pedestrianised section was as crowded and close as the Tangier Casbah. Nevertheless, I sailed steadily up the street, and people got out of my way. It seemed like every second person recognised me – there were nods, salutes, and comments, not all of them positive – *It's Irefucker* . . . *Isn't that the ponce in the poster?* – but any publicity is good publicity as far as I'm concerned. The Christmas decorations festooned across the streets, featuring these giant mock-lanterns, looked snazzy. But maybe everything was beginning to look better under snow.

And then suddenly, outside A-Wear, I saw my salvation. It was so unlikely but so perfect that I laughed out loud. Firbolg thought I was laughing because I was pleased to see him. And, in a way, he was right.

Brían Firbolg used to be a friend of mine. He lived around the corner, on the Ascent. He went to a different school, St Paul's, a Holy Ghost factory down near the American embassy. We hadn't seen very much of each other since sixth year, the year of my metamorphosis. And by that stage I was having major problems with his caution and his crimes against fashion and this problem he had with saliva over-production. The drooling is what really got to me.

I went to Trinity, he went to yucky death – UCD. Yeah, he

was an acquaintance of my caterpillar years. I would have avoided him, or flashed passed him with a quick *hey*, but he was doing something interesting. He was shaking a can. He was shaking an open-top can two-thirds full of money. And I don't just mean coins. My cash-sensitive eyes – keener still with the B-Special kicking in – saw nunny bunnies, joyces, o'connells, and even hydes in there. Firbolg's badge said, *Roomkeepers*, whatever that meant. He had it pinned to a chunky vomit-green sweater (Elephant Man winter collection), but I didn't let that deter me. I stopped and donated my joyce.

'Thanks! Tomás – Tom! Gee, how are you doing?' Niagara Falls were still in business.

'I'm grand, Brían, grand. And how are you doing?'

'I'm fine, fine,' he slurped. 'God, I didn't expect to see you. I heard you were travelling somewhere weird – yeah, India.'

I shook my head. 'Nepal. Been there.'

'And so you're home for Christmas. Your parents must be delighted.'

'They are, they are.'

I was going to suggest going for coffee but I felt jittery enough as it was. I just couldn't have sat still. The coffee talk would just have to happen out on the street.

'So what is this – your final year in Engineering?'

'Yeah, that's right.'

'How's it going?

'Pretty tough, most of the time. But when we engineers decide to enjoy ourselves we enjoy ourselves!'

'I'm sure.'

'Last month I went on the Eng Soc trip – basically a big piss-up – to London. When we came back we saw your poster at the airport. Some of the guys, well, they had some choice things to say about you – or it. But I told them that I knew you from way back and that you were decent.'

The telling of this tale had saturated his unevenly shaven chin.

'Why, thank you, Brían, I'm touched. You know, we must go for a few pints or something over the holidays. We haven't exactly seen a lot of each other over the past few years.'

'I'd like that, Tom, I really would.' He stopped nodding his head and started shaking it. 'I've got a lot of questions to ask you. I hear so many things about you, and so little of it fits with the Tomás Iremonger, I mean the Tom Iremonger I knew.'

'Yeah, we need to talk, no doubt about it. But listen what's this Roomkeepers business?'

'The Roomkeepers? They're Dublin's oldest charity. The Impecunious Roomkeepers Society. They've been around for two hundred years, or something like that. Have you ever seen that house they have up near the Castle?' I hadn't. 'My Uncle Simon has been involved with them for years.' Firbolg pointed out a portly man standing near a tone-deaf orchestra of buskers belting out 'Do they know it's Christmastime?' They make the musician currently 'entertaining' me with his twee take on 'The Holly and the Ivy' look like Prince. I seemed to remember meeting a thinner version of Uncle Simon years ago at Brian's house. 'I got involved a few years ago,' continued Firbolg. 'In fact, I saw you here on Grafton Street this day last year.'

'You did?'

'Sure did. You passed right by. You didn't see me.'

That was it. I seriously doubted I was going to get one of those cans into my hands, no matter how psyched I was.

'Christ, I'm sorry – I didn't mean to be rude. I must have had something on my mind, last-minute shopping, perhaps.'

Firbolg laughed. 'Oh, it's quite forgivable. You were with Teddy Doyle's daughter.'

I checked my surprise as best I could. 'You know Mainie?'

'Oh, no, not really.' Firbolg coloured. 'I've seen her picture in the paper. But I have met her father. Uncle Simon knows him. He usually comes by here every year and makes a very generous donation.'

I was shaking my leg now to try and get rid of some of this dense energy that was building up inside me. I felt like I'd just knocked back fifteen hammerhead espressos. This was good shit Bish had given me. I couldn't stand here in the middle of Grafton Street for much longer. I had to spring into action. So I went for it.

'But you know, Brían, I think it's so cool of you to do this collecting thing.'

'Cool? No, it's nothing. It's just a bit of fun. This morning Percy Tóibín did his radio programme from outside Bewley's, and he actually interviewed me for a minute.' I tried to look jealous. I think those RTE personalities are the saddest characters in the western world. It takes more than woolly sideburns and a Robin Reliant to make a personality, in my humble opinion. Firbolg continued, 'And when you stand here all day on Christmas Eve you meet everybody you ever knew. Everybody's back. Even you, Tom! Makes you think what kind of place Dublin would be if people didn't have to emigrate.'

I grunted in response, and got the conversation back on track, 'I think you're being far too modest, Brían. I'm not sure I could stand here and do what you do. I'm not sure I could stand here and ask people for money.'

'Are you *kidding*, it's easy! A child of five could do it – no offence.' He was frothing at the mouth.

'No offence taken, Brían.'

'Honestly, you just stand here and shake your can and shout, *Help the Roomkeepers, please!*'

'Yeah, I can hear them!'

'And people just *give* you money, Tom. It's Christmas

Eve. It's hard *not* to collect money. The only problem is that sometimes these poor unfortunate poor people come up and ask you for money and you have to explain to them that you can't just redistribute it straight away.'

I shook my head. 'Unreal. But back to the collecting business. I'm not sure I'd do as well as you're doing. You must have some special knack or something.'

'No way! You'd do brilliantly.' He slapped his forehead. 'Why didn't I think of this before. You're the IDA guy. You're a virtual celebrity.' Firbolg was now a man inspired. 'Tom,' he said, 'I know this is may be a little out of order. I know you're a busy guy, especially on a day like today when you're just back in town. But could you help us out for a little while – just an hour, say? We're about half a dozen collectors short this year, and that means we probably won't beat last year's total. You see, we have this big thing where we always beat the total from the year before.'

Hoping he wouldn't notice the pneumatic drill my left leg had become, I pretended to consider it carefully. After about five seconds I smiled and said, 'Sure I'll do it.'

Firbolg smiled back victoriously. 'Let's get you kitted out.'

We went over to his uncle, who was standing guard over yellow buckets full of silver and copper.

'Uncle Simon, you remember my friend Tom from Cedar-of-Lebanon Road, don't you?'

Firbolg's chubby uncle took me in for a long moment, and then beamed as if he'd just translated a difficult foreign word. 'I do indeed! Little Tomás Iremonger – would you look at him now.'

I wanted to ask this guy why he wasn't doing Santa Claus at a mall. But I let it pass. I was very close now to what I wanted.

'That's me!' I said, my chirpy reply made possible by the sneachta.

'What are you up to these days, Tomás?'

Flying, fucking, dropping, snorting.

Firbolg answered for me, 'Tom's a sort of symbol.'

Uncle Simon smiled. 'Good retirement plan with that kind of job?'

I was pressing my right Umberto Boccioni leather boot on top of the left by now. Either I was going to collect money for their stupid charity right now or I was going to explode.

'It's nothing to do with work. Tom's on the IDA poster that you see when you land at Dublin airport.'

'No joke? Well, that sounds like a grand gig. Half the people walking down the street must have seen you then.'

'And they're going to see him when he collects for us.'

Uncle Simon beamed at me. 'You're going to help out?'

I nodded rapidly.

'Ah, that's grand!'

So I got a badge and an open-top can with some rattling coins. I made the sacrifice of blemishing Nico by pinning the badge on her lapel. I wanted to dive into the crowd and get to work, but I knew that would look suspect after being so shy about collecting just a few minutes before. So I followed Firbolg out into the middle of the street and stuck close to him to begin with. Shaking my can at masturbation speed to release some of that pent-up chemical energy, I worked the crowd with my taupe-brown (and undoubtedly dilated) eyes. People either gave me knowing looks or looked away, but nearly everybody I stared at gave money. And serious money too – pound coins, nunny bunnies, joyces. Anybody who did no more than lose their loose change I gave a drop-dead look. A few ten-pence pieces popped out of the can I was shaking it so intensely; I didn't bother to pick them up.

After a while Firbolg came up behind me and slapped me on Nico's shoulder. I tolerated that.

'You're doing great, Tom!'

'It's not as tricky as I thought it would be.'

'What did I tell you. Those punts are burning a hole in people's pockets on Christmas Eve.'

'I think I'll strike out on my own a little bit.'

'Good idea. We're too close together. Stake out some territory for yourself. But don't go off Grafton Street – that's where our licence says we have to collect. Go back and deposit the money with my uncle once your can gets really full.'

'I hear you!'

So I went solo – launched out on my own, went for the hard sell. What did I do, walk up to people and hassle them for cash? No way. That's not my style. I treated this charity gig like the Smirnoff Young Designer of the Year Show. For that display I'd also got revved up chemically – a few snorts of Semtex backstage in the Atrium, compliments of the master of ceremonies, Mr Ardal McQuaid. Every foray down the runway had been an event, even when I had to wear the rubber suit made by that mad bitch from Limerick. Now I was back on Iremonger's original runway – Grafton Street itself.

I strutted back and forth between Bewley's and HMV. Shoppers gave me space; they parted like the old Red Sea. And I didn't have to say a damn thing. I didn't invoke the name of the Impecunious Roomkeepers once. I just gave them the eye, holding the can left then right. The money came pouring in – rarely anything less than pound coins, plenty of nunny bunnies and joyces, two danny boys, even a walrus. And they were giving the money to *me*. I could have done it without the badge. Some kid asked me for my autograph, but I told him later; I was on a roll and I didn't want to stop.

Among the dozens of people popping money into my can I recognised a Progressive Democrat TD, two ex-girlfriends, and a guy from Trinity whose Irish Poetry after Yeats notes

I'd borrowed and never given back. Eventually my can was close to overflowing, and so I had to go back to Uncle Simon and his yellow buckets. I thought he was going to kiss me or kiss my feet when he saw the damage I'd done. Simon put the can on the ground, and, squatting hugely, his elephantine ass stretching the seam of his brown slacks to breaking point, plucked out the notes and stuffed them into a bulging wallet. The pound coins were cascading into one of the yellow buckets when Firbolg arrived. His uncle looked up at him and smiled shrewdly. 'Your old friend is quite an asset!'

Firbolg laughed. 'What else do you expect from Ireland's Greatest Resource?'

I was delighted. If I were capable of blushing, I would have done so.

Then it was back to work. And this time, I knew, it was serious. The buzz from the rubber bullet was wearing off already (Bish was right about my tolerance), so I put everything I had into my strut. But no fear. The punts poured in just like the first time. I had Grafton Street in the palm of my hand, and I was milking it dry.

But now it was time to get off my main drag. I had to settle up with myself, and for that I needed a little privacy. First making sure that neither Firbolg nor any of the other collectors were in sight, I slipped into Johnson's Court. I used that passageway as my catwalk for a little while as well, catching some choice customers coming from the Powerscourt townhouse centre and out of Appleby's jewellers. At first I thought I would slip in the side-entrance to Bewley's and take the elevator to the toilets on the top floor, but I had forgotten about the side-entrance to Clarendon Street church right opposite it. That, I realised, was exactly the kind of place I was looking for.

I went through the archway, crossed the little court-yard and went up the steps to the side door. (I guess that's the first time I've been inside a church since we went to see Uncle Columb MC the old man's funeral.) I expected a dark chapel with a few old women praying to candles and statues, but the church was doing a pretty brisk business. Maybe I shouldn't have been surprised – this is the last shopping day before Christmas, and religion is the original dodgy product; you can imagine what it's going to be like there during the sales next week.

Men and women, young and old (but nobody I knew, and probably few people who would recognise me) were kneeling by their Switzer's and Dunnes Stores bags in the pews. Others were checking out the nativity scene by the altar, even though the straw wasn't off the little main man yet. Side chapels looked like they had their regulars. For a moment I considered putting the heavy can under Nico's wing, but then snapped out of it. First Rule of Cool: if you act suspiciously, people suss you out. In any case, I was just a charity worker stopping off for a quick spiritual espresso, wasn't I?

The back of the church was much quieter, and nice and shadowy. Enjoying the resonance of my Boccioni heels on the stone, I walked by a noticeboard with adverts for pregnancy and pilgrimages and the priesthood (they sure could have done with an Ascendancy make-over) and along by the confessionals. I sat in the last pew and put the can down on the ground just behind the kneeler, and keeping half an eye on the other supplicants. Getting down on my knees, I lifted a danny boy and three joyces, enough to see me through an evening of mad pinting.

It didn't matter that the light was bad back here. At a touch I can tell what currency, what denomination is in my hand. It's a gift, I guess. Deutschemarks have this leathery quality while yen are always silky; a washington doesn't have the backbone of a hamilton. Punts are just varying degrees of pulp, but I was still very satisfied to be lining the designer pocket of my jeans with them.

Put it this way – it was commission. I had skimmed fifty quid, yes, but already I must have collected three, four hundred. Most of that money would have walked right by the other collectors, would have been spent in Principles and Next. That's the nature of disposable income. I should know. And on top of all that, I was going to go right back out onto Grafton Street and do one more show, without any chemical help – the buzz from the B-Special was history. My take would end up being no more than ten per cent. The Impecunious Roomkeepers were getting a bargain. They were lucky to have me.

At the archway on my way out I came face-to-face with Mainie Doyle. I was not surprised to see her. What Firbolg had said about Christmas Eve was true: everybody was here. Town was an extension of the airport. And, I realised at that moment, I'd been looking out for her all afternoon. But for the second time today my heart – that least Iremongerish of my organs – started thumping. Maybe it was because she had caught me coming out of a church. In any case, I was nothing but nonchalant.

'Hi, you.'

She just stood there for a few seconds, as if she were immobilised by the three Brown Thomas bags she carried. I smiled. BT bags are very Mainie Doyle. I think she must have been born wrapped in a Brown Thomas bag. In the unlikely event of Mainie ever being reduced to the status of baglady, I know what she'll be carrying her worldly possessions around in. Years ago, when her supermarket king father – Super Doyle himself, Mr Edward 'Pinkie' Doyle – had his cashflow briefly choked by the croissant war with the other major stores, her friend Melanie Cosgrave swore to me that she'd seen Mainie *ironing* an old BT bag at the Doyle mansion, Tír na nÓg, in Dalkey. But today it didn't look like she had any cashflow problems. Today Mainie looked heavily invested in. Her short, exquisitely styled black hair had more body and gloss than ever before. No expense had been spared to be in season: she wore a thick olive-green woollen jacket patterned with geometric reindeer (by Louise Jouissance, I reckoned). Lipstick, mock-turtleneck, ribbed stockings – all holly-berry red.

Finally she spoke, 'So it's true – you're back. What made you change your mind?'

'I didn't change my mind.'

'Oh, really? I seem to remember you saying, the night before you went away, at that global wake we had for you in the Buttery Brasserie, that coming home at Christmas was a cliché, and that you were going to have no part in it.'

I had to smile, realising how much I'd missed Mainie giving me a hard time.

'Well, my mature recollection of the evening is that I did say that coming home at Christmas was a cliché, but not the rest of it. I like keeping my options open, Mainie, you know that.'

'So how are you enjoying the cliché?'

I shrugged. 'I'm trying to breathe new life into it.'

'So, it was wonderful to see you in Prague, Iremonger.'

Oh, you evil woman, Mainie Doyle.

'Hey, what's the deal? Did you have a bunch of those ex-communists spying for you in the old town?'

'No, but the trail of weeping women and bar owners was hard to ignore. Thanks for getting in touch.'

'I fully intended to – seriously.' I wasn't lying. 'But I had no number for you. I wasn't even sure you were still there. And besides, I was gone within forty-eight hours.' All true, but I buy those reasons as much as she did. I'm not sure why I didn't get in touch with Mainie in Prague (I've hung out with loads of other people from our scattered circle these last six months, by accident and by design). Maybe I was . . . saving her for Dublin. Something like that.

Wisely, she abandoned the subject of our non-rendez-vous in Prague by tapping the tin badge Firbolg had given me.

'What are you up to, Iremonger? Collecting for the Roomkeepers, hanging around churches?' Mainie's black eyes went into what I call x-ray mode. I know, from experience, that the worst thing you can do in this situation is BS her. Even vintage Iremonger BS doesn't always fool Mainie Doyle. So I just smirked and said, 'BTE.'

And all Mainie could do was give me a sardonic *touché* expression in return. BTE stands for Bourgeois To Explain. It's something my father says. One thing Mainie and I have in common is how unlike our fathers we are (even more than we're unlike our mothers). But we have both adopted one killer line from them. Mainie's – and it's so effective because she says nothing else like this – is, *Shot by a ball of your own shite*, a line that really doesn't lend itself to being reduced to initials. But BTE's neat. And pretty profound, I think. Of course the ironic thing is that my father, who probably inherited this line from his father, the old man, is the most bourgeois person I have ever met in my life, with the exception of my late grandfather. Go figure.

Mainie attempted a come-back to my vintage line.

'I guess it would be too bourgeois to explain how the last six months have gone for you.'

'Not at all. That would be just a case of presenting facts. No, I'd be only happy to catch up. I've been looking for-ward to it.' What I was really looking forward to was getting invited to her party, and being really off-hand about accepting.

'Yes, we must do that before we leave town again. I presume you *are* leaving town again.'

'Of course.'

'Well, it certainly has been a surprise seeing you, but I've got a lot more shopping to do.' She made light of her BT bags. 'I'll give you a call in the new year.' She trotted towards the steps of the church. Okay, I thought, if this is the game she's playing, I'll play along. I turned on my Milanese heels and called after her, 'We can get together before that, I'm sure.'

Mainie stopped and turned around. 'Oh, can you fit me into your schedule? I would have thought you were going to be too busy breathing new life in the cliché that is Christmas.'

I shrugged. 'Some traditions are venerable.'

She shook her head very firmly.

'Oh, no, Tom. No way. One thing I've given up is going to smoky, insane pubs on Christmas Eve. Besides, it always ends up with you and Dylan stoned out of your minds playing that video trivia game in the Horse Show House and getting stroppy because you can't remember the name of the Japanese stock market. Tonight I'm doing my drinking back in Dalkey. I'm leaving town at six.'

'Which means you'll have a little down-time between now and then.' I couldn't believe it – this was very unIremonger of me, to be so insistent about hooking up with someone, even Mainie Doyle. But to my surprise that's the line that did it.

'Okay,' she said brightly, 'let's make it afternoon tea. You can buy me afternoon tea at the Shelbourne, Tom Iremonger.'

We arranged to meet at quarter past five, and I watched her go up the steps and into the dim lobby of the church. Amazing thing about Mainie – well, one of the amazing things about Mainie – she's still a believer, or so she says, an *à la carte* Catholic who one day, I suspect, when she's older and done living and being a very contemporary woman, may just ask for the set menu.

*   *   *

The time now? Well, put it this way: I've reset my watch, but the Tzara has this evil feature, an outer dial, that tells me that it's precisely 6:41 in Paris. (While I was away I happened to leave the dial set on Greenwich Mean Time, London time, Dublin time.) So if we were meeting at the Café Flore, Mainie would be seriously late. I order a third pint of Fursty. I defend Mainie's empty armchair. And plot a piano string lynching for that follicle-fake torturing us with a super-schmaltzy version of 'O Tannenbaum'. Jesus, I never realised waiting was such hard work.

After I left Mainie at the church, I hurried back to Grafton Street. I figured Firbolg would be getting anxious. Indeed he was. I met him coming off Lemon Street. He wasn't carrying his can.

'Tom! Where on earth did you go?'

'Oh, I just explored a few of the lucrative side streets.'

'But I told you – we don't have a licence to collect anywhere but Grafton Street. The society could get into hot water if the guards stopped you.'

'Don't worry.' I smiled. 'I can deal with the police.'

But he didn't find that amusing. In fact, he looked more troubled. No way did I want to end my collecting on a note of suspicion – it's the professional in me.

So I said to him, 'I'm sorry. I guess I got a little carried away. I tell you what, let me deposit this money with your uncle and fill one more can. I'll stay on Grafton Street the whole time and you can shadow me every step of the way.'

Firbolg hummed and hawed about this.

'Think of the amount of Roomkeepers you'll make happy,' I added. (I really must find out who the hell these Room-keepers are. They have an evil name.)

It worked. Firbolg went for it. I was back in business. But that last can was hard work. My strut lacked spark. The only effect I could now feel from the B-Special was a parched throat, and no way could I slip into McDaid's for a quick one, not with Firbolg watching me. On top of all that, night was falling rapidly. Even with the pseudo-Victorian Grafton Street gas lamps on, I sensed that most people were failing to recognise me now. It took me an hour to get the can up to a decent level, twice as long as it had taken me to stuff it the first two times around. Handing it over to Uncle Simon, I saw that it was 5:06. I was back in Firbolg's good books again. No, sorry, understatement. I was Firbolg's god again, and both he and his uncle begged me to come to the 'post-count piss-up' in Gleeson's on Booterstown Avenue.

'Sorry, gentlemen,' I told them, 'but I've made plans for this evening.'

'That's a pity, Tom,' said Simon, 'you've been a tremendous help.'

'It was nothing, really.'

Firbolg had a bright idea. 'Hey, why don't I phone you next week to tell you what the total is!' In his excitement Firbolg squirted my face like one of those little atomisers they hand out in First Class, except it wasn't Evian he was spraying. 'Maybe we could go out for a pint of Bass to, you know, celebrate.'

'Sounds great, but for now this deputy's got to hand in his badge.'

Firbolg smiled. I think he thought I was making some allusion to the games of our shared childhood.

I never did get Uncle Columb's present, but that's tomorrow's problem. Today I don't have any problems because Mainie Doyle has just arrived. *Knew* she would show. Mainie negotiates her way gracefully across the crowded room. She's gotten rid of all but one of her Brown Thomas bags. I stand up. She allows me to kiss her cold, fresh cheek. We both sit deep into our opposing armchairs. Mainie orders Earl Grey, telling me she doesn't have time to eat.

'So,' she says, slipping off a pair of Isotoner gloves, 'how are your parents?'

I make a show of considering this, and conclude, 'They seem fine.'

'*Seem* fine?'

I smile and try not to shift around in my armchair.

'Well, to tell you the truth, I haven't seen too much of them so far. They picked me up at the airport, of course.'

'That's where you spent most of your quality time, isn't it?'

'Well, it didn't work out that way with my parents. I guess I'll take care of that later. Might as well, since I'm back.'

I'm about as uncomfortable as I can get. I mean, borderline blushing. High time to change the subject,

'So, how are Teddy and Lucia doing?'

'They *are* fine. Daddy's insanely busy, of course, to the point of making himself sick. Mummy's busy worrying about him and being Lady Captain. Both unpaid full-time jobs, you know.' Mainie consults her slim Rolex. 'You know, I was serious about not having much time. I *do* have to meet someone at six. You were anxious to catch up, if I remember correctly. Why don't you start? How has it worked out?'

She means the anti-odyssey. I lean back in my armchair and throw my hands out philosophically. 'So well, Mainie, that it defies linear narrative.'

'Oh, God, we're not back to more of your post-modern nonsense.' Mainie is a graduate of the Department of Business, Economics and Social Studies.

'I'm just being honest. I told you I was making a major commitment to living in the present, and I followed through on that. I wasn't doing it for the sake of posterity, so what can I say about it now? I went everywhere, did everything, saw everybody.'

She stares at me and says, 'Everybody except me in

Prague.' I kind of freeze, until she smiles, and I laugh, mostly with relief.

I shake my head. 'You're an evil woman, Mainie Doyle. Well, now that you know all about what I've been up to, let's hear about you.'

Mainie's order arrives, and once she's poured herself a cup of tea, she does begin to tell me how she's getting on. Wonderfully, is the bottom line answer. As if that comes as any surprise. Mainie didn't even have to do the Milk Round in college last spring. Arthur Anderson; Goldman, Sachs; Chase Manhattan all came looking for *her*. Forget about golden hellos; those tight-ass suits were putting down platinum welcome mats.

In the end she went with the offer from Riddly, Motion, the London media consultancy firm. She was excited about the prospect of working in Eastern Europe and RM's plans to eventually open a Dublin office. Mainie had done promotional work for Lick 95FM here in Dublin one summer – how well I remember us cruising around St Stephen's Green in a black Land Rover (Mainie driving; I can't) emblazoned with the station's Rolling Stones rip-off logo – and so Riddly, Motion sent her off on her first assignment in September to Prague to help set up an FM station there, Velvet 101.

She's amazed how quickly the Czechs warmed to the concepts of target audience, easy-listening favourites, station identification. Velvet went twenty-four hour a fortnight ago, just as she was packing for London again. She tells me all about the fabulous people she's working with in the London office, some of them from Trinity, and how it looks like her next foreign assignment could be Istanbul this spring, revamping state television. The sound track to her monologue is a slow version of 'Ding Dong Merrily on High'. I order another Fursty. With great discipline I am resisting the urge to blurt out the question, *So what are you doing on New Year's Eve?* So instead I ask another question on my mind, one that can be put a little more playfully,

'So, did you *meet* anyone while you were in Prague?'

She considers this, playfully, with her tea cup in both hands close to her lips, takes a sip, and smiles as she puts the cup down again. 'Well, there was this cute guy at the Irish Trade Board dinner.'

'Oh, really. Is that who you're drinking with tonight?' I intended that to sound playful too, but it didn't quite come out that way.

After a pause, Mainie replies firmly, 'No. That's a different somebody.'

'I see.'

Mainie checks her watch again, then looks at me squarely and says, 'So what are you doing on New Year's Eve?'

I am not expecting the question at that moment, to put it mildly. But I still do a fairly superb job at being off-hand. 'Well,' I sigh, 'I don't know. I sometimes think my parents have the right idea – sit at home and do virtually nothing. It's the arbitrariness of New Year's Eve that gets me. I'm all for starting a new tradition where you have this massive party on February the 24th. Yes, February the 24th. Mark it in your calendar. A new tradition. In fact, why doesn't everybody come home *then*. The weather would be a bit better.'

Mainie's giving me this smouldering smile. 'Do you seriously have any plans for the evening of the 31st of December?'

I shrug – I'm not going to let her off so easily. 'Well, sure. Bish McQuaid is running a club called 1916 that night. I can't imagine anywhere better to be.'

'Oh, really? Well, maybe I'll be there myself after midnight.'

This is going a little too far, but all I can say is, 'I thought you didn't like Ardal.'

'But you'll be there to protect me, won't you?'

I stick to my jammed guns. 'Why, yes I will.'

Mainie finishes her tea and reaches for her BT bag. We stand up together. I'm a little shaky on my feet, from the B-Special and the Fursty. 'Well,' she says, 'I guess we'll bump into each other in the next few days.'

'Sure we will . . . where?'

I can't believe it. I can't believe I said that last word. Iremonger doesn't ask those kind of questions. That's more like a question . . . Tomás Michael would ask. I send an executive order to my body not to blush. I pretend that nothing out of the ordinary has happened. But Mainie is smiling.

'Where? Oh, I don't know. I'll be at the Forty Foot Swim tomorrow morning. But I'm not sure that's an Iremonger kind of event.'

I can't believe it again. Maybe that was an Iremonger question, after all. Maybe it was instinct that made me ask her where she was going to be. My brother-in-law, Finbar, does that suicidal swim every Christmas morning. I watched him do it once years ago when he was my sister's fiancé. He'll be there – Finbar has a heavy swimming habit – and so will I.

I shrug. 'You never know.'

Mainie gives me a big PR kind of smile. 'It was lovely to see you, Tom. Have a lovely Christmas and a prosperous new year.' Well, that just about gives away the crap about meeting me at 1916. What the hell does she think she's up to?

And this time we just *shake hands*. I have never shaken hands with Mainie Doyle before, and I hope it will never happen again. I want all of her, or nothing.

She leaves. I call the waitress back over. 'What's the damage?' I ask.

As I wait for my change, something causes me to shiver. At first I think it's an aftershock from the drugs, but then it happens again and I realise that it's the music, the goddamn piano. It's not one of those corny carols Baldy is playing now. This music is slow, hushed, spooky, decidedly minor key. And it's something I know. I turn and stare at the pianist. He's playing with such concentration, a focus that is alien to me. I barely acknowledge the waitress when she comes back with my change. I stuff it into my CK jeans pocket and rise. I approach the piano slowly and softly. I have to know what this music is called. And I wonder why I have to know. When I reach the piano the old-timer has his eyes closed. I want the music to be over so I can ask him what it is, so that I can put a label on it, but, at the same time, I don't want it to stop. As the last, fragile chord dissipates, the old guy opens his eyes on *me*, as if I'd been beside him the whole time.

'You liked that,' he says with a little smile.

I nod tentatively. 'I think I sang it once. What's the name of it?'

He raises his eyebrows a little. 'That's the Coventry Carol. About the killing of the innocents.'

'Of course,' I mutter.

I put a pound coin in his tip jar and split.

3

Angels

It's coming up to seven, Tzara-time, and we've taken over the snug in Keogh's. Close-up on Dylan. He looks like a young Andy Warhol – *before* the wig, when you could see his prematurely thinning blond hair. Dylan's talking about this NYU chick he met at the Kip, a new Irish bar (for the new Irish) near Tompkins Square Park. He's got potentially big news. For several years Dylan has been refining something he calls the Perfect Girlfriend Principle. And it looks like Ms April Gottlieb may meet all the major criteria. The rest of the mad pinting gang are giving encouragement. Listen in, 'Then I find out she thinks Seamus Heaney is vastly over-rated.'

'Promising.'

'Next I discover that she likes early Martin Amis better than *London Fields*.'

'Very promising.'

'And finally she tells me that *Pulp Fiction* doesn't even come close to matching *Reservoir Dogs*.'

'This could be it, Dylan.'

'Did you ask her about U2?' Roderick asks.

Dylan looks at Roderick disdainfully. 'Oh, for Christ's sake, I didn't want to in*sult* the girl.'

Roderick and Dylan wanted to go pub crawling, but I was too restless for that. So we went pub surfing instead. We had a pint in every pub that we passed that one of us (well, Iremonger, mainly) wasn't barred from. And we drank without prejudice: in gay bars, in pubs that play traditional music, even on the Northside. I almost got drunk.

Closing-time found us in McDonagh's at the suburban end of Leeson Street. (What Mainie'd said about the Horse Show House and the video trivia machine made me worry that we were sinking into a rut.) We'd hooked up with two mad pinterettes – Rachael Cunningham and Selina Walsh. Rachael's back from Washington, where she's doing something with the World Bank; Selina's back from Kyoto, where she's doing the Teaching English as a Foreign Language scam.

Selina had sent out a few signals when we were in O'Dwyer's earlier, but I didn't respond. Astonishingly, I found I was not in the mood to seduce or to be seduced. Now there was talk of hitting the clubs, maybe checking out 1916, but, for once, I was realistic, pointing out that it would be next to impossible to get a taxi home in the early hours of Christmas morning. What I didn't say is that I wished I was back in Paris, maybe mad pinting in Rooney's near the Pantheon.

We were the last to leave McDonagh's, at about eleven-thirty. The plan was to walk up to the Burlington and share a taxi home; we were all going in the same direction. Unfortunately, about half the population of South County Dublin had the same plan. We joined a long, loose, humourless queue along the black railings of the hotel. When a taxi finally appeared, two guys in tuxedoes almost came to blows over who was going to get it. Dylan tried to sneak into the hotel to order one, but was stopped at the front door. And forget about buses – the bus stop was deserted, the last 46A having left town at something like nine-thirty. It began to drizzle, and none of us had brought an umbrella, except Selina, who then realised she'd forgotten it about three pubs back.

Roderick spoke, 'Let's walk up to Eddie Rocket's in Donnybrook and see if we can use the phone. My old man might come out and get us, if he's not too pissed.'

Nobody else has a better idea, so we trekked up Morehampton Road, slowly getting wet. Roderick gave his toque to Rachael – a closet romantic is de Brun.

Just as we reached the diner, a car pulled up behind us. We all looked around. It was a trusty Martello Cab, and someone was getting out. Roderick was at the passenger door like a shot.

'Owenstown Hill. Then Blackrock and Monkstown.'

The rest of us had the taxi surrounded.

'Well, okay, I'um goin' down to Dun Laoghaire, anyways. But how many of yeh are there?'

'There's five.'

'Sorry, no can do. Four's the maximum.'

'Ah, c'mon, it's Christmas.'

'That's my point, son. The guards are out everywhere.'

'But under the Bona Fide Traveller Act of 1931 you have a right, if not an obligation, to take all of us.' I'm not going to say it to him, but Roderick would make an excellent wig. Must be in the genes.

'Cut out the bolix. One of yeh will have to stay. Decide quick who it's going to be. There's plenty more who want this taxi.'

He was dead right, of course. A small, speculative crowd had come out of Eddie Rocket's. Several other people inside the diner were standing up.

'Well, obviously it's between the three of us,' Dylan said.

Rachael and Selina didn't argue with that; they got into
the back seat. Dylan looked at Roderick and me over the
roof of the taxi. He sighed, ran his hand through his thin,
damp hair, and opened his mouth.

I cut him off. 'You guys get in the taxi.'

They looked at me in amazement.

'Are you *sure*, Tom?' Dylan asked.

'Yes, I'm sure. My parents are at a dinner party on
Eglington Road. It's only a five-minute walk from here. I
can get a lift home from them.'

'Are you sure they'll still be there?' Roderick asked,
searchingly.

I slapped him on the back. 'Absolutely. I'll have to drag
them out of there. Get in, Rod. I'll phone you tomorrow.'

He did it. As I watched the taxi pull away, I wondered
what the hell I was doing.

It was starting to rain now for real. I *hate* getting Nico
wet.

I stand in the rain at the bottom of the avenue, the Protestant
church on one side, the National School on the other. What
am I doing here? I tell myself I'm drunk after all, not to read
too much into it. But I really don't buy that. Drink doesn't do
that kind of damage to me any more; my tolerance is off the
chart. I simply trash the question from my mind, and start
walking. At least I'm getting a lift out of this.

The tent of tall evergreens keeps most of the slanting
rain off. Intermittently plops land on Nico's shoulders; I
smack the drops away. The avenue is lampless, and my
eyes, neon-spoilt, have considerable difficulty adjusting to
this serious dark. Soon I can't hear the traffic on the main
road any more. If it weren't for a faint orange quality in the
sky, I'd swear I was in the country, approaching some Big
House.

I remember, involuntarily, all the other times I've walked

this avenue in the dark: going to listen to (but never to speak in) debates against the Class A girls schools – St Agnes, Victoria, Blessed Virgin – and walking back down afterwards in the heady company of females; arriving early, with some other minor characters, for performances of the fourth-year play; sneaking up, with a dozen others, to dismantle rugby posts after a long-night's drinking in Fitzpatrick's (they were very strict about age there – you had to be under eighteen or over sixty-five) to celebrate the end of our classroom careers. These aren't bad memories, but they still make me feel queasy. They signal that I'm flying into a web of memory, a destination I'm not prepared for. I slow to turn back, and then put one Boccioni in front of the other again. I have to get back to Cedar-of-Lebanon Road, right? I'm just being a tad sensible.

The tent of evergreens ends and the avenue swings around the school's vast front lawn. I cut across it. The only other time I've been back here since the last day of the Leaving was with Dylan one January night during our first year at Trinity, the time of the big snow. We got stoned on some powerful Turkish ganj in the middle of the lawn, swirling around as the snow swirled around us. You could hardly see the school. As usual, Dylan did the decent thing by not asking me any questions about my old life. It was evil.

The far edge of the lawn is whitened by the lights of the community house, which really was a Big House. Quinlaven told us the history of this land in class one time.

I can also see the mute ruddy glow of stained glass, and that's the light I head for. I pass the vast tree – don't ask me what kind; I'm hopeless with the names of natural things – overhanging the avenue's turn. Cars are parked tightly up to that point. Stepping off the grass, I bang my shin against the bumper of a BMW and let loose a little blast of American Anglo-Saxon. Torchlight finds my face.

'What are yeh doin' der?'

'Nothing,' I reply, shielding my eyes. 'I'm here to find someone.'

'Are yeh a pupil here?'

'Yes. Well, a past pupil.'

I hear the heavy wrinkly with the torch snort even though he's still five, ten metres away. 'Past pupils are not invited. There are too many of yeh. That's whuy I'm here.'

'But I *am* invited. My uncle is saying mass.'

'What's his name?'

'Fr Iremonger. Fr Columb Iremonger.'

The torch went off.

'Why didn't you say so in the furst place? Go on, so.'

'Thanks, man.'

Walking towards the chapel, I glance at the dark facade of the school's main entrance. My father would always drop me at the back gate before eight, and so I would have to wait there on the steps, with the regular flock of earlybirds, until Brother Kelleher, the huge bald bursar, unlocked the double doors at about twenty past.

As I go up the steps of the chapel, I look over once again and see Strongbow's leather barrister bag sitting next to one of the rough-hewn granite columns. The porch is deserted; the bro has opened up; everyone has gone inside to the classrooms. Except me. I'm still standing outside, in the November chill, brooding over Strongbow's instruction to me, issued with a smile in front of his cronies from fourth year, the year ahead of us: *Carry my bag, Fish.*

I enter the oratory. It's decorated with dried flowers, the work of the mothers' club. I can see silhouettes against the stained glass flanking the thick chapel doors – standing room only, as usual. The choir launch into the Gloria – the mass is just cranking up. Jesus. Most midnight masses are over by midnight, but not at Berchmans, oh no. The old boredom begins to seep into my system, and for that, I discover, I still have a very low-tolerance level. Well, both my hair and my beloved jacket are pretty much soaked from crossing the lawn, so I've got something to do.

I go through another heavy door and walk along the parquet of the corridor that connects the chapel with the heart of the school. Feeling like an intruder, I go as quietly as I can. The fluorescent lighting is only half on – just enough to get you to the bog and back. I pass the vestry, the teachers' room and the teachers' boxes, the tiny supply shop where I sometimes helped out and where I bought – never pilfered – plywood rulers that soon broke or were broken.

In the main corridor I glance at shadows – the spiral staircase that leads to the library, the doors of the gym, the doors of the 1983 extension, the modest trophy case in the entrance hall – and then turn and walk towards the toilets, at the very end of the corridor. This brings me past the classroom where I spent my second year in the senior school, a long noticeboard with career information (medicine, law, financial services, the priesthood), a poster advertising a debate on the future of social welfare, and another commemorating a bunch of Jesuits killed in El Salvador.

The toilets are free of their term-time stink. Or perhaps Berchmans boys are a little less animal now than they were five years ago. One thing's sure – that row of hand dryers is new, which means I don't have to use one of those grey towels, which look as scummy as ever. I dry Nico first, then my hair, then check myself out in the mirror. They're right, my mother and my dealer, my cheeks are a little on the concave side. I look better in the poster. Maybe I should surrender to a little of my mother's force-feeding in the next few days.

I quit the toilets. Opposite, next to a glass case with a stuffed fox still staring fiercely – or is it fearfully? – after all this time, are the wooden steps that lead to the prep school. I almost cross the corridor and climb them, but instead walk back in the direction of the spiral staircase, deciding to crash there until mass is over. Ten seconds later I'm turning the doorknob of Senior 2A's classroom.

I step inside and flick the light switches. The fluorescent bulbs blink several times, then give full, steady light, whitening the edge of the senior thirds rugby field. A dark expanse of them lie beyond this one. Berchmans always had way too many rugby fields.

The blackboard has become a greenboard. The old wooden desks, so easy to inflict with graffiti – *Fish is Queer, Fish is a West Brit* – have been replaced with laminated tables. But the smell – the smell is still the same, the smell of . . . apple cores decaying behind radiators.

Up front, that's where I sat. And they stood around me, after Quinlaven's class on the Plantations – Carl Pollen, who'd spent a year at Irish college; Mark Daly, whose father had come to our door canvassing for Fíanna Fáil; and Luán McKeone, son of Liam McKeone, the historian and broadcaster, and closet provo, according to my father: the tacit princes of the class. Strongbow, their king, stayed in the background, leaning against the radiator, smiling.

McKeone did most of the talking, 'Licking up to Quinner again, Fish.'

'My name is Tomás. And I wasn't licking up to him. I just agreed with him. You can agree with a teacher, you know. It's a free country.'

'It's a fucked-up country with Free-Staters like you and Quinlaven in it.'

'All I said was that the Unionists have a good argument too.'

'If they don't want to be part of this country, they should leave. End of story.'

'And what if they don't want to leave?'

'Then they should be loaded up on cattle trucks and sent back to Scotland where they belong.'

'You don't really believe that, do you?'

'Yeah, I do. And prod-lovers like you should be sent back with them.'

'Then why didn't you say any of this in class?'

Contempt swelled in McKeone's eyes. I scrunched up, thinking he was going to hit me. It was Strongbow who saved me, or saved me for himself. 'Leave the fat little blue shirt alone.'

I turn off the lights and get out of there. The door booms shut behind me. Now the idea of sitting in the gloom of the spiral staircase, surrounded by memory, doesn't seem so appealing. So I go back to the oratory. The choir start up again, *Praise the God of all creation, God of mercy and compassion/Alleluia, alleluia, praise the word of truth and life!* Christ, the Alleluia – that means that they haven't even got to the goddamn gospel.

The I hear his voice, doing the introduction. A little muffled out here, but still distinctive. That wistful, knowing tone. Suddenly, I want to check out my uncle, see if he still looks the same. It would beat standing around in this miserable oratory, staring at the dried flowers.

The chapel is as crammed as I remember it being. Forget squeezing into a pew, there's hardly any standing room back here. But over the sea of furs, Crombies, and black blazers I can make out Uncle Columb at the pulpit. His hair has turned white.

I'm standing with the very people the security guard wanted to keep out of the midnight mass – past pupils of recent vintage, who come up here for a laugh after the pubs close. Many of the profiles around me are faintly familiar – boys three, four years behind me, all now undergraduates. One of them, acne-afflicted still, turns to me and whispers loudly, 'Hey, Iremonger, how's it going? I like the poster!'

I shush him. My uncle's reading the gospel. Now, don't get me wrong. I'm not listening for content. Trinity-smart, I know how chronologically dodgy this nativity story is. It's the voice that gets me, that sad knowningness, as if he can't get out of his mind what will become of that child.

'This is the Word of the Lord,' he adds slowly, as if someone in the congregation had raised an objection. The parents and pupils say praise to You, Lord Jesus Christ and begin to sit down even before he's invited them to. I can now see most of the concelebrants seated behind him. I recognise Fr Drum and Fr Myers and Fr Harrington (hard to miss those rank eyebrows). What are names for the white items they've got on? Words come back to me: soutane, alb, amice, stole, but I can't remember what's what.

Uncle Columb's now telling the crowd who he is, 'I've been a Jesuit for almost forty years, and a missionary in Africa for almost twenty-five. But I've also had a long attachment to Berchmans. As a scholastic, I taught French here for two years – indeed, you could say I *learned* French at Berchmans.'

Polite laughter from the pews; heavy mock-laughter from the boys at the back; I give my spotty little fan a cold, sideways stare – that shuts him up. Uncle Columb continues, 'After final vows, I returned to the school for a year as pastoral adviser to the sixth years. Then it was off to Remoko. Happily I had a living connection with the school when my nephew Tomás was a student here. He graduated just recently.'

Mr Acne gives me a smile and a nod, but I ignore him. I'm perplexed. Is my uncle mixed up about me graduating from Berchmans and from Trinity, or is five years ago really just 'recently' to him? To me it's more like a lifetime. Or another life.

'But for the most part I have been losing touch with Ireland. It's wonderful to come home, but when you only get back once or twice a decade like I do, it's hard to say you really know the place any more. I still find it a novelty to be driven across the toll bridge on the way over from the airport. To give a more profound example, I'm still trying to understand the complexities of this Golden case because you only pick up so much listening to the BBC World Service. I'm sure that it's going to take some explaining, in the same way that things I really care about in Remoko – the future of coffee-bean production, AIDS education, discrimination against the minority tribe – would take me most of Christmas to explain to you.

'The extent of my involvement in Remokoan life led me recently to take a major decision, one that was not easy: to apply for citizenship. Even after all these years, I began to suspect that I was holding something back, avoiding the deepest commitment I could make; still, in my heart of hearts, trying to live in two countries. A wise Swiss Jesuit once told me that if you tried to do that you ended up living nowhere. But it took me many years to *taste* the truth of that adage.

'So, think of me, if you like, as a visitor to your country. Which means you're going to have to act as my guides. I have many questions, as I said before. Questions, indeed, about tonight's gospel. What moves me most about those chapters from St Luke are those shepherds. Who do the angels appear to? Not to Augustus, the most powerful man in the world, nor his lieutenant, Quirinius. Not to the high priest of the Temple in Jerusalem. Not to any priest at all!' Polite and mock-laughter again, but not from pizza-face.

My uncle shakes his head. 'No, they appear to those miserable shepherds. So here are my questions: if the nativity of Our Saviour had not taken place in first-century Palestine, but instead had been delayed until tonight and was about to take place in twentieth-century Ireland, who would the angels appear to? Would they appear to anybody in this chapel? If not, why not? What's wrong with us here in Berchmans? Why would we be ignored, overlooked? Has it something to do with the awesome display of foreign horsepower in the carpark tonight? How do we make ourselves fit to receive such news? Who are the real shepherds among us?

'Let us rise and profess our Faith.'

The congregation rises quickly, as if they've been waiting for his cue. I think Uncle Columb's stirred things at Berchmans up a little, which is all right by me.

'We believe in one God, the Father, the Almighty, maker of heaven and earth, of all that is seen and unseen. We believe in—' Thank you, that's quite enough. For once Iremonger wants to be unseen. I slip back out into the oratory.

I have a suggestion for the pope. If you gave the mass some serious editing, you might bring a lot more people my age back into the fold. After the sermon (which, as Columb had shown, has possibilities) I think you should cut to the chase – the consecration, right? Lose the prayers of the faithful, the offertory hymn, the mystery of faith, the lamb of god, and all the rest of it. Make it snappy, twenty-three minutes max (the length of a sit-com minus the ads).

I nearly OD'd on boredom waiting out in that oratory, sitting on the hard parquet, Nico leaning against the granite wall, getting up from time to time to peek in and see how things were progressing. Communion took so long that I was certain people were going up for seconds. Then towards the end the choir started that carol I'd heard earlier in the day. I put my fingers in my ears, but instead heard *us* singing it, the choir of a decade ago, when I had still been a soprano. Our voices charged the air of the chapel like incense.

But I've got to hand it to my uncle – who couldn't be

blamed for the music – he wrapped things up pretty snappily after that. 'Joy to the World' got me up on my feet – we'd always done that as the recessional hymn; Uncle Columb and his gang would be heading back to the vestry. I stood over by the dried flowers, expecting a flood of people to come out those doors. But it wasn't going to be that simple. Nobody came out, not one single pissed past pupil. From inside I heard the choir burst into 'The Boar's Head', this fruity Elizabethan carol that Devereux, our music teacher, had introduced into the choir repertoire when I was a tenor in sixth year. But it wasn't just the choir singing it now – that was definitely the past pupils in the back joining in and murdering it. I guess that had become a tradition in the years I'd been away.

And for some reason I found myself, very quietly, singing along,

> Our steward hath provided this
> In honour of the King of Bliss!

I even remembered, in a phonetic kind of way, the Latin of the chorus.

But I shut up fast when two kids in blazers came out of the chapel and started opening up doors, letting in the chill of Christmas morning, as the congregation applauded the choir and the past pupils cheered themselves.

Then people couldn't get out of there fast enough. I leaned meanly against a granite wall. Yes, I got a lot of looks, the whole gamut of recognition from parents who'd known me in the prep school to kids who knew me as Ireland's Greatest Resource. Officially I was on the look-out for my parents – my ticket out of here – but I couldn't help searching the crowd for guys from my own year. I'd seen very few of them since the Leaving. They'd virtually all gone to yucky death, sticking to the suburbs. One sad character had gone beyond yucky death – Sligo Regional Technical College. There were two other exceptions – I had gone to Trinity, and St John Strongbow had got into Cambridge.

But I couldn't see anybody from my year. Instead I saw a certain Bavarian hat. My parents looked pleased to see me, to an embarrassing degree.

'Hu-ho, speak of the devil,' said my father.

'You came,' said my mother, squeezing my hand.

I shrugged. 'Yeah, well, I was in the neighbourhood and—'

'Your uncle will be very pleased.'

'See, Sinéad,' my father said, 'he can make up his own mind.'

Suddenly my mother was a tad narkier. 'I can tell you have a few pints on you,' she said.

'I had a drink before I came up here, yes,' I replied edgily. No way was I taking the rap for the bad singing coming from the back.

'The important point is that he's here,' my father told her. 'The how or why doesn't matter.'

'I suppose so,' she replied, casting a critical eye over the dry-flower arrangements behind me.

I'd had enough of this. 'So, is Uncle Columb going to meet us at the car?'

'No,' replied my father, 'he's going to meet us at the community house.'

'Excuse me?'

'We've been invited over for a glass of mulled wine,' said my mother, sounding like we'd been granted a private audience with the Aga Khan. I'd forgotten she had this thing about priests.

Just then I did spot one of my class, Bull Madigan, a simple, rather ineffective bully, leaving the chapel with his parents and a string of younger brothers. This was obviously an ecumenical exercise on their part because I remembered rugby as being the Madigans' religion. The family, including the mother, reminded me of the bulls of Pamplona (I ran this summer, you know). Maybe talking to Bull – for the first time in almost five years – would perversely cheer me up.

'Okay,' I told me parents, 'I'll meet you over there too. There's someone I need to talk to.'

I caught up with the Madigans on the porch of the chapel and called Bull's Christian name. He turned around and looked at me curiously.

'You're . . . the guy at the airport.'

Was this irony? I remembered Bull having great difficulty with the concept in English class.

'It's also me,' I said.

He looked at me like I was a matador playing tricks.

'What? Don't you recognise someone you were in school with for ten years?' I'd meant that to sound wry, but a quiver of emotion came into my voice.

Tentatively he got it. 'Iremonger? Tomás Iremonger?'

'Yes, that's Tom Iremonger up there all right,' I replied assertively.

'Christ, I don't believe it! . . . Fish doing an IDA poster.'

The last time I'd heard that name was four years ago outside the Stag's Head. The guy who said it had gone down with a Class A kick in the crotch. But this wasn't outside the Stag's Head. And maybe Madigan wasn't being deliberately offensive. Even in school there had been speculation that his IQ had been affected by too many collapsed scrums. Bull continued, 'I saw it when I came in from Heathrow last night. Never put two and two together.'

That did not come as a heart-stopping revelation. A young blazered steer appeared on a lower step. He had been sent to fetch his big brother.

'Listen, Fi–, I mean, Tom, I've got to go, but it was great

to see you again. I'll look out for you in airports. Happy Christmas.'

'Yeah, to you too.'

Our hands met like locking front rows.

He smiled and turned into the night.

But I remained in the porchlight. Headlights and engines were coming alive all over the car park. So that was one less character from the old life who needed a little taste of the new and improved Iremonger. Problem was that Bull Madigan had been way down that list, not even in the top twenty. (Yes, somewhere in my glossy back pages I kept a slowly shifting chart. Guess who was number one for Christmas, as he was every Christmas.)

I felt a calm hand on my shoulder. I turned around.

Up close I could see three intense furrows ploughed into his forehead that I didn't remember from before. Also, his grey-blue eyes, the same colour as my father's, seemed smaller, but more photogenic. No fiftysomething Jeremy Irons now, more of a sun-burned Milan Kundera (I still dig writers' faces; the back cover of books is where the real action is, if you ask me). Yeah, his face was a blend of Polish film director and Polish pope. But the only sign he was a priest now that mass was over was a small silver cross on the lapel of this beige summer suit he was wearing. Out of uniform and out of season – I did recall him making those fashion statements in the past.

'Uncle Columb,' I said. 'Aren't you cold?'

He smiled richly. 'Tom. It is "Tom" now isn't it?' I nodded readily. 'Tom, I think you're too old now to be calling me "Uncle". Call me Columb.'

Just Columb – it fit. The sound of it described him well.

'I can do that,' I said.

An awkward silence (awkward for me, I guess) grew as we waited for the door of the community house to be answered. I looked over my shoulder. A cortège of red lights was moving down the avenue, the sweep of front beams silhouetting the big tree. Why hadn't I asked Bull for a lift?

The ancient priest who answered the door I could only remember as Fr Freeday. For years Berchmans boys had been counting on his imminent death as an excuse for cancelling school.

'Hello, Father,' I said, 'you're . . . looking well.'

'Thank you,' he smiled. And I swear he winked. 'This way, please.'

The first time I'd been in this high-ceilinged hall had been fifteen years ago, the night I came with my parents for 'a little chat' with Fr Andrews, the doughy headmaster of the prep school. Then the marble busts of Loyola and Xavier had towered over and intimidated me; now they were nothing more than chunks of cold fashioned stone. On the wall hung portraits of the Jesuit patron saints of youth. I didn't have to read their names: Kostka, Gonzaga, Berchmans himself. Pale-faced boys in ruffs. Over the years, coming to the community house on some errand, they'd always looked disturbingly effeminate to me. Now what struck me was how deadly serious they were. You could see it in their eyes, Berchmans in particular. A young man with a mission. At twenty-two I had outlived them all.

Fr Freeday lead us into the drawing room. About two dozen people were small-talking or helping themselves to food and drink. My parents were over by the bay window, talking to Toiletbrush – Fr Harrington. He spotted me and his thick brows (flecked with grey now) went bounding up his forehead in an expression of ironic surprise. I smiled back feebly. Couldn't wait to catch up with him.

I'd only been in this room once or twice as a schoolboy, but straight away I had the feeling that something wasn't quite right, that something was missing. I panned the walls. Above a bookcase hung a portrait of a very Mexican-looking Christ. It was bordered by an inch or so of wallpaper a shade paler than the rest – another painting had once hung there, and now I remembered what it was: a time-darkened old-mastery picture of Christ being arrested. That's what was missing. I guess the Jesuits are revamping their image. Columb poured himself a ladleful of mulled wine; I dished out a full glass. Turning around, I spotted Harry Quinlaven sitting by himself in a deep armchair in the far corner of the room.

'Coming over to talk to Bill Harrington?' Columb suggested.

'Yeah, sure, in a minute. I think I'd better say hello to another one of my old teachers first.'

Quinner was drinking what looked like straight whiskey. I wondered if I should call him Harry or Mr Quinlaven.

'Hi,' I said, 'remember me?'

He pulled on his red Rasputin beard – shot through with grey now and peppered with crumbs of stilton cheese – and did his sardonic sniffing thing of old.

'Well, well, Mr Iremonger. Do sit down.'

The last report I'd gotten on Quinner was one night in the Buttery in Trinity from a guy who'd been two years behind me at Berchmans. Seemingly Quinner was going through the mid-life thing, which must be even worse if you're a school teacher. Anyhow, he told me Quinner's bad times had started out with him breaking an arm chasing a student who'd put a banger through his letter box on Halloween and culminated with him getting off with a Blessed Virgin girl at the debs in the Burlington. Amazingly he hadn't been fired but had taken a year off teaching to get his head together. This ex-Bercher had told me all this to amuse Iremonger, but it had the reverse effect: it sobered me up and made me feel sad and embarrassed for Quinner. If I had to think about Berchmans, he was one of the first people who came willingly to mind.

'So . . . how's it going?' I asked.

He sipped his whiskey. 'It goes, it goes. You know we have a new headmaster this year?'

'Oh, really?' I replied, trying to sound interested.

'Yes, Mr Coyle. Over there by the mince pies.'

I looked over and saw a bearish man with a Late Jim Morrison beard, somewhere around the forty mark.

'A *lay* headmaster?' I said.

'Yep,' replied Quinlaven, sipping his whiskey. 'Happening in all the schools. It's the man-power shortage in the society.'

A headmaster who wasn't a Jesuit – it didn't seem right, although I didn't quite get why I cared. Maybe it was because Berchmans was now something less in my imagination.

'I guess you must be finished with Trinity by now,' Quinlaven said.

'You knew I went to Trinity?'

'Oh, yes,' he sniffed. 'And I heard you didn't do history, Tomás.'

I was beginning to regret coming over to talk to him. The mulled wine had a metallic tang. 'Yeah, that's right.'

Quinlaven was shaking his head. 'A great pity. It's sad to see talent going to waste.'

'Talent?'

'I still remember that essay you did on the assassination of Kevin O'Higgins.'

I nodded my head slowly, remembering.

'Yeah, I was pretty happy with that. But to tell you the truth, Mr Quinlaven, by the time I got to Trinity I'd had enough of Irish history. And that was a large part of the syllabus, even there. I studied Pure English instead.'

He smiled and sniffed. 'And so what are you doing now with your degree in *Pure* English?'

I shrugged. Maybe a man like Harry Quinlaven would understand the Iremonger Project, but even with him it would take a lot explaining. And it's BTE.

'Not much,' I smiled.

He didn't smile back. He drained his drink.

'A pity,' he said. 'A real pity.'

4

On the Morning of Christ's Nativity

Inside the Senator, coming home along the Stillorgan Dual Carriageway. When we finally got out of Berchmans (for a while I thought they were going to make me sit the Leaving Cert all over again), Columb elected to share the back with me; I'm sitting behind my mother. From sporadic banter between the brothers, I've picked up that the business about Columb becoming a citizen of Remoko was old news to my parents. He probably told them about it in one of those thin blue aerogrammes with the brilliant stamps that arrive at Cedar-of-Lebanon Road every four or six months. When I was a kid, and still fascinated by my uncle's life in Africa, I used to ask my father to read them aloud because I could decipher maybe one word in four of Columb's spidery writing. My mother would be listening too, and I remember her sometimes making a comment I've never quite got my mind around: *That fella would throw a sprat to catch a salmon.*

'So does this mean that you'll have to give up your Irish citizenship?' I ask.

For some reason, I find this idea disturbing, dangerous.

'No,' Columb smiles. 'I don't think that will be necessary. No need to tell Dublin about this. But I will be travelling on a Remokoan passport.'

I wonder what kind of bold declaration the Remokoan Minister for Foreign Affairs makes on the inside cover of his travel book.

'And when is the . . . transformation taking place?'

My uncle laughs and my father snorts.

'Soon after I get back in February.'

'You're staying that long?'

'You want me to go sooner?'

'Oh, no, that's not what I meant. I just thought you'd be going back right after Christmas, like I am.'

'What date are you leaving, Tom?'

Great question – I can break the news to my parents without having to talk to them about it face-to-face.

'Probably New Year's Day, if I can get a flight.'

The way Columb slowly looks away from me and at the back of my mother's head I know something's up.

'That is,' I add warily, 'if there's nothing going on here.'

My father snorts richly. 'Just a little something.'

Silence. I want someone to explain to me what's going on. 'Mum?'

My mother sighs and turns around as best she can. 'Well, this is what we wanted to talk to you about, Tom. For most of the time you've been away, Daddy's been having some indigestion problems. Dr Keegan thinks it may be a hiatus hernia, but he wants your father to go in for some tests just to make sure. So he's going into the Simmonscourt Clinic the first Tuesday of the new year, the third of January. Should be out of there within a day or two.'

What a time and place to have to deal with this. Some stunt. I'm not exactly sure what a hiatus hernia is or what it does to you, but I'm willing to go along with Keegan's diagnosis.

I look at my mother and my uncle and shrug construc-
tively. 'Well, I guess I'll be hanging around a little bit
longer.'

Over her shoulder my mother says, 'I should hope so.'
Faintly, I hear my father sucking air through the side of his
mouth.

My mother punched the white buttons of the control con-
sole and the electronic voice of the new TeleGuard alarm
system intoned, 'Status: home.'

I talked back, 'Whatever you say, friend.'

'We call him Tom,' my mother said. 'He's got your
American twang.'

I smiled and hissed, 'Doesn't sound a bit like me. Anyway,
what did you pay for this?'

My father gives me a lopsided smile. 'Enough to keep you
in the style you're accustomed to for several weeks.'

'That much, hey? Well, I hope he does strip searches.'

'And breathalysers, too,' said my mother. 'Listen, I have
a turkey to take care of, you should get yourself to bed. You
have a big family day ahead of you tomorrow.'

'Yeah, I'll crash in a little while.'

So she went into the kitchen. It was just myself and my
father and Columb standing there in the hall. *Hall* – the
space seemed hardly worthy of the name. Every time I come
back to this house after a long absence – my J-1 summer
in New York, my TEFL summer in Barcelona, a couple of
times last year living in rooms – it always seems smaller, less
substantial. Now I felt like I was standing in an elevator. And
Columb had his eyes on the antique barometer on the wall
as if he were watching floor numbers change. I think he was
still preoccupied with the fight we'd just seen coming off the
dual carriageway. It wasn't a big deal, really. Just a couple
of guys pissed out of their minds in a little holiday dispute.
No weapons, not much blood. I mean, if this were New York

. . . Suddenly he turned around and offered me his hand. I shook it warily. He stared at me with this spacy little smile.

'Tom,' he said, 'thank you for coming to hear me preach.'

Was he subtly taking the piss? Jesuits do that all the time.

'Yeah sure, no problem.'

'I think I'll retire also,' said my father. 'Tom, I believe the bellboy put your luggage in your room.'

'Great. Thanks.'

He followed Columb up the stairs. They looked like some old gay couple hitting the sack.

A stiff drink and a stiff cigarette were my main priorities. I opened the drawing-room door, and saw the old artificial Christmas tree, all lit up. I wasn't in the mood to look at dumb decorations, but there would be no mini-bar in my room tonight. I turned on the overhead lights to dim the intensity of the tree. A Christmas hamper lay on a table near the drinks cabinet. As hampers go it was a stingy deal, but one item caught my attention – a bottle of Kells, the new cream liqueur. That's what I wanted. Not a shot of Jameson's or Sheridan's or even Bailey's – I wanted to try this new poison; it might go pretty well with a Roland. So I took the squeaky cellophane off the hamper (the card said it was from my father's 'lonely colleagues at AM') and poured myself a healthy inaugural glass.

It tasted just like Bailey's, but what the hell. I grabbed an ashtray, lit up a Roland (T – 178), laid Nico down comfortably on an armchair and crashed on the couch. But that damn Christmas tree was posing away in the corner. The other marvel in the room was the crib. I tried to fix my attention on it instead. The crib had been custom-made by father to fit into a space in the funky shelving system he'd designed in the seventies (on the highest reaches of which you could see the heads of the sleek, slender, dark-wood statues Columb used to bring back as gifts).

My father had constructed a chip-board box, then lined it with heavy black paper, crumpled at the edges and fringed with spray-on snow. The holy family were over-nighting in a huge rectangular cave. You could dimly make out animals in its shadowy corners. The whole thing looked like a stage design for a nativity play by Beckett. It was a downer, I didn't want to look at it. But neither did I want to be distracted by that tacky tree.

I stood up to go turn off the fairy lights. But instead of just crawling under the tree and hitting the plug switches, I found myself staring at the branches. The ornaments I'd made as a kid in Montessori school were more noticeable than I ever remembered them being, certainly more so than in recent years when I got involved in the decorating process as a means of containing my father's nostalgia. This year my sad paper lanterns, my spastic Santa, and my wrong-headed angel were dangling from the best branches – strange fruit, indeed. I put my juvenilia in the shadow of my sister's intricate beadwork baubles and ingenious pipe-cleaner gnomes. One thing I couldn't change was the top of the tree. Traditionally a plump fairy wearing a Mary Quant-style mini-skirt Triona had created from felt when she was four was impaled there. This year it was nowhere to be seen. In its place, illuminated by a red fairy light, was my asymmetrical glittery cardboard star.

I got down on my knees – to check out the presents; I had completely forgotten about my presents. There was a respectable stack of wrapped gifts underneath the tree. I rooted through them, looking for the dark paisley-patterned paper (I wanted something *un*seasonal) I'd requested from the Bloomindale's gift-wrapper. My gifts were not there. I looked underneath the curtains, behind an adjacent arm-chair – nada. I couldn't think why my mother wouldn't have put them under the tree. Before extinguishing it, I took a long lung-fuck drag on my Roland. I knocked back my Kells. Then I went to ask my mother what on earth had happened to my gifts.

She was doing something to the turkey that reminded me of sex I'd had with a Canadian girl in Marrakesh. More home improvement: they'd retiled the kitchen floor coral-pink.

'Off to bed finally,' said my mother, disengaging from the bird. 'You should drink some milk or water. You'll get dehydrated after all that beer.'

'Sure,' I replied. 'Listen, Mum, wasn't there a CeltEx delivery sometime this week?'

'No.' A quiver of suspicion in her voice.

'You didn't even find a ticket saying they'd tried to make a delivery?'

I didn't quite manage to muffle the rising note of disbelief in my voice.

'We didn't get sight nor sound of them. What were you expecting, drugs?'

Her smile, when it came, was forced. I faked one back.

'Yeah, that was it, drugs. Tons of them. A seasonal hamper.'

Chill, Iremonger, I told myself, this is not your highest priority. It felt good to change the subject.

'Anyway, Mum, I guess what I really came in to ask you was what time Finbar goes down to the swim.'

'Why are you interested in the swim all of a sudden?'

I shrugged. 'I'd like to start Christmas with a splash.'

My mother sighed. 'I don't think we're ever going to get a straight answer out of you.' Turning back to her turkey, she added icily, 'The swim's at midday. I guess that means you might be up in time to phone him yourself in the morning.'

'I guess.'

She continued to operate on the turkey like I wasn't there.

'Well,' I said, 'I've got presents to wrap. You got any more wrapping paper?'

'Everything you need you'll find on the dining-room table.'

'Cool. Well . . . Good night.' It was almost a question.

She half-turned around and said good night in a weird, quiet way. I got out of there.

When I turned on the dining-room light the dimmer was down low. I left it that way. Beneath my Boccioni boots, new parquet and throw rugs.

On the wall over the mantelpiece hung the old man's portrait. The old man's old man, to be precise, Anraí Iremonger, but in my mind always *the* old man. If my father ever makes it to ninety (he's only about two thirds of the way there), maybe then he will finally succeed his father in being the old man. But not till then. And I've got a feeling he's not going to make it that far.

I didn't pay the painting much attention. By Maurice Fitzgerald, RHA, son of an old friend of my grandfather from his days at the Ministry of Internal Affairs. First thing, it isn't the old man I knew, even though I was about sixteen when the painting was done. The old man I knew didn't have that honed passion, that puritan stare. Second of all, I guess it gives me the creeps. Ultimate horror movie cliché I know, but I really did feel like those small pale green eyes were watching me. (Why not? This whole trip has the makings of a horror movie, my own private horror movie.) My mother was right. Everything I needed was there. I went upstairs.

Nico is hanging from a wooden hanger. I am lying on a crisply made bed. The statements from Tara Bank that were waiting for me in a neat pile on my desk (beside my old set of house keys on the key-chain with a leather tongue and a fat metallic I) are in my wicker wastepaper basket, unopened, shredded. In the air still the faint flavour of new paint. The chaos I created in the weeks between moving back from rooms and moving out of Ireland – gone. That's not to say that everything is in its place. My mother has some pretty neurotic ideas about where things should go, but I'm not complaining, everything has *a* place, at least, and a lot of crap has been stored away. There was a lot of junk in this room – books, clothes, letters – that I wasn't looking forward to dealing with, but now I'm not even sure I can even find any of it. You see, I threw a lot of stuff out in the weeks before I left (artifacts dated 1 to 5 BI: Before Iremonger, or from the early Iremonger Era), but I hadn't quite finished the process.

For example, that Jim Morrison poster has got to go. True, I learnt a lot from old Jimbo. Back in the embryonic Iremonger days, my last year in Berchmans, *No One Here Gets out Alive* was a kind of bible for me. The guys he read as a teenager – Rimbaud, Nietzsche, Celine, Colin Wilson – well, just take a look at my bookcase; not even the beats or the deconstructionists replaced them in my affections. He lost weight; I lost weight. He urinated into a wine glass at a college party; guess what I did. Venice Beach became my idea of heaven. I knew the words to 'Horse Latitudes' off by heart (and wrote poems about weird happenings in the Irish Sea). The day my first year results came out I was a hazy pilgrim at his chaotic grave. Yeah, Mr Mojo Risin', he was one of the singing masters of the Iremonger soul. But I've gone beyond influences and role models now. Iremonger is an original. The poster has to go. What if I died? I know my mother would do exactly what my Aunt Miriam, my mother's sister-in-law, did when my cousin Paul died of cancer in the eighties, aged twenty-one: keep the room exactly like he left it, a museum, a shrine. His possessions define him. It's funny to think, but the things in that room, the jackets of his paperbacks, the political stickers on his bathroom mirror, his ties and trousers, are becoming dated now. His room must have a coherent retro-look. I wonder if his mother still goes in there every day, like she forced herself to do at the beginning. When I heard about that I got much more upset that I ever did at Paul's funeral.

To work. Personally I think that the exchange of gifts on Christmas morning is a pretty hollow ritual; I could survive without getting anything from my family, but I don't dig the idea of sitting around the living room later today telling some sob story about how I'm going to sue the ass off CeltEx. Then again, I've been in much tighter corners than this, sweetheart. Only a few nights ago I was cornered by two Arabs near Place Pigalle, hassling me for francs. I asked them in viciously broken French (I adore the violence I do to that language) if they'd ever heard of my hometown, Belfast, if they knew what kneecapping was. They replied, backing away, that they had to leave now and they hoped we all could meet up again under more pleasant circumstances. If I can preserve my testicles, surely I can improvise a few Christmas presents. Iremonger is a resourceful guy, his own greatest resource.

I haul my sad suitcase out from where my father has stowed it – I can see him insisting that he can manage, struggling up the stairs with it – under the sink. I lay it down in the middle of the floor and line up the combination on the little golden lock: 1-2-7. Why did I choose that? Because it is the combination that my family has always used for suitcase locks; this is one number I can't forget. And why has my family always used that combination? Because the twelfth day of the seventh month is my father's birthday. Yes, my father was born on the anniversary of the battle of the Boyne, the day of the Orangemen's marches. When I was a kid this was a source of shame to me. *Why?* Did I think if I told my friends, my classmates – wrong word, far too chummy – the date of my dad's birthday they'd think he was secretly a Protestant, that he paraded around his bedroom wearing an orange sash and a bowler hat? That it was just the kind of sweet ammunition Strongbow was looking for? Apparently so. It was bad enough that he had given up going to mass.

This July 12th, his sixty-first birthday, I was in New York. I'd CeltEx'd him a gold-nibbed limited-edition Wendell and wanted to phone him and get his reaction to it. But things did not go according to plan. I'd been in a blizzard of Aspen Snow in a Chelsea club the night before and was coping with a shrill headache and slow nosebleed caused by the meat cleaver lodged deep in my sinuses. For several hours I lay on a futon in the Charles Street studio of Sufi, the Micronesian model I'd hooked up with. A red phone lay near by, my Eurovox calling card on top of it.

I could not remember my parents' telephone number, my old number. My suitcase with its Iremonger ID tag was uptown, (in a Park Avenue apartment that's become a kind of flophouse for the elite of the new Irish, those deeply in the know), but it would not have been difficult to get hold of Irish directory inquiries. A stubborn unexpected pride held me back. I may have left home, but this was going too far.

About six-thirty I tentatively declared my nosebleed to be at an end and felt well enough to venture out of the apartment. The streets were shadowy, but the day's heat was oozing back out of the brownstones. I walked the intimate blocks of the West Village, crossed 12th Street and stepped onto one of the rotting wharves that pointed towards the Jersey shore. There was a welcome breeze coming off the Hudson. I passed a few mellow or wistful gay couples out for a stroll as I went to the very end of the wharf, where I sat cross-legged, alternately peering down through a gap in the boards at the Guinness-coloured water and looking out across the broad river at the declining sun. My mind grew hazy. This was perhaps the most peaceful moment I had known since leaving Dublin. And, just as I had completely forgotten what was bugging me, I stumbled across the number in my mind. Too quickly I got to my feet and almost put a foot through an absent plank. I raced back down the wharf, smiling benevolently at two moustachioed men necking, and hurried back down a darkening Charles Street. Bursting into the apartment I found Sufi home and missing me. I told her I had to phone Dublin before anything else. She wanted to know if there was some kind of emergency. I told her, yes, in a way there was. Moments later I was talking to a Eurovox operator. My mother answered after three rings. She told me it was quarter to one in the morning, that my father's birthday had been over for forty-five minutes, and why was I phoning now after three weeks of silence? I had no answer for her; all I could say was that I just wanted to talk to my father. Groggily and a little grouchily he accepted my congratulations and thanked me for the pen. He told me that my mother would really appreciate it if I phoned back in the morning. I promised I would. But next morning I caught a flight to LAX from Newark, without using my Eurovox card again.

Enough. I've got to be careful. Memory is dangerous. Memory is a drug. Memory is bad shit. And as Dylan once told me, only half-joking, I have an addictive personality. So – open that suitcase. Get to work.

I was woken up at some unspeakable hour by the sweet melody of 'Away in a Manger', broadcast by the bells, the electronic bells, of Owenstown Hill's parish church, St Joseph Stalin's. Undoubtedly the sweetest feature of this community service was the slight delay every fourth or fifth note designed to convince my fellow parishoners that the bells were being rung by real fallible humans just like themselves. Miraculously, by retreating deep into the shelter of my duvet I managed to sink into unconciousness again. I had no such luck when my mother knocked sharply on my door, calling me by *that name*, at 11:15 (Irish time, I was stuck in Irish time). It was too early (still) to protest. I pulled on the pair of limp silk Paul Smith boxers I'd shed at 3 AM – I'm strict about sleeping naked – and shambled to the door. I opened it sparingly; I would gain nothing in letting my mother see what I'd done to my room overnight.

'If you're planning on going down to the swim you'd better get some clothes on. I phoned the Wogans. Your brother-in-law is going to be pulling up outside the house in five minutes. He won't wait for you.'

I smiled faintly at my mother. 'Happy Christmas to you, too.'

My mother was wrong. I was the one who ended up waiting. I didn't mind; I was happy for an excuse to get out of the house quick. It was a bright winter morning, with an almost Parisian clarity, a fine day for watching masochism, and for hanging out with Mainie Doyle. I was looking pretty good considering I'd only had time to throw on a Hugo Boss turtleneck, an old pair of black 501's, and Nico; slapping some duty-free Zeus on my moody bristles was my only vanity. About twenty to twelve, a late-model Stalwart came cruising down Cedar-of-Lebanon Road at a Christmas-morning kind of pace. Finbar pulled up. I got in. Garth Brooks was mushing out of the speakers. I experienced the crushing eagerness of Finbar's handshake – an absolute greeting. I'll say one thing, I'm glad I'll never have to confront him in a water polo match. A teddy bear on dry land, my *beau frere* is reputed to have administered several primitive vasectomies playing for the Martello Mariners.

We set off for the coast.

'Where'd you get the new wheels?'

I'd already heard from my mother that Triona had traded in her second-hand Darma for a new Juno, the same model my mother drove.

'Company car.'

'Are you sure you didn't feck it in the city centre?'

I speak like this the rare times when I'm alone with Finbar. I don't pretend it's natural – I can hear a hint of a Dublin accent coming into my voice when I talk to him, for god's sake – but it's something I've perfected in the decade he's been legally connected to me. It's a pastiche, I guess, of the locker room and Friday night in O'Rourke's, or what I imagine Finbar and his peers say in the locker room and O'Rourke's, with a little Bosco thrown in for good measure. In any case, Finbar goes along with it, and that's the way I deal with him. Don't get me wrong, basically I like the guy. He is, to use a Finbarism, a decent skin. The jock side of him I can tolerate (god knows I had to put up with enough of it at Berchmans). It's the other side of him, and most of my sister, that I have trouble with.

Finbar and Triona are both thirty-three. When he is not crushing testicles in the water or hands on dry land, or being the kind of family man featured in ads for life assurance, Finn slaves away for Tara Markets behind the green glass of the Financial Services Centre; my sister mainlines motherhood and still works part-time for Leinster Bank.

Yuppies? Not really. They are racing towards middle age, embracing it. Finbar's wiry red hair seems to be in tactical retreat. If they have any serious personal agenda, any big plan for power or profile, any erotic ambition left, you would never guess it. Now it's all to do with the children. It's all about the children. It's Sibéal this, Kieran that. There's a speech I've been itching to make to my sister and brother-in-law for about five years. It goes something like this:

Why do you sacrifice so much of yourself for your children? So that they can grow up and sacrifice themselves for their children? So that *they* in turn can grow up and sacrifice themselves for *their* children? What's the point?

What generation gets to break open the piggy bank, gets to fuck without repercussions, gets more than a few years of freedom, gets to put itself first, gets to *live* a little? Well, I am that generation. I have declared independence. I'm doing this not only for myself, but for all the repressed generations at my back. I'm releasing centuries of spunk and spleen – coming for my country. And I shouldn't be coming alone: Ireland needs an army of Iremongers.

That's what I want tell Finbar and Triona. But they'd only get upset, my sister in particular. And besides, I actually kind of like them. They're my anti-role models.

Picking up speed on the dual carriageway, Finbar said, 'I think this is very brave of you.'

For one tiny transcendent moment I thought he was reading my mind and alluding to the Iremonger Project. Then I touched base with reality again.

'Brave why?' I asked.

Finbar took his eyes of the road and smiled at me.

'For thinking about doing the swim.'

'Wait a second, Finbar. Who gave you that idea?'

I guessed the answer. 'Your mother.'

'What did she say to you on the phone?'

'That you'd got this notion into your head that you had to go down to the swim today and maybe you were planning on surprising us all by getting into the water. I knew she was joking, but I brought an extra pair of togs and a towel, just in case.'

'Well, I'm sorry to disappoint you, but I don't think it'll be cold enough for me this morning. Maybe next year.'

Finbar laughed. 'That's what you say every year.' He shook his head. 'You don't know what you're missing. You work up a wicked appetite in the water.'

Traffic around the Forty Foot was outrageous. We had to park several streets away.

'If we could only get *five per cent* of these people into the water,' Finbar brooded as we walked down the roadway of Sandycove Avenue.

'Their London Fog coats would certainly keep them warm,' I replied.

It was a throwaway line, but pretty accurate. Triona had dragged me to a Christmas Morning Swim when she and Finbar had been dating, about a decade ago, I guess. Spectators back then were finely wrapped; now they looked like some giant *Vogue* photoshoot. Roderick and Dylan would be here. Dylan's mother would be here, working the crowd. The swim had become *the* place to be 'round midday on Christmas, *the best way to escape that Christmas day claustrophobia*. And I was pissed about that. I didn't want anybody to think I was here because I was following fashion dictates. If I cared to, I would be the one setting the cutting edge agenda for Christmas morning. If I'd spent it hanging out in the Kish lighthouse some people would be planning to spend Stephen's Day there. I had Finbar as an excuse, but a pretty sad excuse he was.

The Irish Sea was trying to act all innocent, looking calm and blue, almost Mediterranean. But it wasn't fooling anybody. Even if it had been the Mediterranean, it wouldn't have mattered. I don't do seawater. We walked down the broad concrete path that goes past the Joyce tower, Dublin's ultimate photoshoot backdrop. Down below, at the Forty Foot, pale bodies – I could almost see the gooseflesh from here – were already clambering onto the steep rock that is the starting point of the swim. The heads of a few informal swimmers bobbed in the water.

As we reached sea level, Mainie Doyle, wearing a thick cobalt-blue cable rope sweater, stood out from the crowd. I was just about to tell Finbar I'd see him later and nonchalantly orchestrate a crossing of paths, when I saw who she was with. And I was sure that they saw me. I must have frozen on the spot because it was Finbar who said, 'I'll see you later.'

I snapped out of it enough to say, 'No.'

He smiled. 'You're coming with me?'

I stared at him, uncomprehendingly, and then realised he was providing me with a brutal salvation.

'Yes. I mean, give me the keys. I mean, please give me the keys.'

He put a kind, crushing hand on my forearm. 'Tom, hold on, hold on. What's the matter? You look like you've seen a ghost.'

'Don't ask me to explain, Finn, please. All I can say is I really want to do the swim. *All* I can do is do the swim.'

He shrugged tolerantly, then sighed and shook his head as he looked at his watch. 'You're cutting it fine. They do begin on time most years.' He put a heavy set of keys in my hand. 'Run.'

I was happy to. The last time I'd ran had been a few months back when a deal went wrong one night in Les Halles. I ran faster than that now, oblivious to the bundled-up beautiful people. I wasn't thinking much about Mainie, I was thinking about *him*. I was remembering him, all the way back to the car.

I remembered the morning in late September St John Strongbow walked into the Senior 2A classroom for the first time. For a few minutes it was just him and me. I was reticent, offhand, not because I was scared of him – even though I noted that Carl Pollen was no longer the tallest guy in the class – but because he was so embarrassingly polite, so embarrassingly *English*, like something out of Children's BBC. I thought that befriending him might lower my already modest social standing in the class. For the next four years, I wondered if things would have gone differently if I'd had enough confidence to make friends with him while I had the chance, that first morning, if that loyalty would have meant anything to him later.

I know I began to regret my wariness as soon as two of the lads arrived – Luán McKeone and Mark Daly. I thought they would start to take the piss out of him straight away, but they didn't. True, they were amused by his handshake, but besides being very polite, very Home Counties, he proved to be unshakable. And they responded to that. I watched them, dismayed. It was chemical.

Things happened sickenly fast after that. Strongbow could have gotten a pass from Irish class but didn't, and learnt more of the language in two months than I had done in seven years. (He went through a phase where you were obliged to call him Seán.) He had a better French accent than Mrs Grennan, coolly corrected Mr Hynes when he quoted Keats, and knew more about the subjunctive in Latin than Fr Dooley.

But popularity at Berchmans – more accurate to call it power – didn't derive from being a smartarse, even a super-smartarse. He made an impact outside the classroom, as well. Contact lenses replaced John Lennon glasses. Even though he had no apparent love for rugby, Strongbow became a devastatingly accurate penalty kicker on the Junior Cup Team. He declared his tastes: in music, the Clash; in terrorism, the INLA. But the crowning moment came about six weeks after he arrived when his grandfather died. A picture of the funeral made the inside pages of *The Irish Times* – Strongbow and his family and all these bigshots from Fíanna Fáil. Old man Strongbow had been in the GPO in 1916. (So had my grandfather, as a junior clerk; he got marched out of the building about ten minutes after Pearse read the Proclamation from the front steps.)

After that he was the aloof king of our class. One of his first acts was to christen me Fish. Or rather, what he did was shorten an old, occasional twist on my name – Fishmonger.

The first time he called me by that abbreviation (in the dangerous minutes between teachers) I must have winced because Mark Daly's eyes lit up with glee, and I knew I was stuck with it. Not such an impossible nickname to live with, you might say, but I didn't see it that way. It made me into the slimy creature I feared I was.

Soon after that he left his leather bag by the rough-hewn granite column, left it with clear instructions as to what should be done with it. What did I do? I stared at the substantial bag for a good five minutes, arriving classmates passing me and asking me what the hell I was doing standing out in the cold. I muttered something about not feeling well, turning my face away so that they wouldn't see the hot, furious tears welling in my eyes. I willed them back, and then picked up the bag and carried it in.

By the time I reached the Stalwart I was completely out of breath. A furled green towel lay on the back seat. I lay Nico down in its place. No way was I going to risk leaving her in the changing area, not even with somebody 'keeping an eye on her' – she would walk like *that*. I threw my Tzara down on the front passenger seat. Five minutes to midday. I locked the door, took several deep breaths, and began to run back. At least Nico is safe. That's what I said to myself, over and over again like a mantra, as I dashed back down to the Forty Foot. At least she's safe.

5

Beasts

I'm busy getting the briny taste out of my mouth with the aid of Ulick de Brun's eighteen-year-old scotch (Roderick's old man has a case of this crap, one of the little rewards for aggressively representing those Fine Gael pols in the Potatogate inquiry), I'm busy sluicing that potent juice through my still frigid teeth when who should arrive and make a queen bee line for me but Carmel Carraig-Dubh. Carmel Carraig-Dubh and her latex face. Once upon a time she was a beautiful woman (check out the photographs of her in the sixties); now she looks like something out of *Spitting Image*. I think it's an almost wilful transformation. It would make Carmel Carraig-Dubh's decade to be on *Spitting Image* because her vainest illusion is that she's famous – notorious – in Britain too, a confidante of Princess Di, the next Nigel Dempster, Lady Thatcher's lesbian lover.

She should be content with what she is: the most dangerous woman in Dublin. Every time I see her parading my way, every time I kiss her rubbery cheeks like I'm about to do, I have mixed emotions, no – scrambled emotions.

Just like Ardal McQuaid, Carmel is a pusher. And just like

him she's strictly Class A – dealing Class A people, in her case, or what passes for Class A people in this town. The vast majority of her customers are decidedly not Class A people. About half a million of them score her dope every Sunday; my mother, for example, reads 'Dove Tales' in *Ireland on Sunday* as soon as she gets back from mass. Then there is the slender minority who are eligible for her premium product – the kick of seeing your name in bold face, and maybe even your beautiful face, on Carmel's tasty page. Yeah, the first time I saw the name **Iremonger** was one of the sweetest moments of my life. And the first time I saw my demi-monde monochrome face there – better than supermodel sex.

But there's a downside, a dark side. Carmel Carraig-Dubh has about a one per cent purity level. She's as insecure as she is dangerous (I guess they are one and the same thing). You can be banished from the columns of 'Dove Tales', sent into social cold turkey, on a whim, or on less than a whim. Or even worse, you can be poisoned on the page. No one is safe. I've seen it happen to Taoiseachs and DJs, novelists and media nuns. My friendship with Dylan means very little to his mother. I'm smart enough to know that I'm fair game now, a player in my own right, one of the big boys. (The way Carmel sees it, it's nothing personal, just business.) I've become blasé about seeing my name in her column, but I'm sensitive to the damage she can do. Just watch me do some sophisticated arse-licking. And watch closely because it's the only time you'll see me do this.

'Tom – sweetie! – Happy New Year!'

'Happy New Year to you too, Carmel. You're looking great. I met Daniel Day-Lewis in Avignon and he made me swear to give you a kiss from him.'

'Oh, Iremonger, you're too much. And getting in the water this morning – *so* brave. What on earth possessed you to do it?'

Carmel asks the question with this moist, knowing smile.

If anyone can read minds it's Carmel. I respond with a vintage Iremonger shrug.

'I was bored.'

'Well, I can tell you your appearance sent a wonderful *frisson* through the crowd. You looked good in those Speedo togs. Ireland's Greatest Resource, indeed.' She gives me a languid wink. That, I can assure you as a veteran reader of Carmel's prose, was one of her subtler remarks. I give her a tolerant smile. She continues, 'Don't forget to pick up a copy of *Ireland on Sunday* next week, on New Year's Day.'

'No fear.'

She strokes my arm and says, 'Listen, I want to hear all about what you've been up to – from *you*, so don't you dare leave Dublin before we have a proper chat.'

'I wouldn't dream of it, Carmel.'

'Splendid. Well, before I go I simply must talk to Ultan about this IRA fellow he's defending. He's meant to be a wonderful poet, the next Seamus Heaney.'

'You're leaving already?'

'Sweetie, I have five other drinks parties to go to before sitting in on three different Christmas dinners.'

As I kiss her synthetic cheeks goodbye, I'm wondering if I should sleep with Carmel Carraig-Dubh. I've never had sex with a post-menopausal woman before – speculated about it, of course – but it might be worth it. She might be eternally grateful – might. It would be like taking out a pricy insurance policy.

Roderick cruises by and pours me some more of that Class A whiskey. I want to ask him to reconfirm what he told me when we were leaving Sandycove – that Mainie Doyle has graciously accepted his invitation to the house and will be making an appearance. But I don't want to be seen in need of reassurance, even by Roderick. Or perhaps especially by Roderick: he swears he picked up nothing about Strongbow on the exile grapevine, never even heard of the guy, but I don't know if I believe him. De Brun doesn't always level with me the way I'd like him to. He sometimes has these messy conflicts of loyalty. Could be what's going down here.

Dylan has drifted in to the party (his movements are complex, more complex than mine, which at least adhere to flight timetables); after a quick word with his mother he comes over to BS with me. That helps kill time. As we talk about the swim – Dylan giving my performance a rave review – I scan the walls of the huge, high-ceilinged drawing room we are in. This house was built by this big-time West Brit Augustus Smerwick a few years before the Act of Union was passed and the shit hit the fanlight. Painted on the wallpaper are delicate scenes of Grand Tour destinations: Paris, Heidelberg, the Swiss Alps, Florence, Venice, the Bay of Naples – all painstakingly restored with Potatogate money. And I think to myself, Augustus Smerwick would have understood the Iremonger Project. My father once explained to me that these young aristocrats, these eighteenth-century Iremongers, had the choice of going to Oxbridge or hitting the Italian trail. Now, I guess, it's a choice between graduate school and going global. These take-offs and these landings, these one-night stands and sublets, these circlings and reversals – put them together and what you've got is a post-modern Grand Tour. And I guess that makes me a post-modern rake.

Roderick's old man is escorting Carmel Carraig-Dubh from the drawing room when Mainie and Strongbow come in. He's wearing Lennon glasses again. Mainie has her hair tied back in that retro Robert Palmer video style. How long has it been since I've had the simple – and exquisite – pleasure of running my fingers from side to side across her head when she has her hair like that, the gelled-strands like the strings of a harp? Six months, at least. Far too long.

'Who is that guy?' Dylan asks.

'That's Strongbow,' I reply.

'You know him?'

'Yeah, but he doesn't know me.'

Mainie and Carmel delicately clasp hands and shadow-kiss each other's cheeks. They talk warmly. Carmel glances back at me – that moist smile again; Mainie does no more than glimpse. By now the conversation between Dylan and me has dried up. Mainie introduces her new man to Carmel, who begins to paw him and question him closely. Strongbow is carrying a prop I find hard to square with the Strongbow I knew – a compact video camera. (If he were carrying a copy of Chaucer I wouldn't look twice.) I'm further disturbed by the black leather flight jacket he's wearing: an allusion to Nico? I almost cheer when I look down at his feet. The guy still wears *sensible* shoes.

Strongbow hands the camera to Carmel Carraig-Dubh. She's pretty confused by it too, doesn't know what button to push, which end to look in. Finally she puts her eye to the viewfinder. For a moment I think she's taping Strongbow's crotch, but then I get it – she's watching replay. I snap out of it (I'm one of the watched, remember, not a watcher) and, with enormous discipline, slip into the de Brun's big woody kitchen. First Rule of Cool: the more you want somebody, the further away you have to stay, the other side of the world if possible; if they pick up the scent of desire, you're done for. I'm burning to know what's on that videotape – is Iremonger on that tape? – but I'm not going to stay in that drawing room and let those women read my mind.

The de Brun's fridge is crammed with supercans of Fursty; Roderick and a young Law Library crowd – the devils and the junior counsels – are in here getting pissed and passing around a discreet joint.

'Toking with your toque on, Roderick?' My nonchalant pun is much appreciated.

'Hey, Iremonger,' says the scion of a big shot Fíanna Fáil barrister family. 'I didn't know Ireland's Greatest Resource could swim. Take a seat and tell us what it was like, you mad bastard.'

I do so. I sit down and hold court.

'You see, it all began as a bet with my bother-in-law. He said that a Trinity boy like myself didn't have the balls to get into the water on Christmas morning, let alone complete the swim. Well, now he owes me a bottle of Kells, the new cream liqueur.'

'But what about the cold?' asks a pretty devil. 'I think I'd have a heart attack if I dived into the Irish Sea in the middle of winter.'

I shrug. 'I was sort of prepared for it. The health club I belong to in Paris has this sadistic plunge pool. I've been training myself to stay down there longer and longer. It makes their Scandinavian sauna an even more intense experience.'

The young lawyers look suitably impressed, and a little stoned.

Knew it – Mainie and Strongbow and the video camera have wandered into the kitchen. First Rule of Cool vindicated once again. I know Mainie, and now I've got a theory about what's going on: Strongbow is a provocation. She's been on the lookout for someone like Strongbow for a very long time – not just a pawn to play with but a rival-Iremonger to brandish, a man who would make me sweat, make me make a commitment, any kind of commitment. Well, she's hit the jackpot with Strongbow, I'll give her that. She mustn't have believed her luck when she came across him (in London, I guess) and he made the connection for her between me and the old me; in other words, the very young me, the discarded, test-run version of myself that Mainie was always discreetly curious about, as if piecing me together – softly, softly – might come in useful some day. Well, that day has arrived. And that's why she must be pissed I'm not making a scene, losing my cool. It's the very least I could do.

Mainie nods casually; I nod casually back. Strongbow pretends he doesn't recognise me, for god's sake. Roderick equips them with drinks, and they chat with him like they've all known each other for ages, like they went through some incredible bonding experience together – a nightmare transatlantic flight, perhaps, or a hostage situation. I sip the Fursty I've been handed and let the pretty devil chat me up.

Eventually Mainie and Strongbow saunter over to the table. But keep me in mind: leaning back in my chair, right UB leather boot resting on the left knee of my black 501s, an indolently sinister smile on my face. Ready for them. Psyched. 100% Iremonger.

Mainie tilts her head to one side and smiles coolly.

'Well, Happy Christmas, Mr Iremonger.'

'The same to you, Ms Doyle.'

'I think you know St John, Tom.'

Ah, here's the moment, at last. I stand up, uncoil myself like a snake, a particularly deadly kind. And what do you know, we're exactly the same height these days. Strongbow betrays his surprise by backing away an inch or two – well, guess who feels *psychologically* taller.

Strongbow finally speaks, 'My god . . . Tom. What a transformation. I wouldn't recognise you.'

His accent has changed again – back to what it was that first morning when it was just us two in the Senior 2A classroom. Or almost so. Now it's more *Late Show* than Children's BBC.

'Sure you wouldn't,' I whisper, a nasty smile on my face. As if he hasn't studied the IDA poster at the airport.

'Mainie mentioned you, of course, and I asked if that was the same Tom Iremonger I was in Berchmans with. But I was carrying around a rather different image of you in my head.'

'Oh really.'

'Well, what are you up to?'

I smirk at Mainie. 'Your girlfriend will explain.' She flashes a sarcastic smile at me.

I tap Strongbow's prop. 'So, what are you doing with the camera?'

'Well, actually, it's how I make my living. Some friends of mine from Cambridge and I have set up an independent film production company in London. I carry this around like a notebook.' Without warning he puts the viewfinder to his eye and the red light goes on. I give the lens my IDA smile, although inside I'm not feeling evil at all. Carrying around a video camera like a notebook? That's what I was going to do. Somehow this guy is stealing all my best ideas. And still trying to push me around with his shadow. Doesn't he realise that Berchmans, and all that went down there, is history?

He stops recording and explains, 'A friend of Mainie's from Prague, Ado Keating, asked me to shoot the swim.'

'Yeah, I was one of the people he beat.'

Mainie squeezes Strongbow's arm. 'Didn't I say that to you, Sinj? Didn't I say that looked like Iremonger on the rock.'

Sinj? I want to laugh out loud and tell Mainie she's got no idea how badly this guy has got her fooled.

'You did indeed,' Strongbow dutifully replies.

'Well, I think that was very brave of you, Tom. Why don't you take a look at the video. See if you can find yourself.

I find Mainie's patronising tone pretty hard to take, but my anger is cancelled by my curiousity. I just can't resist seeing my image, in any medium you care to mention. If someone made a sculpture of Iremonger out of cow manure I'd probably want to check it out. So how can I resist seeing myself on video?

'Is the tape ready to go . . . St John?'

'Almost.' As he rewinds to the right place, Mainie tells me how Strongbow's mother has moved back to Dublin and opened a new antiques shop in Glenageary. I don't even pretend to be interested. It's all I can do not to grab the camera out of his hands.

Finally I get to press playback.

1. *Ext. Joyce Tower – morning*. MAINIE tilts her head and smiles with gorgeous pseudo-impatience when she realises she is being videoed. *Close-Up* of those big black eyes. I want the lens to linger but we *Cut to*: *CU* of an old sign on a granite wall: GENTLEMENS BATHING PLACE. COSTUMES MUST BE WORN. NO SCUBA DIVERS. BY ORDER, MARTELLO MARINERS SWIMMING CLUB. GOVT. LICENCE 1923. *Cut to:*

2. *Ext. Forty Foot – morning*. We get a *Medium shot* of a swarthy teenage GIRL running down the concrete ramp that leads to the lapping water. When she is knee-deep she plunges in, stays down for a good three seconds, then bursts back to the surface. She runs back up the ramp to a waiting towel, hugging herself, scandalised. *Cut to: Tracking* across the placid inlet. Strongbow's *POV* is halfway between the two arms of the little bay. The camera slowly *Zooms in* to a *Medium* on the SWIMMERS, all men, on the steep rock that's the starting point of the swim. There's over two dozen of us up there. I catch a glimpse of myself – my Californian tan stands out against those pale Irish-winter bodies. (I'm also one of the few swimmers not wearing a cap.) *Jump Cut to:* a *Long shot* – a blur of dives and a cloud of spray. *Cut to:* a *Medium Tracking shot* (approximating *Steadicam* solidity) of the pack pounding its way across the inlet to the turning point rock. A swimmer in a red cap that we recognise as ADO KEATING begins to break away. The camera follows him. He touches the rock and turns for home. The camera *Fixes* on the rock. Soon there is a frothy confusion of approaching, turning, and turned swimmers. The camera *Zooms in* for a *CU* and catches a bare-headed, bronzed swimmer who is undoubtedly IREMONGER turning without touching the rock.

I give myself an executive order not to blush. Naturally I want to yank out the tape and shove it down the de Bruns' trash compactor, but I do no such thing. I keep my eye against the viewfinder, blankly watching Ado Keating's victory, wondering what kind of face I need to face Mainie and Strongbow, that bitch and that bastard. This has to be an elaborate trap, maybe set in motion as early as yesterday afternoon in the Shelbourne. I know what that little smile from Carmel Carraig-Dubh was all about now – they must have shown her Iremonger's short cut. I want to know what Roderick knows. I even wonder for a paranoid millisecond if Finbar helped set me up. But the most irrational thought of all has to be when I ask myself, as I watch Ado Keating being presented with a giant bottle of Kells, if getting caught like this is some kind of weird pay-back for the Impecunious Roomkeepers Society. Back in Dublin twenty-four hours, and losing my mind already.

The remaining footage is of Ireland's Greatest Resource flirting with the camera in the very room I'm standing in. He looks unflappable, unassailable. I'm jealous of him, my old self of just two minutes ago.

I press stop, take the sheltering camera down from my face. Mainie and Strongbow are trying to pretend that nothing is going on, but their little routine doesn't fool me. Oh, suss out those barely suppressed smiles when Mainie asks, with polished innocence, 'So, did you see yourself?'

To get flustered now would betray everything I hold dear. 'You didn't get my good side.' I shrug.

Now Roderick arrives on the scene. 'Video of the swim? Can I take a look?'

'Look all you want.' I smile, and toss the little Sony towards him like a piece of fruit. He catches it with a jolt that rhymes with Strongbow's jerking eyebrow.

'Excuse me, friends,' I say, and saunter out of the kitchen.

*   *   *

I'm walking home. As I was leaving de Brun's – slowly, unhurriedly – at least three people offered to give me a lift, but I said no, it isn't far and I want to clear my head. So I'm walking up Owenstown Avenue, trying to get in synch with its tranquillity, walking away from the sea, only Nico for company.

What was on Strongbow's tape, that's what happened. I guess you could call it the truth. At least that's what they are going to *remember*, Mainie and Roderick and Carmel Carraig-Dubh, and god knows how many other characters on this morning's drinkies circuit who got to look at that . . . pornography. It's what they will remember, but it's not what I will remember.

A vague whistle blew. Immediately I heard the percussion of the first plunges. Astonishing how fast those backs in front of me peeled away and fell towards the water. Trying to remember how to dive without smacking my torso on the surface of the water, I crouched down. I crouched down and saw the limb-crowded sea and the foaming green water. And then I felt a hand on my lower back and I was being pushed off the rock. Finbar. The sea rushed towards me, pulled me in deep – seaweed slimed against my face. And the cold? Even worse than I imagined. The cold was a humiliation, a violation. The Irish Sea buggered me.

Almost with noticing it, and without thinking why, I turn right and start to walk down Cross Avenue. Going this way will make my walk five or ten minutes longer. I pass the entrance to Sion Hill (Triona's old school) and the entrance to Willow Park (*alma mater* of the Iremonger brothers when they were in short trousers) and, across the street, the Protestant church's movie-set perfection. All the while I'm fighting the realisation of why I've taken this detour. I turn right again and find myself standing at the modest modern gate of a big white house, its curvaceous facade in profile. I can just about see the stone stag's head and antlers above the portico. The name of the house, a sign on each gatepost tells me, is Dunamase. The signs use the old Celtic lettering. Look at those noose-like Ds.

They brought the Minister back here, riddled with bullets, and laid him on an improvised bed in the dining room. The death watch, the living wake, began. There were token blood transfusions, but no attempt was made to move him to a hospital. Doing my research, I couldn't get over his fatalism, the calm and certain way he talked, even joked, about his death to his wife, his virtual widow. It took him five hours to die. The Wilsons, the old West Brit couple who lived here when I was in Berchmans (probably dead now) gave me tea and cold scones in the dining room. I kept imagining I saw pools of blood on the worn parquet.

Two rangy German Shepherds appear from behind the shrubbery skirting the house – they may have been lying on the front porch or let out the front door – and come galloping across the gravel of the wide driveway. They could clear these gates, if they really got their act together, so I walk away from Dunamase as quickly as I can, my nerve-endings flashing back to yesterday's B-Special. I gotta say I preferred Tripod, the Wilsons' three-legged labrador.

Back on Cross Avenue I head towards Booterstown, as the Minister did. He was on his way to midday Mass. Earlier that morning he had gone down to the Forty Foot for a swim with an armed guard, but now he slipped out of Dunamase alone, and without his revolver.

He passed the house where De Valera, his civil war enemy (but quick to distance himself from the assassination), would live and write our beloved Constitution a decade later. The bay of that house has a grey marble plaque on it; there's no commemorative plaque on the facade of Dunamase.

Even though he died on a hot July day, I cannot help

but imagine the Minister tapping the pavement with an umbrella. The old man's slim black umbrella. Always be prepared for rain, that's his philosophy. He taps the pavement at precise intervals, except when he raises the umbrella in subtle salute to a passerby. A young lad on a pushbike overtakes him so slowly, so laboriously, that he salutes him too. The boy does not acknowledge him. Instead he picks up speed and soon disappears around the corner onto Booterstown Avenue. Maybe he's serving at mass and doesn't want to be late for the parish priest. Moments later, around the same corner walk two tall young men, caps pulled low over their foreheads. Immediately the Minister suspects something, slows, raises the umbrella defensively. When he sees the first shadow of a gun he drops it and runs for his life – he's hit in the side before he's off the grass verge. He staggers across the avenue, and gets shot in the back. He collapses – there, it must have been about there. One of the assassins runs over and empties his revolver into the fallen man.

And it took Kevin O'Higgins five hours to die. That bastard must have been the worst shot in Irish history.

I'm glad I think of that. I laugh, a little hissy laugh, and that breaks the heavy spell I've been under for the past few minutes. Chill, Iremonger. Where do you think you are, Dealey Plaza? So the strong man of the first Free State government bought it here on a quiet Sunday in the summer of 1927. So what? What's it to you? In what way would your life have been materially different if Kevin O'Higgins had lived, had even become Taoiseach?

No difference at all. This place means nothing to me.

I wish I'd brought my Ray-Bans with me.

It was coming up to two o'clock when I got back to Cedar-of-Lebanon Road. Going to the Christmas Morning Swim had been good for one thing: a wave of relatives, a wave of Maguires, had come and gone from the house. But the Wogans were here already: there was the Stalwart. And that was unfortunate because I needed a few minutes to prepare myself for this scene by, say, downing a creamy pint of Kells. The faint whiskey buzz that I'd worked up at Roderick's had completely faded. Tragically, I had nothing illegal on my person; I really would have to get some more of that quite excellent B-Special soon. But I'd have to rely on my inner resources to get me through this trial. It would be a test of character. Sweet Jesus.

It was worse than I'd feared. I was bracing myself to face one relative, one Iremonger at a time, but they were all there together in the hall, sucking me in, surrounding me. It was the kids that did it. My darling niece and nephew, Sibéal and Kieran, six and four respectively. They went apeshit, jumping up and down, grabbing me, grabbing Nico – hands off the leather, fellas! – using me as a climbing frame, sticking their bony limbs into my flesh, dragging me towards the ground, and screaming, 'Tommy! Tommy!' You would think that the adults, my sister, my mother, would try to restrain them, but apart from a few token *go easies* they let the children get away with it. Indeed, the kids' good humour and enthusiasm were infectious; the rest of my family were beaming, even my parents. It was as if I'd arrived in the door from the airport unannounced, as if yesterday counted for nothing.

I sussed out what was going on here. The arrival of Uncle Tommy was inextricably bound up with the idea of presents in Sibéal's and Kieran's minds, exotic presents, American presents. Suddenly I saw it from their point of view, I understood completely, or should I say, I remembered perfectly. I remembered the craving, I remembered the rush. The kids' main man, that fat freak in red threads, had come last night, but they were ready for another fix.

Now Triona lunged at me and planted a kiss on my cheek,

squeezed my arm and said, 'Welcome home.' For a few moments I blinked back dumbly at her – being pulled this way by Kieran, that way by Sibéal – until I realised that this was the first time that I'd seen my sister. Since Finbar had opened the hall door (giving me a sly smile that I took as a kind of Masonic signal from one Christmas morning swimmer to another) and I'd been pulled off the porch, I'd assumed that I'd bumped into Triona sometime in the past twenty-four hours. Apparently not.

I finally responded to her affection with a wooden, 'You're looking good, little sister!'

What was that touch of melancholy in the smile she returned all about?

Sibéal and Kieran were finally quietened by the aura of wrapping paper. The adults organised their stockpiles of generosity. Even Columb had his little pile. (All books, by the look of it. Something told me that I wasn't going to end up with a copy of *American Psycho*.) He sat, by ascetic choice, on the piano stool. I outdid him by sitting crosslegged on the floor in front of the fireplace. I was trying to recapture a little of the detachment I'd felt that October afternoon I spent in the isolation tank owned by my Toronto-Trinity friend Greg Montenotti, the time I tried it without dropping a tab. Get it over with, Iremonger, I told myself. It's no big deal.

'Let's do mine first,' I said. Everybody assented.

Now, logically, the next step should have been to give the kids their presents, get *that* over with, but I found I didn't quite have the balls for it yet. So I started with the older Wogans. The kids were quiet and suspicious.

'Finbar, Triona, this is for you.'

I handed the square parcel to my brother-in-law, who whipped off the wrapping paper.

'CDs!' he said, his face a pastiche of surprise. Then he

leafed through them, hesitantly. Now he was really surprised, really amused, and trying not to show it. I wonder which bemused him more, the lack of cellophane on the cases, or the choice of titles he was confronted with – there wasn't any Garth Brooks in there. 'Look,' was all he could say as he passed them to my sister. She looked at each of the covers seriously, even scrutinising the track listing on one or two of the albums.

'Great,' she said. 'We don't have any of these.'

The CDs were the latest releases from Assisted Suicide, Meat Theater, Blow, Slit, and Meconium.

'Yes,' I mumbled, 'I was hoping.'

'Mummy, Mummy, let me see!' said Sibéal, trying to grab the albums out of her mother's hands. Triona held the CDs to her breast. 'No, Sib, I don't think you'd like them. And you'll be getting *your* present in just a minute.'

I responded to this big hint by throwing a soft package at my father.

'Ho, ho, what do we have here,' he said, sounding like Santa Claus greeting a child at the end of a twelve-hour shift at a shopping centre. He tore it open with his thick-skinned fingers – Christ, even his fingers had that yellow tinge – and unfurled the tie that lay inside. Held it up for all to see, his eyebrows arching with irony. Now he could read the label at the back, 'Colleczioni Hieronymus Bosch. Well, well.'

It had been an impulse buy from the Prado gift shop. (I love gift shops – you get the whole museum in there in miniature; sometimes I head straight for the gift shop and don't bother with the real paintings.) I'd worn the tie only once: in front of the mirror in the bog at the Café Central for about five seconds. It's hard to find a really good Iremonger kind of tie.

'It's the first panel from the *Garden of Earthly Delights* triptych,' I added helpfully; I always read labels.

'It might go nicely with that blue v-necked jumper I bought you in Dunnes Stores,' my mother said.

My father and sister looked at each other; that didn't help the smiles they were wrestling to contain. I guess I would have seen the humour in the situation if my four-year-old nephew had not been staring at me like a child possessed. I sprang to my feet.

'Mum, here, this is for you.'

She looked up at me. 'Ah, Tom, do the kids before me.' Out of the corner of my eye I saw nodding freckles, joggling pigtails. I more or less shoved the gift into my mother's hands. 'I'm saving the best for last,' I muttered.

My mother stared at me from beneath her dyed eyebrows and gave a low acidic sigh. The tension eased, eased for everybody except me and the children, when my mother started to unwrap her gift. Unconsciously, I had put several extra layers of wrapping paper on each, ever more desperate present. It was pass-the-parcel in reverse.

'Well, Sinéad,' said my brother-in-law, 'you'll certainly have worked up an appetite by the time you get to the bottom of that!'

But finally she did get to the bottom of it: the *Iliad*, read by Derek Jacobi. I'd bought it one morning in W. H. Smith at Heathrow during one of the very rare moments of doubt I have about being a post-literary guy. I listened to it during take-off on the flight to Prague, and didn't get back to it. All I could remember now about the story was that all hell broke loose between Achilles and that other guy whose name begins with A because Achilles was pissed off with the lousy gifts he'd been given.

Now my mother was trying to be nice. She was examining the box carefully, just like her daughter had done with the Meconium CD.

'What else did he do again?' she asked.

'The *Odyssey*?' I replied, only semi-suppressing a note of sarcasm.

She stared at me again. 'No, Tomás, I mean this fella, Derek Jacobi.'

Tomás – I didn't like that. No, sir. Fight or flight time. I backed away, holding my hands up in an appeal for peace.

'He's the guy who did *I, Claudius*.'

'That's what it was,' my mother said, and sighed. 'Well, I hope he doesn't read this thing with a lisp . . . Thank you, Tom.'

Sibéal looked itchy with anticipation; Kieran just kept on staring. I decided that this would be an excellent time to give my uncle his present.

'And this is for you, Columb.'

'Thank you, Tom. Thank you.' The way he said it you'd swear that I'd just handed him a cheque to cancel Remoko's debt to the World Bank. He started to unpeel his present. I sat down like Buddha again in front of the fireplace. This was great: it would take him at least ten minutes to get the wrapping off.

But I was to have no such peace. My mother was now making very unsubtle mouthings and gesticulations to the effect that I should give the children their presents now or face excommunication from the family, or maybe plain execution. I tried to ignore these signals. I also tried to ignore the tears beginning to well in Sibéal's eyes. Impossible to ignore was Kieran's evil stare. When my sister, that queen of common sense, finally said in a controlled but firm tone of voice, 'Tom, if you have presents for my children would you please give them out now,' I cracked. From the back pocket of my 501s I produced two ass-rounded envelopes, one marked SIBÉAL!, the other KIERAN! I handed them to Triona. She could do the talking. Pleased, I guess, to see me produce anything, she immediately began to talk up the slim gifts.

'Oh, my goodness, I wonder what Uncle Tommy could have given you.'

To my relief, Sibéal became intrigued. To my despair, Kieran looked like he smelt bullshit. Triona opened Sibéal's envelope. She raised her eyebrows and smiled very deliberately. 'A Eur-o-cheque!' she declaimed in a sing-songy manner. 'For fifty pounds! . . . And Kieran, you get the same!'

Sibéal picked up her cheque and examined it with crafty wonder. At six, she could appreciate the abstract beauty of money. At four, her brother could not. Perhaps if I'd given him some pound coins to bite into, or even a few joyces to sniff and crinkle, he would have been appeased. He opened the envelope like a potential letter bomb, then held its contents in his fist, his worst fears confirmed – this was a dirty trick. His expression turned mushy with injustice. He appealed loudly to me and his mother, 'I wanna cowboy suit from 'merica! I wanna cowboy suit from 'merica!'

Sibéal tried to shake some sense into him,

'It's a *Eur*-o-cheque, stupid. You can buy *ten* cowboy suits!'

Way to go, Sibéal, I thought. But it only encouraged Kieran to go to DEF-CON 4 on the tantrum scale,

'Don' *wan'* euwocheg! Don' *wan'* euwocheg!'

I fled the room. Upstairs in my bedroom I could still hear his screams, and my sister and brother-in-law's muffled consolations. I looked at my silk Paul Smith socks lying on the floor beside my bed and that idea I'd had at two-thirty in the morning of making hand puppets didn't seem so stupid after all.

When I returned to the drawing room, Kieran was merely sobbing but still heartbroken; other presents – from Nana and Pops, from Uncle Columb – had been opened, but none of them had proven to be a cowboy suit from the land of cowboys.

'Here,' I said, trying to contain my anger and thrusting out my right hand from behind my back. 'Here's your real Christmas present. Take it.'

And he took the CD Walkman from my hands, and began to smile.

At which point his sister began crying. I guess I could also kiss my Ray-Bans goodbye. I ran my hand through my thick hair. Then I noticed Columb smiling at me kindly, a neat pile of discarded wrapping paper beside him on the closed piano. 'Thank you for the aftershave, Tom,' he said, holding up a bottle of barely opened duty-free Obsession for Men.

So I gave a lot, gave more than I ever intended to give, gave away parts of *myself*, Iremonger items, and what did I get in return? Fuck all. From my parents – from my mother, essentially – I got clothes, unwearable clothes: crimes against fashion, grotesque parodies of the real thing from the proletarian department stores; I know what my mother's game is: these are clothes that Finbar wears – she wants me to metamorphose into my brother-in-law; she wants me to come downstairs tomorrow morning wearing those beige corduroy trousers she gave me today so that she can say, *You look smashing, Tomás. Real Mod.* (My mother's fashion vocabulary fossilised around the time *La Dolce Vita* was released.)

From the Wogans I received a Braun matte-black travel alarm clock, with a global time-zone map printed inside the lid. They think they know me, that's what gets me. Triona and Finbar think that's the perfect Iremonger gift. But if they really knew Iremonger, they would realise that I have no use for an alarm clock, that when I do have to get up early – to get to airports, to make flights, the only appointments I feel compelled to keep – an infallible, chemical-resistant internal clock always wakes me up. If they knew me well they would know that that global time-zone map is printed inside my *eye*lids.

And from my uncle – get this – from Columb I got a little matador-red paperback entitled *Breath of Christ: Praying with the Jesuits*. I guess prodigal nephews are hard to shop for.

This is neither cool nor kosher – my father is eating even less than I am. His traditional Christmas dinner would be big enough to feed a whole Remokoan village for several weeks. But this year it looks like famine has struck. He's going really easy on the bird. And making do with a token slice of ham that's lying next to a mere brace of baked potatoes. Bread sauce is represented by a blob. The food looks naked without my mother's famous thick gravy. On the other hand, he's eating a disturbing amount of brussels sprouts. This man is sick.

When I was a kid, I would always try to make the first bite of my Christmas dinner a synthesis of every taste on the crammed plate in front of me. I had to act fast because if Triona or my mother saw me with all that food piled high on my fork they'd nag me about my manners. Today Triona isn't here – it's the Wogans' year to eat with Finbar's parents – and I think my mother would be delighted to see me stuffing my face. Man, is she ever going to have a lot of leftovers.

The conversation so far has been pathetic, painful. I almost wish that the Wogans had stayed; Sibéal and Kieran would have filled in the silences at the very least. Now, normally it's part of the Iremonger philosophy that small talk is for eunuchs and losers, but this dead meal is driving me crazy. I'm sitting with my back to the old man's portrait, but in the lengthening silence I can feel those small pale green eyes watching me, weighing me. Time for some limp wit, 'The Châteauneuf-du-Pape's not bad, Pap.'

My father grunts and smiles. 'Hope so. I just bought two cases of it last month.'

I wonder if he intends that to be a lifetime supply, like the drawerful of size ten-and-a-half odour-eaters he has in his wardrobe.

Columb, who has been attending to his own (moderately indulgent) meal with a eucharistic concentration, now turns his wine glass ruminatively, turning the sticky coaster with print of Christchurch on it upside down. He hums and speaks, 'As I said last night, I've been trying to piece together this Golden case. And I'm still not clear about a few things.'

My father smooths his crinkly grey hair, shaking his head just a little as he sighs and smiles. My mother decapitates a mushroom. This could be good. That sermon last night kicked some ass (the old guy is much more of an Iremonger than I ever gave him credit for); maybe Columb's going to do the same thing again here.

'You know,' I say, 'I'm pretty hazy on this whole Golden deal myself. The last six months I've tended to tune out when people start talking about Ireland.'

'It's well for some,' my mother smiles. She takes a satisfied sip of wine.

My father makes an unemphatic halt sign with his hand and mutters, 'Sinéad.' Then he turns to me and gives me a look that reminds me of the sarcastic patience of Fr Harrington teaching inductive reasoning.

'Do you know where Rossmuck is, Tom?'

'Somewhere down the country, right?'

'It's a huge satellite suburb outside of Galway. The Galway equivalent to Tallaght. Very young population. A lot of problems. A lot of unemployment.'

'Gotcha.'

'Anyway, there was this young priest working down there, Niall Golden—'

'Gorgeous-looking fellow,' my mother breaks in. 'Comes from a very good family in Wexford. The father's a solicitor.'

My father gives her a look – he's the storyteller – and continues, 'He was very active on social issues, very outspoken. I think some of the things he said were a little bit too liberation theology-ish for the local bishop. But he was very popular with his parishoners. Maybe a little bit too popular. He was counselling this twenty-year-old girl, Mary Quigly, whose husband had been killed serving with the UN in Lebanon. Golden got her pregnant.'

'Guess he didn't believe in using condoms,' I say.

'Oh, Tom,' my mother responds with shivery censure.

Columb has a cool question for my father, 'Whose idea was it to abort the child?'

'The girl said she'd kill herself before she had the baby.'

'That's right,' my mother says, 'blame it on the girl.'

'It's not a question of blame, Sinéad. It's all in the letter.'

'I don't think we'll ever know the full truth.'

'Anyway—' My father sighs. 'To continue. Golden borrows five hundred pounds from his local TD and he and the girl fly over to London on separate flights. She goes on Ryanair to Stansted; he takes Aer Lingus to Heathrow. They stay in separate rooms in the same cheap hotel near Victoria station. Waits for her in this tatty little coffee shop while she goes for her appointment in the clinic. They say she met another girl from Rossmuck while she was there.'

'And this girl goes home and spills the beans, right? That's why this Mary Quigly killed herself.'

My father exhales horsily through his lips. 'Shows how much you really know about Irish women, Tom. I guess you've never thought about why those girls interviewed on RTE about their boat trips to Liverpool are always in silhouette. No, the operation was successful—'

'—Interesting choice of word,' says Columb. My father ignores his brother and continues.

'No. Golden must have thought he'd got away with it. But about six months later he's doing the seven-thirty folk Mass and preaches a very firm pro-life sermon to back up a pastoral letter on the subject he's just read. A week later

Mary Quigly writes a letter of her own: a long letter to her parents explaining everything. She then takes a fatal overdose of sleeping pills. Two weeks later her father rings up *The Phone Show* and reads Percy Tóibín and the rest of the country the letter.'

'Jeez,' I say. And think, I've been missing out on some action here.

Columb is rotating his wine glass. 'The other thing that I wanted to clarify was this: How long did it take before he admitted all this had happened?'

'He didn't try and deny it.'

'How could he?' my mother asks.

'He did this big confessional interview on Pat Kenny a few nights later,' my father explains. 'The bishops weren't pleased.'

'Pity about them,' says my mother.

'What do you mean, Mum?'

She stiffens. I half-expect her to say nothing at all; my mother is not afraid to ignore my questions. But, after toying with her butter knife, she speaks, 'If the bishops were doing their jobs properly they'd deal with fellows like Golden when the rumours start, not wait until some tragedy happens.'

I have never heard my mother talk like this before. In the past, if she disagreed with the church she did so without rancour and without fuss, voting Yes for divorce on her way to ten o'clock mass. I've heard her get a little sarcastic, a little exasperated, but that angry tone – that's new. And if the hierarchy are pissing off people like my *mother*, they must be in big trouble.

Columb nods slowly and says, 'This does appear to be a bad time for the church in Ireland. But St Ignatius would say that in a time of spiritual desolation you must focus by keeping in mind how good spiritual consolation was, and pray for its return.'

'Yes, but that doesn't do poor Mary Quigly much good,' says my mother. My father is shaking his head and smiling to himself with his eyes closed. I know what he's thinking. It's one of my father's major principles in life that it's futile to argue with a family member about anything to do with taste, religion, or politics. He learned his lesson about that by having the old man as a father. These days he has a kind of jaded tolerance for what other people think. Tolerance doesn't come into it for me. I think the only honest thing to do is push this as far as it will go.

So I say, 'She wouldn't have been desolate at all if she hadn't had such a guilt trip about the abortion in the first place.'

My uncle fixes me with a clinical grey-blue stare and says, 'You agree with the decision to abort?'

'Absolutely, Columb. No way should she have gone through with that pregnancy. It would have been pure cruelty.' Funnily, it's only after I say the word *cruelty* that I really mean it, that I really *feel* it.

My mother tuts and shakes her head. She also voted Yes in the abortion referendum; some things haven't changed.

Columb broods and nods. 'It was a horrible situation all right. But the abortion was still . . . an abomination.'

Woh. Now *there's* a strong word. I wasn't prepared for a word like *abomination*, not from the new version of my uncle at least. I don't know how to respond. I don't know what to hit back with. Columb said it calmly enough, but you could tell that he meant it and felt it long before he said it, long before he came to this table.

You know, maybe I should have just kept my mouth shut, like my father. This is not the way I expected things to turn out. I guess after his Berchmans performance I expected more from Columb: a more enlightened attitude even on something like abortion, a little relativity – a little of that goes a long way – a little more give and take.

No such luck. I'm dealing with a theological street fighter here.

'Whatever,' I say, and pick up the Châteauneuf-du-Pape to pour myself a second glass. I tip the bottle too fast and fill the glass to the brim. Both of my parents stare at me. As I put the bottle back down on its silver coaster I almost wish they'd say something, break this fresh tension. I almost wish they'd say what I can hear my grandfather say behind me, echoing one of the few flashes of displeasure he ever directed against me:

'Tomás, that's an ignorant glass of wine.'

6

Immaculate Conception

What have I been up to? Oh Christ, it's been a crazy week, but I think it's finally shaping up the way I want it to. Let's grab a coffee in Bewley's and talk. Better still, let's grab a pint or two of Fursty in the Stag's Head and talk. A lot of Ballygowan has passed under the bridge.

This is Saturday, right? I find it hard enough to keep track of the days, but at this time of the year it's nearly impossible. The essential thing is that it's also New Year's Eve – Mainie's party is tonight, and I'm going. Just how I'm going I'll come to later. Let me start with a status report.

I've got a ticket to ride. Christmas Day having fallen on a Sunday, the week kicked off with a double whammy of bank holidays. A lot of the shops in town started their sales on Monday or Tuesday anyway, but the places I really needed to go didn't open until Wednesday. That morning I took the 46A into town disturbingly early; I got off at the Green end of Grafton Street well before midday. I walked purposefully to the Diaspora Travel office at the corner of Dawson Street. (If I'd had my Wanderlust card with me on Christmas Eve I would have done it then.) As soon as

I walked in the door chick radar picked me up; the agents were insanely busy (what with people trying to change their flight plans, people offering bribes to get tickets out of the country), but I saw two of them exchange glossy little smiles: Ireland's Greatest Resoure was here. I got into one of their lines. When I reached the counter, the girl – Kate Moss after a good Christmas dinner – greeted me warmly, like an old flame she'd mostly gotten over. Then we got down to the serious business of air travel. I knew next Friday was the first comfortable day I could leave, all going well. Kate consulted her computer.

'I see one seat available on a lunchtime Aer Lingus flight. Leaving Dublin 13:10; arriving Paris, Charles de Gaulle 15:15.'

'Anything on another airline?'

She checked. 'No.'

This didn't come as any surprise. I mean, if everybody comes home for Christmas, they've all got to leave again; arrivals are not the opposite of departures; they are part of the same deal, the same journey. Dylan, Mainie, Strongbow – they all made their departure plans months ago, I'm sure. I guess I'm lucky a space was free, or had opened up, on the Aer Lingus flight.

'Okay,' I told Kate, 'put me on that plane.'

'Will do. And what about a return date, sir?'

'This is one-way.'

'Oh, really? Because it's actually cheaper to get a return.'

'As I said, one-way.'

I put the ticket on my Wanderlust card. Next stop for me was the bank. Yes, I was finally facing up to my biggest responsibility – to find out how much money I had; ripping up those statements had been no more than a delaying tactic. And talking about delaying tactics, on the way to my branch I stopped off in Bewley's, Westmoreland Street, and held court there for over two and a half hours.

And as I posed, brooded, and flirted, I kept on thinking what a pity is was that every day couldn't be a bank holiday. But finally, at about ten to three, ten minutes before closing time, fuelled by a half dozen mugs of coffee and the odd sticky bun, I decided that if it was worth finding out at all what this beautiful transcontinental lost weekend had cost me so far it was worth finding out today. So I went over to Tara Bank to ask what the damage was.

Assertive stamps echoed around the main office. I liked this joint, the brown marble columns – doric? corinthian? don't ask me – the high ceiling, the distant pink stucco; I felt my money, the Iremonger fund, was safe here; nobody but me could steal it. This is where I had come one gentle morning in late June to buy my Eurocheques, my AmEx traveller's cheques, and, best of all, my inaugural portfolio of foreign currencies. It reminded me of the variety packs of Kellogg's cereals that my mother used to buy me sometimes as a kid, except that now, instead of deciding on a whim to eat Coco Pops instead of Frosties, I would decide whether to spend dollars on Bourbon Street or francs on the rue St André des Arts.

This is the place that I had thought about whenever I got a little stressed about how much money I was spending, or how fast I was spending it, or why I was spending it so fast. I thought about this office, this great hall, thought about those brown marble columns, their solidity, their certainty, even dreamed about them. They made me feel better, chilled me out.

Forget about Trinity, this was my real nurturing mother; this felt like home. So imagine how pissed off I was when the teller, a pimply, gangly teenager wearing a brown knitted tie (he reminded me, reluctantly, of Brían Firbolg) told me I would have to go into the student office. I told him I wasn't a student any more. He responded sulkily that that's where my account still was, that I'd never transferred it over. I turned on my Italian heel. Bastard didn't even recognise me. He probably only travelled by Sealink.

The student office. What can I say. Remember that line of Brando's in *Apocalypse Now* – the horror, the horror? I never thought I'd have to deal with this place again. It never occurred to me that my account was specially linked to this office by some financial umbilical cord. All along, when I had been dreaming of those brown marble pillars, my money had been languishing in this dive, managed by morons.

There was no marble or stucco in the student office. Instead, its whitewashed walls were decorated with framed posters of art house films big five years ago, the most obvious Doisneau prints you could think of, that old Jim Fitzpatrick image of Che Guevara, and busy, bubbly adverts for Tara Bank itself. On counters either side of the room and hanging from black brackets screwed into the ceiling right above the tellers' heads were Hitachi television sets, all tuned to European MTV (an oxymoron, according to Dylan), where a Dutch VJ with long blond hair was gurgling away. On one of the counters brimming coffee pots, caf and decaf, sat on hot plates; beside them was a little sign composed of coy Indian ink calligraphy that read *Help Yourself!*

If these people really wanted to be cool, I had often thought, radically cool, they would let me help myself to some free money. When it came to financial institutions, I wanted to deal with Kafka, not Madonna. Today it looked like I would have to deal with Derek MacReady, student officer supremo. Derek had light brown hair and a loud mole on his left cheekbone. He and Finbar sometimes played together on the corporate water polo team, the High Kings. I was greeted like a long-lost brother.

'Tom Iremonger, great to see you! Finn said you wouldn't be back in town. You're looking as good as your poster!'

'Why, thank you, Derek. Got a little business to attend to.'

'Alrighty. What can we do for you?'

'Well, mainly I want to get my account switched over to the main office—'

'No prob.'

'But first I need to find out what my balance is.'

'No prob. But first I'm going to have to see some identification.'

I guess I gave him a very stiff look. What the fuck was this? Why did Derek MacReady need to see my ID? At the same time, I had this odd feeling that his request was only fair, that it was surprising nobody else had made this demand since I'd come through Dublin airport five days before. Then Derek reached over the counter, that mole coming close enough for me to count the number of hairs planted in it, and slapped Nico on the shoulder.

'Only kidding, Tom. Gotcha there!'

I attempted a smile.

Taken in by Derek MacReady. Jesus.

'I'll have it for you in just a seccy.'

It took longer than a seccy. It took more like sixty seccies. I didn't like the look on Derek's face (not that I had ever liked the look on Derek's face) as he scrolled down through the digitised particulars of my account with his jittery mouse – an uneasy frown. When he got to the end of the statement, the bottom line of the Iremonger Project, he scrolled back up again and took a second look at the numbers. I leaned on the counter but looked away from his monitor. I hoped he wasn't going to do something rash like swivel it in my direction. I didn't care now to see the glowing orange record of my excess. In fact, if I'd had any guts, if I'd been 100% Iremonger at that moment, I would have just sauntered away from that counter, saying to hell with my balance – if you got too stressed about money, money sensed that, money smelled your anxiety, money figured out that you couldn't handle money, and money split. If you kept your cool about money, money came your way. Look at my grandfather's inheritance, for god's sake. How much thought had I given that baby before the day my father broke the good news that at long last he was putting the Raglan Road property on the market and was going to carry out the old man's deathbed wish: that the money be split four ways, between my parents, my uncle, my sister and me, and that I should use the money to in some way 'further my education'. I'd got that financial fix just when I'd needed it, no sweat. I hadn't spent more than two consecutive minutes at Trinity worrying about the future, and look what kind of graduation party I'd been able to give myself; why should I worry about it now? Like my mother said, the day I found out about my impending wealth, *You always land on your arse, Tom*.

I should have just sauntered out of there, but I didn't. I remained leaning against the counter, staring at the mahogany laminate, yearning for a Roland. By the time Derek MacReady finally reached for a slip of paper – the back of a withdrawal docket – to write the balance down, I was convinced that the fuzzy estimation I'd been carrying around in the back of my mind that I had, after all those Eurocheques I'd written and direct debits of my Wanderlust bills, about four grand left in my account out of the original twenty-one, was hopelessly optimistic; maybe it was going to be no more than half that. Derek slid the slip, folded, across the counter to me. I stood up straight, snapped out of it as much as I could, injected a little of that Iremonger insouciance into my attitude. I picked up the slip. On the printed side of the docket, in the office-use-only portion of the form, a word caught my eye, a little bit of bank jargon – *narrative*. Well, this was one story I didn't want to hear, especially the ending. It was too linear, too realistic for my liking. A bloody tragedy. Derek was watching me, pretending not to. I unfolded the slip, glanced at the figure, balled it, flicked it into a metal wastepaper basket under a table six feet away.

I smiled. 'Thanks, Derek.' I turned to leave.

'Tom, didn't you want to transfer the account into the main office?'

I turned around. 'Nah, I'll do that some other time. I've really got to go.'

'What about a little chat about financial planning?'

'Some other time, maybe,' I shouted over my shoulder. I'm glad I didn't mention that I needed to retrieve my Puntpower Card because he probably would have physically restrained me from leaving.

I was the last customer left in the Student Office. The gurgling Dutch VJ was introducing a video by my favourite band: 'I Still Haven't Found What I'm Looking For'. I marched to the door that lead out onto College Street. It was locked.

'It's after three,' Derek shouted over Bono's bellowing. 'They'll let you out at the main doors.'

It wasn't easy walking through the main office again. The busy clerks (busy ignoring my presence) the brown marble columns, the high and mighty ceiling – I found it hard to deal with them again. Either I had betrayed them or they had betrayed me, I couldn't quite figure out which yet. An old porter – was that a knowing smile on his face? – unlocked the door and let me out. When I heard the locks turning again behind me, I felt as if this was a permanent exclusion, or, at the very least, that I wouldn't be let in there again without showing him the colour of my money. I had been ejected from the temple. Excommunicated from the faith.

I walked as coolly as I could down the steps and back onto Westmoreland Street.

According to Tara Bank's computer, I was thirty-six pounds and twenty-four pence overdrawn. Iremonger was in the red.

I took immediate action. I went up to the Wanderlust office, where I got some good news – the balance, the negative balance, that Derek MacReady had given me included the direct debit of this month's Wanderlust bill; it had gone through on December 23rd. Even with the plane ticket back to Paris and those wretched presents from Bloomingdale's, I had over four grand to go before maxing out the card (my inheritance had qualified me for the Conquistador level). I was in control of four thousand pounds: I was in control. I got a cash advance for one hundred quid. Those joyces felt good to the touch. I think I even smelt them before putting them away in my Gucci wallet.

In the wallet I found an old Telecom callcard – Christ, Joyce's mug on that too; what agency is he with? – and went to the phones near the Tart with the Cart to touch base with Cedar-of-Lebanon Road.

My father answered the phone with a faint, gravelly voice, a *yellow* voice.

'Hey, Dad, it's me, Tom.'

He acknowledged my existence wearily.

Why so cool towards his only son? Well, I guess I have an explanation. Things had been a little tense at home. Dylan had thrown a little afternoon drinks party on Stephen's Day (or, as Dylan, that West Brit *manqué* insists on calling it, Boxing Day). Carmel had gone down the country with one of her toyboys to a party at Butler Castle in Kilkenny and Dylan had seized the opportunity to entertain his friends at Frascati Court (an exclusive little development of townhouses opposite Blackrock Park) without the Dove there making everybody feel like they were in a parade.

He was as excited as a fifteen-year-old by this free house. Dylan's father? We don't talk about Dylan's father, poor man. He's better off in that monastery.

It turned into a very heavy session, even by Iremonger standards. Roderick had procured a half-ounce of rich Moroccan from one of his King's Inns buddies (he does a very good Ian Paisley impression when he's stoned). But tonight alcohol was the star of the show. Alcohol was calling the shots. We started drinking a little before three and I stopped drinking a little before three, or so I'm told. I was too busy drinking to take much notice of the time. I mean, I was *working* at drinking, putting my heart and soul, all my creative energy, into it. A vintage Iremonger performance, according to Roderick. I didn't even allow the prospect of getting laid – candidate: Joanna Swift, been after me for years – interfere with the task at hand. Maybe if Mainie had been there I would have been distracted. But Mainie wasn't there.

A quick confession – not really my style, but I feel obliged to say this: when I started this thing (at the back of my mind) deplaning on Christmas Eve, I thought every second scene was going to be sex – bonking and blow-jobs all over the place, a little S&M here, a little troilism there, with some dialogue and fashion talk thrown in. Maybe even a few cameo appearances from family members. But it's not working out like that, is it? I'm *very* sorry. I intend to set things right as soon as possible, make sure you get your money's worth. But for now, back to the party.

My drinking was a kind of Grand Tour in itself. I launched myself gently, with a little chardonnay – French, Chilean, Californian. Then I went around the world on eight imported and distinctively bottled beers. (Ever try Joker Beer from Nigeria? Don't.) Happy hour I spent shuttling back and forth between Scotch and Irish. By dinnertime (selflessly surrendering my slices of gourmet pizza to those who had the munchies real bad) I had arrived in Margaritaville. After that, as the party shrank to a committed core of serious drinkers and tokers, I was more or less on standby, drinking unfussily whatever came my way – Spanish champagne, obscure Czech liqueurs, German dessert wine, even Budweiser. Sometime after midnight I got closer to my rural roots in the form of a shared half-bottle of poteen that Dylan located in Carmel's closet. My itinerary becomes distinctly hazy after that. I have these fragmentary memories of drinking Norwegian wine and Qatari lager, but that can't be right. I do remember Roderick insisting around two o'clock that we order a taxi and all go off to 1916. But Dylan had collapsed in the kitchen at this stage and I wasn't in the mood for dancing. In fact, I may have spent about five minutes chanting the mantra, *My dancing days are over, my dancing days are over*.

Roderick and Joanna did head out to the club, though in the end they only got as far as his house. As far as I could tell, I was the last guest left. I sprawled on Dylan's spacious velvet couch, staring at a framed photo of Carmel Carraig-Dubh sharing a light-hearted moment with Charlie Haughey at some awards ceremony, all seven continents distilling in my liver.

I woke up feeling grotesque, unbelievable, bizarre, unprecedented. According to my Tzara, it was a little after midday Irish time. I felt sick. Then I remembered I was back in Dublin and felt really sick. Then I remembered I'd been dreaming about Strongbow, Strongbow and Mainie, and got sick.

In the context of that potential PR disaster (the legend was that Iremonger was constitutionally incapable of throwing up, no matter what he ingested, smoked, or snorted), I was in luck. I made it to the downstairs bathroom in time; there was no sign of Dylan or Carmel or anybody. No visual sign, at least – somebody had been praying to the porcelain god already (that distinctive incense was in the air), and I very much suspected it was *mein host*. I made my supplementary offering as discreetly as I could, then washed my mouth out from Carmel's brass fittings for a good three minutes.

Her son was no longer comatose in the kitchen. Dylan's real funny about people coming into his bedroom, so I left him a note on the big rough-wood kitchen table thanking him for his hospitality and telling him that if I didn't see him during the week I would definitely see him at Mainie Doyle's party.

As I walked unsteadily up an almost deserted Owenstown Avenue, unbidden a metallic grey Peacock pulled up. Maybe it's because I've been revelling in foreignness these last six months that I didn't think twice about the driver, a sallow-faced man in his late thirties, everything about him – white grandfather shirt, light-grey suit, matte-black beard – neat and trim. He beckoned me in a way that made it impossible to think about refusing the ride. I just nodded and got in.

'Where are you going?' The question was not unkindly asked, but right away I got the impression that this was not the kind of man who, as they say, suffered fools gladly.

'Owenstown Hill.' In the car there was the faint aroma of . . . roasted peanuts.

'I'm driving back to the embassy, but I can bring you to the top of the avenue.' He had learnt his English in America or from an American. Our accents, in other words, were virtually the same.

'Sure, that would be great.' Now I was getting curious about my driver. 'That would be the . . . Iranian embassy.'

'Correct. My name is Mr Kashan, second secretary.'

I nodded slowly. 'My name is Mr Iremonger.' I felt I should add a title, a clipped description of what I did, who I was, but I realised that I couldn't do so. That he had a title and I didn't made me kind of jealous.

There was so much I wanted to ask him – what he thought about Salman Rushdie (he was more likely to have read the book than I was), what he thought about Ireland, what he thought about *me* – but neither of us said anything for the rest of the short journey. As we passed Cross Avenue, I looked straight ahead.

When I got back to Cedar-of-Lebanon Road I realised I'd dashed out the night before – Roderick was beeping the horn of his mother's Freelance – without my keys. I'd been hoping that I could slip upstairs and crash out again without having to deal with my parents. Luckily, my parents weren't in the mood to deal with me. My mother answered the door, only looking in my direction long enough for me to register a scowl on her face that was equal parts hurt, indictment, resentment. For a few moments I felt incapable of setting foot in the house, their house, and stood sheepishly on the porch's chequered tiles, even though she'd disappeared into the kitchen. Then I was the one who felt resentment, of a perverse kind, I realised. Why hadn't she stood her ground? Why hadn't my father come out to confront me? Where were their principles? For this was one of the core commandments that they'd clung onto – perhaps only eclipsed by *Not in my house* – as the Iremonger onslaught gathered momentum through my college years: *If you are not coming home, phone us*. Simple as that. Doesn't matter where you are or who you are with, phone us, let us know you're alive. No questions asked (though that came later; at first there were questions, until they became too uncomfortable to ask).

The first time I failed to come home and phone home, the night the Leaving Cert results came out, they hit the roof – no, they put their heads right through the roof: my father gave me a red-faced lecture on my recklessness and its effects: insomnia and dark imaginings for them; a grounding and allowance-suspension for me. I guess the next time must have been the night I went into town to wait outside the offices of *The Irish Times* on D'Olier Street for the place-offers supplement to be published. (That was the night I met Roderick, the night we discovered we'd be going to Trinity together, the first night I got stoned.) This time the lecture turned into the first, and last, shouting match I have ever had with my father, and, I suspect, the only shouting match I will ever have with him. Not a word passed between us for nine days; he left it to my mother to dole out the prohibitions. Only when my grandmother had a heart-attack, death's dress rehearsal, did we start talking again. After that, my grounding was quietly forgotten about, and I ventured forth once again.

Into Freshers' week. The week Roderick introduced me to Dylan Carraig-Dubh and Dylan introduced me to Ardal McQuaid (not yet the Bish in those days). The week I introduced myself to Mainie Doyle, on the sunlit steps of the 1937 Reading Room, not realising I was being watched by the Special Branch, still shadowing her in the aftermath of her father's kidnapping.

I remember very clearly walking through Front Arch that Monday morning, remember it clearly because I told myself I was going to remember this, because this was the moment, the moment when the shell broke open, the moment when life really began, the moment when I (Iremonger) began. I walked through the cavern of Front Arch, past the glass panes of the Players' noticeboard, under which countless notes marked IREMONGER – URGENT! would be left over the next four years, into the soft October sunshine, and sauntered along the arcade formed on the cobblestones of Front Square by the booths and tables of Trinity's extra-curricular world, everyone from the Jolley Geology Society to the Rock Nostalgia Club wanting me to join. Later in the day, drunk on Tara Bank promotional Furstenburg, I joined both of them, I joined everything, but on that first strut down my first runway, I didn't stop at all. I was joining myself; there was Iremonger waiting for me at the end of the alley of stands, which, I fancied, was a festive guard of honour.

Friday night was the Freshers' Ball. I ended up staying in somebody's rooms in Botany Bay, and getting laid for the first time (though not by Mainie Doyle, that would come much, much later – once the Special Branch had been called off). When I came home Saturday lunchtime, it was my mother who gave me hell; my father only muttered, *You're wasting your time, Sinéad,* as he carved through the leathery skin of a sausage.

I guess you could summarise my parents' reaction to the evolution of Iremonger like this: first there was punishment, then there were threats, and now there's only silence.

So that's what lay behind my father's reluctant recognition as I talked to him on the Telecard phone. I guess I felt a little bit pissed off by his attitude and wished that if he had a problem with me he would speak his mind, but at the same time I was in a hurry to take care of my own agenda.

'Listen, Dad, any calls for me?'

'Let me check with your mother,' he replied unenthusiastically. Muffled conversation. The phone was picked up again awkwardly. 'Two calls. One was from Mr Carraig-Dubh. He wants you to meet him and your other associates at five o'clock at a place on Molesworth Street called Le Café Vert.'

'Got it. Who was the other call from?'

Here my father's tone lightened, 'The other call was from your old friend Brían Firbolg.'

'Brían Firbolg? What did he want?'

My father needed to consult my mother again. Waiting for him to come back to the phone, this wimpy little voice inside me answered the question: the money, he wants the Roomkeepers' money, the Roomkeepers want their money. Then my father came back on the line with a sensible answer.

'He phoned to tell you that the total was up six hundred pounds from last year, whatever that means. And he was wondering if you'd like to meet him for a drink.'

I smiled. Of course. That pint I'd promised him. The guy just wanted to get in some Iremonger-time. (Who could blame him?) He knew nothing about the finer points of the financing deal I'd done for those Roomkeepers of his. Of course he didn't.

'That's good to know, Dad. Well, I guess I'd—'

'Just a second, Tom, your mother's asking me a question.' More muffled conversation. 'She wants to know if she should keep something on the hot plate for you.'

For a moment I didn't know what to say. 'Tell her no thank you,' I said softly. 'I won't be back till very late. Tell her not to worry.'

I arrived at Le Café Vert right on schedule – forty minutes late. I smiled when I saw the name on the canopy over the entrance; when I left in June this establishment was still called MacSwiney's, an old, old hangout of the mad pinting gang. They'd gutted the place and transformed it into an evil neo-art-nouveau bar, all writhing black iron and acid jazz. The joint was booming. Plenty of money about in Dublin, even after Christmas. Maybe a whole bunch of people had inherited money from their canny, puritanical grandfathers. Chick radar picked me up as soon as I walked in. I located Dylan's and Roderick's table in the chiaroscuro lighting. A waiter came over to take my order. A waiter in MacSwiney's, for fuck's sake. I wasn't too sure what I thought of that. Nevertheless, I ordered a double Pernod for myself, pints of Fursty for the boys.

'Well,' said Roderick, 'what's the deal? You want to get a lift out to Mainie's?'

How was I going to get out of this one? Roderick always chauffeured me around Dublin when he could get the Freelance. Why wouldn't I want to drive out to Dalkey with him on Saturday? Then I remembered something. An invitation to a Mainie Doyle party followed a classic formula. (I had seen so many prominently displayed on the mantelpieces of West Brit and pseudo-West Brit girls who lived together in rooms; I had in fact rarely ever received one because usually I didn't *need* one: I was Mainie's date, Mainie's consort, an insider in the invitational process.) The white card – embossed border, black calligraphy, a work of art – always invited a named couple or a named person and unnamed guest. Roderick and Dylan would be bringing women, even if they weren't the girls they intended to hook up with at the party.

'How are you going to fit six people in the Freelance?' I asked Roderick, enjoying a quiet triumph.

It didn't last. 'Oh, don't tell me you're going to bring a date, Iremonger,' he replied. 'That would be cruel. We all know the person you want will be there already.'

I smiled sarcastically at my friend, then, sensing my executive order not to blush was, to my astonishment and further embarrassment, not being carried out to the letter, I turned my face into the fashionable shadows of Le Café Vert.

'Now,' I said, 'where has that goddamn waiter got to?'

I had never known trouble like this before. I wasn't (and

am not) worrying too much about my financial situation – I could arrange half a dozen go-sees like *that* back in Paris and was sure I could pull in some money through modelling by the end of January; a copy of the IDA poster was all the portfolio I needed. Not that the prospect of Iremonger finally breaking into the international modelling scene, something people in Dublin have been predicting for so long, way before the Ascendancy gig, really turned me on now. It seemed too much like . . . work. And I wasn't sure if I could deal with the strenuous requirements of the trade – beauty sleep, early mornings, being co-operative – in the foreseeable future.

But my immediate problem was Mainie Doyle. The more I thought about that invitation, or its absence, the more I obsessed about that party. I came to the conclusion that she was playing an elaborate game with me, that the party was, just like this Strongbow liaison, probably conceived as a means of getting at me, sending me a message, messing with my head, looking for my attention. Well, it was working. The obvious thing to do, if you were Iremonger, was to obey the First Rule of Cool and ignore the party, stay away, get invited to something cooler. But the problem, it became clear as the week progressed, was that there was nothing cooler happening around town. It was rumoured that two other people, Mainie-wannabes, had cancelled their New Year's Eve bashes when people now invited to the Doyle party started cancelling on them. It was rumoured that SuperDoyle had hired the Guinness Jazz Band to play. It was rumoured that Carmel Carraig-Dubh would be there for midnight.

I heard these rumours as I and the other mad pinters pub, party, and club surfed our way around Dublin, fuelled by more shipments of B-Special from the Bish, on those indistinct interlude nights between Christmas and New Year's Eve.

By Thursday I'd heard more talk about that party than the IDA poster. Most of the people I met, the women in particular, assumed Mainie and I were still intimate and that I was therefore virtually co-hosting the party. It was an easy assumption to make. So many people coming back were simply picking up their Dublin lives where they'd left off in June, or trying to, and they believed everybody else was doing the same.

Even those who knew about Mainie's liaison with Strongbow assumed that I'd received my invitation and had chosen my companion for the evening. I did nothing to disabuse them. The downside of that, of course, was that nobody was even going to think of inviting *me*.

I couldn't even bring myself to tell the truth about my invitationless state to either Dylan or Roderick. In fact, I avoided all serious subjects with the mad pinters. I didn't want to talk about the future and I didn't want to talk about the past. I made a joke out of everything. I reckoned one serious subject might lead on to another and another and on to the most serious subject of all – Mainie. Besides, often I was too stoned or wired to talk about anything.

For all the pubs and parties and clubs we went to I never bumped into Mainie or Strongbow once. So many times I nonchalantly nodded when somebody told me they'd just left or were expected. I neither tried to avoid them or find them. I tried to continue as if I were the centre of the universe, the trajectories of other heavenly bodies being of minor interest. But one time, in the bathroom of a house on Serpentine Avenue, I put a fluffy pink towel to my cold, wet face and breathed in Maud Gonne, Mainie's balmy signature perfume. Iremonger is not a superstitious kind of guy but at moments like these I began to suspect that this whole trip back to Dublin was cursed for some reason. The plot or the curse – I wasn't sure which came first.

Something else that happened on Thursday night, or

early Friday morning to be more precise, also freaked me out, though it had nothing to do with the Mainie Doyle situation.

Let me fill you in a little on the party I was coming home from. The mad pinting gang, chauffeurred by Roderick, had gone up the mountains to Johnny Fox's pub. From there we were invited to a party that was about to happen in a big house up near Kilgobbin. The girl who was giving the party was the daughter of some Labour Party minister and uncool about controlled substances in her house, so the three ganjateers decided to smoke the rest of the evil ounce Dylan had scored (from an Ardal-imitator at Strictly Suspects the night before) in the garden. It was cold as fuck outside – Roderick almost chickened out – but as clear as the morning I'd swam for Mainie in the Irish Sea. We walked down the sloping garden, through a windshield of trees – I'll take a wild guess and say they were beech trees – and stood before an old ha-ha fence (the perfect place to get stoned, Dylan opined). We lit up and looked out. The orange lights of Dublin lay below us, from the functionality of the suburbs to the intensity of the city centre, then out along Sutton's amber bridge which became Howth's weaker fairy lights; at the headland's tip, however, was a white star that blazed and faded, blazed and faded.

'Beautiful,' Roderick commented.

'Why would you want to live anywhere else?' Dylan added.

'You're both stoned,' I replied.

After that we went back inside to sample some of the Minister's liquor. Drink and dope proved to be a problematic cocktail. By the time the party had peaked, I guess about two-thirty, and we had decided to hit the road, Roderick was trying unsuccessfully to hide his paranoia about being over the limit. I told him to chill – we'd heard a lot of horror stories about the guards' drink-driving campaign, but we'd not seen one check-point with our own eyes; and besides, he was in better shape to drive than he had been the previous night. Even so, the Freelance crawled back down the mountains and into the suburbs five miles under the speed limit, skirting main roads where possible.

It must have taken us the best part of an hour to get back to Cedar-of-Lebanon Road. As we pulled up outside the gate of my parents' house, Dylan said, 'Looks like there's a party on here too.'

A prickly wave was already going down the backs of my arms and legs – the porch, hall, drawing room, bathroom, and my parents' room were all lit-up. Something had happened to my father. With some effort, I put Iremonger back in control.

'My folks are probably doing a little retro-parenting by waiting-up for me.' I wasn't exactly sure what I was talking about, but Dylan and Roderick seemed to find it both amusing and convincing. I saw a shape behind the bevelled glass of the front door and one of the pink curtains in my parents' bedroom squint. I released my seatbelt and was about to open my door when we heard this car roar around the corner behind us onto Cedar-of-Lebanon Road. Dylan, who was in the back, identified it, 'It's the fucking cops.'

Shock! went the central locking as Roderick said, 'I've got to get inside Iremonger's gate. They can't pursue you onto private property.'

The garda car had slammed to a halt right behind us.

I grabbed his arm. 'Relax, de Brun. I know how to handle these guys.'

'I'm way over the limit, Ire!'

'That's nice to know.'

As soon as I stepped out of the Freelance torchlight hit my eyes.

'Identify yourself,' said the torch-wielding guard. His partner was getting out of the driver's seat.

I was too confused – the dope, the drink, the dazzle – to say anything at first. I just brought a splayed hand up to shield my face. Then I noticed the other guard approaching Roderick's window.

'Tomás Iremonger,' I blurted out, 'I live here.' I even wished I had my passport on me, to confirm all this.

It must have had a ring of truth about it. The guard switched off his torch. White discs floated across my eyes. The other guard was knocking on Roderick's window. What kind of trouble had I got him into? Probably nothing the Tort King couldn't get him out of.

It was then that both cops were distracted by a familiar but unexpected voice – Columb's.

'It's all right, guards, that's not them – that young man does live here. And those are his companions.'

The first cop shone his torch in the direction of the voice. Columb was standing in the gateway bundled in a slapdash ensemble of his and my father's clothes. He looked both comical and dignified; the guard quickly turned off his flashlight once again.

'Are you the young man's father?' asked the other cop, now leaning on the roof of the Freelance.

Though the streetlighting was poor, I'm sure I saw a smile steal across my uncle's face. 'I do not have that honour, Guard.'

This is what had gone down as we crawled back from Kilgobbin. About three-fifteen the TeleGuard alarm had gone off – an excruciating sound, according to Columb. Earlier that evening my father had thrown up his dinner and had gone to bed feeling very weak. When the alarm went off he'd staggered out of bed (as my mother fumbled with the remote control to turn off the sonic torture). She and my uncle convinced him not to go downstairs. Columb did, as my mother phoned the guards and pleaded with her brother-in-law to mind himself. He couldn't find any signs of a break-in, but the guards were already on their way.

After their fussy arrival, my uncle invited them in, telling them my mother was anxious for reassurance. They obliged, informing me off-hand that my friends could go. I told Roderick to get out of there, that I'd phone him tomorrow; he didn't stick around to chat. The cops told my mother to contact them at Dundrum station if we did find any signs in the morning of an attempted burglary. My mother said she would because the system had never malfunctioned like that before.

'Tom does his job,' she muttered.

The cops looked at each other.

I got very little sleep. Better to say I just gave up on sleep about eight-fifteen and went downstairs to make myself a cafetière of Bewley's French roast – this was as sophisticated as coffee was going to get in my parents' house; they distrusted espresso machines. Blurrily I looked out the kitchen window – the light outside was leaden – and saw my mother inspecting the lower reaches of the garden wall, down by the apple trees. She was wearing the shabby once-ecru padded anorak of my father's that Columb had worn when he came outside to talk to – and rescue me from – the cops five hours before.

The coffee was ready by the time she came back into the garage. A metallic creak froze me mid-plunge. It was just the sound of the handle of the thick door between the garage and the kitchen turning, but for some reason it freaked me out a little. My mother came into the kitchen and I plunged down to the grounds.

'What are you doing up?' she asked, astonished but pleased.

I turned around and shrugged. She hadn't put on her make-up or done her hair yet. I didn't want to see her like this. She looked worse than she'd done at three o'clock in the morning. She looked like she had been in a fight. 'I guess I couldn't sleep because of the alarm going off.' That was part of it. 'Want some coffee?' I asked mechanically.

She hesitated for a moment and then said, 'Yes, why not. Get out cups and saucers and spoons and everything. Do it right.'

I felt too tired to do it anything but her way. We sat down and I poured the coffee.

'Thank you, that's fine,' she said sniffily.

'So, see any evidence of a break-in?' I asked.

She scrutinised me for a moment to see if I was making fun of her (I wasn't, not this time). Then she answered me cautiously, 'No. The house looks fine. But there are some fallen bricks on Mrs Donlan's side of the wall.'

'But haven't they been there for years?' I didn't mean this to sound as combative as it came out.

'These were *new* bricks, Tomás.' I winced when she called me by my old name – I mean, she knew very well I wanted to be called Tom all the time – but I decided to, once again, let it go; she was probably stressed out about my father. The coffee tasted stale.

Simultaneously, she took out her king-sized Gossamers from the deep pocket of my father's anorak and I took out my Rolands (T - 90) from the baggy Levis I'd thrown on. This lightened things up. She thanked me when I fetched two ashtrays and when I gave her a light from my Zippo. Her ashtray featured a photo of the marina in Marbella, the first foreign place I'd ever been, almost twenty years before. Low-tar and unfiltered smoke mingled in the space between us. My mind began to drift, and I realised why I'd been taken aback by the sound of that door handle turning: in that dozing state that I'd gone into on so many long flights I'd sometimes sworn I'd heard my mother opening the kitchen-garage door, only to open my eyes and discover it was only the hostess extracting the passing service cart from a jam.

Suddenly my mother stabbed out her still tall Gossamer on the tiny yachts.

'If they tell me he has cancer I'll die,' she said as she stood up. She left the kitchen without looking at me, without giving me a chance to respond.

I'm very grateful to her for that.

The thing to do was not panic. Okay, I had thirty-six hours to get an invitation to this party – any kind of invitation. Gatecrashing was not an option. Iremonger does not gatecrash. True, Iremonger sometimes *arrives* unannounced at a party or an opening or a show (often straight from the airport), but that is different, a surprise, a bonus, for all present. Showing up where you're not wanted without a valid excuse – that's gatecrashing.

Now, I know my Mainie. On the face of things, my non-invitation is a snub. But deep down she wants me to be there tonight – wants that more than anything. Because for me to make it past her father's security apparatus would be a sign of real commitment. This party is a test, a trial. And that's fair enough. I'll admit it – I've never had to sweat or suffer for Mainie Doyle before. She's been this . . . casual miracle in my life. Yes, it was fair play to throw down this gauntlet. That's not, however, the way I was seeing things most of Friday.

I sneaked that bottle of Kells upstairs and spent the rest of the morning brooding in my bedroom, listening to my entire collection of Tom Waits tapes (an early Iremonger favourite). If the worst came to the worst, I could always bribe the security SuperDoyle would have on hand. But that was not going to be cheap. In the afternoon I crashed out. I would need to be on my toes that evening, that eve of New Year's Eve, alert to any window of opportunity, ready to do some sly social engineering. If I could just be myself, 100% Iremonger, then surely everything would fall into place. Of course, that was the philosophy I'd been using for the past week, and I was still no closer to getting an invitation to Mainie Doyle's party. But I didn't linger on that insight. I just crashed out instead.

I was woken by the sound of the piano. Though muffled by the floorboards, my father's style was distinctive – mildly jazzy, sentimental, over-sustained. Even though he had a large stack of sheet music stored away under the seat of the piano stool, he returned with a mellow obsessiveness to maybe a half-dozen standards he'd been trying to perfect as long as I could remember. I could name them, no problem – 'Misty', 'The Girl from Ipanema', 'Stardust Memories'. But I always got confused about which one he was playing at any one time. Like right now. I'd heard him play that song a thousand times – its mood and melody bringing to mind an art-deco bar somewhere sub-tropical where a bartender in a pressed white jacket shook up killer martinis while you waited for your femme fatale (a place that perhaps I'd been looking for these past six months and had yet to find). I couldn't remember the title of the song, but I wasn't too bothered. This was the first time I'd heard my father playing the piano since I'd come back. It cheered me a little. Maybe it was 'What a Difference a Day Made'.

Dylan phoned about six-thirty. He and Roderick were in town already.

'This is what's happening tonight: Vivian Buckley's party on Ailesbury Road (she really wants you to come) and there's a new club, Irregulars; Marc Murphy really wants you to come to that; Joey Gregory is spinning.'

Everybody wanted me to come to everything except

Mainie Doyle's party. 'Let's put in an appearance at both, I guess.'

'My thoughts exactly.'

I told Dylan I'd meet them in Hogan's around eight-thirty (sometime after nine, Iremonger Standard Time). Five minutes later the phone rang again. I picked up the cordless thinking it would be Dylan again, relaying some change in strategy for the evening. But it wasn't. It was Firbolg. I was surprisingly pleasant.

'Well, hey there, Brían,' I said, 'Happy New Year.'

'I hope I'm not interrupting your dinner or anything, Tom.'

I was in fact done with dinner, having briefly joined my parents and Columb at the kitchen table and eaten a few token slices of smoked salmon. 'Well, I'm sure my mother can keep it hot for a few minutes,' I told Firbolg.

I could hear him slurp anxiously at the other end of the phone. 'Oh, don't worry, I won't keep you long. I was just wondering if I could take you up on the offer of that pint tonight.'

'Brían, I'd love to, but I've already made plans for tonight.' That line came out automatically, but it sounded a little weird since I was so used to brushing off second-rate babes with it.

'Oh, really? That's a pity because I wanted to ask your advice about something.'

'Well, ask me over the phone – we can have that drink some other time.'

'I'm not sure I can ask you over the phone,' he sipped. 'It's kind of embarrassing.'

'Try, Brían.'

He took a few big gulps of himself and finally said, 'It's like this. That girl, Mainie Doyle?'

Suddenly the whole world shrank to Firbolg and his streaming mouth.

'What about her?' I tried to say that as nonchalantly as I could, but it came out sounding very Bad Cop.

Firbolg gulped again. 'I've been invited to her party.'

I swallowed hard myself. Then, putting every Iremonger fibre in my body to work, I said very blandly, 'Oh, that's great, Brían. Good for you.'

'Yeah but Tom,' Firbolg whispered into the phone (I wasn't sure if that was static or spittle I was hearing), 'I don't know who to bring!'

Those were possibly the sweetest words anyone had ever said to me. I wasn't interested in explanations – the when, the why, the where of how he'd gone and done the incomprehensible: get an invitation to Mainie Doyle's party. No, that could come later. Right now I just wanted to exploit the situation as quickly as possible.

'No, you're quite right, Brían,' I said gravely, 'this problem is too sensitive to be talked about over the phone. Meet me in the Mount Anville House in half an hour.'

The Mount Anville House is a ten-minute walk from my parents' house. I hadn't set foot in the joint since the night the Leaving Cert results came out. The place was still catering to the hordes of Southside brats just above or below the drinking age; every year some kid got killed or killed somebody else in his mummy's Swan driving home drunk from there. They'd added yet another lounge since I'd hung out here (Iremonger in embryo) and this one seemed to have been designed to attract an older crowd: it had waiter service and had been expensively fitted out in mahogany, brass, and bevelled glass; brewing and distilling memorabilia were displayed in illuminated glass cases. According to Dylan, there was this company making a killing stripping down old-style bars in far-flung parts of the country and reassembling them in Dublin, where publicans had merrily destroyed such decor a few decades before to make way for Formica and plastic. That's where I should invest my money, he'd told me, in Dublin's fickleness. It was a sure thing.

Firbolg was waiting for me there, almost hugging a Guinness. (I'm proud to say I hadn't gone and done something rash like show up early.) I ordered a JD straight.

'I'm sorry to say I don't have much time, Brían,' I told him. I'm sorry to say I really had all the time in the world to deal with this matter.

'Oh, that's okay. I really appreciate you rearranging your evening like this at short notice.'

'Don't worry about it. Anything for an old friend. Anyhow, first things first. How did you get invited to Mainie Doyle's party?'

Firbolg nodded rapidly, sipped himself, then his drink. 'Well, it all goes back to Christmas Eve. Remember I told you how Mainie's father likes to give to the Roomkeepers?' I nodded. 'Well, about ten minutes after you left who should walk down Grafton Street but the two of them. While Mr Doyle was chatting with my uncle, Mainie asked me if I was a friend of yours, and I told her how that afternoon had been the first time I'd seen you, or at least talked to you, in years and how you'd been a real trooper collecting for the Roomkeepers. Then she told me she was planning this party for New Year's Eve and would I like to come. Of course I said yes and she said she'd get an invitation to me next week. And guess what, Wednesday morning it arrived – hand-delivered by some guy who works for her father. I was pretty excited, I'll tell you, Tom; I reckoned she was going to forget about what she'd said on Christmas Eve. Up to then it had looked like I was going to spend yet another New Year's Eve watching Percy Tóibín with my parents. Well, when I read the fine print of the invitation, so to speak, I saw that I had to bring a guest. I haven't been going out with anybody lately so I phoned up this girl I know from engineering, but she said she'd already made plans for New Year's.'

I reckoned that Firbolg hadn't been out with anybody ever, but I let that one pass. 'Did you tell her it was Mainie Doyle's party you'd been invited to?'

'Yeah, I mentioned the name, but it didn't seem to make much difference. I don't think Ursula reads *Ireland on Sunday*.'

I sipped my JD and sighed. 'I know exactly what the problem is, Brían.'

'What?'

'Well, it's like . . . telling a nun that you're holding a half kilo of uncut Peruvian snow.'

Firbolg sucked uncomprehendingly. I tried again, 'It's a case of pearls before piglets! The kind of girl you're likely to encounter, Brían, may occasionally treat herself to an avocado sandwich from the SuperDoyle deli, but the closest she'll ever get to Mainie Doyle's world is seeing her name in Carmel Carraig-Dubh's column.'

Firbolg looked a little hurt by this, and sought comfort in his Guinness. Go easy, Iremonger, I told myself. Don't blow it.

'That's not to say that you don't deserve to date the kind of girl who *does* move in Mainie's circle. So I tell you what, why don't just forget about any of the girls you've known before and focus on the future. Because tomorrow night, my man, is the first night of your new social existence. Because tomorrow night you're showing up at that party with *Iremonger*.'

Firbolg gulped and smiled. Then his excitement became shaded with doubt.

'But what about your date, Tom?'

I was prepared for this. 'Oh,' I sighed, 'I'm essentially post-dating.'

While Brían Firbolg absorbed that concept, I savoured another.

I am invited therefore I am.

7

Star

I guess I should tell you about something. Something that has been happening that hasn't happened for a long time. I have been remembering my dreams – vividly, almost frame by frame, blow by blow. And what have I been dreaming about? Strongbow. And my father. Sometimes both of them together. Here's one of the better ones:

Dusk. Pouring rain. The Bombardier stops at the top of Cedar-of-Lebanon Road. I tell the fat, sweaty bus driver that my jacket will get wet if I get off, but he just grunts and tells me that I have to go home. I step down onto squelching grass. Icy rain hits my face. Then I notice him under a tree, its black bark glistening. The rain has brylcremed his jet-black hair to his skull. This is the twenty-two-year-old Strongbow, but he is still wearing the striped purple-and-gold Berchmans tie. I call his name, but he doesn't acknowledge me. I go right up to him – my eyes level with his chin – and say, Don't you recognise me? He stands rigidly still, eyes glaring over my head, his cheeks ruddy, the way they always are when he is cold, or contemptuous. I give up, and storm off down my road.

When I reach our gate I stop. A strip of light indicates that the garage door is ajar. The only other light on in the house is in my parents' bedroom. I suddenly remember that my father is in bed, sick, alone, and that I was meant to be at home looking after him.

As the taxi from Martello cabs speeds along the Stillorgan Dual Carriageway, Brían Firbolg turns to me jerkily and says, 'Tom, I've forgotten something.'

I convert dark thoughts into light sarcasm, 'The invitation?'

'No,' he slurps, shaking his head and smiling. 'It would be a bit much now if *both* of us had forgotten our invitations.'

'Yeah, that would be a bit much.'

'No, I've forgotten which of Mr Doyle's hands has the missing finger. I shook the right one, I mean the correct one, on Grafton Street on Christmas Eve, I think. He was wearing gloves that day. But I reckon he won't be wearing gloves tonight, and I don't want to start things off on the wrong foot, so to speak.'

'Chill, Brían. Teddy doesn't really care if you try to shake his dud hand.'

'I would have thought it was a horrible reminder of what they did to him.'

I laugh. 'The most horrible thing that happened, the way that Teddy tells it when he's drunk, is that the company paid.'

'They *paid*?' Threads of saliva become suspended across Firbolg's open mouth.

'Dublin's worst-kept secret, my friend. They paid a matter of hours after Lucia opened that jiffy bag and took out two thirds of her husband's little finger.'

Firbolg shakes his head. 'Bloody animals. To think somebody could believe that has something to do with patriotism.'

I don't reply. I don't want to get involved in a discussion about the North (and I can see from his profile that the taxi driver is itching to say something).

'So, Tom,' Firbolg says, 'which hand is it?'

'The left,' I lie.

The taxi grinds up Merano Road on Dalkey Hill, reminding me of the funicular ride I took when I was in Lyons. Or was it San Sebastian? The road has been narrowed, almost to the point of obstruction, by the lines of cars that extend right down to the stone-walled bridge over the DART rails. I go over the storyboard of this seduction (the only kind of narrative I really care for). I've been working on it all week. It has, I believe, a classical simplicity:

1. Iremonger makes a dramatic late entry (less than half an hour left of this defining year), charming his way past Teddy and Lucia Doyle, acting light-hearted and aloof when he encounters Mainie Doyle and Strongbow.

2. He retires to a bathroom and gets a little inspirational buzz going with the help of the B-Special prescribed for him that afternoon by Dr McQuaid in the bog of the Trotsky Sandwich Co.

3. He hooks up with a young lady, the virginal type that has in the past made Mainie so jealous.

4. In the post-midnight confusion Mainie asks seriously to have a word with him in private; they go to the kitchen.

5. Mainie's lecture turns to lust.

6. Using the back staircase, they reach the first floor, then sneak up the regular stairs to Mainie's bedroom.

7. Having stolen Mainie away from Strongbow, Iremonger himself steals away, less than a half-hour into the new year, into a waiting taxi from Martello Cabs.

This is a big-budget production. And no, the most expensive item above the line is not the choice chemical from Ardal; it's this goddamn taxi. Well, *you* try to book a taxi in Dublin for this late on New Year's Eve without having to resort to bribery. But the bottom line is that I don't care – I don't care about the cost. If I had the whole of my inheritance over again, I believe I'd spend it all to get what I want tonight – Mainie Doyle, one more time. Why? I'm not exactly sure. It's not love. (Iremonger doesn't fall in love.) It's not even lust. Yes, it's got something to do with her. But it's also got something to do with him. It's got something to do with the past. And it's all about me.

But forget about all of that for now. What you are about to see is an hour of vintage Iremonger. No, of Iremonger surpassing himself.

When we pulled up outside Tír na nÓg, the insanity of any notion I'd had of gatecrashing this party was impressed upon me once again. Even though it had been over a decade since Teddy Doyle had been kidnapped and had the little finger of his right hand hacked off by an INLA splinter group, security was still very tight. In fact, it was tighter than I'd ever seen it in the four years I'd been a frequent visitor to this house. These days, I guess, the Doyles fear gatecrashers more than they do terrorists.

I paid the driver, tipping him lavishly and reconfirming my pick-up time: 12:30 AM, Jan 1. A bouncer in a monkey-suit and overcoat, a moonlighting cop undoubtedly, was there to meet us on the pavement.

'Got your invitations there now, gentlemen?' A Cork accent. My grandfather's accent – my other dead grandfather.

Firbolg fumbled in the breast-pockets of his ill-fitting rented tuxedo, his excess saliva flowing over his lower lip, threatening to freeze into little icicles. 'Yeah . . . sure . . . just a second.' Despite the temperature (it was, as the old man used to say, baffling me as a child, *too cold to snow*),

Firbolg got all hot and bothered looking for the precious white card. For a moment I thought that he *had* forgotten it, and wondered if the bouncer took Wanderlust. But then Firbolg found the invitation in his trouser pocket, sweeping it out triumphantly. 'Here!' he sprayed.

The burly bouncer took out a pocket torch and examined the invite. Were the Doyles putting watermarks on the goddamn things now?

'That'll do,' he said, handing it back to Firbolg. 'But what about you?'

I met his stare insouciantly, let the languid vapour of a sigh fade between our faces. I'd known this moment would come. 'I'm his guest,' I shrugged. 'It says on the invitation, Brían Firbolg plus guest.'

He looked at me closely. I wondered if he'd been given special instructions to look out for Iremonger, keep him off the property at all costs. But Mr Moonlight merely smiled. 'Go on, so.' He took a walkie-talkie out of his coat pocket. 'Two late arrivals at the ball, Charlie – Prince Charming and Cinderella.' The tall, spiky gates behind him began to trundle open. 'Have a nice time, boys.' He winked as we went by.

I didn't care that he thought Brían Firbolg was my bitch. I was in. That's all I cared about. I was in.

'I thought he was going to give you grief because you aren't wearing black tie,' Firbolg whispered excitedly.

'Brían, would you quit worrying so much? Make it your new year's resolution. As I told you, I consider myself post-fashion.'

In fact, I'd simply fucked up – been caught off guard. Mainie had only thrown one black tie before, her twenty-first. She was certainly getting ideas about herself.

'Well, it *is* a nice jacket,' Firbolg said.

Walking up the driveway, I could see other burly figures lurking – in the rockery, in the gazebo, under the granite walls. 'What a house,' said Firbolg, when Tír na nÓg came properly into view. He's right, I thought, what a house indeed. Oh, compared to what I'd seen and slept in over the past six months, real châteaux and gilded mansions, the Doyles' gabled, late-Victorian three-storey pile was nothing to write home about, but tonight I wouldn't have swapped it for Versailles. Already I could hear a shuddering techno-beat and muffled shouts. The curtains in the ballroom were open, throwing multi-coloured pulses and pulsing silhouettes out onto the empty veranda running the length of the house, its fairy-lit balustrade echoing the Sutton isthmus, which could be glimpsed through a screen of branches. Last Bloomsday out on that veranda I had gotten slowly and deliciously wasted on Bombay gimlets, tipped back in a recliner, Blazes Boylan straw hat tipped forward over my eyes. Right at the top of the house, the dormer window of Mainie's bedroom was also illuminated. I remembered the first morning I ever awoke in that bedroom (Teddy and Lucia had gone to their timeshare in Antibes for a week to escape the misery of Dublin's January). They missed the sight of the city under heavy snow, and there was no better place to survey that rare world than Tír na nÓg, especially from the window of Mainie's velvety nest. The white arms of Dun Laoghaire pier reminded me of the old man's pipe cleaners.

Well, I would be back in her boudoir before the last fog horn out there in the bay had faded. My finest Iremonger-sensors told me so.

The hall door of the house was off to one side, approached through a conservatory. Yet another moonlighting cop stood among the potted plants and palm fronds; he merely indicated with a sour nod that the front door, with its bevelled and stain-glassed plant life, was open.

The hallway was booming – people flirting, drinking

Teddy's potent punch, manically catching up with each other after six scattered months. Chick radar picked me up. *Guy* radar picked me up. I fielded an IDA question while Firbolg handed his old Cleary's overcoat to the coat-check girl, who took it as if she'd been handed a dirty rag. I gave her Nico's lambswool lining, which she took as if it were a late Christmas present. I was so late arriving – my Tzara told me that there were only twenty-one (opportunity-rich) minutes left in this wrinkly year – that Teddy and Lucia were not there to receive guests, as was their habit when Mainie was throwing a big party. But that was okay with me. Deep down I realised that if Mr and Mrs Doyle, perhaps inspired by some rash thing their daughter had said, really didn't want me there, I would have been spending midnight waiting for that taxi on Merano Road, no matter about my technical legitimacy through Firbolg's ticket. But once I'd melded with the party the Doyles, Lucia in particular, would be much less willing to risk a scene. I knew this family, better than my own.

Firbolg stood hesitantly on the threshold of the cacophonous, parqueted ballroom – the spacious heart of the party, filled with about seventy or eighty dancers, drinkers, posers – staring at his beautiful and relaxed peers inside as if he had come across an undiscovered civilisation.

'Well, there's your black tie for you, kid,' I said.

Every guy had individualised his outfit. Some wore tails or loud cummerbunds, others psychedelic waistcoats. Tuxedos were spiced with florid buttonholes. It was the girls who were all in uniform. Little Black Dress orthodoxy held sway. Some of the LBDs, I judged, were freshly torn out of the cellophane they'd come back in from their post-Trinity Ball dry-cleaning. Others, even more risqué, had been brought back from the fashion capitals for their Dublin début. But for both sexes the deconstruction of formality was continuing apace. In wearing Nico, I was, as usual, simply a step ahead.

The ceiling was pregnant with balloons. I spotted Roderick. I spotted Dylan. I found it hard to spot a face I didn't recognise. But there were two faces I didn't see. The soul of the party, its Yin and Yang, was elsewhere.

I slapped Firbolg on the back. 'Go in. Enjoy.'

'Where are you going?' he said, almost aggressively.

'Nature calls.'

I left him there, teetering on the edge of pleasure, and went to find a little privacy. Knowing this house and knowing parties in this house so well, I didn't bother with the downstairs toilet but climbed the wide staircase, with its carved mahogany posts, to the first-floor bathroom. When I got to the door I heard a thunderous rush of urine, followed by a rumbling flush. I realised there was only one (guy) I knew who could piss like a Nietzschean superman, and that was SuperDoyle himself. I began to trot back downstairs – getting buzzed could wait a few minutes. Too late – I should have remembered that Mainie's father was also the only Irish person I knew, apart from a few drug dealers and politicians, who wasn't hung up on the idea of washing his hands; the man who had introduced the kiwi fruit and the jalepeño to Ireland, who had revolutionised dinner parties in Dublin 4 with moderately priced quality Californian chardonnay, didn't have much time for personal delicacies. Teddy Doyle was on the landing before I had reached the return.

'Is that young Iremonger slinking away?'

I turned around and smiled as shyly and sweetly as I could.

'Yes, Mr Doyle, it is.'

'Well, cut out the fuckology and come up here and say

hello. And for God's sake don't call me Mr Doyle. Mr Doyle was me father!'

I climbed back up the stairs towards the bulk of Mainie's father, pleased for two reasons. First, I was obviously not going to suffer the unthinkable Iremonger indignity of being asked to leave a party because I was not welcome. Second, this reminded me of the very first time I had met SuperDoyle, the first time I came to this house, a fortnight after the Freshers' Ball, a few days after Mainie and I had started going out together (yes, there was a time when we did things the conventional way). He'd offered me his right hand to shake, something he always did, Mainie told me afterwards, to his new business partners and her new boyfriends, to see if they'd flinch. (Trust Teddy to turn a loss to profit.) I didn't flinch. Now I wondered how Strongbow had fared.

Teddy grabbed my shoulders, shook me a little, as if something loose inside me might rattle. There was more vigour in the four and a third digits of his deformed paw than other men have in ten.

Apparently I was still solid – Teddy laughed, the great grey bar of his moustache rising. True, I'd never seen Mainie's father in anything but a robustly good mood, not even when the croissant war really put the squeeze on his cashflow. But it was that animal heartiness, together with stories I'd heard from Mainie and around town about his volcanic temper, which made me wary of the man. No, say it straight, Iremonger: I was ever so slightly afraid of Teddy Doyle, the way I had been of my father so many years before.

'Looking good,' he was saying, 'not as good as your poster. But looking good.'

'Thanks, Teddy. How's Lucia?' I asked idly.

'Sure why don't you come and ask her yourself!'

Before I could answer and make my excuses, four fingers

and a stump were manoeuvring me to a small drawing room that Mainie's parents seemed to use exclusively as a retreat during their daughter's parties. The TV was on, tuned to RTE; Lucia Doyle was drinking white wine, chilled in a bucket beside her armchair, her legs crossed. She was wearing a martini-olive green evening gown with floral appendages – the dress shrieked Bibi McGurk, Lucia's favourite Irish 'couturist'. A chartreuse pump dangled from the big toe of one foot. Her signature big henna hair was a little lopsided – she looked like a high-class madam bowled over by the amount of business she was getting. When she saw me, she put down her glass gladly and rose, beckoning me forward with both hands. I kissed her on both cheeks. It was like kissing a guy. That's the thing with Mainie's mother – she looks like a very impressive sex-change operation, a queen turned into a gypsy queen. You keep on looking out for an Adam's apple.

'It's so good to see you, Tom,' she smiled wistfully. 'We weren't sure when we'd see you again.'

Why? I wanted to ask, desperately. Because I was through with Dublin? Because I was through with Mainie? Because Mainie was through with me? What had Mainie told them?

But these were questions I could not ask. Iremonger doesn't ask desperate questions.

'It's good to see you,' I replied, 'you're looking great, Lucia. Better than any of those little girls downstairs.'

'That's what I said to you, wasn't it Teddy, darling?'

SuperDoyle, who had sat down and was opening a supercan of Harp, assented with a saucy grunt.

'Then what are you doing up here watching the Percy Tóibín Show when all the action is downstairs?' I guess I was talking to myself as much as her. I was itchy for a hit. I was itchy for Mainie. But here I was instead, with the minutes of my precious hour slipping away, talking to her wrinklies instead. It was like I had stayed at Cedar-of-Lebanon Road. But I knew I couldn't let my impatience show. I still didn't want to fuck with Teddy or his wife in any way. Hence the charming Iremonger routine.

Lucia grabbed my wrist, a sure sign that revelation was on its way. 'Oh no, it's not Percy Tóibín this year. He's sick. Carmel told us that he has cancer.'

'I think we've seen the last of Percy Tóibín doing the New Year's Eve programme,' Teddy sighed.

'I believe she's here tonight,' I said.

'She *was* here,' Lucia answered. 'She paid us a flying visit – literally because Tony O'Reilly sent a helicopter for her. I think she left her son behind as a kind of representative. In fact, she was asking for you. She was very curious about where you'd be tonight. She asked Mainie if you were coming here.'

I laughed lightly and added, as inconsequentially as I could,' And what did Mainie say?'

'Mainie said she didn't even know if you were still in Dublin.'

I wanted to sigh with relief. Good answer, I thought, good answer.

'Well, somewhat to my surprise, I still am. And I guess I'd better make the most of it and get some partying in. So I'll leave you two in peace.'

'Right yeh are, Tom,' said Mainie's father, not getting up. 'We'll be down for midnight. We'll see you later.'

I started to walk towards the door.

'Oh, Tom,' called Lucia, 'one more thing.' I turned around. 'In case I don't get a chance to talk to you later, in all the noise. How's your mother? We haven't seen her around the golf club in weeks and weeks.'

I nodded slowly, trying to think of something. 'Yeah, so she tells me. Well, she's been a little preoccupied lately.

My uncle is home from Africa and she's been looking after him.'

Lucia nodded sympathetically. I knew she didn't believe me.

'Well, give her my best. Tell her I hope she can make it for the Lady Captain's Winter Classic on the 19th. We're raising money for the Impecunious Roomkeepers this year.'

She smiled with an exaggerated sweetness.

'I'll be sure to tell her, Mrs Doyle.'

This time the bathroom was free. From Nico's most intimate pocket I pulled out my baggy of B-Special. I cut two lines on the green Italian marble of the wash-hand basin with a little antique pen-knife I'd picked up in Geneva and snorted them with a rolled joyce. Oh, I wanted to give Bish McQuaid a round of applause straight away – this was nasal champagne. I put the rest of the sneachta deep within Nico once again, flushed through force of habit, and unlocked the bathroom's fat lead key. Already that fine powder had been converted into Iremonger-energy. I was ready to do my thing. I was ready for Mainie Doyle.

I knew where she was. My party-animal antennae told me. The bar room, or, as Lucia insisted on calling it, the Yeats room. It was her idea that Teddy should commemorate his victory in the croissant war by buying at Sotheby's a small Jack B. Yeats oil painting of this Firbolg type brooding on a park bench while two doe-eyed, old-fashioned fashionable babes sitting on the neighbouring bench laugh and gossip. Personally I could think of better ways to blow three hundred grand but, as my father likes to say, there's no point arguing with other people's taste. I don't know why I'm wasting my breath explaining this because the painting that was there now, during the party, was nothing more than a reproduction. If I hadn't known that, however, I would never have guessed. I wondered what Strongbow could see that I couldn't see, now that he was in the SuperDoyle loop.

He and Mainie were standing near the bar, holding casual court, like she and I had done so many times before. But it wasn't jealousy that upset me – it was what she was wearing. I had fully expected that she would be dressed allusively – wearing something that was a heartbreaking (in her dreams) reminder of some highlight in our history: perhaps the silky sapphire Donna Karen number she'd worn the night we'd gone to Carravaggio's, our favourite Italian, to celebrate the sale of Raglan Road, or one of the benchmark dresses she'd worn to the Ball (girlfriends came and boyfriends went but Mainie Doyle and Iremonger *always* went to the Trinity Ball together). Tonight she was wearing a sequined, knee-length LBD with matching tuxedo jacket that I reckoned to be Givenchy but had certainly never seen her wear before. I just couldn't work out what kind of signal she was sending me.

The way Strongbow was dressed also got to me. His tuxedo was as conservative as Brían Firbolg's, but retro cut, crisply pressed, elegantly worn. His collar was wing-tipped, his hair brylcremed back. He was Merchant-Ivory. He was F. Scott Fitzfuckingerald. I felt . . . eclipsed by him. After all these years, back to being overshadowed by Strongbow. I almost regretted that I was wearing Nico and not something a little more Louis Copeland, a little more IDA. But did I let it show? Of course not. As I sauntered over to the bar, I made insouciance look like a state of anxiety.

'Hello, Tom. Welcome to the party.' The tone of her voice and smile was confident, amused, jaded. What a wonderful facade, I thought.

'Hey, Mainie. Thanks for having me. Hey . . . Sinj.'

Strongbow nodded at me very politely. Excusing myself, I went to the bar and ordered a Bombay gimlet, watching out of the corner of my eye for a reaction from Mainie;

there was none. Out of the corner of my other eye there was better news – the kind of girl that would drive Mainie crazy was staring at me from the other end of the bar. I turned and gave her my most devastating Iremonger smile – I had no time to waste. Her reciprocal smile disappeared into a long glass of Southern Comfort.

'What's your name?' I asked her.

Aoife Wren told me and, after a hesitation, approached me, attempting to look sultry. She had a compactly pretty face with notable brown-sugar eyes, she had a decent body, but I knew she was a virgin: she lacked that fluent sexiness that women like Mainie have. But she had ambitions in that direction – the way she moved her bare, freckled shoulders told me more than I needed to know about Miss Aoife Wren.

'I'm Tom—'

She provided my last name with an exclamation, as I thought she might.

'I've heard so much about you,' she continued. 'And I've seen you in the airport, of course.'

I nodded an *of course* of my own.

'Is it true you brought Samuel Beckett to a nightclub just before for he died?' she bubbled.

I sighed. 'That story has become a little distorted with time.'

'I'd love to hear the real story.'

My Bombay gimlet had arrived. I knocked it back. The holistic hum that I had walked into the room with was already fading – looked like I needed to stoke up the fire in my brain.

'Oh, you will, some time. Why don't you tell me about Aoife Wren first.'

She did, and I nodded along – I knew it all already. St Agnes girl. Still in college, Economics and Spanish at yucky death. Summers working in London, Boston, Barcelona.

Couldn't wait to graduate, to get a full-time life abroad. Wanted to come back and raise a family here, of course. I nodded vaguely. I was thinking about the poster of Mainie Doyle in *Cara*.

Suddenly people were checking their watches and stirring – the tacit countdown had begun. One minute and thirty-five seconds, according to my Tzara, which also showed me that the new year was getting old on the Continent.

'Shouldn't we be moving into the ballroom?' Aoife asked tentatively.

'Sure,' I replied quietly. I looked around slyly. They were no longer in the room. How long ago had they left? I felt the B-Special fizzle away in my system. I felt uninspired.

'Well, shall we?' Aoife Wren said pertly.

'Absolutely,' I responded, distracted.

We walked across the emptying room arm in arm, but in the hall I said, 'Aoife, I'll join you in a minute, but there's something I've got to do first.'

'It can't wait?' she asked timidly. 'It's almost midnight.'

I was already on the stairs. 'Nature calls.'

On the cream tiling near the wash-hand basin I spotted a drop of blood – I wasn't the only one who'd come to use this convenience. I could faintly hear them shouting the countdown as I cut the rest of the Special into three lines. As I hoovered the first I could faintly hear them shouting the countdown to midnight. The second I snorted to the accompaniment of 'Aul' Lang Sigh'. Faraway fog horns celebrated my final line. Happy New Year, Iremonger.

Coming down the stairs the Special really began to kick in. I had to hang on to the banister, my hand anchoring me in case the rest of my body decided to dive into space. In the hall Dylan stopped me.

'So, Jesus, it is true – you are here.'

'Here and there.' I tried a nonchalant shrug, but my shoulders leapt up as far as my ear lobes.

'Hey, what are you up to, Iremonger?'

'I'm having a religious experience.'

'You got any more?'

'As my little nephew says, *allgone*.'

Dylan smiled sourly. 'Happy New Year to you too, Tom.'

I hugged myself to control the chemical carnival going on inside me, remembering that I had a serious matter to discuss with Dylan Carraig-Dubh.

'Did your mother have fun here?' Real question: Did she ask where I was?

'Yeah. She's really fallen for that Strongbow guy. You can expect to see his name in bold print next week.'

'Is the Heinz helicopter bringing her back here?'

'I seriously doubt it. The party's in Kerry. But don't worry.' He winked. 'I'll tell her that you made it, finally. She was kind of curious about where you were. Anyway, you can find us in the bar. Roderick's just introduced me to a very strong Perfect Girlfriend candidate. I think she may be the one!'

'Know what you mean,' I muttered as Dylan walked off towards the Yeats Room.

Aoife Wren was waiting for me just inside the door of the ballroom.

'Happy New Year!' She kissed me on the cheek. I kissed her back on the lips. She looked a little stunned. The DJ was playing the acidy remix of one of the big Dub-Lin hits of the dead year, an obsessive beat, a virginal voice, a loop of addictive melody that had followed me from Ireland, through the white-hot clubs of the Western world, and back again. My heart was imitating the rhythm. I began, choicelessly, this vertically oriented, industrial dance that often emerged from my body on occasions such as this.

Aoife began to dance too, but hers was ballet in comparison. And then the music faded out. My system was screaming encore. But other people were applauding, cheering, turning their attention towards the turntables.

Feedback, and then its polar opposite, Mainie Doyle's amplified voice. The DJ handed her his mike. Teddy and Lucia were standing behind her, smiling benevolently. Mainie was about to make a speech.

'Well, it's the new year, everybody!' Another cheer. Mainie, a thank-you addict, started in on the appreciation routine. I started moving through the crowd, drawn not by what she said, but the way she said it – the soft melodrama of that South Dublin inflection, with hints of Trinity and a J-1 summer in New York. Iremonger radar picked up some chicks and guys giving me some funny looks; maybe I got a little bargy – I guess the B-Special was affecting my normally fluid co-ordination. I stood as close to the front as I could without looking like some Mainie Doyle flunky. Only then did I realise that I had dragged Aoife Wren with me, like a teddy bear. 'Oh, hi,' I said apologetically.

'Let's listen,' replied Aoife, posing her suggestion as a fragile question.

'Sure.'

I tried to concentrate on the content of what Mainie was saying, not just the music. I caught this much,

'. . . and can you imagine what this city would be like if all of us lived here the whole time? Not that it would be like Christmas week fifty-two weeks a year, but there would be an incredible buzz . . .'

The incredible thing was that my buzz was fading again, and I had no more Ardal powder to fall back on. It might have been good shit that he'd sold me, but it was also the quickest shit I'd ever snorted, and that meant that it was ultimately bad shit. And considering my present needs, it was the worst shit anybody had ever sold me in my life.

And if things didn't work out the way I wanted them to, Bish was in deep shit.

Mainie was now telling everybody how in the coming year she would be travelling incessantly, basically living on an aeroplane, but that she was going to be based in London, and how everybody on their way home tonight should not only put an up-to-date address in the guest book in the hall, but also pick up one of the little green cards with her new Notting Hill address. 'Or should I say, *our* new address,' she said coyly, extending one of her lithe arms. 'Come here, Sinj.' Applause broke out as Strongbow emerged elegantly from the shadows. There was a disturbing warmth in the way Mainie's parents clapped and smiled. Teddy flung out his right hand – Strongbow shook it instantly, vigorously. He was rewarded with a paternal four-fingered slap on the back. Strongbow then took his place beside Mainie Doyle in the coloured pool of light around the turntables. They put their arms around each other lightly. Without quite deciding to, I was leading Aoife Wren through the crowd towards the door of the ballroom.

'But I want to hear what he says,' she tentatively protested.

'Trust me. He doesn't say much. Just stands there and looks pretty.'

We were standing in the hall by now.

'Where are we going?' asked Aoife.

I had this sudden desire to suggest that we go into the dining room and trash the long buffet table that would be laid out there, the fruit of the SuperDoyle flagship store in Dun Laoghaire, smashing the large Waterford crystal bowls of Teddy's chunky punch. But this proved to be the last flare up of the Special. I had a much better idea. Or a less desperate idea. I started walking up the stairs.

'Where are you going?' Aoife asked.

I turned around, smiled down at her, and kept on

climbing. For a scary moment I thought I had misjudged things badly but then, as I reached the first-floor landing, I heard light, rapid footsteps behind me. Aoife Wren stopped on the return, looking up with a nervous, curious face. 'Should we be going up here?' she asked.

'Yes, we should.'

I started to climb up the stairs to the second floor. Aoife Wren was catching up with me fast. Outside Mainie Doyle's bedroom I spun around and gave her a demonstration of superdelicate kissing. About two minutes later she broke the light connection and looked into my eyes. She looked as if she had been the one taking drugs.

'So the rumours are true,' she said.

I shrugged bashfully and, without looking around, turned the doorknob, and started backing into the room. Scandal ran across Aoife's face. 'Whose bedroom is this?' she whispered.

'This is a guest room.'

I left her there on the threshold and went and lay down on the queen-sized antique brass bed, a bed that was too small for me to ever get a comfortable night's sleep in, but that was perfect for snug fucking. The light from the landing illuminated, among other things, her collection of Madame Alexander dolls. For years she had been searching for the Thai doll. On my travels I always kept an eye out for it. Maybe this year I could dedicate myself to finding it.

'Are you sure this is a guest room?' Aoife said.

'I've stayed here many times.'

That convinced her to come in and close the door.

'Do you mind if I leave the light off, Tom?'

'I'd prefer it that way, Aoife.' I came so close to calling her Mainie.

What was I doing? What was the story, now that my storyboard was smashed? Well, I did have a plan. I didn't exactly have a hard-on for it, but under the circumstances I couldn't think of anything else. So, Plan B: I would leave my calling card. I would leave blood on the sheets.

How did it work out? Let me put it this way:

Late last summer, this École Normal Superieur chick named Odile I was seeing brought me to a Vietnamese restaurant on the rue du Dragon, off the Boulevard St Germain. She asked me if I'd ever eaten shitaki mushrooms. I hadn't. With a mischievous smile she recommended I try them. I did. And could scarcely believe my tongue. That texture, those contours – uncanny. But now, down on Aoife Wren, all I could think about was . . . eating shitaki mushrooms.

I was speechless. I couldn't bring myself to say, *This has never happened to me before*, mostly because it was true. This had never happened to Iremonger before. It was against my nature. By *definition* this couldn't happen. Finally she spoke, 'It's okay, Tom. It really is. In fact, maybe it's better like this.'

Now I found my voice. 'Better?'

'Yes. I'm not sure I wanted to go the whole way. Not with you. I mean, not tonight.' It was as if she'd had a short-lived B-Special rush too.

I got off the bed and started to dress quickly. This involved taking off Nico, putting the rest of my clothes on, and putting on Nico once more. I could see Aoife reaching for a lamp.

'No. Please. As you said, better with the light off.'

'Okay,' she replied, very softly.

I made out from the dulled phosphorescence of my Tzara that it was approaching 12:30.

'Jesus.'

'Are you okay?'

'Aoife, you're going to hate me for this, but I've got a taxi coming about two minutes ago.'

She drew breath in wistfully. 'No, it's okay. Go. I'll come downstairs in a few minutes.'

I pulled on my Boccionis balancing awkwardly on the other leg.

With my hand on the cold doorknob something inside me collapsed. I turned around. She had pulled the duvet off the floor and over herself and had turned away from me.

'Aoife?'

'Yes?' was her hesitant and muffled reply.

'This is just between you and me, right?'

It was so silent in that room during the long moment that followed that I could hear raucous laughter rising from the driveway and a rumour of rhythm from the ballroom.

'Right,' said Aoife Wren.

Rounding the return between the first and ground floors, I changed my pace, simulated the Iremonger saunter as best I could. Good thing – the party had spilled back into the hallway, and a lot of upturned faces smiled a big wink at me. I wasn't about to disillusion them. They made way for me, particularly the guys, a fluid guard of honour. By now I had a smile tacked on my own face, but my eyes were fixed on that bevelled, stained-glass front door. I wanted to charge through them, that transient gang, get out into the night as soon as possible. A good thing Mainie or Strongbow, or Teddy or Lucia, or even Roderick or Dylan didn't get in my way just then. I would have had no choice but to shove them aside.

The coat-check girl presented me with Nico's lambswool lining like an offering.

I felt a hand on my shoulder. I froze, then turned around very slowly, ready to strike. It was Firbolg. I had totally forgotten about Firbolg. I sighed.

'I guess you want to share this taxi with me back to Owenstown Hill.'

'No!' he replied gleefully.

'No?'

'No. I'm having a very nice time, Tom. In fact,' he slurped conspiratorially, 'I think I might get lucky?'

'Get *lucky*?'

'Yeah, you know – get off with a girl. She started to talk to me in that big room with the bar. Turns out she's in UCD too. Studying to be a vet. Came here with her sister. They're all out of punch in there, so I'm going to the buffet room to get two more glasses.'

'That's great, Brían.' I slapped him on the shoulder. 'That's absolutely wonderful.'

'Well, thanks for making me come!'

'My pleasure. Anytime.' I started to turn around.

'You're leaving?'

'Other parties to go to, Brían. Other parties.'

'Oh, of course. Well, Happy New Year, Iremonger!'

I didn't return the compliment. Neither did I write an up-to-date contact address in the guest book or pick up one of Mainie and Strongbow's little green cards.

Outside on Merano Road, no taxi. I lit up a Roland (T - 71) and tried to ignore the moonlighting guard from Cork.

'Good party?' he asked presently.

I took an impossibly long drag on my Roland and blew out through a tiny aperture in my lips before mumbling, 'Wonderful. I was the life and soul.'

I heard a car labouring up the hill. Yes, indeed, it was Martello Cabs. At least they hadn't let me down.

Speeding along the dual carriageway an old familiar echoing piano riff came on the radio.

'Turn that off,' I snapped.

The taxi driver pretended he hadn't heard me. Ol' Bono started to sing,

All is quiet on New Year's Day
A world in white gets under way
I want to be with you, be with you night and day
Nothing changes on New Year's Day

I sighed. 'Please.'
He changed the station.

8

Saviour

This is not a sight for sore eyes – my mother sitting at the kitchen table wearing a pair of upside-down glasses with saucer-sized lenses and lavender-and-white plastic frames. They belonged to her spinster sister Nora, and are now part of her eyewear-of-the-dead collection. You see, no matter who dies in our family, my mother will insist, after a suitable grieving period, that their glasses are just the right prescription for her to read with, regardless of whether the loved one was near- or far-sighted. She even has the old man's pince-nez somewhere. In the past, my father has made dark jokes about his bifocals, but not since I've come back. Nora's are her favourite, and they really get on my nerves. They magnify her eyes, blow them up. And as she looks up now from her newspaper, the effect is intensified by her ironic surprise.

'Look at himself. What are you doing up before midday?'

'Happy New Year to you too, Mum.'

'Let's hope it will be, Tom,' she says ruefully, reaching for the king-sized Gossamer that has been sending up bland smoke from the Marbella ashtray. 'Let's hope it will be.'

Something else is bothering me. 'Mum that's not *Ireland on Sunday* you're reading.'

She looks up at me again with amused googly eyes. 'You're right, Tom, it's not. I knew there was some reason we sent you to Trinity.'

This is no time for second-rate sarcasm; she knows that as well as I do. This is an unprecedented situation, a major break with tradition: my mother is reading one of the British newspapers – and *The Observer*, to boot – before *Ireland on Sunday*. And that's the one paper I don't see in front of her on the table.

'Where is *Ireland on Sunday*?' I demand.

My mother scrutinises me with huge shrewd eyes. 'Do you know what's on the cover?'

'On the *cover*?' It takes me just a moment to absorb this. 'Yeah, I can guess.'

'Your father has it,' she says, turning a page. Tradition has been shattered. 'He's sitting inside in the drawing room with your uncle.' Tradition has been trampled in the dirt.

'Dad's up already?'

'Well, he went to bed just after midnight.'

I choose not to remember what I was doing just after midnight.

'I'm going to take a look at it,' I say as I turn and leave the kitchen, as much to myself as to my mother because I am now in two minds. I am, of course, obsessed with the idea of reading about myself in the paper, particularly in a high-brow rag like *IoS*, particularly if I've made the front page. But if I've embarrassed or upset my parents, particularly my father, then I'm going to be pissed with myself. That's a feeling I haven't had in a very long time.

My father being up this early on a Sunday – another

bad sign. Usually he doesn't stir out of the bed until he has done a thorough reconnaissance and selective reading of the block of British newspapers my mother brings up to him after she gets back from ten o'clock mass in Booterstown; she keeps the trim *Ireland on Sunday* downstairs for herself. (Above the masthead of each paper, in newsagent scrawl, is some garbled version of our name: Iremoner – Iremaner – Iremoney.) The leaps my father must make across the political spectrum as he goes from one Brit broadsheet to another don't phase him. What does annoy him, to the point of threatening continuously in the past few years to cancel our order, is that *The Sunday Times* now produces its own Irish edition, distorting the authentic item now being read in the Owenstown Hills of North London and Buckinghamshire; he fears *The Observer* and *The Sunday Telegraph* will go the same way. 'When I want Irish news, I read an Irish newspaper,' he likes to say. He gets around to *IoS* in the late afternoon, muttering editorials to himself as he skims through it.

But this morning he hasn't been able to stay in his bed. He's been forced out of it to face the Irish news, the Iremonger news. I really don't want to go in there and deal with that. But at the same time I've got to know what that bitch wrote about me. Is there a photograph? Have they reproduced a still from Strongbow's video?

At the door of the drawing room, hand on handle, I stop. It sounds like my father and uncle are arguing. I can hear my father say quite clearly, 'I've given up trying to understand you. I think you're actually *pleased* that the Iremonger name is being dragged through the mud.'

My uncle's voice is much more subdued. He says something like, 'In Remoko there's an insect called the sun ant. During the rainy season it lives deep underground—'

'Ah, Jesus, Columb, enough about Africa. Get to the point.'

After a short silence, he does, 'There's something inevitable about the discovery of the truth, Rich.'

'This isn't the truth.' A thumping sound. 'This is only half the story.'

Way to go, Dad! I wasn't expecting my father to be so emphatically in my corner. Now I can go in. My entrance is announced by the brittle lowering of the handle. In fact, I wasn't expecting my father to be in *anybody's* corner, given his attitude towards arguing with family members. My uncle is sitting in the armchair at the other end of the room exactly as I imagined he would be: long, thin legs crossed, fingertips joined prayerfully. My father is not as together as I imagined him. He gives me a haggard look over his shoulder. And there in his hands is the front page of *Ireland on Sunday*. Below the masthead and above the main headline, in a space that the paper habitually reserves for a titillating story with a veneer of newsworthiness, is the headline, SHOCK OVER DUBLIN'S HOLOCAUST DIASPORA SHAME. In the left-hand corner, partially obscured by my father's thumb, is an old photograph of my grandfather.

'Happy New Year, Tom,' Uncle Columb says.

'Hey, same to you,' I reply, hovering near my father, wondering how I can get out of here. I've wandered into none of my business. What can I say?

'Dad, are you done with the Lifestyle section?' I ask breezily.

His face sours. 'This is all a joke to you, I suppose.'

I bring my hands up defensively. 'No, not at all. How can I make a joke out of something I don't know about?'

That long Iremonger arm of his puts *IoS* in my hands. I shrug reasonably, – last thing I want is a fight – sit down on the couch, and unfold the paper. My father and uncle are watching me: my father's off-white eyes distrustful and hurt-laden; Columb staring at me like he's checking out my soul, the way I check out a woman's body. Under these circumstances, it's more comfortable to read, to focus on my homework. Although I've never seen this photo of the old man before, I've seen others like it: working at his desk in the department wearing a three-piece tweed suit, sober tie and pince-nez, hair grey-streaked, face vigorous, thick fountain pen in his hand, matters of State before him, civil servant of a black-and-white world. *This* is the man in the painting. The caption underneath reads: *Iremonger: Christian*. The article is by Kyle Collins, *IoS* Heritage Correspondent.

The wartime Department of Internal Affairs actively obstructed desperate attempts by Jewish refugees to escape Hitler. That is just one of the dramatic revelations contained in newly declassified government documents. Under the new Freedom of Information Act, signed into law by President Robinson last summer, thousands of files previously exempted from the 30-year rule can be published as of today. Officials at the Office of Public Records gave journalists initial access to the former secrets for the first time on Friday.

The new information casts further light on the prejudicial way government officials, including ministers and top civil servants, dealt with applications from European Jews to settle in this country before, during, and after World War II.

The most startling evidence of the government's negative attitude towards the refugee crisis comes in a series of memos written by the Secretary of the Department of Internal Affairs, Anraí Iremonger.

In 1935, Iremonger became the youngest ever civil servant to hold that top position, the same year an Aliens Act made his department the responsible ministry for processing residency visa applications. In 1938, Iremonger issued a confidential memorandum stating that it would be departmental policy to apply immigration law 'less liberally to Jews than other applicants' because 'any substantial increase in our Jewish population might give rise to an anti-Semitic problem.' In December 1938, a month after *Kristalnacht*, a night of Nazi-organised terror against Jews and their property, Iremonger personally reviewed requests from three German Jewish doctors and their families. One was accepted, on the grounds that the doctor had 'Christian relatives in this country'.

Even after the war and the discovery of the death camps, Iremonger's line did not soften. In June 1946, the Chief Rabbi of Ireland presented the department with a proposal to care for three dozen orphans of Auschwitz at Butler Castle in County Kilkenny. The entire cost of the operation was to be funded by the Jewish community in Ireland; the Chief Rabbi offered guarantees that the children would be relocated if permanent homes could not be found for them in Ireland. Iremonger instructed his officials to reject the plan, explaining that 'it has always been departmental policy to regard a large Jewish population as a potential irritant in the body politic.' This decision was ultimately overruled by the Taoiseach, Eamon de Valera.

That's it – I've read enough. Why does all this crap have to come out on New Year's Day? Why not on February the 24th? I fold the paper and put it to one side. My father and uncle are watching me in their different ways, waiting for me to respond. I shrug. 'Well, that's not cool.'

Columb lowers his fingers, smiles richly, and says softly, 'To say the least.'

My father is not smiling. 'Ah, you don't know half the story. You didn't even *read* half the story.'

As a gesture, I pick up the paper again, look at that exact

man in the photograph. A question swells inside me. I look up at the man's eldest son, his jaded imitation. I hesitate, 'So . . . you don't think he was, like, anti-Semitic?'

For a long moment my father closes his bulging eyes and sighs, a prayer for patience. 'No, Tom, he was not anti-Semitic. Your uncle here is probably too young to remember this, but I haven't forgotten my father's reaction when he heard Richard Dimbleby's reports on the BBC from Belsen. The man was close to tears. Was that the reaction of an anti-Semite?'

Columb clasps his hands together, adopts a brotherly tone. 'Risteárd, I know Daddy wasn't a racist. And that's not what we should take from the article.'

My father clucks and sighs with exasperation as he squirms and fidgets with his belt. 'Ah, Columb, I didn't come down in the last shower. I know what the implication is, and so do you.' Then a surprising aside to me, 'These Jesuits are big on implication.' I support him with a strained smile.

Columb is unruffled. He's brought his fingertips together again, a little tent of meditation. 'Well, what I took from the article was that if Daddy was guilty of anything, it was a failure of the imagination. A failure to make connections, a failure to bring the conscience of the private man who was moved by those reports on the radio – which I do remember, by the way – together with the sense of duty of the public man. I think it's true to say that sometimes Daddy identified too closely with his job, that he was too much the civil servant. Too eager to be merely the instrument of his minister.'

All through this, my father has been itching to speak. 'I wouldn't accuse my father of being guilty of anything, especially since the man is not here to defend himself, something that the editors of that rag might have remembered before they splattered his name, our name, all over the front page.' The door opens – thank god – and my mother comes in; my father continues without even looking over his shoulder. 'The one thing I've always tried not to be is judgemental. I don't judge the living' – I swear he glances at me as he says that – 'so why should I judge the dead?'

My mother has walked over behind his chair. She touches my father's shoulder and stares at both me and my uncle. 'I knew this would turn into a fight.'

My father squeezes the hand on his shoulder. 'A discussion, Sinéad. Just a discussion.'

My uncle lowers his fingertips and shrugs his shoulders. 'An argument, perhaps.'

'A fight I'd call it. And this is no time for fighting.'

No one argues with that. My mother turns to me. 'I hope you're coming up to Triona and Finbar's for lunch.'

'Sure,' I reply. 'When are we going?'

I've been doing something that doesn't come naturally to me: keeping a low profile. Roderick and Dylan have phoned a bunch of times, but I've told my mother to say I'm out. She's had a lot of lying to do. I've been in ever since we got back from lunch at my sister's, two days ago. I don't think I've spent this long at home since that time I was grounded in the nascent Iremonger days. I ask myself the same question that nagged me at the airport, way back on Christmas Eve: what am I doing here? This time many reasons suggest themselves. But *many reasons* doesn't cut it with me. There's always *the* reason, isn't there? I've always had a talent for sussing it out in others. It's myself I can't suss out. So I've been keeping a low profile, wondering why I'm keeping a low profile, wondering what the hell has grounded me this time.

It was my father who grounded me last time, and it could be argued that once again he's the reason why I've been staying in. That's certainly what my mother thinks – that this Howard Hughes act is a quiet display of filial solidarity. In my father's hour of unspoken need. In her hour of unspoken need. I wish.

She hasn't come right out and said so, of course. But it's in her twinkly eyes and tender smile every time the phone rings and I remind her to cover for me. All that's required is a simple lie, but she puts a great deal of dramatic energy into informing Roderick or Dylan about my absence and unknown, and probably unknowable, whereabouts, speaking in a telephone voice worthy of the queen. I haven't heard such bullshit since I stood in line at INS pre-clearance at Shannon airport. So much for her honesty-is-the-best-policy mantra. This newly revealed talent makes me wonder what else my mother has lied about in her life. (It makes me wonder about her life.) As Lou Reed says, You can't always trust your mother.

Her tacit gratitude is making me edgy, but for now I think I can resist ruining her illusion. To tell the truth, it's not because I want to be drawn into the bosom of my family that I don't want to talk to Roderick and Dylan. I don't want to talk to Roderick or Dylan (or any of my other old satellites) because I don't want to see them. And if I go out, go out anywhere worthy of the name in the incestuous fishing village that is Dublin, I will see them. Wish to Christ I was in vast Lalaland. Maybe that's what I'll do. As soon as I hit the ground at CDG, I'll book a flight to LAX.

And why don't I want to see them? Well, I go through phases – particularly late at night when I'm trying, unsuccessfully, to wash away my burgeoning insomnia with the best my parents' drinks cabinet has to offer – I go through phases when I think that they are *in on it*, particularly de Brun. What exactly *it* is I cannot say – the plot, the intrigue, or simple *understanding* I first sniffed in

Roderick's kitchen after the swim. At other times, usually during my drained daylight life, I tell myself that this is all just chemical- and booze-induced paranoia. But maybe *that* is just wishful thinking. Even Iremonger has enemies, you know.

So I don't want to see them, the bastards. But I also don't want them to see *me*. They'll have seen the story about the old man, and maybe found out the truth about New Year's Eve. I don't want them asking questions I can't even ask myself. And there are other things, things that make me feel . . . less than myself, things that make me wonder how I can look Dylan or Roderick in the eye.

The Strongbow story, for one thing. When I finally got a chance to look at 'Dove Tales' – at Triona's house, retreating into the downstairs toilet to read it in private – I discovered, to my relief and despair, that there was no mention of me, not directly anyway. I had to resort to deconstruction (at least they taught me one useful skill in college) to find any hint of my existence. Iremonger was there by implication in a long, fawning passage about the bold-faced Strongbow, Mainie Doyle's new 'beau'. Here's the highlight: 'Not only is St John well connected, superbly educated, and drop-dead gorgeous, he is also an immensely talented young film director. I saw evidence of this with my own eyes at **Ulick de Brun**'s barrister-infested post-swim bash, where St John let me take a look at some crisp video he'd just shot down at the Forty Foot. Revealing images, folks. All I can say is that when it comes to swimmers, length really matters.' Well, there you have it, don't you?

Strongbow, yes. I'd put my money – or my credit line – on him being the reason for these Iremonger blues. As long as I'm in this town I'll feel like I'm in his shadow, whether he's actually here or back to London. Strongbow's shadow – I've been there before, and I don't think I can deal with it again. Once I find out what the results of my father's tests are, I'm out of here. Dublin is history.

Of course, my Strongbow problem is closely connected with my Mainie Doyle problem. There are compelling reasons to believe that she is the reason, and that she is the one behind this . . . Iremonger trashing.

One other possibility, of course. The Bish. That fuckology specialist. I've little doubt that McQuaid deliberately screwed me with that last batch of B-Special. My tolerance level can't be that high. But why? What's in it for him? Maybe Strongbow paid him off to set me up – to please Mainie. So much for four years of loyal friendship and patronage. Well, now Ardal is the one who's going to pay. That's another thing I've been doing these two long interior days: psyching myself to deal with Bish. Pulling myself together. I need to be at least 90% Iremonger to pull this off because dealing with Bish means going into town, stepping on stage.

Half an hour ago I left a message on his answering machine in college and with his parents in Killiney. I'm waiting for his call.

But, hey, don't think that these past two days have been uneventful. For one thing I got to spend quality time with members of my family. We may not have been in the same room much, but compared to the rest of this holiday season we've been positively intimate. And last night I even had a frank exchange with one of them – my grandfather.

It was probably closer to dawn than midnight; I wasn't wearing my Tzara. Search me why I ended up standing in front of his portrait, knocking back the last drops of Kells, the dimmer on the overhead light way up high this time. Maybe I wanted to see if he looked different in the depths of the night. He was suffering from insomnia just like me, but it didn't seem to bother him in the least. He looked just as sure of himself as he did in the daylight.

'Hey,' I said, holding up the bottle so that those pale-green eyes of his could read the label. 'Did you know that this shit has been sacred for centuries?'

My grandfather neither confirmed nor denied any knowledge of the holy nature of my drink.

'I thought you might be interested. I thought you were big on things sacred. Sacred honour. Sacred trust. The Sacred Heart of Jesus. The sacred nature of the foetus. Everything in the sacred department.'

The old man suffered me.

'Yeah, all life is sacred. That was your mantra, wasn't it, during the abortion wars? All life is sacred. End of story.'

Now I saw a glimmer of cold pity in those pale-green eyes. That condescension had stopped me before, but not this time.

'Pity you couldn't have applied your great principle to people who weren't Irish, who weren't Catholic.'

His image smouldered, and I could tell exactly what he was thinking – *Give me back my money, you ungrateful little pup*.

It was then I asked myself what the fuck I was doing standing there talking to acrylic paint.

Even more exciting is the reading I've been doing. Yes, I gave into a nagging nostalgia for books. I've been quite the scholar these past two days, taking a refresher course, Iremonger 101. Been going to night school, thanks to my insomnia. Basically it's involved rereading – or, more precisely, attempting to reread – all the classics from the Iremonger cannon, the texts that helped make me who I am. But all the old favourites have left me cold. I've gone right through the top shelf of my bookcase – Rimbaud and Jim Morrison, *On the Road* and *The Outsider*, Jean Cocteau and *Junky*, deconstructionists and minor beats – without anything gelling with my mood. Some top-shelf tequila is what I need.

Last night about four a.m., giddy with boredom, I even picked up that little red book Columb had given me as a Christmas present. Just for laughs. The introduction said that the book had been structured so that it could be used as a companion to St Ignatius's Spiritual Exercises. That was nice to know. Flicking through it I was amazed by how many of the names I recognised: Faber, Xavier, Berrigan, Edmund Campion, Arrupe and Teilhard de Chardin, Gerard Manley Hopkins – those trippy poems *prayers*? – and my main man, young John Berchmans. My eyes rebelled against reading the longer prayers – too thorny, too intense. But they couldn't help but get through the shorter ones, some of them very short, I mean William Carlos Williams short (the subject of the longest paper I ever wrote at Trinity). I didn't enjoy reading them, but somehow I couldn't help it; I kept on flicking those pages, and my eyes kept falling upon these little prayers, these pious epiphanies. What were they about? The usual crap: devotion and vocation, sin and forgiveness, death and resurrection. The things I had left behind. The things I had left behind so long ago that I could barely remember ever regarding them as a big deal. And lying there on my bed, fully clothed at six or seven or eight o'clock on a winter's morning, I felt vaguely jealous of Iremonger-types – if there were any – who'd been around in my grandfather's or even my father's time and for whom quitting the Church had been a big deal, something you could make a scene out of in a movie, perhaps. For me, brought up in the era when the high point of mass was some retarded hippie your sister fancied singing and strumming 'You've Got a Friend' during communion, it was a non-event.

But one thing. I've got to admit that I can't get one of those miniature prayers out of my mind, that I have quite unintentionally *committed it to memory*. It's by this Jesuit named de Mello. I'm sure Columb knows his stuff (not that I'm going to ask him). Prayer goes like this,

> Both what you run away from— and yearn for—
> is within you

On one level I'm telling myself that's paradoxical bullshit; on another level I can't stop those words running through my head. Most irritating of all, I hear them being spoken in Columb's voice, my uncle's calm, melancholy cadences. With the bloody Berchmans choir singing 'The Coventry Carol' in the background.

So, okay, the last two days haven't been so hot. But today is going to be different. Today, refreshed by no less than two hours' sleep only lightly flavoured by nightmares, I am going to get my shit together. And get some good shit. The very best shit. Which some might say is also the very worst shit there is – the big H.

You see, I've decided it's time to get serious about drugs.

What else is there left to do?

Twenty minutes to midday the phone rings. I pick up in the kitchen. My mother picks up in her bedroom.

'I've got it, Mum.'

Hesitantly she says, 'Are you sure, Tom?'

'Yeah, no problem. I know who this is.' And I do, even though the person on the other line hasn't said a word yet. I can see him smirking and running his hand through that designer-wild red hair.

'Oh, okay then.' She replaces the handset awkwardly.

Slick silence. Psyched by him returning the call I maintain it: he breaks it.

'How's it going, Iremonger?'

'Never better, Bish.'

'That's good. Not used to getting messages in the, eh, imperative. I can only assume this is an emergency.'

'Oh, not really. I just wanted to talk to customer service.'

'Always here for you, Tom. Always here with good advice.'

'That's funny because I got some really shitty advice around midnight New Year's Eve.'

'What happened, turn into a pumpkin?'

'No, I turned into a problem. A big problem. Your problem.' Now *that* sounds more like it. That sounds more like me. Ardal is silent for a moment.

'I see. Well, how can you be solved, Iremonger?'

'Lots of free advice.'

Ardal sighs. 'I'm not sure I'm in a position to dish that out right now, Tom.'

'That's a pity.'

Bish bites. 'And why's that?'

'I'm only going to be in this town for another four days, Ard, but that's more than enough time to bump into everybody we know and tell them why my Christmas was an anti-climax.'

Sigh followed by smarm. 'Tom, this is getting a little bit out of hand. Why don't we meet for lunch and try to work this out over a few bottles of overpriced bottles of Pouilly Fumé at Robespierre's?'

'Keep it simple. Thomas Read's Café. 1:15.'

'Tom, I don't think I'll be able to make it that soon.'

'Well, I'll be there, Bish. And I'll be in the mood for conversation.'

In the silence that follows I see a strained smirk stretching across his face.

'Okay, I'll humour you. 1:15 it is. Thomas Read's.'

'Don't be fashionably late, McQuaid.'

For the first time in two days, I slip into my skin, I slip into Nico. For a few moments an erection pushes its weight around in my green AE boot-cut jeans. I wonder if I really need what I need from Ardal today. Then I remember Strongbow and Mainie and all the rest of this yuletide horror story, and I sink and shrivel. My kingdom for some horse.

Downstairs again, I open the kitchen door, but stay on the threshold.

'Mum, I'm going into town to meet someone for lunch.'

My mother looks up from the back page of *The Irish Times*; she's a real student of obituaries. Today she's wearing Aunt Kitty's wing-framed flamingo-pink trifocals. At any moment they could could take flight from her nose. 'Who?' she asks bluntly.

Trying to look her straight in the eye (it's not easy with all that bevelled glass in the way), I reply, 'Mainie Doyle.'

She starts to reply immediately, then hesitates, then almost smiles. 'Still seeing her?'

I shrug. 'I'm not seeing her. Just having lunch. She's leaving town tomorrow, going back to London.'

'So I read,' my mother replies with wry authority. 'Well, what time will you be back? That's the important point.'

I hold the palms of my hands out, sincere broker of my time. 'See, that's the thing. This could be a long goodbye. I thought I'd meet you down there. Dad's already said that would be fine with him. He said I'd just be in the way while he was settling in anyway.'

My mother stares at me. I'm positive that she's about to reject this fragile yet dynamic plan of mine, but to my surprise she says, eyes already back on her column of alphabetical dead, 'Off with you. But don't get there later than half past four.'

'No problem.'

The smile I give my mother I leave on my lips even after I close the kitchen door. I turn to the mirror over the sideboard in the hall and check myself out properly for the first time this year.

I would make a beautiful corpse.

9

Shepherds

The temperature had nose-dived during my mini-hibernation. Nico kept me warm. Dame Street, as always, was polluted with petrol fumes and the screech of Bombardier brakes. Even so, I had more time for this Dublin street than most. I was almost fond of it. Stretching from Trinity's braced facade past Temple Bar (an area I had helped make fashionable) up to the Castle and the rise that led to Christchurch, it – and not the scuzzy expanse of O'Connell Street or even the catwalk of Grafton Street – was the city's jugular, its real main drag. I got a kick out of its peculiarities, like this pedestrian crossing I was waiting at right now. This had to be some failed pilot scheme because I'd never seen, or more precisely never heard, anything like it anywhere else in Dublin. Every time the little green man lit up, a fat chick's voice blared out a blurred message. It wasn't until my third year in Trinity that I worked out that what she had to be saying was, *Traffic on Dame Street has been signalled to stop*. But as I stepped out onto Dame Street this time I swore I heard her say, *Raffish young aesthete sadly picks up his cross*. Go figure.

Crossing the street was a diversion – Thomas Read's was straight ahead, but I was only ten minutes late and determined to go back to my old Iremonger ways and make the Bish sweat a little, make him think I could take or leave this deal. Coming out of the Wanderlust office a few minutes before – another Conquistator advance of crisp joyces in my Gucci – I'd remembered what Firbolg had told me about the Roomkeepers house. Why not go check it out. Just to kill time.

Firbolg was right – Palace Street was tiny, not worthy of its name; no wonder I'd never noticed it. Maybe fifty metres from the corner of Dame Street was the high side gate of the Castle. The side of the street I was on was nothing but grey bank exterior. On the other side was a row of tall Georgian houses, all but one of them bricked up or half-demolished. That of course was a pretty typical Dublin sight. The remaining house, which I now stood opposite, was notable for more than just having survived. On its redbrick facade was the copy,

IMPECUNIOUS ROOMKEEPERS
SOCIETY.
FOUNDED
A.D. 1790

And even though it had survived, so far, the Roomkeepers house was in pretty shaky condition: paintwork peeling; windows cracked; carvings weather-worn. This wasn't a charity: this was a charity case.

A light, a bare bulb, came on in one of the front rooms on the first floor. I crossed the street, went up the stone steps – the top one half-crumbled – and tapped the claw-shaped brass knocker two tentative times against the flaking turquoise door. Nothing happened. I knocked twice more. I heard that first-floor window unlock and lift with a stiff screech. Straining my head upwards, I stepped back down onto the street quickly, almost losing my footing on the broken step.

'Can I help yew?' A business-like but good-humoured Northern accent. It belonged to a heavy, erratically balding man wearing a grey v-necked jumper. For some reason it made me anxious to see him leaning out the window.

I really didn't know what the hell to tell him. I was just killing time.

'Hey there. How's it going?' I shouted up.

'Slowly.'

I sure could have used a little recognition from the IDA ad as an ice-breaker here. I guess the angle was all wrong for him to recognise me.

'So this is where the Roomkeepers used to be,' I said, still wondering what the hell a roomkeeper was.

'You've got an eye for detail, son.'

'So . . . who are you?'

'I'm the new owner.'

'Oh yeah? What are you planning to do with the place?'

'What else would you do with a place like this? We're restoring it, as best we can. Not that many like it left in this town. You should see the stucco in the old reception room.'

Here, surely, was my cue.

'Well, that's the thing – could I see it? I'm kinda early for an appointment.'

'Not today, son, I'm afraid. It's too dangerous. We've most of the floorboards up downstairs, and I don't have the insurance to pay if yew break an ankle. But tell me this, what's yer name?'

I told him.

'Iremonger,' he mused. 'Where have I heard that name before?'

Automatically I opened my mouth to suggest the journal-istic endeavours of Carmel Carraig-Dubh, but then stopped myself and shrugged, 'I'm not sure. There's more than one Iremonger in Dublin.'

'Och, I'm sure there is,' he said, the thick honey of his accent making it seem as if he didn't believe me. 'Well, Mr Iremonger, if you're passing this way again in a few months, stop by and ring that aul brass knocker again. I'd be happy to give you the grand tour then.'

I lowered and shook my head. 'Thanks, but I don't think I will be.'

'Next Christmas then. We're here for good.'

And with that he pulled his head back inside and began to lower the window. At first it jammed several times, protesting with shrill squeaks, then guillotined down to the sill with a rumble. The man from the North turned his back on me and disappeared from view, but I stood there on Palace Street looking up at the empty window a few moments longer: I'd figured out why it had troubled me to see the new owner lean out like that. Eons ago on holiday with my parents we stopped one night at this old Big House near Mallow in County Cork that had been converted into a hotel. I was leaning out the same kind of window when my father told me to always be very careful of those old-fashioned frames because one morning when he was twelve, home sick from school with the flu (and, I knew, with his father hard at work in the department and his mother dead two years), his bedroom window had come down on top of him and pinned him to the sill, and Madge the housekeeper was so deaf that it wasn't until the postman arrived an hour later that he was set free.

I checked my Tzara. Fifteen minutes late. I realised, to my regret, that I'd forgotten to ask the man from the North for his definition of what a roomkeeper was. But it was too late now. Fifteen minutes was pushing the envelope with

Bish, even in these circumstances. It was time to go buy heroin.

My mean main man is digging into a bowl of steaming mussels when I arrive at Thomas Read's. He's sitting between the bar with its high, Continentally stocked shelves and the fat pillar papered with posters for art house movies I saw months ago in Paris, *version originale*. Bish wipes some white sauce but not the smile away from his mouth. He rises about an inch out of his chair – great formality for him – and extends the billowy arm of a dead-rose red silk shirt. His handshake is firm. If he thinks this Mr Nice Guy act is going to make me forgive even one punt of his debt to me, he's sadly mistaken. Time to get on McQuaid's case.

'Been doing a little bargain-hunting in the sales, Ardal?'

I sit down. He responds with a smile.

'No. Bought this Christmas Eve in Lacuna. You know what I think of sales, Tom.'

I do indeed. This is one of the things I learned from Bish, and made part of myself: the price-aura principle. Buy something cheap, you look cheap. When the girl in the Perry Street vintage-clothes store told me that Nico was on special – a ten per cent discount – I simply wouldn't hear of it. No way was I wearing a steal on my back for the rest of my life. Just think about it. A $200 shirt is three times as classy as a $100 shirt. If you want to have a million dollars, you've got to look like a million dollars first. All this Bish McQuaid taught me. It's tragic that it's come to this, but what can I do? The Bish has pissed me off big time.

Waitress comes over – black tee-shirt, bobbed blonde hair, small but effective breasts. I vaguely recognise her. She may have been a fresher at Trinity last year. I may have slept with her. She recognises me.

'*Haigh*, how *ah* you?'

The West Brit accent is so OTT it's got to be fake. This

is the kind of girl who thinks just because she's got a Protestant father (who agreed to bring the kids up as Catholics anyway), she's a scion of the Ascendancy. The kind of girl who Dylan talks about as PG material. The kind of girl who when she's waitressing in Manhattan on her J-1 tells curious customers that she's *Anglo*-Irish. The kind of girl who says bitchy things about Mainie Doyle, that gross grocer's daughter, but secretly feels inferior to her. I know her type. They've caught me on every rebound these past four years.

I tell her I'm doing just fine.

'And what would you like?' she asks with rehearsed charm. With these girls you get the idea that at any moment the affable facade is going to crumble and that they're going to tell you they were not born to be your slave.

On the counter are these glass bowls full of oranges and fat lemons. What would I like? Something stinging and pure.

'A *limon pressé*.'

It takes her a moment to figure out what I'm talking about. Then she subtly colours. 'Oh,' she says, turning on her heel, 'no problem.'

I shrug for Bish. 'You see, a very simple request. My needs are simple.'

He sips his white wine with a smile. 'Simple is the last word I'd use to describe your needs, Tom Iremonger.'

I have no time for this, but remain as cool as that wine looks. 'I know what I want. And truly knowing what you want is ninety-nine per cent of getting what you want.'

Bish smiles again. 'I'm flattered.' Flattered because I'm quoting him. 'But I'm also disappointed, very disappointed, Tom. You used to say that's one thing you'd never do, that's where you drew the line.'

'Lines are for losers.' I've been waiting to use *that* line forever. 'Besides, this won't be the first time, I assure you.'

Bish gives me an arch look. 'Cocktails don't count, Iremonger. We're talking *intentionality* here.'

I swear sometimes Ardal forgets whether he's making a deal or sitting in a philosophy seminar. It will be his un-fucking-doing. My sigh expresses my low-tolerance patience. My stare is directed towards the counter, where the bardude is taking his own sweet time preparing my bitter drink. Bish runs his hand through his Medusa hair, looks around him cautiously. He's finally getting the message.

'You're really serious about this, Iremonger, aren't you?'

'Dead serious.'

And so is Bish. He cracks open a mussel. 'You know our relationship will never be the same again if you play this card. No more favours. No more free advice.'

I shrug. 'Since I won't be in Dublin it hardly matters.'

Now he manages a smile. 'Oh, hardly. But you can pay for your own drink.'

Yes, I was being tough, but also fair. As we were leaving Thomas Read's, I acknowledged that the deal would have to be sub-contracted, out-sourced. Bish was not in the horse trade, but I knew that he was acquainted with some gentlemen who were. I knew because in his own indirect, laconic way he'd bragged about it in the past.

So Bish had a call to make on his cell phone. For the sake of privacy we crossed Dame Street to Millennium Park, a pretty big name for a place that's no more than a niche of statues, cobblestones, terraced grass and dormant flowerbeds. The statues were a trio of broken, blunted but still imposing female figures – goddesses, muses, personifications, I couldn't remember which, though my father had once told me about them, about how they'd stood on top of Earlsfort Terrace when he was in yucky death, and when yucky death was still in the city.

But we turned our backs on those hefty chicks and got down to business. When Bish's call was answered, he asked for Locky. Locky took his time coming to the phone. But when he did, Ardal was super-polite. It was disturbing; I'd never seen him step so far out of character. It was also a little thrilling because my gut told me this was the real thing.

'It's kind of a late Christmas present for an old friend of mine,' Bish was saying. He'd dropped the South Dublin polish from his voice (not to mention the Trinity tone), but was being careful, it appeared, not to put on any false proletarian airs. The result was what you might call a Mid-Liffey accent. Talk about a telephone voice.

After listening carefully to what had to be a set of instructions, Bish turned to me and said, 'Three o'clock, Parkgate Street.'

He didn't wait for my assent. He had his mouth open to confirm the rendezvous when I grabbed his arm and told him to wait. Bish gave me an eloquent look. Bish's look told me I had just torn up the Rule Book of Cool and pissed on it. He took an awesome breath and told his counterpart, 'Locky, I'm very, very sorry about this, but could I phone you back in half a minute?'

Locky was apparently kind enough to grant this request. Bish stabbed the illuminated end button, then assaulted me with a stare. 'Iremonger, what the fuck is the matter with you?'

'I don't like the sound of this Parkgate Street.' No, sir, I did not. Now, obviously I was taking *nothing* for granted. I wasn't taking Bish's co-operation for granted, and I certainly wasn't taking this Locky character for granted. Parkgate Street sounded way too Northside for my liking. This was a sensitive business. I didn't want to piss anybody off if I didn't have to, but I seriously doubted I would get what I wanted if I didn't bring this whole thing back into *my* world. This deal would only go down to my liking in a place I felt cool in. Since I wasn't planning on having my snort-fest – forget needles, sweetheart, don't even talk to me about needles – until after I was done with my father, there was something to be said for arranging a time in the bog of some club on Leeson Street, but my instinct told me to delay no longer than I had to, to keep my eyes on the prize. How much better I would feel, for example, during the small talk at the Simmonscourt Clinic knowing that I had something heavier than a few lines of B-Special snug in Nico to get me through the night.

Bish was shaking his head. 'I really think you've lost it. Do you have any idea how far out of your depth you are?'

Well, I didn't like that. I didn't like anyone suggesting I had depth. I stuck to my sweaty guns.

'Call him back, Bish. Call him back and tell him the time is fine but that the place will be the cloisters of the Royal Hospital, Kilmainham.'

Bish ran his hand through his rank Versace hair and held it taut, staring at me all the while. 'Let me get this straight. You want to buy heroin in broad daylight at the Irish Museum of Modern Art.'

'Yes, and in the courtyard to boot. Hit redial.'

When he finally took his hand out of his hair to do so, it was like the top of his head had erupted.

Christ, early *again*. Five to three. This is getting to be a nasty habit, another sign of decline. I pay the taxi and walk under a fan of stone-carved weaponry into the cloisters of the Royal Hospital. Hospice is more like it because the only way the old Brit soldiers who came here ever left again was boots first. Nobody ever got better coming to the Royal Hospital, Kilmainham. No one here got out alive. Now it's IMMA. IMMA indeed. I'm a-waiting for my man.

The courtyard is deserted. Nobody here – yet – but me and those dozen or so clay pygmy figures out there on the sand. Each statue has its own little zone, demarcated by a single strand of rusty barbed wire. To say the pygmies are naked is an understatement. You could tell their sex a mile away. Those in-your-face genitals make rue St Denis porn look demure. The males wear masks that remind me of those neglected Remokoan statues in our living room. From the neck down, though, these figures, some with blunt terracotta hard-ons, look nothing like anything Columb ever brought back to Ireland.

But they're nothing compared to the clay chicks. The females remind me of a sick joke we used to tell in Berchmans, the one about a woman being nothing more than a life-support system for a cunt. Well, these little women both confirm and deny that definition. The rest of their bodies seem to swirl around that fundamental orifice. Dylan once joked that I was vaginacentric. So are they, but in a completely different way I can't quite articulate. Their fierce, simple faces say it better.

I light a Roland (T - 54) and begin to pace the cloisters. High above the hospital, the puttering of a helicopter.

Some figures are in the centre of their space, some close to the wire. Some face another figure, male or female; some have their backs turned. I can't decide if the installation is a profound commentary on post-modern sexual identity or if it's total shite.

Soon, however, I've got something else to worry about – that chopper. It sounds as if it's circling the museum now, at an ever-decreasing altitude. What the fuck is going on? I can only think of one thing: it's army air corps support for some big gardaí sting operation – with Iremonger, the greatest offence against the state, as its target. Bish has fucked me around. And he's probably a mere agent of

Strongbow. And guess who's pulling Strongbow's strings. Oh, chill, Iremonger, chill.

Now the copter is hovering right above the courtyard. Against my better instinct, I step out of the cloister and onto the sand – nothing but vintage solid grey Dublin sky up there. But still I continue to hear the phantom helicopter get closer and closer. Surely the sand will start swirling around any moment as the monster lands.

And suddenly I want to kick myself with the wing-tips of my Boccionis. I see where the sound is coming from – speakers have been placed at open windows on all four sides of the courtyard. I've been the victim of a quadraphonic illusion. When did I start to become a victim?

Half an hour later I'm on my sixth Roland and listening to the helicopter tape loop for the twelfth time. I decided shortly after three o'clock (H-Hour) that I needed to interpret the concept of meeting in the courtyard very liberally. I've been all around this place several times, inside and out, east wing and west, from the abstract to the figurative and back again. Security must think I'm casing the joint for an art heist, or lifting goodies in the gift shop at the very least. But I'm not sure there's much worth stealing here. I'm only interested in buying. But nobody is selling what I want.

I stamp out the Roland on a flagstone. Not even Mainie Doyle did this to me (unless, in some way, she's doing this to me now). It's hard not to think of all those satellites of mine, male and female, that I've left standing under the blue clock at Front Arch. Now I know what it feels like, to be stood up. The horror, the horror, as Brando says.

What can I say? I haven't felt this pissed off since I had to deplane and recheck my luggage at Stansted on a British Midland flight to Amsterdam because some idiot with a boarding card had gone AWOL. Fuck you, Bish McQuaid. I'm not done for yet. I'm going to use every last ounce of influence I have left in this city to pay you back for this, and to get to the bottom of it. And I have other contacts in Dublin. I'm pretty confident I can score once I'm back in town tonight. But first I have to visit another hospital.

The quickest way out of here and back to civilisation is to get a taxi from the rank outside Heuston Station. So I walk down the evergreen-lined driveway of the museum, past an unmanned security Portakabin, and turn left onto the winding road that leads to the main road. Hedges, stone walls, silence, isolation – you'd swear you were in the middle of the countryside. Nasty. Unnerving. I should have ordered a taxi from the lobby of the museum.

It's with some relief, therefore, that I hear a city sound, an engine behind me, an arrogant engine. I turn around. A sports utility vehicle, a metallic grey Paratrooper that I saw in the car park is zooming in my direction. An awesome machine. Suddenly I want to learn how to drive more than I want to snort heroin. Maybe that's my problem – I've been a passenger too long.

Unfortunately, I don't have time to chase down the repercussions of this thought because the Paratrooper does not juggernaut past me as I expect; instead it brakes fiercely and comes to a halt just a few feet ahead of me. Something tells me that the occupants of the Paratrooper, obscured so far by tinted windows, are not stopping to ask directions. I stop, adrenaline squishing through my system – my split-or-bullshit mechanism is kicking in. The front passenger door swings open and this Bull Madigan type wearing jeans and an Old Belvedere jersey jumps down. A smiling Southside face, not one of Locky's boys – bullshit it is.

'How can I help you, friend?'

Belvo Boy's broad fist slams into my right eye in response.

Added to my astonishment that I've just been punched –
after all those close shaves in the Tenderloin and Alphabet
City and Place Pigalle I'm finally made to suffer in my own
lovely Dublin – is my astonishment that I'm still on my feet,
though barely. A trippy nebula rushes endlessly towards my
closed eye; my cheekbone is already throbbing in protest.
What I'm dealing with here – among other things – is the
reality of disfigurement. Jesus, now I'm hungry for that
modelling career I could have had, just like *that*.

'Stand up straight, Iremonger,' I hear a calm voice, a
touch of the country in it, say behind me. At this moment
it sounds very like the voice of reason, so I try to do what
he says – and get a mindfuck of a headrush. Christ, if Bish's
crap had worked like this on New Year's Eve none of us
would be here right now. Suddenly I find myself falling
backwards, only to be caught and put back on my feet
by the no-nonsense arms of the Voice of Reason. 'We're
getting in the Para,' he says with easy authority. And it
looks like I'm going along with what the man says.

Belvo Boy takes charge of me as the Voice, whose sandy
hair and serious build I can now see with my one good
eye, unlocks and lifts the hatch door of the Paratrooper;
aluminium arms pump it skyward. I get thrown on the
hairy floor of the storage area, legs still dangling out over
the back of the vehicle. The back seat has been pushed
down to maximise my comfort.

'Crawl in, stay down.'

I comply with the first part of Belvo's blunt instructions immediately, but reserve the right to mess with the
second.

The door comes down with another bicycle-pump hiss,
followed by a clinical clunk. As soon as the front doors slam
shut, *shock* goes the central locking system, the Paratrooper
starts like a lion clearing his throat, and we're off. I turn
over and at first see nothing but bare branches through

tinted windows. Then a wrench, large enough to turn off a Manhattan fire hydrant, emerges over the passenger seat, followed by an arm wearing the colours of Old Belvedere. I get the message, and roll back over, careful to keep the swelling side of my face off the prickly ground.

At the end of the country road the Paratrooper turns right. We must either be heading into town – which I doubt – or heading for the Northside. Great, now I'll get the best of both worlds.

The pert sound of a cell phone. The Voice answers, and listens. 'Yeah. Okay. I'll go in through the last gate.'

Last gate. Well, it wouldn't take a Trinity graduate to figure out what they're talking about. They're taking me to the park, the frigging Phoenix Park. And not to see the llamas in the zoo or Mary Robinson in Áras an Uachtaráin or the top brass in Garda Headquarters. I'm too aware that the park has its dark side where tourists get stabbed, nurses get bludgeoned, politicians get blow-jobs. A new emotion – possibly panic – has risen in my throat, forcing me to say these slurred words, 'Money. I've still got money.'

Belvo taps me on the head with the wrench and says, 'Shut up, poster boy.'

Then another bump; the road surface becomes smoother. I think we're crossing the bridge.

I think we're on the Northside.

The rare glimpses I take up at the tinted window reveal nothing but winter branches rolling by, and that fat wrench hovering above me. We seem to be going around in circles, and we seem to have been doing so for a quarter of an hour, as if the park were some miserable maze. I keep on imagining the headline in the next edition of *Ireland on Sunday* – IRELAND'S GREATEST RESOURCE MISSING; GARDAÍ FEAR FOUL PLAY. But no mention of my demise on Carmel's page; that is perhaps my greatest fear.

Finally we make a right turn – or what I think is a right turn; they've got me so disoriented now that right and left are as relative in my mind as right and wrong. The road, if it's still a road we're on, becomes uneven and gritty. Still those trees overhead. And that supersized spanner. We come to a stop and the Voice cuts the juice. Silence. Suddenly a few more circuits of the park doesn't seem such a bad proposition. Christ, keep me in suspense – screw finding out about what happens next.

Sadly this is not an option. I'm expecting the Voice to run around and open up the rear door while Belvo keeps me covered with the wrench, but I sense neither of them make a move.

Shock go the locks, hiss goes the hatch door. A shadow falls across me. My throbbing head tells me it's Bish's shadow and it's Strongbow's shadow and it's my grandfather's shadow. I dare not look.

And then the shadow speaks, 'You can get up now, Iremonger.'

It's McQuaid. Well, of course it's McQuaid. I hear the driver's door open and slam solidly.

As coolly as I can, like a lover reaching for a post-fuck cigarette, I roll over, pull myself up. Bish laughs, lowers his head and laughs into his billowing dead-rose shirt, the studied tousle of his hair an inadequate veil for his glee. Oh, this is more, far more than I can take. I think my ego has clocked out for lunch because the question left resonating in my mind is, Isn't he cold on a day like today? He's lost the umber barn jacket he put on as we were leaving Thomas Read's.

Abruptly the Bish is done laughing.

'Get out,' he snaps.

I crawl out. Bish backs away (in a curious motion), leaving the Voice to take hold of me, which he does, almost reassuringly, in his firm, no-nonsense manner.

Belvo clambers out after me, dropping the wrench with a mighty thud on the floor and bringing down the hatch door. I hope, faintly, that this might mean that the heavy shit is over. But I'm not counting on it. I'm not counting on anything, or anyone.

Belvo grabs my free arm and snarls, 'Let's go, Iremonger.' But he doesn't scare me (not that I'm going to let him know that). He's a sad amateur compared to my other handler. What is this, training day at the mob? No, it's Bish I'm really scared of, I'll admit it. My old friend Ardal who's now behind me, out of sight. I keep on wondering who's behind *him* and out of sight. If the answer is nobody, I've still got my hands full. In a situation like this Bish can be . . . touchy. Though the result of his touchiness this time, I suspect, might be more than my omission from a guest list.

We're on a profoundly obscure road, winding and pot-holed. The only other vehicle around is the Bish's beloved purple VW Beetle, Prudence. I guess someone could come cruising along and save my photogenic ass, but in my belly I know it's more likely that a squad of Mounties is going to ride down the road.

Escape? Don't even think about it. Not only am I still woozy from that belt Belvo gave me, but the Voice's confidence had drained me of even the dregs of mine: I think I'd feel less helpless wearing goddamn manacles.

A soft *here* from Bish and we turn off the road and onto a crude, curving path. I'm getting mud on my Boccionis – that's the most specific thought I have on how much this situation sucks – I'm getting mud on my Milanese leather boots. My heart is beating metallically in my hollow chest.

Off the path. Through the trees. I'm vaguely annoyed, or saddened, that I can't identify them. I'll say they're beech trees.

Through long grass. To a pond. It's the colour of my bathwater after coming in from rugby practice years ago at Berchmans, too shy to shower in the changing rooms. A lot of fucking good memories will do me now. Why won't the past get off my case? Can't it see that I've got my hands full right now dealing with its crony the present?

I can't handle Bish walking behind me any more. I look over my shoulder, try to turn around, try to speak, 'Look, Ardal, this has all been a big . . .'

Belvo and the Voice grapple Nico with both hands, one of them kicks my feet from under me, and the knees of my green AE jeans go into the moist, green earth. Belvo gets me in a half-nelson and is doing a pretty good job of wrapping my left arm backwards around my neck when Bish, unenthusiastically, calls him off. Belvo and the Voice back away, and before I've really had a chance to check out the symbolism of the scene I find myself on my knees before Bish's feet. Looking up I see red hair fringeing a sour smile.

'Oh, yeah, big misunderstanding all right – on your part, Iremonger. When you breezed back into town on Christmas Eve, did you ever for a second consider that you might not be coming back to the same town you left in the summer? Did you ever stop and think as you were pulling this bullshit stunt that maybe the rules had changed in your absence?'

No, of course I didn't. The whole Iremonger Project is an attempt to avoid stopping and thinking. Trainee assistant managers in SuperDoyle with stutters stop and think. The Brían Firbolgs of this world stop and think. My father has spent his whole life stopping and thinking, and look at his reward: a premature pension from American Machines. Iremonger doesn't stop and think. Pull the plug on me if I do.

But I don't tell any of this to Bish. I don't say anything. I don't even shrug. I don't know what the fuck to do.

Bish puts his hand behind his back and calmly pulls out a gun. A matte-black, snub-nosed fucker of a pistol. It looks like the real thing, and at the same time too much like the real thing – there's a black plastiky brilliance about it. I look up at Bish's face. He's smiling with relish now, and seems to read my thoughts.

He speaks lovingly, 'A Christmas present. From Ardal to the Bish. Like it? A Steurenagel 17. German precision engineering – the Porsche of pistols. Semi-automatic, double action, hair-sensitive trigger. Right now the magazine is holding fifteen nine-millimetre bullets, each one with a grooved, concave tip to maximise impact damage. In fact, one of my colleagues here' – he nods towards Belvo, looking on with glee – 'was saying earlier this afternoon how they look like little assholes. How appropriate, I remarked, for Iremonger. Or should I say, for To*más*.'

I don't have the resources to even start dealing with that last insult. All my attention is focused on that gun, which is becoming more miserably real by the moment. I've turned to stone, here on my knees in front of Bish McQuaid. Even if I could react, I don't think I would. I know the script of this scene is out of my hands. And no one is going to ask me to sit in on the rewrite. Better to kneel here and concentrate on what I'm feeling. What do I feel? Fear, yes. But not an unprecedented fear. I've tasted this flavour before. What is it? What is it?

It's the fear of what will happen to me if I don't carry Strongbow's bag inside. An overdose amount.

Part of me wants to tell Bish to go ahead and pull that trigger. Maybe part of me has been telling Bish to do that from the very beginning of this deal.

'Now,' he says, with ominous ease.

I manage a hoarse reply, 'Now what?'

With his non-death-wielding hand, the Bish rakes back

his Medusa hair with sensuous slowness. 'Now' – his eyebrows dance – 'give me your jacket.'

'N—?' I gag on her name.

Bish's attitude snaps.

'No?' He makes a big show of clicking off the safety. 'Is that what you're saying, Iremonger?' Standing over me now, grabbing a handful of her precious leather, hauling my face towards the snub-nose of the Steuernagel. Ice-cold contact. Oh, that gun is at least real. Please don't piss yourself, Iremonger, like some loser in a sad Stephen King novel. Die dry, dude. Bish is so close that I can smell Obsession for Men wafting from the silk folds of his shirt; I wish, crazily, that Columb, of all people, were here to set things right, make my world sane again. The gun is pressed so tightly to my cheek that if I leave the scene of this crime alive I may well be bringing a nine-millimetre indelible imprint with me. 'You think I don't have the balls to do it?' Bish is ranting. 'You think it would cause me any great pain to rid Dublin, rid the world, of Tom Iremonger? You think I'd loose any sleep over that?'

I want to shake my head – something tells me that truth is my last defence left – but I dare not; any sudden movement may be my last.

Bish flings me back down to the ground, causing me to land awkwardly on my right hand. I would never have guessed he was so strong. it's as if the two henchmen flanking him, (gloating Belvo, stolid Voice), are lending him their energy. Or maybe he's just that pissed with me.

Wincing from the fresh pain in my wrist, I hold out my good arm (I'm on my knees again). 'Here, take this genuine Tzara. It's worth far more than my jacket. It's got this dial that—'

'Your choice, Tommy boy.' Bish sharpens his aim. 'It's that jacket or your ass.'

Freezeframe. What happens next is action-packed, but

beyond the reach of any camera. All the drama takes place on that dark soundstage within myself. I don't know, five, maybe ten, seconds go by. But by comparison the time I've spent back in Dublin up to this moment is just the blink of an eye. It all happens here. Not that I'm sure I understand what happens. Something to do with that part of me that wants to tell him to go ahead and shoot diminishing, loosing a hard-fought, six-month-long arm wrestle. But what exactly gains the upper hand I do not know. All I can say for now is that I hear the sound of Nico's chunky zipper coming undone and feel her being wrestled off my shoulders and see that McQuaid and his goons have kept their distance, though they look ready for Iremonger tricks.

There are no tricks, not this time. After completing the delicate operation of getting to my feet, I walk forward slowly, Nico cradled in my arms. Bish snatches her without ceremony. With a wave of the Steuernagel he tells me to back away. I do so reluctantly.

And then the gun is gone and Bish is trying her on. This I cannot watch and so I turn and stare at the muddy bathwater of the pond.

'Fits grand,' I hear the Voice say.

'Yeah,' grunts Belvo. 'Suits you, Bish.'

Then silence. I can imagine the glances they are exchanging at my expense.

'Not the end of the world, Iremonger,' Bish patronises. 'You can keep the wallet. I hear a whispery thud. I don't want your grandfather's Nazi gold.'

But I'm beyond provocation now. I shrug to be done with response, to be done with them. I just want to be alone.

Soon I get my wish – I hear the brushing of long grass; casual, fading voices; two vehicles starting up and driving away; and then nothing but the faint backdrop of city traffic.

So, no more Nico. What does that mean? Well, for starters, that I'm getting damn cold; this is *nippley* weather. My Mossimo tee-shirt and Hugo Boss mock turtleneck aren't doing the trick. No lambswool – that's what it means, most immediately, to be without Nico. Whatever else it might mean I don't want to think about right now.

Well, there seems to be no point in hanging around here and freezing to death since I just made this major life-affirming move by giving up my fucking jacket. Let's get out of here. I hug myself unlovingly and start to walk in a different direction to the one where the Bish and his boys had their wheels parked. Call me paranoid, but I just can't bring myself to walk in their footsteps, no matter if that's the most direct route out of this jungle. Say if they've left Belvo behind to finish me off?

I walk through a small, dense wood of dead trees, down a slippery slope, through more trees – and then out into a vast field, dotted in the near distance by young evergreens and suspicious deer, marked at the far end by a huge white cross set against the darkening eastern sky. I have found my bearings with a vengeance. Forty Acres – isn't that what this place is called? – is deserted. I head towards the papal cross.

What I remember first is the *second* last time I was here, the weekend before he came. This space had been transformed into a vast ranch, the whole area divided into wooden corrals. Long splinters jabbed my dungarees as I clambered over fences. I was a cowboy; Dad and Uncle Columb were big-shot ranchers. The comparison was not that wild. As they strode along one of the grass avenues that the Papal vehicle would drive along, the brothers surveyed the scene with a proprietary air.

'They've done a grand job,' said my father, referring to Dublin Corporation. Whenever he'd talked about them before he'd called them 'a right shower'.

'And they did it so fast,' I chipped in.

'Ah, you can be sure, Tomás, that plans were laid for this longer than three weeks ago. But it's a fine job by any standard. They've done us proud. A pity that cross'll be up for just one Mass.'

'They'll never take it down,' Uncle Columb quietly predicted.

I look up once again at the once temporary construction.

We got up in the night. Sleepy, thrilled, I stared out from my bedroom window. Kitchen light washed our back lawn; gnarled limbs of the apple trees at the bottom of the garden protruded out of the misty darkness. Bedroom and kitchen lights were on, coming on, in nearly all of the surrounding houses.

In our house it was just Mum, Dad, and myself getting up to go and see the Pope. Uncle Columb was actually going to be saying Mass with him (I imagined them on the altar together, Columb handing the Holy Father a white serviette as I had handed him one when I had been his altar boy). He had spent the night at the Jesuit residence on Hatch Street. Triona had gone to Galway for the Youth Mass (how jealous I would be, despite the excitement of the Phoenix Park, when she came home a few days later, glowing, and told us how they'd given the Pope a ten-minute standing ovation when he said, 'Young people of Ireland, I love you'). Grandad, already sickly and ancient, was going to watch the Mass on his RTE-only TV in his comfortable little house in Sandymount (for months afterwards he would bore me with his extended comparisons and contrasts between the Papal visit and the Eucharistic Congress of 1932, in which he had played some important lay role).

Everyone else I knew, in Berchmans, in Owenstown Hill, was going to see the Pope by bus or by train. But we went to the Phoenix Park in a limousine. Dad's first cousin, Cornelius Iremonger, was an undertaker. He and his wife Ellen were my godparents and had no children of their own. Their limo was a designated vehicle, with a coveted blue sticker. That meant admission into a blue-zone corral, very close (and yet still very far away) from the high altar and the higher cross.

Into the miraculously blue late-September sky (my mother said she'd never seen an Indian summer day quite like it) flew the Papal jumbo and its escort of nimble fight planes (*Irish* fighter planes!). Somewhere in the swollen head of that 747 was the first Pope ever to visit Ireland. The Jumbo banked heftily, the fighters tipped lightly, maintaining a tight trail on either side of the Aer Lingus plane. All of this above forty acres of corralled spectators. My heart pumped with anxiety and pride.

In the beginning the Papal plane; at the end, the Popemobile. My father – who even then spent Sunday mornings working his way through the English papers while my mother dragged me to Mass in Booterstown – Dad ran alongside the Pope cheering and waving, leaving the rest of us behind.

I look over to my left and see the American Ambassador's residence. In spite of myself, I smile. In one area the Corpo did not do a fine job. The toilet facilities on the day were, as my mother put it, hopeless. The word spread, however, that women who just couldn't wait were making do with a ditch in front of the stone wall of the Ambassador's house. Ellen and my mother went off to investigate, and came back about ten minutes later with an urgent request that their husbands and their long coats come with them. I wanted to go too, but my mother insisted that I stayed with a group of nuns she had befriended in our section. Reluctantly, I agreed.

These nuns were scary, or even scarier than normal

nuns. They were from a reclusive order, let out especially for the day. Some of them were very old, as old as my grandfather. But they were all excited, charmed by everything. They acted as if they'd been entrusted with a little prince, asking me shy questions about myself and my school that even I sensed were naive. They had a simple picnic laid out on thick tartan blankets, and they insisted I share it. I wasn't hungry but ate none the less. Bread-and-butter sandwiches. I didn't want to take any of the sweet things because I was afraid they might not have a chance to eat them very often. I was relieved when my parents and godparents returned.

I'm close now, about as close as I was that day.

On both sides of the altar a thin white line of concelebrants mounted the platform, surplices – that's the word – blowing gently behind them. But nowhere in that endless procession of priests could I make out my uncle. He had become his function.

I reach the concrete remainder of that stage, climb a few steps, look around. My father lifted me up – not without a struggle, and not for long – to scan the black sea of people behind us. The whole of Ireland had to be here.

I wasn't too far off the mark. A million people in this one place at one time. No way would that ever happen again. Not even for a free U2 concert. This papal mass never comes up in conversation but virtually everyone I know must have been here that day – Dylan, Roderick, Ardal, Carmel, Firbolg, Mainie. All of them. Maybe even Strongbow.

The base of the cross is covered with magic-marker graffiti:

IRA – INLA FOR EVER – TALLAGHT GANSTAS – MUSHER WAS HERE – SHITE

You'd think that since they bothered to keep the thing up the Corporation would keep it clean. But that's not my problem. I have other problems. Namely, my hand hurts, my eye hurts with an attitude, my Rolands were also in Nico, I'm beyond cold, and it's getting dark already (the light in Ireland is such a loser). So if you'll excuse me, I think I'll try and find a way out of this wilderness.

10

Found among Doctors

I eventually got into a taxi outside Heuston Station just after 4:15. I promised the Sumo-sized driver a ten-quid tip if he could get me to the Simmonscourt Clinic by 4:30. The guy looked like he had to be lowered by crane through the sun-roof of his Saint every morning, but he proved to be a very agile driver, cutting through the back streets of the Liberties – streets I'd never seen before in my life – to avoid the building rush-hour traffic. He had the knowledge all right, the Dublin knowledge. I faintly envied him.

Once we crossed the Grand Canal, things slowed up, and there was little he could do about it. As we crawled through Ballsbridge I could see him checking me out every so often in the rear-view mirror (I must have looked worse than he did), but he had the savvy not to ask any questions. It was almost 4:40 by the time we swung into the parking lot of the clinic, but I gave him the joyce anyway; at least he hadn't let me down.

I cleaned off my Boccionis as best I could before going through the revolving door. The lobby looked more like the reception area of an advertising agency than a hospital – marble floor, low leather couches, dark-glass-top coffee tables with copies of *Architectural Digest* and *Exotic Escape*, walls covered with densely corrugated brown paper and reproductions of unprovocative abstract paintings. It hadn't looked like this when I'd been here five years ago, when the old man had died. Of course back then it had simply been called the Simmonscourt Private Nursing Home; some make-over they'd given it in the meantime.

A guy about my own age with a Caesar-style haircut and wearing a tight white coat was manning reception. He looked a little startled when I approached him.

'This is a *clinic*,' he said sniffly.

'I know that, thank you.'

'The nearest emergency room is down at St Vincent's.'

I covered my right cheek gingerly. 'Oh, my face. That's nothing. Ran into an old friend. I'm here to see my father. Risteárd Iremonger. He's the one who's sick. Would have checked in just this afternoon.'

Caesar Boy gave me this little smile. 'Iremonger, you say?'

Woh, stop the lights. What was *that* all about? Was he just being stroppy, or had he read the article in *IoS*? Either way, I decided to play it cool, or the closest approximation to cool I could still manage.

'Yeah, that's right – Iremonger.'

He checked a clipboard. 'Yes. Mr Risteárd Iremonger. Room 3.18.'

I thanked him with more sincerity than I'd intended. As I walked towards the elevators I realised the source of my gratitude – my father was not staying on the fourth floor, the top floor, the floor where they'd moved the old man after his first, meaningful weeks of treatment (and just before my mother began praying to St Jude). No, they hadn't sent my father to the top floor. Not yet, anyway.

Two young, plain nurses in the elevator already held the door for me. As we rode up, I remembered that this was the very place we'd found out that he was dead. It was the early hours of Sunday morning. Uncle Columb and my parents and I had gone to bed late, close to one o'clock, only to be woken by a phone call at three; he was very low, they said. My mother asked me if I was sure I wanted to go, but seemed satisfied when I said that I did. What she didn't know was that I wanted to be present at my grandfather's deathbed vigil more out of a sense of curiosity than loss; I'd never had the opportunity to be that close to death before. We drove to the nursing home through a cloudburst, rain bouncing off the deserted lanes of the Stillorgan Dual Carriageway, my mother repeatedly telling my father, *go easy, Risteárd, go easy*. When we arrived at the nursing home, he insisted on letting us out at the entrance so that we wouldn't get wet, and then parking the car. A middle-aged nurse, a picture of serene seniority, was waiting to unlock the front door for us. We waited silently in the modest lobby for my dripping father. And in this large lift, going up to the top floor, it was me – yes, Christ, it was me – who asked, *How is he?* As the doors opened the nurse told us gently but unflinchingly that Mr Iremonger had in fact passed away a few minutes before we had arrived.

Stepping out on the third floor I got the impression for the first time that I was in a building with some medical purpose. The floor was tiled with marble in the immediate vicinity of the elevator only; after that it was good old linoleum. That disinfectant-and-piss hospital smell was faint but unmistakable, and it gave the place a stamp of seriousness. There were even a few people in dressing-gowns and looking a little off-colour floating around. Plexiglas signposts guided me to Room 3.18 in half a minute. I paused, however, outside the closed door, hand-combed my hair and took several pathologically deep breaths before knocking.

'Come in!' I heard my parents respond in unison.

Tentatively, putting my left side forward, I did so.

They had each been marking time with one of their little addictions. My mother, who was sitting in a wood-and-leather armchair on the far side of the bed, wearing a brown satiny suit and Aunt Nora's upside-down glasses, cut the sound on the Australian soap she'd been watching. My father, sitting up in bed, looking too settled, too much like a patient already, put down the crossword he'd been working on, undoubtedly *The Daily Telegraph*. Apart from its clinical floor and its spaciousness, the well-lit suite looked like many a mid-price hotel room in the States I'd crashed out in. From the window you could see the darkening roofs of the RDS. The old man's original room had been much smaller – to my father's exasperation, he had always maintained some cranky resistance to joining the VHI – and much darker, and just above the grinding and booming of the nursing home's delivery bay; but the old man didn't seem to notice, or care any more.

'Well, well, look who came in from the cold,' my father said, less sarcastically than he could have. My mother was not so forgiving.

'Tom, Columb, and Triona have gone *home* already.'

'What does that matter?' I replied, trying to be as uncombative as I could. 'I finally made it. And visiting hours aren't over yet.'

'It matters because—' She didn't get to finish her lecture. The room was too well lit and those dead-aunt glasses too powerful for her not to notice my swollen eye-socket before too long.

'To*más*' – on that killer syllable she sprang to her feet— 'what happened to your face!' Instantly, she was on her way over to check out the damage.

Why is that name always spoken at moments when I can't complain about it? Right then, for example, I had to devote all my energy to downplaying the significance of this bruised eye.

'It's nothing, just a little . . . accident.'

'Show your father! Show your father!'

My mother's perfume aura arrived a second before she did – a startlingly assertive scent, something Continental, sexy; frankly I wished she would go back to spraying on a little Aisling. That smell seemed so weirdly mismatched with everything else – those goofy glasses, the Aussie soap, the West Brit crossword, these looming tests; I just didn't get it. Was she losing it?

Definitely. She took a firm hold of my chin and turned my blemished side towards my bed-parked father. Great – I was finally getting to do some more modelling. My father winced, sucked air through his lips. I suddenly wondered why I thought I had any right coming here, late and damaged, adding to his anxiety, their anxiety. Not showing up at all would have been the predictable thing. I doubted they would have been too surprised if I'd just slipped out of town, gone stand-by.

Maybe that would be the best thing for everybody – if Iremonger just simply disappeared.

My mother let go of my chin and asked what I should have seen in the taxi on the way over, if I had been thinking straight, was the inevitable question, 'And where's that jacket of yours? You haven't taken it off since you came back to Dublin. Where is it now?'

My parents weren't stupid. It was obvious some violence had happened me. The shrewd thing to do – or so I figured – was to give them a taste of the truth, make it plausible, so they could get over seeing me like this (since I'd been dumb enough to show myself at all) and concentrate on other matters.

'Basically I got robbed,' I said, remembering to look her straight in the eye.

'Jesus-Mary-and-Joseph! Where?'

'Town.'

My father sat forward. 'Where in town?'

'Palace Street,' I told him, making sure not to throw in a lame shrug.

'Where's that?' my mother demanded.

My father ruefully enlightened her, 'Right next to Dublin Castle.' He had the knowledge too. 'Sweet Jesus, you're safe nowhere in this town. Not even in your own bed.'

He believed me; that was the important thing, I guess. Whether my mother did I still don't know.

She wanted to know more. 'What happened, Tom? Did you get the guards? Tell us!'

I didn't know which was harder to take, her charged, dizzying perfume or her helpless, overwhelming concern. You could smell both of them. Drained of energy and invention, I shook my head, looking down at the marbly linoleum and the caking residues of mud on my Boccionis. 'No, I didn't bother to waste my time, and their time. It was just some pricks (sorry) from up past Thomas Street – from Katanga Land. You've got to be careful in that part of town these days anyway. I should have known better. Maybe I have been away too long.'

'What's that got to do with it?' my mother replied. 'You were robbed. You were *hurt*, Tom. You have to tell the guards.'

I looked up at her and smiled sadly. Her innocence was touching. 'That wouldn't change anything.'

'Still—'

'He's right, Sinéad,' my father rumbled. 'The boy's right this time. He'll never see that jacket again.'

I had my mouth open to express my unanticipated

gratitude for him siding with me at such a delicate point in this tricky conversation, but the bluntness of his pronouncement about Nico – a death sentence – literally took my breath away. My silence was my mother's opportunity to speak again, 'Well, I still think the proper thing to do would be to report it.'

As my breath came back to me, I was tempted to confess that what I'd given them was a rip-off. Only 20% pure at best, cut with all kinds of crap. I wanted to blow their minds with the real story – that I had been fucked around by one of my own kind, set upon by my own set. But I just couldn't. I still couldn't get my tongue around the whole truth.

With a saliva-trembling sigh, my mother turned around and walked back to her seat. My father, sagging on his throne of pillows, said that I might as well sit down. I pulled up the twin of my mother's armchair and sat down on my father's other flank. He made a half-hearted attempt to resume his crossword, but after a few twiddles of the pen put the paper down again. He joined my mother in staring at the silenced Australian soap.

The current drama involved some kind of communication problem between a shirtless, bronze-torsoed teen-aged boy with spiky blond hair and his neo-flower-child girlfriend as they walked along a deserted, wave-bombarded beach. A close-up revealed the girl's abundant chestnut hair to be sporadically woven – the dull handiwork I'd seen performed by countless alternative girls (some wearing patterned dresses like her, some wearing denim, all wearing Doc Martens) on counter-culture concourses from the Pompidou Centre to Haight-Ashbury. I thought of their cardboard signs and their cardboard equipment. And the thought depressed me. Did I really want to go back to those hang-outs and those hangers-on?

The boy and girl had worked it all out. Close-ups of shy smiles. Long shot of them walking down the beach together, away from camera, holding hands. Australia was starting to look good. I'd barely penetrated the Southern Hemisphere before. I began to daydream about the possibilities of Iremonger Down Under, fighting off the nagging suggestion that my parents were waiting for me to speak, to ask questions, to ask the right questions. I kept on staring at the TV, now showing an ad for Barry's tea.

I was more than relieved to hear the sharp report of a knock at the door – I turned my head to see it immediately open. The name Dr Arthur Guiney was sewn in cursive blue letters beside the right lapel of his white coat. He was a little man (already I was irresistibly on my feet – yes, me, Iremonger, standing respectfully, anticipating something), maybe no more than five six, five seven, but with an impressive French compactness about him, as if, pound for pound, he had the energy of three men. He was one of those fit wrinklies whose bodies hold back from ageing at a spare fifty-five. The surviving strands of his straight black hair, streaked with grey, were brushed back rigorously across his reddish scalp. The frames of his glasses were also black, the square plastic kind I had seen my smiling, trim, dark, handsome father, a youngish family man, wear in softly coloured photos from the sixties, from before I was born; glasses worn by Buddy Holly and moonshot-era NASA mavens and stuffed shirts late at night on RTE reading the *Nuacht* till about the late-eighties. Dr Guiney had clearly never seen the need to change his style. And I wouldn't have been surprised to learn that he'd gone thirty years without needing to strengthen his prescription and without getting a scratch on those lenses. I was on my feet, my mother was on her feet and walking towards him, and from the way my father said, 'Ah, Doctor,' I knew he would have been on his feet too if he could have. He was certainly sitting upright in the bed again.

Why did I feel so much more secure all of a sudden, after just a few moments in this man's presence? I wasn't expecting him to save Nico. I wasn't expecting him to perform miracles. Iremonger doesn't believe in miracles.

The doctor's voice came as no surprise – kind but assertive, 'You look like you've settled in well, Mr Iremonger.'

'I have, Doctor. I'm very comfortable. I wish I'd been here over the whole of Christmas.'

Guiney's response was a genuine but economic laugh. My mother and I faintly smiled. He turned his attention to us, her first. 'Hello again, Mrs Iremonger. Happy New Year to you.'

'And to you too, Doctor,' she replied, shaking his hand. 'I'm so glad that Risteárd is in your hands.'

Me too, me too, I found myself thinking. In his safe, sure hands. The doctor turned to me and offered that right sure hand: I offered my left undamaged hand. His shake was firm but not crushing, and all the more reassuring for that. 'I'm Tom, Doctor.'

With a tight smile, he replied, 'Ah, yes, the globetrotting son. I've heard a lot about you.'

With a wavering face I let him know that maybe I wasn't too much to write home about just now.

'A nice job somebody did on your eye,' he pronounced.

I shrugged and tried to smile. 'Botched plastic surgery.'

To my surprise, this earned another one of his compact laughs. Then he got down to business. 'Please, sit down.' We did, both a little reluctantly, I sensed. Guiney continued, 'The main reason I'm here is to go over the procedure we're going to be following over the next few days. Risteárd, you've heard most of this before, but I think this would be a good time for your wife and son to get an overview.'

'By all means,' my father calmly assented.

'Early tomorrow morning we're going to wheel you down to the diagnostic centre and take some x-rays and, most probably, do an ultra-sound. If they reveal a blockage of any magnitude – and as I said to you before, from your bloodwork I suspect that they will – we'll put you under straight away and do a biopsy. And I should be in a position to come up and talk to you about that some time after lunch on Thursday.'

As he spoke, I discovered that *cold sweat* is not a figure of speech. I broke out in a cold sweat all over. Cold sweat soaked through the armpits of my Mossimo tee-shirt, the inner leg of my woolly Brooks Brothers boxer shorts, even the ankles of my silky Paul Smith socks. The Irish Sea on Christmas morning was nothing compared to this drenching. It was the word *magnitude* that got to me, that made my bowels flutter.

I was glad I was sitting down because my right leg started to jitter, and I was able to lean forward – as if I needed to pay any closer attention to this explanation – and quell it with my throbbing hand. Added to this damp dismay was the fear that my parents would see that I was losing my cool and turn their attention to me. Or even worse, that Guiney would start checking me out again. But no, the doctor got on with his frank preview and my parents nodded soberly, almost professionally, at all that he had to say.

Then Dr Guiney was excusing himself and my mother was on her feet once again wanting to shake his hand and thank him once again for stopping by to talk to us; and my father was earning another one of Guiney's economical laughs by telling him he'd be seeing him for a working breakfast in the morning; and I was also getting to my lead-weight feet – the rest of my body feeling paper-thin, headrush blackness fluttering on the margins of my eyesight – and having my good hand concisely shaken by his. He looked up at me, cobalt eyes crisp behind those perfectly preserved lenses, and said, 'Take care, young man. We don't want to be dealing with two patients at the same time.'

'I'll certainly try,' I responded. My voice was a lot calmer, more familiar that I expected. The old me, the classic Iremonger, was putting up a fight.

Dr Guiney was gone, for now, closing the door succinctly behind him.

I turned to my parents. My mother was a study in pensive elegance, sitting forward, legs crossed, chin resting on a plinth of fingers, looking at my father, her brown eyes liberated from those glasses, which now hung from her neck. It was hard to say where my father was looking. He'd tilted his head on the pillow in such a way that those big square bifocals were glazed with fluorescence from above. His lips were too dry. His face was too thin. His cheeks were too pale and too yellow at the same time, like the discoloured keys of the out-of-tune piano the old man used to have in the drawing room (though he always insisted you called it the parlour) of his bijou house in Sandymount. He was all wrong, all wrong, my father. I had to break this silence.

'Y'okay, Dad?'

He snapped out of it, lifting his head and flexing his eyebrows. (They needed a trim; he was beginning to look like Fr Harrington.) 'Fine, fine,' he replied. 'I was just thinking about what Guiney said. I appreciate his honesty. If there is something interfering with me plumbing' – that descent into Dublinese made me cringe inside; it smacked of smokescreening – 'then we need to know straight away, and get it sorted out.'

We? It made me uneasy to think that I might be part

of a team. I could only think of the number of B-team scrums I'd collapsed at Berchmans. The truth of course was that my father was on his own. And that was a pretty gloomy thought also. *We* were on the sidelines, my family and I, and no matter how hard we shouted or how hard we prayed, we could offer no shelter to the lonely full-back, waiting for the high, slippery leather ball, and the onslaught of enemy forwards. I imagined them wearing the colours of Old Belvedere. I saw Strongbow leading the pack.

'Keegan is very sure it's a hiatus hernia,' my mother said assertively, as if we'd never heard that diagnosis before, as if it hadn't been the official story all through Christmas, and god knows how long before I came back.

'Well,' said my father, a little testily, 'Keegan isn't Guiney, and that's why we're here. We'll just have to wait and see.'

My mother sighed and got to her feet. 'You're right, love, we'll just have to wait and see. In the meantime, I think I'll just take this fellow home and sort him out with a bag of ice and a hot dinner.'

I didn't protest; it didn't take a Trinity graduate to figure out that feeding me would be a therapeutic deal for her. And, funnily enough, for the first time in I didn't know how many months, or years, the idea of a hot dinner, home-cooked, suddenly sounded pretty appealing. My mother bent over and kissed the glossy top of my father's forehead. 'I'll drop back in about eight to see if you're all right.'

In the funeral home, I had followed his example and kissed the old man's forehead. It was like kissing a bowling ball. Triona kissed his lips. Flakes of skin came away on hers; discreetly she brushed them away, redid her subdued lipstick. Up to that moment, his long-expected death and the sight of his dead body had been an anti-climax for me, almost a non-event. But now my stomach churned, and, for a few minutes, I knew what death was.

'There's no need to drive all the way back, Sinéad,' my father was saying, 'I have enough here to amuse myself.'

'Ah, sure what else would I be doing.' My mother gave me a little wink. I wasn't sure how to handle this conspiratorial gesture, wasn't sure I deserved it. I smiled back as affectionately as I could. My father smiled at her too; he looked tired now, but reassured by this banter, and all that lay just underneath its surface.

'Okay, so.' He picked up his biro and his *Telegraph* again. My mother was walking over to me.

'See you tomorrow then, Dad,' I said, trying to sound up-beat but not moronically so. My mother, standing beside me, nodded with cautious approval. This inspired me to add something, 'I'm sorry I showed up so late.'

'Oh, better late than never.' He took one wry eye off his clues. 'And besides you weren't to blame.'

'Well,—' I stopped myself from getting too confessional. 'Well, yeah, circumstances beyond my control, I guess.'

'Come on so,' my mother said, a stiffness entering her voice.

Another round of goodbyes, and we were gone.

Outside the door, I thought I was going to get an earful about this whole mugging crap. But we walked back towards the elevators in silence, although it wasn't exactly a free ride for me; as we passed the nurses' station at the T-junction of corridors, I remembered how, when I could get away from the rest of my family, I would ask the nurse on duty, as solemnly as I could, how much longer Mr Iremonger had. Her answer was always sensitively put and professionally non-committal, and I was always secretly disappointed. I had tickets for a sold-out Waterboys gig on a looming weekend.

When my mother did speak, it was as our down-elevator arrived.

'Oh, there was a call for you just after you left for town.'

I didn't respond till we'd stepped inside and I'd pressed the G button. Whoever it was – Dylan, Roderick, Firbolg – I really wasn't in the mood for socialising, not with anybody in this town at least. But I made a lame attempt to care. 'Oh, yeah?'

'Oh, yes.' The way she savoured those words turned my head. 'Your girlfriend. Apparently she didn't know that she was meant to be meeting you for lunch.'

'Ah,' was all I could manage by the time the doors opened on the ground floor. My mother strode out into the lobby. I followed her coolly – I didn't want to give Caesar Boy the satisfaction of seeing me scramble after her. I did that once I was through the revolving door and out into a sharp winter night.

'Mum, it wasn't a deliberate lie, when I said I was going to meet Mainie Doyle for lunch; you've got to understand that it was just a kind of shorthand for—'

The sharp chirp of the Senator's alarm being deactivated – nasty sound – cut me off. My mother strode to the driver's side; I hovered by the front passenger door; our eyes met over the rain-beaded roof. 'I really don't want to hear it,' she asserted. And I believed her.

I had forgotten what a sure driver my mother is – it's her fear of flying that has come more readily to mind these past six months – and I was encouraged, comforted even, by her cool negotiation of the rush-hour traffic. And there were some vintage assholes on the road. Once we reached the dual carriageway, I felt that the atmosphere was calm enough to ask, gingerly, 'So what did Mainie actually say?'

For a long moment my mother did not respond, conspicuously concentrating on the traffic. 'She said, funnily enough, that she'd like to meet you before she leaves.'

My heart, Iremonger's enemy, began to pound with fright and excitement. The first thing I would do when I got home was tear into my second last pack of Rolands. I certainly didn't have to worry about hanging up my jacket.

The Feast of the Epiphany

I brought the portable phone up to my bedroom and sat at my desk. Its surface, the wood pale yellow like my father's face, was strewn with boarding-card stubs, foreign coins, glossy maps of city centres and subway systems, books of matches from trendy trattorias and be-seen-in bistros. This desk had served me right through Berchmans, right through Trinity. Of course, it was during the Berchmans years that the real work had been done. This is where I'd lost myself in history, where I'd cursed calculus, and where I'd got up close and personal with *Peig*, an autobiography in Irish which is my nomination for the worst book ever written.

Peig was this peasant who lived on some miserable rock of an island off the west coast. At the start of the book she says she's got one foot in the grave, and as I struggled, *Gaeilge-Bearla* dictionary in hand, through her descriptions of drinking buttermilk and dancing jigs and reels and losing yet another fisherman son – Paudeen Mike or Paudeen Seán – to the sea, I fantasised about shoving her all the way in. But somehow your education wasn't complete unless you spent a lot of quality time with that old shawl-covered witch.

I punched Mainie's number. (I forget my PIN but six months later her ex-directory phone number is still fingertip-fresh.) When nobody had picked up after four rings I came *that* close to killing the call; with every unanswered purr my nerves' anticipation that someone would answer grew, and so did my realisation that I didn't know what the hell I was going to say to Mainie.

Sixth ring her mother picked up, sounding like the queen, sounding, in other words, like her usual self. No, you couldn't accuse Lucia Doyle of having a telephone voice.

'Hey . . . Mrs Doyle. It's Tom Iremonger here.' Then I added absurdly, 'Mainie's friend?'

'Mainie's friend and *mine*,' she replied. It occurred to me that she might be drunk. I visualised her standing there in a palomino tent by Bibi McGurk, glass of tilting Chianti in her other hand, henna hair matted like dough, her made-up face the canvas of an action painting. 'How can I help you, dear?'

'Well, would Mainie actually *be* there?' I was not trying to be sarcastic; that's just the way it came out. It was like my voice was breaking all over again.

'Why, yes, I think she is,' Lucia said with soft, boozy warmth. 'Let me go find her.'

She put down – or dropped – the phone with a muffled clutter. I expected to hear her operatically calling her daughter, but there was silence, not even static, on the line. As it lengthened, lengthened into a minute, more, a voice in my head told me – *Iremonger* told me – forget it, forget it, fuck the SuperDoyles and their gourmet daughter. But just as I was about to take his advice, a quiet click indicated that an extension had been picked up.

'Hello?' Mainie said, in a calm pretence that she really didn't know who was calling. Before I spoke I saw her. In the Yeats room. Perched on a white leather couch with her legs tucked behind her. Wearing a favourite pair of old Levis and a subdued cashmere *faux*-turtleneck by Ungaro. Strongbow silent in the background.

'Yeah, hi, it's Iremonger, it's Tom. You called. I'm returning your call.' The words were right but the tone was all wrong.

A pause – to smile, I could almost hear her smile.

'How are you doing, Tom?'

'Great. Getting ready to leave, you know.'

'I didn't get a chance to say goodbye to you on New Year's Eve.'

'I had a taxi waiting – other commitments.'

'Of course. Well, it was kind of you to put in an appearance.'

'Oh, any time. What's on your mind, Mainie?'

I had answered that question a gazillion different ways myself in the last fifteen minutes, and come up with everything from Mainie wanting to offer me an abject apology for not inviting me, her old flame, her essential flame, to the party – to Mainie announcing her engagement to St John Strongbow.

'I heard about your father, Tom.'

This hit me harder than Belvo Boy's punch. I had never once considered, or allowed myself to consider, that her motivation for calling me was compassion. And I simply didn't know how to handle it – Mainie's *pity* – other than one way: put the bullshit generator into over-drive. Within seconds I had put together this story about how it was my uncle who had gone into the Simmonscourt Clinic, how he had come home from Africa especially to get treatment for a potentially malignant tumour in his stomach, how it was nothing but the best for those Jesuits.

I had got as far as saying, 'Well, you see it's a pretty weird coincidence,' when the line was disrupted by static and clatter – someone hanging up on the original phone.

This threw me, threw me further than it should have, and I stumbled and hesitated and soon knew that I'd blown it. And although Mainie would have undoubtedly listened politely to the rest of my lame story and politely believed it and said nothing more, I wasn't going to be satisfied with that. No way was I going to be happy with getting away with this fiction on the basis of pity. Suddenly honesty seemed to be my only defence.

'Well, I guess it's not a pretty weird coincidence after all. My uncle is home from Africa and I'm home for Christmas but all that was planned long before we knew that my father was going in for tests.'

'So you were coming home for Christmas all along?'

She had me. She had me so many ways that all I could really do was go with the flow.

'Yeah. In a way. But back to my father. It's just tests. He's fine, in great form. And he's got an awesome specialist taking care of the situation.'

'Dr Guiney.'

'Yeah, Dr Guiney. How do you *know* all this, Mainie?'

'Where do our mothers meet, Tom?'

'The golf club, of course. Why didn't I think of that?'

Probably because it was so much part of my mother's world, and how much time did I spend thinking about my mother's world? But since the year I started at Berchmans, she's been religously playing eighteen holes – two rounds of Killiney's hill-hugging, development-hemmed course – every Tuesday, Wednesday, and Thursday morning in seasonal weather, so much so that Mrs Donlan, our ancient neighbour, once had to be dissuaded that Sinéad Iremonger had a day job. She also goes up to the club for frequent lunches, dinners, and bridge nights, but never with my father. This is the cause of no tension, just something established, informally, a long time ago. He has no interest in golf and in the goings-on at the club; she has no interest in getting him interested. But I guess we're missing out on something, my father and me. Some formidable networking must go on, up in that club house on Killiney Hill where our mothers meet. Jesus, they probably know more about our lives than we do. Our circle has been shattered and scattered, only coming back together again for exercises in over-compensation such as this Christmas, but our mothers are always here (except when they're in Tenerife) – comparing notes, trading stories, fusing rumours, slyly bragging. And being economical about certain truths (Blanaid's bulimia, Jimmy's legal situation in Kuwait, Tom's whereabouts). And quietly missing us. And . . . roomkeeping.

Mainie was going on about how her mother had been very concerned that she hadn't seen my mother up at the club for so long and how she had just found out about my father going in for tests and how she wanted Mainie to pass on her very best wishes to both of my parents. I started thinking about the last time I'd gone up to the club, not to caddy for my mother, as I had done in my early teens, but to pick magic mushrooms with Ardal one Friday night during our first spring at Trinity. Then Mainie got around to saying something which got my full attention, 'You know, I'm leaving tomorrow evening, flying back to London. I'd like to meet you.'

With those five magic words Strongbow disappeared. Mainie was now speaking from her bedroom too, lying on that pillow-rich brass bed. The Official Iremonger Rulebook of Cool flew out of my hands, and I said rapidly, 'Sure. What about tonight? I'm free.'

She laughed, not unkindly. 'I'm not, I'm afraid. Besides, I'd rather meet you in the daylight. Tomorrow morning, for coffee.'

'I can live with that.'

'This Christmas has been such a whirlwind, I haven't had time to see half the people or do half the things I wanted to.'

And yet she wanted to see *me* again. 'Why don't we meet in the cafeteria at IMMA, there's this sculp—'

'No!'

She laughed again. 'What's the matter, Tom? Have you turned completely against culture?'

'No, not quite, Mainie,' I replied, recovering a few grams of composure. 'It's just that I've already seen that sad installation and I have no desire to see it again.'

Her voice betrayed further amusement. 'Okay. No problem. I'm sure I'll see it some other time. But prove to me you haven't got something against high art. Let's meet at the National Gallery.'

'Now that I can handle.'

We set a time – eleven, time enough for me to spend a very satisfying hour with Mainie and still make it to the clinic before lunch and catch my family. We concluded our conversation cordially. I then rooted through my Coach carry-on and lay down on my bed with *Cara* magazine.

Okay, let's get an establishing shot of old Iremonger arriving at the National Gallery this Wednesday morning – ten after eleven; I had enough self-respect today to be late – for this throw-me-for-a-loop rendezvous with Mainie Doyle. Iremonger, dressed in polished Boccionis, self-washed and self-pressed Armani chinos, and a horse-chestnut suede jacket bought at Dallas-Fort Worth airport (an ersatz-Nico) and worn only once before, is walking along by the tall black railings, through which can be seen that solid fart Dargan, poster boy for the Victorian Age, on his granite plinth, and behind him the grey façade of the gallery itself, jazzed up a little by some round windows and these odd blocky pillars holding up the portico.

When I entered the lobby this wrinkly green coat behind the cloakroom desk, looking like some mass murderer doing community service, stared at me as if I were barred from the place, which is not true, although I was once warned by the restaurant manager that he'd call security if I didn't stop hassling the staff for a seventh mini-bottle of Californian chardonnay to wash down the side order of coleslaw I'd bought for lunch. The lady behind the information desk, on the other hand, actually gave me a smile as I crossed the glossy lentil-coloured marble. It was a quiet morning at the National Gallery of Ireland.

As soon as I stepped into the first of the Irish rooms I spotted her straight ahead in the last one, in the real Yeats room. She had her back to me and was wearing a camel-coloured coat I hadn't seen before, but I knew it was her for sure. For one thing, Mainie chooses her mark carefully – she gives herself excellent direction. For another, for as long as I'd known her Mainie'd had a thing for Jack B., more so than her parents. They had played it safe with that pretty straightforward park-bench scene, but Mainie's taste ran towards the late, crazy canvasses in that final room. I didn't know how many times that first winter we were in Trinty we'd hung out by that monster canvas she was standing in front of now – I could never remember its bloody title, some abstract word – before we went into the restaurant, (where the Special Branch duo had already parked their broad arses for a cup of tea).

Passing through those brothel-red chambers, my Boccionis booming on the parquet, I barely registered the paintings. The only thing that caused a blip on my radar besides the back of Mainie's tight, glossy hair was the portrait of Lady Laverty. That class A aristocratic face of hers is the same one that appears every time you hold an Irish bank note up to the light – that's right, she's the babe on the watermark, dolled up (or should that be, dolled down?) to look like Cathleen Ní Whatshername, the peasant essence of Ireland, a pin-up Peig.

Iremonger enters the Yeats room. Besides Mainie, no one

else there except a tiny old green coat, eyes fixed on the floor as if the art were on the parquet and not on the walls. Mainie turned around, an ad director's ideal of calm confidence. Her jacket was felted cashmere, with an emphatically stitched shawl collar. Underneath she wore a silk blouse with seventies lapels and precision-pressed pants, matching sage. Make-up and scent – assertive. What a production. My money's on Mainie to be the *next* watermark.

That glint in her eye, that slight pursing of the lips I interpreted to be Mainie resisting a comment about my purple eye – and letting me know she was letting it pass. When she did speak she said, 'I wasn't expecting you so soon.'

I shrugged (I don't know what else to do other than the old Iremonger routine). 'I got lucky with the buses. And I knew where to find you – in front of . . . *Conflict.*'

Now a full-blown smile. '*Grief.* You could never get it right.'

Could never – I didn't like that past tense, but I didn't show it. 'I have trouble with abstract words,' I said.

'You used to think it was an abstract *painting.*'

I hiss-laughed, remembering. 'Yeah. Where would I be without you, Mainie. And I just thought the guy was just stoked up on something. You destroyed my innocence. But I still think you're BS-ing me about that mourning-mother figure. I see the house. I see the horse. I see the fallen soldier. But she's simply not there.'

'The trick is to stay with it, Iremonger. Step back and stay with it.'

We both stepped back. I stayed with it for at least another fifteen seconds.

'You're BS-ing me. Let's get that coffee.'

'Oh, let's.'

The restaurant in the National Gallery of Ireland is, in Mainie's words, *a bright, sane place*. Mainie, a bright, sane person, lives for bright, sane places. I do not. I found the décor kind of annoying (I'm sure the cafeteria in the Simmonscourt Clinic has that earnestly contemporary lighting and laminate set-up), but I also found it tolerable because I remembered all the fun lunches Mainie and I'd had here, our conversation a haberdashery of gossip and fashion feedback. It was a shock to be assaulted by pleasant memories for a change.

Mainie insisted on paying for our coffees – a pay-back for afternoon tea at the Shelbourne, she said. That was fine because I was running low on cash again and I noticed that they didn't take Wanderlust. While she was dealing with the cashier, I made a bee line for our usual table in smoking – or our old table, should I say, since Mainie turned her back on tobacco last spring – beside a bronze sculpture of these two leaping fish.

By the time she joined me, I had a Roland up and running (T - 31). I knew she was a little pissed, but she didn't say anything, just flashed this top-shelf fake smile. I didn't touch my coffee; Mainie flirted with hers, her little finger, its nail painted ruby, caressing the glaze of the mug.

Then she asked the inevitable question, 'So, any more news about your father, Tom?'

Sticking with the script I'd bashed out on the bus, I replied nonchalantly, 'Oh, yeah, some *good* news, actually. Guiney – his specialist, did I tell you about him? *Great* guy – he says Dad's problem is that he's got a hiatus hernia. That's the whole deal. Should be out of the clinic in the next few days. After that he's just going to have to be real careful about what he eats from now on. But, then again, isn't that the case with all the old dears?'

Mainie didn't answer my question. Instead she squinted a little as she sipped her drink. 'Hiatus hernia – sounds nasty.'

'Sure, but compared with what it could have been . . .' Something in my abdomen did a backflip; no way was I touching that coffee now. But I didn't show it. I'm sure I looked like a guy who had bowels of titanium. However, I was hoping to Christ I didn't have to cut this conversation with a pilgrimage to the porcelain temple. I like to keep the excuse of a bog stop in strategic reserve.

Mainie was, naturally, highly diplomatic about the whole thing, now that she was done prying. Well, I'd figured out *her* motivation for showing up here this morning. Now all I had to do was figure out exactly what I thought I was going to get out of it. 'I understand,' she said, nodding her head.

Time to test her a little – see how much she'd miss me, see what the Iremonger-void would be like in her life. Also, it would be quite bearable to change the subject.

'So, Friday I'm out of here.'

Mainie let me see a smile before she suppressed it. I decided to call her on this one. I was getting a little tired of this Mainie Doyle smile-fest.

'What's that all about?'

'What time on Friday?'

I shrugged. 'Lunchtime-ish.'

'Well, watch out for St John. He's on a midday BA flight back to London.'

'I'll be there to kiss him goodbye. So, tell me honestly, you pleased to be leaving, getting back to reality?'

'I know what you're saying, though I don't know how you'd know too much about reality, Tom. But anyway, yes, it will be nice to get back to my life. Once I get off the ground in Dublin I'll be fine, excited in fact about getting back to London. It also helps that I'm travelling BA – a clean break; Aer Lingus is all very well coming home. In any case, it's what you have to go through to get off the ground that I don't like. I hate having to go through that goodbye scene with my parents at the airport. This time I'm vowing to do it in the restaurant because I just couldn't stand doing it at the boarding-pass check place last time.'

'But Mainie, it's not like you're never going to see them again. You're home all the time. And you're only in London, for god's sake.'

'*Based* in London. Where you keep your summer clothes you can't call home. But even if I were *only in London*, I'd still have the same problem. London is a deceptive place, Tom – you know that. Just because it's not, you know, *abroad*, doesn't mean it's close to Dublin, even if you can get from Notting Hill to Dalkey Hill in less than three hours. Oh, you can fool yourself that you're keeping up with what's going on in Dublin – you can go to your London-Irish dances and meet some of the old Trinity crowd for brunch in Covent Garden on Sundays and get your same-day *Irish Times*, but that's not the same thing as living your life in Dublin. It's not even close. And see, that's my problem at the airport. It's not that I think the old pair are going to get run over by a bus before I see them again. At least, that's just a very small part of it. It's a realisation that this is just, on a certain level, *unfair*.'

At this point I rolled my eyes, more for all the people who were not here to hear this than for myself. I just felt it was the decent thing to do.

'No, I'm serious, Iremonger, hear me out. Maybe *unfair* is the wrong word to use. But isn't it sad, even for spoiled brats like you and me, who maybe could survive here economically, that we have to go away, or, in a strange way, have to choose to go away.'

'Please explain to me, Mainie, dear, how we *have to choose* to go away?'

'Because even if we stayed, half the people who really mattered to us would be gone. It's like I said at the party – perhaps you didn't hear this – Dublin would be buzzing if the natural thing were for people to stay and make a life for themselves after they've graduated.'

I shook my head. I also caught sight of those fish, those

brown marble fish. All the times we'd come in here for coffee or to dabble at lunch, I'd never really paid them much attention. Now the ugly fucks were beginning to bother me. Luckily, I had a good question for Mainie.

'But why Dublin? Why does it have to be Dublin? I don't know how many times we sat here – right here – and bitched about this city.'

'Dublin's not perfect. It will never be perfect. It will certainly never be New York or Paris or even London, despite some people's best, or worst, efforts. But that's not the point. It's all to do with *roots*, Iremonger. Don't you see? Everyone has their own Dublin. Everyone de*serves* their Dublin. Parisians, no matter what they say day-to-day, would never dream of leaving Paris.'

I let that one pass. No use challenging Mainie on her generalisations, I knew that much. All I did was snort, 'Roots.'

'Yes, roots.'

I found myself looking at the fish again, I couldn't help it. The two of them were swimming against the brown current. Or, more accurately, the upper, longer fish was leaping, cresting the muddy stone water; the bottom fish was a different story. The bottom fish was having a hard time. The poor fucker was really struggling. Can a fish *drown*? Because, quite honestly, that's what he looked like, a drowning fish.

Suddenly I felt terrible, like my whole body was a bowel. Time to push the radical button. Time to pull something out of the bottom of the Iremonger bag. Time to use the J-P Sartre strategy. Cool as I could, I made this announcement, 'West door, Hagia Sophia, 1:15 p.m., next St Patrick's Day. Be there. I will.'

From the sad little smile she gave me I knew immediately it had totally backfired. But I'd got no choice now but to stick with my bullshit.

'Tell me, Tom, why are you going to be in Istanbul on St Patrick's Day?'

Go down BS-ing – that, I guess, is the Iremonger philosophy in this kind of situation.

'It's the one place in the Western hemisphere I'm pretty sure I won't have to risk seeing a bloody parade.'

I was pretty sure this was going to provoke at least some kind of reaction from her, but instead I got the silent treatment. Even worse, it was the *sad* silent treatment. The only thing she did was tap the blond wood top of the table with a single ruby nail. I didn't know what to say, so I made a big production out of cranking up a fresh cigarette. It also helped me keep my eye off those frigging fish; these Rolands are my support group. Finally Mainie looked up at me and stared, a rumour of moisture in those black poster eyes of promise.

She gave me this crap, 'Tom Iremonger, can you *afford* to do this for another year?'

'Don't worry about my bank balance, Main.'

'That's not what I was talking about. I'm sure your grandfather left you very well provided for.'

From the way she said that and the way she wouldn't quite look at me as she did, I knew she'd seen the story in the paper. So now I had plenty of reasons to be a touch mad. 'Christ, Mainie, I thought you of all people would have a little respect for what I'm trying to achieve.'

The word *achieve* sent her bold brows leaping so high that for a second I thought she was going to shriek with amusement. And Mainie's got some shriek, let me tell you. But instead she just said, 'Since when has *dossing* been an achievement? Because that's all your famous anti-odyssey adds up to, Tom. Getting laid in Los Angeles, getting stoned in Barcelona – it's all just dossing around, getting nowhere, fooling yourself that the future doesn't matter. And your so-called friends are just such total cowards that they won't tell you the truth, even though they're slowly waking up and smelling reality themselves.'

I leaned back in my chair, gave her a smile with a little mean twist. Did she think I hadn't heard all this before? Well, I had, at least half a dozen times, (even if it hadn't been so blunt). But I guess only Mainie Doyle, who had listened for so long and so supportively to my blossoming philosophy in college, could throw it all back in my face like that, like cold coffee. Transcontinental dossing. Christ, I thought, what a *cheap* interpretation. I would never have believed that Mainie Doyle of all people could be so cheap.

After too much of a delay, this is how I replied, 'And I suppose you think it would have been a good idea for me to have toddled along to the milk-round interviews.'

Mainie stared at me again, then sighed acidically. 'Okay. Let's say it's ten years from now. You've finally exhausted your inheritance and your luck. What if you have kids to support? Do you ever think about that?'

'Certainly I do. And I can assure you that that won't happen.'

This amused Mainie big time. 'What, did you buy yourself a vasectomy while you were away?'

I gave that one the smile it deserved. Then I looked over at the sculpture again. My eyes focused – involuntarily – on that lower fish, that bottom feeder.

'Okay, Mainie. I'll humour you with a hypothetical. Say I do sign up with the Mainie Doyle Project: I have a kid and lock myself away behind the green glass of the Financial Services Centre. I have a nice time, I get fat, I join Killiney golf club, but basically I'm living for the future, living for him. And so he grows up and graduates from Trinity, and just as he's on the brink of discovering the depths of himself, he has to go behind the green glass so that he can have a kid who can grow up and graduate from college so that *he* can go behind the green glass and prepare for the next generation. What's the point? When does it end? Why can't it end with *me*?'

Mainie calmly folded her arms and leaned forward on the table. A keen smile now. 'You know who you remind me of?'

'Who do I remind you of, Mainie?' My money was on McQuaid.

'Niall Golden. *Father* Niall Golden.'

Now that one, I'll admit, I was not expecting. Auto-irony kicked in, 'Sure, Mainie, he's my role-model.'

Her lips glistened as she wrestled back a smile. I decided anticipation was the best form of defence at this stage. 'Well, go on, say it.'

'Say what?'

'Say what you always say.'

'Oh, that you've shot yourself with a ball of your own shite?'

Normally it made me laugh to hear Mainie, with her rarefied accent, say that word, but not now.

'That's the one.'

She gave an ironic pout. 'But Tom, you did that back on Christmas Eve at the Shelbourne.'

'How, might I ask?'

'I was about to ask you to my party, but you told me you had other plans.'

I shrugged and smiled, and looked over at the fish. No, I hadn't shot myself with a ball of my own shite. I was swimming in it.

Conversation was pretty much an anti-climax after that. Mainie left about ten minutes later, pleading a shopping date with her mother (rumours of further reductions on YSL bolero jackets at Brown Thomas). I lingered in the restaurant, sacrificing a few more Rolands to the cause (T - 27), and then made my way back slowly through the Irish rooms; I was in no rush to get home.

Well, I tell you, it was a bit of a revelation. All those years going to the National Gallery, and I'd never really been up close and personal with the *paintings*. I gotta tell you, there's a lot more going down there besides Jack B. Yeats. All those other Yeatses, for a start, either painting or posing (now *there's* a family it would have been a blast growing up in). And then there was this landscape that my father's always talking about, *Dawn in the West* by this guy Paul Henry. Always going on about Paul Henry's famous blue hills. Well, breaking news – those hills ain't blue. They're *teal*. And I can say that with absolute authority because I must have looked at that painting for at least thirty seconds. Don't you just hate it when people refuse to be precise about colour?

I didn't scrutinise the other paintings so much, and I've got to admit that even though I only left the gallery about half an hour ago (I'm upstairs on a Bombardier, heading for the clinic, smoking my second illegal Roland), they've sort of merged in my mind – big houses and fishing boats, flower girls and fairies, red coats and revolutionaries, priests and ponces in wigs – they've broken out of their frames, all become part of the same mad canvas. Christ, I hate to think about the kind of dreams I'm going to have tonight.

In the car park of the clinic, I walked by my mother's Juno and my sister's – they were side by side. This made me feel guilty, somehow. As I entered the lobby I saw my sister coming from the elevators. My first thought was to get back in that revolving door; to begin with, I didn't want her giving me grief for being late (they'd been there since about 11:30). But all I did was slow my steps. Caesar Boy was on duty and watching me, and smirking, I swear. But here's the thing that really got to me – the way Triona reacted when she saw me. She gave me this big sad *loving* smile. It was chilling. What the hell had I done to deserve that? I tried to smile back in kind, but I think it came out kind of shell-shocked. We met near the low leather couches.

'Hey,' I greeted her.

'Hiya,' she replied.

Straight away I was scouting her brown eyes for tears, but saw none, though there were dark crescents forming under her eyes that her make-up failed to hide.

'Do you want to sit down for a minute?' she asked.

I didn't but said sure.

We sank into the soft leather of separate couches, then both leaned forward in unison. I looked over to see if Caesar Boy was minding his own business. Amazingly he was.

'So, what's the damage?' I asked.

She laughed nervously at the way I said it, looked down at the dark glass of the coffee table a moment, and then looked up at me calmly.

'Well, things went well. It was very straightforward. But there is some kind of blockage. Guiney did go in and do a biopsy. You know what that means?'

'No diagnosis yet.'

'Exactly. Dr Guiney's going to meet with Dad tomorrow morning, and there may be some news then.' She paused. 'You'll be around then, won't you, Tom?'

'Yes. Of course.' That was a little bit snappy, so I toned things down. 'I'm flying out Friday lunchtime; that is, if everything's under control here.'

'Of course.' She stood up, so did I. 'Well, I'd better pick up Sibéal and Kieran from their other granny. Mum and Columb are upstairs. They put Dad under a general anesthetic, so he's really drowsy still. But he'll know you're there.'

'Good, good.'

'I heard about this,' Triona said as she touched the edge of my spoilt eye. I winced away. She didn't get offended. I wonder if she was remembering what I was – the cut knees and elbows she repaired when I was a kid and she was almost a grown-up.

'I'd better get up there,' I said, looking over towards the elevators as if they were departing trains.

'Do,' she said.

I reached forward and kissed her quickly on her thin cheek. I began to walk away, but she tugged the arm of my false jacket.

'You know maybe tomorrow morning we could have a coffee or something. They've got a very nice cafeteria downstairs.'

'Sure,' I replied.

But there's no way I will. I think it would be easier for me at this time to have coffee with Bish McQuaid than with my sister.

According to my Tzara, it's 4:22 a.m. in Dublin: clubbing-time in New York, bedtime in Paris. I've woken up to take a breather from bad dreams. Reading, for the hell of it, my uncle's little red book:

Both what you run away from – and yearn for—
is within you

And guess what, for about the first time since I hit the ground on Christmas Eve, I'm right about something. This morning I didn't have to get up close and personal with Triona. I got up close and personal with Columb instead. Not in a coffee shop, thank god. No, somewhere with a little more breathing space – Owenstown Hill Park. (Though it was uncomfortable there in other ways.) How did Iremonger get himself in another one of these situations? It happened like this. I emerged from my bedroom with most of the morning mercifully wasted. Columb was downstairs in the drawing room, looking through *The Irish Times* as if it were an artifact from some extinct civilisation.

'Where's my mother?' I asked him.

'Playing golf,' he replied, and he said it just right: surprise, amusement, and a touch of admiration all in his voice. Apparently she would be back around midday. We would have some lunch together, and then go down to the clinic.

Columb folded the paper carefully, as if it were an altar napkin. 'I was just considering a walk around the park, to kill the time. It looks like the rain has stopped. Why don't you come with me?'

He smiled, but those intense grey-blue eyes fixed me in such a way that I knew I had been given a soft command.

So off we went, the odd couple, Columb wearing my father's padded anorak, Iremonger not wearing Nico. I've gotta tell you, at first, going up the hill, it was pretty painful. Priests like him and people like me aren't good at small talk, at the best of times. Things got better as we finally walked up the steps into the park, or so I thought.

'Tell me, Tom, who thought up that poster at the airport?'

I laughed for the first time in days. 'Now which poster would that be?'

'Promoting the Industrial Development Authority.'

'Ah, I think I know the one you're talking about. That's the work of Ascendancy.'

I knew this was more than just casual curiosity on his part, but I was happy to tell him about how the agency and its creatives worked; I made a number of references to Renaissance workshops and medieval cathedral-building, stuff I remember from BBC2 documentaries I used to watch with Mainie. As I lectured, we walked along the lower portion of the park's perimeter tarmac path, overshadowed on one side by the sloping wood of old deciduous trees (don't ask me to get any more precise than that), overlooking on the other a final line of thin trees, an old ha-ha fence, and the backs of the shops on Lodge Road. Running through the wood were muddy tracks created and maintained by countless children's bikes, including Firbolg's and mine.

'I take it they're rather expensive,' said Columb.

'Sure. The best is always expensive. But giving them twenty grand would be like giving another agency forty. You get more than your money's worth.'

'Maybe I will.'

'Excuse me?'

He smiled, but said nothing for another ten steps or so. That's when I knew Columb was going to pull something on me for sure.

'I came into a little money earlier this year.'

'Oh, yeah, of course . . . his money. But I thought it went straight to the Js because of that vow of poverty deal you have.'

'Yes,' Columb said slowly, smiling again. 'But I am *part* of the Js.'

'So you were in the loop.'

'In the loop?'

'Part of the decision.'

'Yes, indeed, I was in the loop, as you say. Or I *am* in the loop. Nothing's been decided yet. I *thought* when I came home that I was simply going to get banker's drafts prepared for the Remokoan Family Institute AIDS education programme. But when I saw you at the airport, Tom, I started having other ideas. Say if you could take that twenty thousand pounds and turn it into fifty or a hundred thousand, through the power of advertising.'

I was paying very close attention at this stage, and I didn't like the way he'd just said *you*. A man like Columb never left language to chance.

'So . . . what's the plan?' I asked.

'The plan, possibly, is to use the money to launch an

advertising campaign on behalf of the AIDS education programme. Posters, radio, even television. Do you think your friends at Ascendancy would be interested?'

'Well, it wouldn't exactly fit their typical client profile, but, sure, why not.'

'Would you be interested in acting as liaison between them and me?'

So, the missionary man wanted to give *me* a mission. Suddenly what my mother had said years ago made sense, and helped me make sense of what was going on right here and now: my poster was the sprat, and I was the salmon.

That was clear, but also grim. I began to sweat more than when McQuaid had pulled that gun on me. I was dying for a Roland, but for once I'd left them back at the house (for some reason I felt uneasy about lighting up when I was alone in his company).

'Well, sure, I can make a few calls before I leave on Friday, or whenever. I guess I can set you up with some go-sees, since you're likely to be around longer than I am.'

I thought this lack of commitment was going to produce a pretty icy response, but he just said quietly, 'We'll talk again.'

A few paces later we were overshadowed by stone instead of wood – a mound of granite boulders and broken white pillars that years ago had been part of the gates of the old estate, down by the dual carriageway. Firbolg and I had called them the Rocks. That highest boulder was the summit of our world. From up there you had a commanding view of the suburbs, the city, the bay. Past the Rocks Columb and I were into the open half of the park. Here the wind picked up. It seemed to be blowing down from the dark rims of the mountains, indistinct beyond the deserted playing fields. Emerging below us now was the blurry panorama of grey Dublin. The only landmarks I could pick out were the Eiffel Tower-shaped aerial down at RTE and the Stalinistic phallus that was yucky death's watertower. I knew if I looked sharply I might see the Simmonscourt Clinic, but instead I looked away and asked Columb, 'Did you tell me one time, maybe when we were walking up here when I was a kid, that you used to come up here before Owenstown Hill was even finished?'

'We used to come up here before the housing estate was even begun, Tom. That was before the war, when my mother was still alive. All of that' – he swept a dismissive hand along the houses of Lodge Road below us – 'everything beyond the park here was open country. The little cottage down there by the Mount Anville gate belonged to the estate's chief gardener. In a clearing in the woods there was an abandoned belvedere. And there was a stream between the woods and where the church is now.'

A river running through a rural Owenstown Hill – he might as well have been talking about another geological age, I found it that hard to imagine. I kind of regretted never having done a project on this for Quinlaven.

When we were close to the Mount Anville gate, he stopped and looked back at the bay.

'Can't even see Ireland's Eye today.'

'Or Lambay,' I added, brightened by remembering the name of the other island out beyond the thin strip of Sutton.

'I remember one very clear summer day Daddy pointing out the Mourne Mountains to us on the horizon.'

Now, forget the stream, this definitely was a little surreal.

'You can see the *North* from here?'

A very thin smile from Columb. 'Maybe only back then.'

We skipped lunch. My mother didn't get back from golf till one o'clock, and there was a consensus, hardly spoken, that we should forget about food and come straight down here. My mother had driven to golf in the Juno, but she wanted to take the Senator to the clinic. I was kind of touched by that; it seemed an expression of loyalty, of hope.

So we've driven down here in my father's new car. My mother suggested, quietly but firmly, that I should let my uncle sit up front, and I certainly didn't give her any grief about it: fine by me if I have to take a back seat. Conversation consisted of a Q&A session between Columb and my mother about women not being allowed to join golf clubs as full members; the cringe factor was high since she really didn't want to talk about it, she was just being polite.

My mother leads the way through the revolving doors. In the lobby Caesar Boy greets us courteously, and that cold sweat washes across my brow again. I nod back at him solemnly. What does he know that I don't?

Elevator opens, and in there already is this young nurse, a skinny red-head, her face a freckle-fest. I sense her radar picking me up in spite of herself. She gives us the same courteous nod CB did. I don't like this. I don't like this at all. I don't like the doors closing. I don't like the silence. What does she know that we don't? For this is the place bad news is broken, isn't it?

But the freckly nurse has nothing to say to us, and stays on board the elevator when the doors open on the third floor. And we have nothing to say to each other as we head for Room 3.18. Two nurses are standing behind the station at the T-junction of the corridors, and as we approach them, one sees us and whispers to the other, who looks up and smiles at us uneasily. Now that is *not* my imagination.

'Hello, how are you?' they and my mother say simultaneously. She speaks in her telephone voice: not a good sign.

After knocking almost as confidently as Dr Guiney, my mother pushes down the large metal handle and opens the door, revealing a room gloomy without its fluorescent lighting. Entering last, I hear her say in a baffled, amused tone tainted with tension, 'Where is he? Risteárd?'

I'm about to tell her to do the obvious – check out the bathroom – when I see what she's talking about. We're standing in the middle of a vacated room. The bed has been tautly remade, the bedside table cleared of coins and biros and bags of dates and dried apricots, newspapers are unfurling in a brown plastic bin. Columb goes through the motion of knocking on the bog door – no reply. My mother opens a cream laminated closet – nothing but the jangle of bare wire hangers. She closes it again, turns around and says, slightly smiling, slightly stunned, 'Well, this is the best yet.'

A thought flashes on and off in my mind like a neon sign, and it takes more strength that I expect to stop myself from blurting it out – they've taken him to the top floor. I stare out at the slanting roofs of the RDS until Columb speaks, 'There must be a reasonable explanation for this.'

Yes, they've taken him to the top floor.

'I'll go and ask at the nurses' station,' he adds.

'Do,' my mother says. 'Do.'

But Columb doesn't: a confident knock on the open door is followed immediately by the *tock-tock* of the light switches being thrown on. Dr Guiney emerges from the short passageway formed by the bathroom, followed, as the fluorescent bulbs flash to solid, by my father, dressed in a familiar ensemble of Dunnes Stores browns and off-whites.

'Dad?' I say, expressing our shared bewilderment.

'Son?' he replies.

He has his hands in his trousers pockets, trying to look as casual as his clothes, testing a rakish smile on his carefully shaven but still yellowish face. Guiney lets him by.

'Hello,' my father says. 'You fellows are early. I was planning to be downstairs in the lobby, bag in hand. But our spies spotted you.' He's really getting into this now, whatever *this* exactly is.

'I only played nine holes,' my mother replies, in a choked kind of way.

Suddenly my father's eyes are slick. 'See, I told you. I told you, Sinéad – you should always keep up the golf.'

Then they are in each other's arms, and a warm sweat causes me to make sure the roofs of the RDS are still there. When I look back at my parents they are looking towards Guiney, who, standing close to Columb, looks like a fellow priest. My mother asks the doctor, 'Does this mean what I think it means?'

Guiney opens his mouth, then stops himself with a smile, and points his short, authoritative arm towards the two leather-and-wood chairs that have been pushed back to the window. My mother is the only one who sits down, but that's good enough for Guiney. He gives us the prognosis: 'Risteárd and I have just come back from the diagnostic centre. I was showing him the x-rays we took Wednesday morning, the ones that showed up the blockage. They show what a tricky little spot it's in, down in the bile duct. It will take several months of treatment to get rid of it. But the good news is that the biopsy revealed that it's benign. Resection – surgery – won't be necessary, we hope. Instead I'd like to get Risteárd here on an out-patient basis to receive the new sonar treatment twice a week for the next five weeks. That should take care of the problem. Well,' – he takes a token glance at his clipboard – 'I'd better get back to the centre. Mrs Iremonger, it's been a pleasure.'

My mother's on her feet already. How to describe her now . . . emotional and controlled at the same time. Graceful. Yes. My mother is graceful.

'Doctor,' she says, 'you've been wonderful.'

'I've had a wonderful patient,' he replies, and you can tell he's getting really formulaic now. I guess the cured, or the saveable, bore him a little. But when it's my turn to shake his hand, he looks at me shrewdly and says, 'Good luck on your travels, young man.'

'Thank you,' I reply. 'Thank you for everything.'

He nods with curt modesty, but there's no way that even Guiney, with his x-ray vision, can understand how much that *everything* includes. For one thing, the good doctor has handed me my boarding card.

12 ∫

Flight

This time, the toll bridge route. But once again we're in the Senator and my father's driving and I'm the émigré of honour in the front seat. Once again my mother is in the back seat, but this time she's got Columb for company – it's a big party seeing Iremonger out of the country; I'm surprised, as we speed along the coast road, that we don't have an escort of gardaí outriders, that there aren't cheering crowds lining the pavements and sea wall. I'm sure there's a lot of people relieved to see Iremonger go. I know I am.

So, the rest of yesterday, my last full day in Dublin. We were hanging around the lobby of the clinic when my sister finally got there. I tell you, if you think the scene in 3.18 was emotional, you should have seen Triona downstairs. Tear overdose time. Needless to say, my mother joined in. In fact, for a moment or two I thought they were going to drag me into it too, but then I lit up a Roland (T - 14) and felt decidedly better after a few deep chilling drags. Caesar Boy was too busy being discreet behind a post-Christmas copy of the *RTE Guide* to give me any crap about the No Smoking signs. My mother did that for him.

The Iremonger clan was officially in festive mood. We drove down to my parents' idea of a cool restaurant (you know, the kind of place that's just totally focused on the *food*) – Roman's Bistro in Ballsbridge. Actually, it wasn't too bad – a pretty good cover to get started early on some dedicated drinking. (After my recent adventures in Tír na nÓg and the Phoenix Park I was through, for now, with mood alteration of the illegal variety.) I toyed with some kind of pasta primavera while taking care of my own private half-bottle of Chianti and sampling the Frascati the rest of the table was sharing. Everybody was being so incredibly upbeat that I got no more that a few looks from my mother, although one time, after I'd poured the Chianti pretty abundantly, my father muttered, 'That's an ignorant glass of wine.'

I just nodded and smiled (making sure I wasn't *smirking* – he's always had a problem with my smirking), almost pleased that, consciously or unconsciously, he'd picked up on the old man's phrase. And I could understand my father being a little narky. Here he was, in one of his favourite places of indulgence, and he was having the starter niçoise salad as a main course – doctor's orders. I let it pass. Yes, I let it pass.

No, the worst moment of the meal was Columb's creation. My father asked him if he had taken care of his bank business okay, and Columb couldn't quite hide how pleased he was with the question.

'As a matter of fact, Rich, I've had good reason to delay going to the bank.'

My father trampled and swallowed a mouthful of salad. 'Oh, yes? Tell us more.'

Columb smiled thinly, turned and fixed me with those grey-blue eyes. 'Tom? Would you like to tell them?'

Well, I didn't like that. I didn't like that at all. That broke the First Rule of Cool. My father was now bulging his crème-caramel eyeballs at me. I stiffened myself with a hearty sip of Chianti, and said, in monotone, 'Columb wants to spend his money on hyping one of his African charities. I'm going to get the ball rolling with a few calls this afternoon.'

But to my surprise, my uncle looked satisfied, my sister curious, and my parents encouraged. For the next five minutes it was like a fucking Beatles-at-JFK press conference, with Columb as the quiet Beatle, and Iremonger having to be cute, funny, and cruel. You'd swear that I'd announced that I was going to King's Inns or something.

Thankfully, lunch began to break up even before the dessert trolley rolled by because Triona had to leave and pick up the kids from their other granny. Unfortunately, before she left she announced that, given the day that was in it, she would be having a 'celebration and going-away' dinner at her house that evening. She was going to make sure Finbar was home early, and do some special shopping at the SuperDoyle flagship store. My parents were delighted, though you could tell my father's emotions were a little mixed up at the prospect of having to go easy at another feast hours later. Columb seemed happy to go with the flow. Thanks to the Chianti, I too was beginning to go with the flow, and so I was pretty gracious about Triona's bright idea. In fact, if you merged those two party concepts together, you got a going-away celebration, which was what my whole day was about. Why not spend some more of it with my family?

After a little cloying dessert wine, I made my excuses and left Columb and my parents to finish their regular coffee. I caught a Bombardier into town and took care of Iremonger business there, mainly in O'Neill's, the Dawson Lounge, and the International Bar.

Some secondary errands got taken care of also: I popped

into the Wanderlust office to make a final withdrawal of punts (withdrawal without penetration – there's the story of this sorry Christmas in a nutshell) and to get a cache of francs for when I hit the ground at CDG. I stepped into Diaspora Travel to re-confirm my 13:10 EI 643 departure on Friday, 6 January. And, yes, I even placed a call to Ascendancy (from the pay phone in the Dawson Lounge), leaving a message for Dara Zorkin (an entry-level creative there, no great loss to bother him) to give Columb a buzz at my parents' number.

By the time I got over to Triona's in Marley Forest, I had a pretty considerable buzz going myself. My mother got suspicious immediately, but I was able to smokescreen my sobriety by horsing around with Sibéal and Kieran in the Wogans' new extension. My darling niece and nephew were keen to show me toys they'd bought with my Eurocheques – a Mainie Doyle doll and an Iremonger Man, accessories not included.

Dinner was like lunch all over again, except that the predictability-level was cut radically by the presence of the kids. They were happy to have their grandfather back out of hospital, but the novelty of having him well again – that's the way it had been explained to them – soon wore off, and instead they latched on to the novelty of their uncle going away again. The kids weren't really into the seafood lasagna my sister served up (I couldn't get enough of it, home-cooking seems to be my new addiction), so that's when the interrogation really began. I fended off questions about my multi-coloured eye and my missing jacket pretty well. The touchiest subject, I discovered, was my itinerary. Already I can't remember what kid asked what; my niece and nephew have become a kind of mega-pest in my imagination.

'Where are you going tomorrow, Tommy?'

'Back to Paris.'

'Why?'

'Because that's where my plane ticket says I have to go.'

'But why do you have to do what your plane ticket says?'

'Because it would be a terrible waste of money not to. I'm sure Mummy and Daddy have told you how bad it is to waste money.'

'But why did you have to buy a plane ticket, Tommy?'

'Because it's time to go away again.'

'Why?'

I shrugged. Mega-pest repeated its question; the Iremonger shrug meant nothing to it. Triona told the creature to eat its fish, but I've got to say she could have interrupted a lot sooner. I got the feeling that she and the rest of the family were enjoying seeing me sweat a little.

Beyond the silt of Sandymount Strand stand the giant barber-shop poles of the Pigeon House power station. That's where the man beside me started his working life, years before joining American Machines. I try to imagine what he did over there, and run this imaginary black-and-white footage, like something from an early RTE documentary, through my mind: a young, lanky version of my father, dressed in a white coat and Buddy Holly glasses, bending over a vast control panel and fine-tuning a thick knob. But I know that's about as complete a picture of the past as my grandfather's portrait.

I want to ask my father about working beneath those red-and-white poles. I want to ask him about trudging through Ireland, planting pylons, on the Rural Electrification Scheme, his next gig after the Pigeon House. I want to ask him exactly why he took early retirement from American Machines. I want to ask him how he feels about his past and his future. I know I've hardly talked to him since I came home. Correction – I've hardly talked to him since I became Iremonger. And I don't know how to begin.

Skirting Irishtown – why did they give this dive that name? Don't they realise that Irishtown can happen anywhere in the world? – my uncle and father start talking about this cluster of miniature three-storey houses that won some award for being decent public housing. I'm tempted to look back and wink at my mother – this is surely more sprat-throwing; Columb probably wants the architect flown out to Africa – but even if I could get away without him catching me, I'm not sure I would. I haven't earned that kind of ease with my mother.

As we go through this warehouse area, I'm cheered by the sight of a Kells – Sacred for Centuries billboard. I guess that's pretty rich since I never replaced the bottle I took from the AM hamper. But I did replace something else, something I'll come to as soon as I can (I want to get *out* of here).

The sight of the river, the black river, makes me feel even better than the advertising. From the back my uncle mutters something, sounds like Greek, sounds vaguely like I might have heard it years ago in Berchmans. I catch my father smiling thinly to himself. On the way up to the toll booth we pass a grimy terrace of red-brick houses. I tell you, no matter what problems are going down in this Iremonger life, I'd rather get sucked out a window at 30,000 feet than end up living in one of those holding cells. Anything but a *little* life, please.

The line of cars at the toll-booth plaza moves quickly. As my father lowers his automatic window, I tap him on the shoulder. He turns, a touch cantankerous.

'Yes, Tom?'

'I've got exact change, Dad.'

He taps open a matte-black tray between us. 'So have I.'

'Shouldn't I pay?' I ask.

My father looks at the silver in my hand, shrugs, and says, 'Yes. Why not.'

He grabs the coins with surprising nimbleness and flings

them into the funnel. My grandfather's money raises the barrier.

Crossing the Liffey, I look up-river and see the wavy turquoise top of Liberty Hall, the restored stone of the Customs House (bright again on another dull day), and the grey compactness of town and its bridges. I think of what Mainie said. That everyone deserves their Dublin, and that this one happens to be ours.

But then we're across to the other side and in the shadow of the Point Depot, and quite frankly I've never been so pleased in my life to be on the Northside.

I had a Martello cab ordered for 7:45 so that I had a reason no one could argue with for splitting from my sister's. It worked beautifully. Three minutes after the driver rang the front-door bell and I casually remembered that I was expected at a party at Anna Livia Carr's place in Wicklow, the very last party of the reunion season, I had put in a pretty decent goodbye scene with the Wogans and was out of there.

But as the taxi headed towards town I began to feel dismal. I totally sobered up for one thing – the drinking I'd done at Triona and Finbar's had done no more than service my buzz anyway. And for another, I couldn't long ignore that something was nibbling away like a Norwegian rat at my heart. And I couldn't completely dismiss the notion from my mind that it was to do with actually beginning to miss the Wogans, even the kids – that I was actually feeling the emotion I'd acted out a few minutes before. Is there such a thing as Delayed Emotion Syndrome? If so, I may be suffering from it. That may be my problem – that I'm a victim of DES.

But wait a second. Perhaps I wouldn't have been so shaky if I had been on my way to something as solid as an Anna Livia Carr party down in Wicklow. That would have been a perfect arena for a night of Iremongering, for being the Iremonger of old. Instead, the only thing I had to look forward to was a vague programme of mad pinting and clubbing, hanging out with whoever I bumped into, as long as they weren't after Iremonger's balls like the Bish had been. I hadn't made plans with anybody. For a start, Christmas Day had been almost two weeks ago and most people with a heavy pay-cheque habit were long gone from Dublin. Of course, my old partners in crime, the mad pinting gang, had more flexible schedules, but I hadn't been returning their calls since New Year's Eve – were they really on my side in all this? – and in the last two days they'd stopped phoning.

What would be the perfect way to spend my last night in Dublin (who knows, maybe my last night *ever* in Dublin)? I could only think of one thing, and that was pretty annoying and pointless since it was already pitch dark. I remembered an evening in June when I left the mad pinters and our satellites and a gazillion other people in Kenny's on Westland Row, all glued to the TV, watching Ireland play a round one game in the World Cup. I just couldn't get into it, so I got out of there. Dublin was deserted. The only person I saw for the longest time was a cop in the distance. I walked through the easy evening light feeling like the place belonged to me. On the quays I heard whistles coming from a pub, followed by a roar, and other distant roars. Ireland had gotten away with a draw, I later found out. Slightly retarded-looking people wearing green-and-white scarves began to spill out onto the street in celebration, taking my city away.

But suddenly, going through quiet Clonskeagh, the idea of drinking depressed me too. The idea of drinking didn't seem evil at all. The idea of drinking made me desperate for a drink.

One thing that I hadn't considered when putting together

my taxi plan was that the get-away car would take me past Berchmans on the way into town. I looked down that dark avenue as we cruised by, and saw myself, Fish, picking up his barrister's bag. Midday. I resolved that I would get to the airport by midday. I would develop an unprecedented compulsion to follow an airline's recommendation about checking in early. And I didn't care if my parents believed me or not.

My pub surfing can only be described as radical. I took a purist approach, creating a circuit of seven booze institutions – the Stag's Head, O'Neills, the International, Keogh's, Dougheny and Nesbitt's, McDaid's, and Grogan's – that I was still welcome in, if that's the right word. I planned to complete the circuit every hour, having a pint of Fursty in every one, and a Roland (T - 10 at 8 p.m.) if I was desperate. The first hour was perfect, though the long trek up to Dougheny and Nesbitt's almost killed me when it turned into a run to make up time.

So by the time I raced back to the Stag's Head, I was feeling pretty proud of myself, much recovered from my little crisis, or crises, in the taxi, though still not feeling particularly affected by alcohol. No matter, still two more good hours of good drinking time left.

The Stag's had gotten pretty jammed since I'd left there fifty-three minutes before – there were a lot more old faces around that I'd reckoned, though I sensed I was causing a blip on only a minority of radars tonight, even with my evil eye. I figured my best bet to get some dedicated drinking done was in the snug, which has its own counter, connected to the main bar. Unfortunately, it's a big snug, with a red-velvet couch that snakes around three walls and plenty of standing room. There were about twenty-five people boozing back there, and one of them was Roderick de Brun, hanging with some of the people who'd been in his kitchen Christmas morning, some of the Law Library crowd. They didn't pay me much attention, or not *enough* attention for my liking, but Roderick stood up immediately to come over and talk to me.

He was in fine form, wearing his oval glasses and gold-threaded toque. And even though he'd put on some more weight over Christmas he still carried it well. Now more than ever, I needed Nico.

'Well, look at who's still here.'

'What do you mean, Rod?'

'The rumour was that you'd been seen at the airport yesterday, getting on a plane to Frankfurt.'

Ah, that was more like it – rumours. I smiled for real. 'I think people are confusing me with my poster.'

'That eye should help them see the difference.'

To my surprise, I actually found this funny. 'I might use that one, de Brun.'

'I guess there's no chance of getting a straight answer out of you about how you got it.'

I shrugged. 'Probably better to wait for the rumours to start coming in.'

'Fair enough. Listen, let me buy you a drink.'

Did he think I was short of money? If so, how did he know?

'Sounds good,' I replied because I was still sharp enough to realise that anything but a casual response would scream financial anxiety.

We found standing space at the counter – people willing to shift themselves more on account of his presence than mine – and ordered Fursties. Roderick noticed me checking out my Tzara.

'In a rush, Iremonger?'

'I gotta be in O'Neill's in six minutes.'

'Oh-kay. I guess I'll just have to make this into some quality Iremonger time.'

My return smile was only lightly salted with sarcasm

because our Fursties had arrived. That was my cue to ask, 'So where's Dylan tonight?'

'Oh, probably ordering a late lunch at some café on St Mark's Place.'

I felt genuinely bad about this, but slugged my Fursty before replying, 'He went back already? That's a shame. Must try and hook up with him next month.'

Roderick sipped his Fursty, then smiled. 'Make sure you have the right address for him. Dylan's moving uptown, and moving in with someone.'

'Don't tell me, he's found the PG.'

Roderick's smile complexified. 'No, I don't think I can tell you that at all.'

'What are you saying, Rod?'

'Well, let's just say that Dylan may have some trouble marching down Fifth Avenue in the St Patrick's Day parade.'

I put down my pint. 'Roderick, no way.'

'Yep. He's Irish, he's queer, he'll be there every year.'

'Dylan *came out* to you?'

'Sure. And he would have come out to you too if you hadn't been acting like Lord Lucan these last few days.'

'Yeah, well, that's unfortunate,' I muttered.

'You missed a great going-away party last night. Not so much an American wake as a heterosexuality wake.'

I was still taking it in. 'Jesus, I wonder if Carmel knows.'

Roderick got all serious. 'No. And you're not to mention it to her.'

'Why not? She'd be really cool about it.'

'That's the problem. If she found out then every week in her column there'd be a reference to *my son, the homosexual*. Dylan doesn't want this to be a fashion thing.'

I nodded slowly, and went back to work on my Fursty. This was a lot to absorb, even though I was, of course, cool about it. So one of my best friends was gay. Why hadn't I picked up on that? Had I picked up on it, and let it go again?

Could I really say he was one of my best friends? Weren't friends people you really knew? Did I really know any of my friends? Enough questions. I decided I would get to work on some answers on the plane tomorrow. There was a time and a place for everything. Just as well because then Roderick quietly dropped another bombshell on me.

'So, how's your dad, Tom?'

I didn't look at him. 'He's fine. He's home.'

'I guess you're wondering how I know.'

I shrugged, looking straight ahead. 'Played any golf with my mother recently?'

'No,' he laughed. 'No, I found out in a very indirect way. My old man went in to see Percy Tóibín. They became good friends when Dad represented him in that libel case against *IoS* after they said Percy had deserted from the British Army in the fifties. Anyway, he went down to see Percy in the Simmonscourt Clinic. Apparently it's meant to be really hush, hush, because he's in bad shape. He's got this private suite on the top floor. He bumped into your Uncle Columb in the lift. Turns out your uncle was his spiritual director at a retreat years ago. He didn't mention meeting my dad?'

'No, but that's not too unusual for Columb.' I drained my pint.

'Yeah, but what is unusual is that you didn't mention it to us. I mean, we're your friends, Iremonger.'

I looked at him now. 'I'm sure there are things I don't know about you too, Roderick. But I tell you what, let's talk about them somewhere quiet like the airport. It's the only place I seem to have a decent conversation with anybody.'

'Woh, what's your problem?'

'I'm late.'

And that basically was it in terms of me talking with Roderick. I didn't even get a chance to ask him anything more about his validation plans, if he still does have any validation plans; looked like he was getting very chummy with those young lawyers. Obviously this Christmas at home has brought us all a lot closer. As I walked up dark Dame Lane heading for O'Neill's, I started thinking about Dylan again. Something was nagging me, and it took me a while to figure out what it was – jealousy. I was jealous that Dylan was gay. Not in the sense that I envied his exclusion from the St Patrick's Day parade, but that he had this formidable fact in his life, something he couldn't ignore or erase. He reminded me . . . of Columb, Columb and his priestly vocation. They both had their cross, their pearl.

We drive across a long, flat stretch of ground between the DART tracks and the bay that must be reclaimed land and enter Clontarf. Irresistibly the date springs into my mind – 1014. Brian Boru killed in his tent by a treacherous Dane just after he had led the Irish to victory over the Vikings. Reverse 1014, Quinlaven told us one time, and you get 1410, the number of the house in Monasterevin where the Herima kidnapping became a siege in 1975. Yes, it's comforting to know that the one thing they can't take away from me is my education.

Just after we turn off the coast road, we pass two large attached Victorian houses, the Alfie Byrne Memorial Nursing Home. I almost cringe as my mother says what she always says, 'That's where poor Granny died.' Her mother, my grandmother. Have I mentioned my grandmother? Seems like I haven't spent a lot of time dealing with my mother's people, dealing with the Maguires. It's been all Iremongers, all the time. What a surprise.

'May she rest in peace,' Columb says.

'Amen,' my father responds, so quietly that maybe I'm the only one who's heard him. For a moment emotion swarms in my throat.

So round two was where my evening started to go all

wrong. For a start, I was put off my game by that little encounter with Roderick in the snug of the Stag's. Later I was escorted off the premises of Dougheny and Nesbitt's for failing to turn the other cheek when this yuppie rugger bugger started heckling the copy of my poster at me. And in between my pace was shot to hell. It was getting close to eleven, winter closing time – well, there's one thing I won't be getting sentimental about – when I finally got back onto Grafton Street, heading for McDaid's. And then something totally beyond the pale, almost unspeakable, happened.

It involved a teenaged street musician. Now, it goes without saying that I despise Dublin buskers, but normally I do the mature thing and keep my distance, letting the appropriate authorities move them along, caution them, interrogate them, beat them with telephone directories, and so on, but this particular gentleman, something of a fashion Chernobyl, seemed to have been deliberately placed in Iremonger's path, almost in the middle of the pedestrianised street. Likewise his choice of song seemed calculated to cause me maximum distress: 'I Still Haven't Found What I'm Looking For'. He had a narrow anaemic face and a parapet of curly, gelled black hair. His instrument – an acoustic guitar so cheap it appeared to have been made out of plywood, precisely out of tune, top string freshly snapped. His voice – that of a drowning seagull.

He more or less stopped me in my tracks, and I in turn asked him to stop what he was doing. He continued to wail away about kingdoms to come and bleeding colours.

'You'll be the one bleeding if you don't fucking stop,' I commented.

He didn't stop but nodded towards the ground. In front of him was a brown plastic guitar cover, sprinkled with a few lower denomination coins. And over his shoulder, down around Bewley's, I saw the dark peaked caps and raincoats of two cops, slowly patrolling and approaching. The Seagull had launched into the song from the top again, climbing mountains and scaling walls. I was quite sure that the cops would eventually put a stop to this obscenity when they got here, but that seemed several agonising verses away, and somehow I just couldn't walk away. I could have put an immediate stop to the torture by grabbing the plywood guitar off him and smashing it to pieces on the red pavement of Grafton Street. I didn't particularly care if that led to my arrest. What I did care about was the possibility of missing my flight if bail proceedings were delayed.

Then I remembered that money was the only thing that made things happen on Grafton Street for sure. I put my hand on the Seagull's shoulder and tilted towards him. That made him shut up and dampen his strings.

'How much,' I said very slowly, 'would it cost to ensure that you *never* play that particular song again?'

He looked at me as if I were a nut.

'Ten quid.' It was more of a question than a demand.

I gave it to him, and for a few minutes felt pretty proud of myself. If I can do some good in this world, I'm happy.

The way things worked out I got no further than McDaid's. McDaid's was the last wave of my pub surf. But that was okay. It was not an inappropriate place to end my last evening in Dublin. For McDaid's had been the mad pinting HQ of an earlier generation of Iremongers, present-tense kind of guys who, it's true, tragically gave into temptation from time to time and put pen to paper. I remembered having to read the fruits of this filthy habit in the short story anthology we studied in third year at Berchmans, stuff about poteen-induced epiphanies and priests pretending to be dead and chickens going to confession. But amid the mythical mahogany and bevelled glass of McDaid's those ur-mad pinters had had their finest hours.

Thinking of all this got me into a traditional kind of mood: I switched to Guinness. Soon I found myself settled into a nice rhythm of drinking a pint in about the time it took the patient, precise McDaid's barman to pour one. At the same time, I got talking to this alcoholic Bosco-type sitting at the bar beside me who claimed he'd drunk here with Brendan Behan in the good old days. I informed him that I was a kind of post-modern, post-literary Brendan Behan. He wanted to know what the fuck I was on about. Foolishly, I tried to explain. He had just about grasped the significance of the word *post* by drinking-up time. Fearing he was going to latch on to me outside the pub, I split while he was in the bog.

Sticking with the tradition theme, I decided, since it was possible to interpret my person as being under the influence of alcohol, that there was only one fitting way to go home: not in a Martello cab but on the last riotous 46A out of town, that vintage Bombardier.

I strutted, a little waywardly, down Grafton Street towards Trinity Circle, braced for both sarcasm and flattery. But nobody said anything, nothing that I heard at least. It had to be that without Nico I was less obviously Iremonger. And the bad lighting didn't help either: those lanterns were still strung above me, but they were turned off. Cheap bastards, I thought. Christmas isn't even over yet.

I have a suggestion: trainee space shuttle astronauts would benefit greatly from boarding the 46A under the influence of fine Irish and German beers, particularly while attempting to find a seat upstairs as the bus does its metronome simulation turning the corner from Nassau Street to Kildare Street – it's the closest I've ever come to experiencing zero gravity, even with all the air miles I've clocked up.

I found myself thrown into a seat behind the stairs. Looking around I couldn't see anybody I recognised. Nearly all of the passengers were just excited kids, high on Bulmer's cider and bad ganj and pure hormones, too young to have been part of my Trinity circle, most of them too young to have even taken the Inter Cert.

A young chick voice yelled 'ride!' and I looked around to see a girl in a green mod flight jacket diving for cover behind the seatback of her squealing friends. Other than that nobody paid me much attention. Now I would have actively welcomed a little slagging on the Ireland's Greatest Resource front. But obviously these kids did not have much business at the airport.

Even worse: the energy level on the bus had plummeted by the time we crossed Leeson Street Bridge. I began to smoke Rolands (T - 6, and counting), more to see if any of the few wrinklies upstairs would complain than to satisfy any craving – my real craving now was for conflict, carnival – but nobody said a word. Instead, some of the kids drank in the dense smoke second-hand; even at that purity level it was undoubtedly better than anything they would be puffing on between their bus stop and home.

At Donnybrook church, the bus finally filled up. The way I remembered it, this stop had the potential to turn into a small war and bring supporting personnel out from the depot across the street, and even some cops from the station in the village. But not tonight. I could hear the driver downstairs giving friendly instructions about finding a seat upstairs and moving down the back. He didn't have to repeat himself. I was scandalised.

As we powered along the dual carriageway, I wracked my blurry brain for strategies, because clearly it was time for Iremonger to set an example, for Iremonger to show these youngsters how it was done. For the longest time the best I could come up with was to start a fire with my Zippo. I had it in hand, flipped open, when that was superseded by another plan, the masterplan, the obvious move. What was the ultimate in self-destructive and obnoxious behaviour?

Do a little busking myself. Put together a little homage to

U2. It was really quite startling to realise just how much of their music I had absorbed, lyrics and all, over the years. I was a juke box of contempt. My assault was chronological. I began with a few fairly acceptable fragments from the early singles and *Boy*. Jesus, I even had some people singing along with me. Then I belted out the most piteous evangelical crap from *October*. A lone voice I was at that stage. Then in Seagull style I tackled the lyrical tautologies of *War*. That had them frowning. *Unforgettable Fire* art-rock phase – the slurrings of 'Elvis Presley and the USA' I found came quite naturally to me. My rendition of 'Bad' was *bad*. This gangly kid had plucked up enough courage by that stage to tell me to shut up. I wanted to hug him and tell him what wonderful taste he had. 'Where the Streets Have No Name' got the driver on the PA telling me to do the same – what a tribute! Only a few bars into *that song*, the one I'd bought the busking rights to, the brakes were on and my friend in the Dublin Bus cerulean sweater was coming up the stairs for me. I protested that I couldn't go until I'd done the monologue from 'Bullet the Blue Sky', that they'd be all the poorer for it. Since he wasn't moved by that I then protested the tight, possibly damaging grip he had on my suede jacket, and promised that I'd go quietly. Meanwhile the kids were showing their appreciation by applauding, god bless 'em.

A farewell plume of Bombardier exhaust sickened me, but also sobered me up a little. I found myself pretty close to home – beside the bridge at the bottom of the Ascent. I crossed it, stopping in the middle to look over the edge at the traffic flashing beneath it. At one point I felt so woozy that I thought I was falling over, and that a hand was lifting the back of my jacket and tipping me over, and that the hand belonged to the dark arm of Strongbow. I held on tight to the steel coping with both hands and told myself to snap out of it. As best I could, I marched up the

Ascent, keeping my eyes on the dim pavement in front of me. Exhausting labour it was.

About fifty steep metres from the intersection with Cedar-of-Lebanon Road, I slowed, then stopped. Across the road lights shone behind white drawn blinds in the extension (what we used to call the playroom) of the Firbolgs' house, imposing on the corner of a cul-de-sac. I crossed a silent Ascent and opened the less silent main gate, which made me look to the rest of the house to see if fresh lights came on. Brían's mother, a high-strung woman who had been obsessed with him and his little brother becoming professional musicians, never did like me much, considered me a bad influence. It had seemed unreasonable way back then, prophetic now.

I passed by his father's late-model Commissioner. His old man was something big in insurance, and got walked all over by his wife. She had this thing against doorbells, and so there was no doorbell on the thick door of the extension. I gave the iron knocker two light taps, but the resulting sound was so emphatic that I was sure I'd wake up the rest of the house. For a moment I thought about splitting across the grass and hopping over the low hedge. But then I heard someone busy with bolts and keys, and the door was being dragged back.

Brían looked as criminally uncool as ever, but behind him, in a room which had been converted from a lino-tiled miniature battlefield into a cozy, carpeted, fairly tasteful den, was another human being, recognisably female, and not, as far as I knew, a family member. In fact, this small, mousy-haired chick was tucking her blouse into her jeans.

'Tom!' he said. 'I had this weird feeling it was you.'

'Hey, Brían, I didn't realise you had company.' I moved back off the doorstep.

'No, no, I'd like you to meet Olga – she's the girl I met at the party!'

'Maybe this wasn't such a hot idea. It *is* late. I'm sure your folks—'

'The old pair have gone to Manchester to hear Timothy play with the Irish Youth Orchestra.'

'Well, all the more reason to get in some one-to-one time.'

Olga now came up beside Brían – she really was tiny, borderline midget. She put a hand on his back and said to me, 'Furry's told me so much about you!'

Furry? Jesus, that did it. I was in danger of throwing up for the second time this tour of Dublin-duty. I wasn't going in there even if he was running a subsidised brothel.

'Yeah, I'm sure.' I replied. 'But for me the First Rule of Cool is not to interrupt other's people's up-close and personal time.'

But Brían begged, 'Just come in for a quick supercan of Harp – we've a bunch of them left over from Christmas in the fridge. Olga won't mind!'

'Wouldn't dream of it. Really, it's a principle of mine.'

Brían shook his head, beaming with bafflement. 'You're something else, Iremonger, you know that?'

I began to back into the dark. 'You kids have fun. I'll check you again.' I turned and began to stride across the grass.

'You'll be around?' Brían Firbolg shouted after me hopefully.

'Sure,' I said over my shoulder.

I was climbing the Ascent again when I heard the door shut and the bolt being drawn. Once again, I found myself slowing and stopping. Why the hell had I called on Brían in the first place? Not to attack the Lego defences of his plastic Germans with my fifty-strong British Eighth Army. Not to drink supercans of Harp and compare notes about Christmas and women.

A crazy fucking notion came into my mind. So crazy I found it pretty seductive. I must have been still drunk – no other explanation. I turned around and walked back past the extension, watching the blinds to make sure nobody was watching me. I stopped below the smaller gate, behind which there was a path that lead up to the main door of the dark house.

Not wanting another creak-fest, I jumped up onto the wall and leapt the spiky hedge, catching one of my Boccionis in the process and landing awkwardly on the soft ground. I cursed my half-twisted ankle, then, in case I'd been heard, hobbled as quickly as I could to the porch. I peeked around a porch pillar to scope out the extension again – no forms in the windows. What was I worried about – they were probably hard at it, or as hard as they could go, on one of the bean bags. I took out my Gucci wallet to check out my punt position. Of course, I didn't need light to do that. I could feel and smell my liquidity. Four joyces, that's what it came down it. Four miserable joyces left, not counting loose change. So little money, as the Bish would say, that you might as well give it away.

Of course I didn't have a pen or an envelope, but if I'd had them I guess I would have written *for the Roomkeepers*, and wondered what exactly the hell that meant. As it was, I just put the notes one by one through the letter box. Brían Firbolg is such an honest bastard that I know he'll do the right thing with them. He may be coming along, that boy, but he'll always be the same in some ways. I know him.

I left by the little gate. There were no witnesses.

You think it makes me feel all warm and fuzzy that I gave him (back) the money? I wish. I wish.

We're doing nicely on the time front. Eight minutes before the morning ends, the Senator enters the grounds of Dublin Airport. In the distance, on top of the car-park pay point, I can see the giant red-ribboned gold lamé-box. I guess somebody forgot to claim their gift.

'Oh, you can just pull up at set-down,' I joke, but nobody laughs.

Unfortunately, the car park is almost as full as it was on Christmas Eve, and we face another long trek over to the terminal building. I'm out of my seat as soon as my father pops the boot, but as I'm hauling out my suitcase Columb appears beside me and takes out my Coach carry-on.

'Travelling light,' he murmurs. He's already said that back at the house when we were loading up the Senator, and I still haven't figured out if it's praise or criticism. Really, trying to understand what that man is saying is like learning a new language – by getting a few hours of instruction every five years.

'You bet,' I tell him again.

And then I turn my attention upward. The cloud cover has muscular ripples in it today, like the sky has been taking steroids. But on the other side I know the clouds will look like magic castles. The other side of the sky is Iremonger-land. All I have to do is get up there.

'Let's go,' I say. *Hurry Up – I'm Melting*!

Big surprise – Departures is booming, doing a roaring trade. Long lines, ragged with relatives, at every check-in desk. Straight away I see faces I know, but I sense I'm not being picked up on as many radars as I was on Christmas Eve. Have they forgotten the poster that quickly? Many familiar faces and profiles, but no Strongbow. Yes, straight away I'm scoping for Strongbow.

We stop in the middle of the concourse, trying to figure out which desk I need to go to, but I get distracted by this line of huge Styrofoam snowmen – runners, skaters, tumblers – on a ledge above us, against the high windows of the terminal. One of them is being winched to the ground by a team of workmen. Back at Cedar-of-Lebanon Road, back at home, our decorations are still up. I imagine my mother stripping the tree, dismantling the trunk, dislodging the crib, packing everything into cardboard boxes and putting them back into the dark hollow under the stairs.

My father has been investigating, the way he likes to.

'You're the third Aer Lingus desk down on this side, Tom.'

'Oh, thanks.' I snap out of it and pick up my suitcase. Come on now, Iremonger, this is it. 'Columb, I'll take that now, thanks.'

The line moves quicker than you'd think – they're the emigration specialists, these Aer Lingus people. My parents and uncle stand back between my line and the next, looking like people at the burial of an acquaintance. My father looks the part most of all, still wearing his Bavarian hat.

I check out a departures screen as I get closer to the counter. It's 12:02:29. My flight is listed, without a gate number, as departing on time at 13:10. Fine. But what I'm really interested in right now are the London flights. Only one fits what Mainie said at the National Gallery: Strongbow must be leaving on BA 1601, departing gate B-23 at 12:40. Shit, that means they'll start boarding about ten or fifteen minutes from now. Don't get me wrong, I'm not looking to have some big scene with Strongbow – I'm not looking to have a big scene with *anybody* at this airport today – but I do want the fuckologist to see me making a gracious exit from the homecoming stage, minus Nico but otherwise intact. (Once I'm up in the air again I can fall apart.)

Now, normally I've got a soft spot for those poor wing-clipped creatures known as ground hostesses, but the old one who gets me checked in is so upbeat I want to tell her that there's serious danger of a make-up avalanche on her face. Tell those warts to get the hell off the slopes. And I thought I'd be feeling euphoria by this stage. And I thought this airport would be good shit.

'So that's seat 22A in Smoking. And they've just announced a boarding gate for your flight, Tomás. B-21 at 12:45.'

That's *Mr* Iremonger to you, witch.

'Thanks,' I mutter.

I go back to my little party of subdued mourners.

'You know who I just met?' my mother says.

'Who?' I reply.

'Froggy Mitchell's daughter, Giséle. Off to Paris on the same flight as you! She's the Kerrygold representative for the whole of France.'

'Great. I'll keep an eye out for her.'

Somehow I reckon Ms Mitchell will be sitting in Non-Smoking.

'What's the plan, Tom?' my father says, looking pretty serious about it.

'I'm not boarding for a half an hour,' I reply, 'but I promised a bunch of people back in Paris that I'd pick up duty-free for them.'

'Well,' my mother replies, getting huffy, 'we'd best walk over with you to the boarding-card place if you're in that much of a hurry.'

I smile, shaking my head, running my hand through my hair, not looking her in the eye. 'No, Mum, no. What I meant was we should go up to the restaurant and have a final cup of coffee together and chill and say goodbye like that. Much more civilised than the boarding-card check point. I have ten or fifteen minutes.'

That sounded good, so now I look at her.

'Okay so,' she says cautiously. 'I suppose that's better than nothing.'

We make tracks towards the escalator. 'Chill,' I hear Columb whisper behind me, and chuckle in his throat.

Upstairs in the restaurant (a generous use of the word) my mother and I conspire together on one thing – a table in the smoking section. On the serve-yourself circuit she and my father have picked up white coffees, I've got an espresso, and my uncle's been convinced to get a Styrofoam cup full of boiling water and a Lipton's teabag. My mother, sitting across from me, takes out her king-sized Gossamers, and that gives me the green light to light up too.

'Running low on cancer sticks there, Tom,' says my father, taking off his hat.

My mother's eyes meet mine for a startled second.

'My very last one,' I confess.

'So that's why you're in such a hurry to get to duty-free,' my mother comments with a puff of sanctimonious low-tar smoke.

'They don't sell Rolands here, Mum – yet.'

And that's about the high point of the conversation until my final pure stick of evil French tobacco is burnt away. Time now 12:23:58. That London flight is boarding for sure. Even though I've been checking out the time on a screen, I make a big show of sadly analysing the face of my Tzara.

'Well, looks like I've got a plane waiting for me.'

'What about your coffee?' asks my mother.

'It was the cigarette I really needed,' I tell her, and she, of all people, has to accept that.

And suddenly we're all on our feet – this is it. Goodbyes and hugs and kisses come fast and anti-climactically. Mainie Doyle, you're a sweetheart, you're a genius – this *is* the place to part – it's too easy. Up here in this smoky perch where you can't see the planes or other families breaking up, goodbye loses its intensity, doesn't seem quite real. Before I know it I'm weaving through tables, then giving the distant tableful of people who happen to be my loved ones a final upbeat wave from the top of the escalator – I can't help but think of Nixon's final wave before boarding the helicopter that took him from the White House – then descending by myself back down into Departures. As I walk through the crowded concourse some of that old airport-lightness enters my head at last. I feel free, I feel headed in the right direction. Hey, I might just catch Strongbow.

The boarding-card check is manic, a bulge of at least twenty people trying to get through, trying to get out of here, get back to their lives, their other lives. Man, they need to Tensa-barrier this place too; it's the one blackspot in the departure process. Already my good mood gets stained. It feels like I'm never going to get through to the other side, to that special space I can see just feet away through the glass walls, my duty-free world.

And then I hear my father's voice calling my name, softly calling my full name. At first I don't turn around, and not because I'm pissed off that he's followed me from the restaurant or called me Tomás, but because, out of nowhere, I'm afraid I'm about to do something that really would break the First Rule of Cool. I squeeze the bridge of my nose with the thumb and forefinger of my right hand, take a deep breath, then turn around.

There he stands, hatless, yellow up to his receding hairline. In some ways he looks worse – certainly older – than when I saw him here on Christmas Eve, when he was still dangerously undiagnosed.

'Hey,' I say, my voice thick.

He takes a deep, stiff breath, staring at me with those buggy grey-blue eyes, and says, 'I forgot to tell you something. Something I wanted to tell you in hospital.'

'What, Dad?'

'That I'm sorry.'

I almost laugh. 'Sorry for what?'

'For failing you.'

'Failing me how!'

'Failing you as a parent.'

I really don't want to have this conversation, especially here and now. But I do feel obliged to say, 'Don't be ridiculous, Dad. You're an incredible parent. You've never stood in my way.'

He looks away, vaguely out at the aeroplanes, and nods for

the longest time, occasionally sucking air through the side of his mouth. 'You've put your finger on it, son,' he eventually says. 'You've put your finger on it.'

Then he slaps me on the arm of my suede jacket, says, 'Good luck so,' and walks away. Just walks away. How can he do that?

I could stare at him receding through the crowd, unnecessarily tempting myself to run after him, or I could get on with this. So I get on with it. I get back in the messy queue and whip out my boarding card. When my turn finally comes I hand it to the guard before he's even handed back the card of the woman in front of me.

An old pro at getting through x-ray machines first time, I've got my rue du Guignol keys and my very last Irish coins in the tray before they even ask me. I cruise by duty-free and down the corridor to the Departures lounge. Seeing the planes up close, hearing the rising whine of their engines makes me giddy. I pause at the glass wall between Arrivals and Departures, but I can't see the IDA poster from this angle. Crossing the pathetic imitation Ha'penny Bridge, I am finally in the horseshoe of departure. I go straight past my gate – real quiet still – and head for B-23. Boarding is well underway. As nonchalantly as I can, I go up close to the queue and check it out. No Strongbow. The bastard probably had priority boarding. He'll probably be in the jumpseat for take-off and landing, hanging with the pilots. No – he'll probably be flying the plane. Duty-free seems a pretty attractive proposition, now that I have all this time on my hands.

I turn around and almost bang into him. Strongbow's running, a viewfinder dancing around his neck, heavy-duty carry-on over his shoulder. But he puts the brakes on pretty fast when he sees me.

'Hello there.'

I nod. 'St John.'

'Are you on this flight too?'

In his voice I hear the echo of the tall English boy who introduced himself to me that distant November morning at Berchmans.

'No, just seeing off a friend, Giséle Mitchell. I'm actually on the next flight out to Charles de Gaulle.'

'Oh, pity. We could have had a chat. We really didn't have a chance to talk properly all through Christmas.'

'No, no we didn't,' I say slowly; it hadn't even occurred to me that Strongbow and I *should* sit down and talk. 'The airport is usually where I go to catch up with people,' I deadpan.

He laughs politely. 'Listen, Tom, I'd better go. I don't think they're going to hold this one much longer. But I tell you what, next time you're in London, give me a call. Phone my office. Look, here's my card. We really must have a proper chat over a pint. Straighten things out.'

As he's saying that, the ground hostess is doing her any-remaining-passengers bit over the PA, and Strongbow has to split.

I head for the Under the Clock bar, near the Ha'penny Bridge, and, since I don't have any punts left, open a tab with my trusty Wanderlust. I line up a large Jack Daniels and try to figure out what the fuck that was all about, as I brood over the cool minimalism of his business card. Arranging to go out for a *pint* with St John Strongbow. Strongbow wanting to have a *proper chat* with me, wanting to *straighten things out*. What's his problem? Why can't he be the Strongbow I carry around inside?

First Republic Films. Wardour Street. The company's logo is a stark blue harp. I file the card away in my Gucci.

I chase the JD with a couple of pints of Fursty, keeping my eye on an info screen, and off my reflection behind the bar. EI 643 climbs the departure charts. At 12:45 exactly I ask for the damage and head for my gate. B-21 is booming.

Straight away I see a few old satellites of mine, bit players. The stage is set for a pretty decent Iremonger departure. But then I hesitate. What is this, *gate*-fright? No. It must be that after Strongbow, and after Strongbow's surprise, other eyes are irrelevant. Departure has become purely personal. That must be it. I walk over to the windows of the quiet neighbouring gate and watch a Lufthansa jet do its sky-strut down the runway.

Back at B-21, a ground steward comes over the PA, 'And now, ladies and gentlemen we're ready to start pre-boarding Aer Lingus flight EI 643 to Paris Charles de Gaulle. Today we'll be boarding any passengers travelling with small children first. Please have your boarding cards at the ready.'

Ken – all stewards are called Ken – looks like he's just done his Leaving Cert, but he's trying to sound like a veteran transatlantic pilot; this departure-power must be going to his head. As for the business of boarding people with small children first, well, the next time I see Mainie, wherever and whenever that will be, I'll admit to her that there is one situation where it pays to have a child, or be a child yourself.

I remember the first time I flew out of this airport alone. I think it was from the gate closest to the bar. I was twelve and on my way to stay with this exchange in Lyons who turned out to be an undiluted bastard with a hard-on for Napoleon. Anyway, Aer Lingus gave me this Unaccompanied Minor status, which meant that my parents, much to my horror, were allowed to accompany me right down to the gate. We went through this big farewell scene when my row number was called, but of course they insisted on staying at the gate until I was on board the plane. Not only that, but while I was queuing to present my boarding card, my mother kept on rushing back up to me, dangerously close to tears, to 'remind' me what to say about the Irish gifts I was bringing for my host family, how to budget my pocket money, and what to do in a half-dozen different emergencies. I couldn't get on that plane fast enough. But then again, I knew I was coming back.

'Now, ladies and gentlemen, thank you for your patience. We'll be boarding the aircraft from back to front today, so we're ready for those passengers with boarding cards for rows 22 through 15.'

Mad rush. You'd swear that airbus was the last helicopter out of Saigon. No way am I going to become an extra in that mob scene. No way am I going to break my neck getting to that air bridge. Seat 22A has my name written on it. I don't need to worry about bin space like a lot of these heavy travellers because my lithe carry-on will fit right under the seat in front of me. I sit down and watch the valiant efforts of Ken and a chick colleague to turn this ragged escape into a proper departure.

A few minutes later things have chilled considerably and Ken's back on the mike.

'Thank you once again for your patience, ladies and gentlemen. We're now ready to board those passengers with boarding cards for rows 14 through 7.'

Same deal as before, but maybe just a little less crazy. After a couple of minutes things are well under control. This might not be a bad time to start lining up. Then again, I'll be in seat 22A long enough. I'll be in seat 22A for as far into the future as I can see. So what if I'm the last passenger to replane? Trust me, by now I know a thing or two about the dynamics of flight closing. They aren't going anywhere without me. They can't with my suitcase.

Soon Ken is back on the PA, 'Ladies and gentlemen we're now ready to board all remaining passengers for flight EI 643.'

This time there's hardly any rush at all. It's mainly suits

who stand up: business class is boarding. Seasoned travellers, like Iremonger, except that I'm going to be sitting at the opposite end of the cabin, in anti-business class.

I still don't feel like standing up and pulling out my boarding card. I'm serious about being the last passenger to replane. It will give me a certain perverse satisfaction. Christ knows there hasn't been much symmetry to this trip so far.

The suits are processed speedily. Ken checks his clipboard, consults his computer, confers with his side-kick, and then reaches for the mike again, 'Would passenger Tomás Iremonger please proceed immediately to gate B-21. Passenger Tomás Iremonger.'

This time the announcement goes out over the general PA system. It can be heard all over the Departures lounge, if not the entire airport. I just hope my family have done the sensible thing and gone home.

Well, here we go. I stand up, pick up my carry-on – and start walking away from gate B-21. But it's okay. I just need to stretch my legs a little before I finally get on that plane. I just need to take a running jump at that air bridge. As I said, they aren't going anywhere without me. They can't. That Stansted incident taught me how touchy airport folk are about Unaccompanied Luggage. They're slaves to security.

I walk around the Departures circus until I come to an Eason's niche across from Under the Clock. I go to the magazine stand and pick up a scented copy of *Momentum*, the first issue of the fresh year. I become engrossed in an advert for Baldassare Castiglione shoes, until I hear Ken on the PA again.

'Would passenger Tomás Iremonger proceed immediately to gate B-21, where his flight is closing. Passenger Tomás Iremonger.'

Okay, I guess they're ready for me now. The aisles must be clear. Time to do my Iremonger routine. I put back the magazine in the wrong place and squeeze my way out of the crammed shop. I continue my circuit around the Departures lounge, though my pace is more purposeful now. I really can't delay my air-brothers and -sisters any longer. As I come full circle I see Ken standing at his high desk scoping the lounge for any sign of the chronically late Mr Iremonger.

I'm just about to acknowledge my identity when I feel this surge in my stomach, then another, even stronger. No doubt about it – the Fursty's coming back up. I pass right by my gate, and bolt for the bog. I am not going to throw up in public. Throwing up in public would be the end of me.

I get lucky, if that's what you want to call it. I make it to the stall in time, it's not too scuzzy, and my aim is true. Three frothy gushes later, I'm feeling some sense of relief, but then I hear Ken calling my name again. That's it – page a man while he's down. Is nothing sacred? Is there anywhere the information can't reach? Is there anywhere your old self can't reach? And I used to think this airport was a place for escaping.

I flush, get off my knees, and cautiously emerge from the cubicle. Nobody pays me any attention. I go to the nearest clean sink and wash out my mouth until the sourness has been replaced by the taste of my fillings. Then I look up at myself. No, this is not the guy in the poster. It's not even the guy in the poster with a bruised eye. This is not Ireland's Greatest Resource. This is an exhausted resource.

I'm not getting on that plane – that, and not much else, is clear. I'm not leaving Dublin today. Maybe I'll be ready to leave tomorrow (with a little help from my friends at Diaspora Travel); maybe it won't be till next week, or even next month (my parents could drive me and Columb to the airport on the same day). I just don't know. I can't look that far into the future. It's hard enough to predict what's going to happen in the next fifteen minutes.

Outside the little boys' room I hesitate. Another bloody decision to make. I could turn left and walk back towards the Ha'penny Bridge – try to slip away from this confusion entirely. Or I could turn right and walk back towards gate B-21 and get this luggage business sorted out. I go right. Don't ask me to explain. It's bourgeois to explain, as my old man likes to say.

Ken is on the phone, but when he sees me approaching he lowers the receiver and says sharply, 'Tomás Iremonger?'

I put down my carry-on, lean an arm confessionally on his desk, and nod slowly.

'Yes, I'm Tomás Iremonger.'

Acknowledgments

Two scenes in the novel are based on historical reality. The description of the assassination of Kevin O'Higgins draws on information in the standard biography of the man by Terence de Vere White. Much of the inspiration for the story on the Dublin government's reaction to the Jewish refugee crisis comes from an article by Andy Pollack in *The Irish Times* of April 14/15, 1995, which in turn draws upon the research of Dr Dermot Keogh, the Jean Monnet Professor of History at University College, Cork.

I would also like to thank the following for their kindness and encouragement: Richard Nevle and my other colleagues at Strake Jesuit College Preparatory; Vivien Green and her associates at Sheil Land; Neil Taylor and his associates at Sceptre; John Padberg, SJ of the Institute of Jesuit Sources; my teachers and friends at the University of East Anglia; the Arts Council of Ireland; David and Karen Danburg of Houston, Texas; and, lastly, the members of the mild pinting gang, wherever the Diaspora has scattered them.

The poem by Anthony de Mello, SJ is taken from *Hearts On Fire: Praying with Jesuits* and is reprinted with kind permission of the Institute of Jesuit Sources, St Louis, Missouri.